CHAF

CW01500540

Commander Dumar looked out through the blast-proof windows of the third-floor operations center. His eyes squinted in the glare of the setting sun, its waning yellow light flickering in and out as the smoke drifted past from the many fires of devastation still burning in the city. Most of the buildings across the parkway from him had been reduced to rubble as a result of the bombardment earlier that day. It seemed miraculous that while so many structures around him lay in waste, his seemed undamaged. It was indeed a testament to the accuracy of Ta'Akar weaponry.

It wasn't just his building that had escaped the destruction rained down upon them by the warship Yamaro. The majority of the structures still stood, some damaged and some not. As he looked out at his neighborhood, it appeared as if some enormous being had walked through the district, crushing buildings with every careless footfall as it lumbered across the sprawling metropolis that was his home.

His city, Aitkenna, was the capital of Corinair. It was the seat of not only the global government, but also of the entire Darvano system, in which the planet was a member. He had lived here for going on thirty years now. He had met his wife here, married here, and raised a family here. His home was only a few kilometers away to the east. The school where his children had been educated lay just beyond. In fact, much of his city was now gone, reduced to piles of rubble and bodies. The lives of the people of this world would be changed forever. The lives of his family would be changed forever. Even though it was all for the betterment of the empire he served, it saddened him, as it was destruction on a scale that few had ever witnessed.

Unfortunately, he was one of those few. This was not the first time he had seen such utter disregard for human existence, and he feared it would not be his last. His home had not been destroyed. This he had already confirmed. Nor had any of his immediate family been injured in this attack, just as he had suspected would be the case.

He drew in a deep breath and sighed as he wondered how many of his men could say the same about their homes and their families. He knew why this secret compound and his home to the east had not been targeted by the Yamaro. As the central operational command post for all the Ta'Akar Anti-Insurgency Units operating covertly on this world, its location would have been marked as 'protected' in the Yamaro's fire-control systems. In addition, as the commander of all Ta'Akar anti-insurgency activity on Corinair, his home would also be on that list. He only wished that everyone under his command could share the same privilege. Had every one of his team's homes been spared, however, a connection might eventually have been made, one that might lead to their untimely exposure. The advanced warning they received was barely enough for them to take whatever preventative measures they felt were needed.

So no one would be the wiser. To any but the

THE FRONTIERS SAGA
EPISODE 4

FREEDOM'S DAWN

Ryk Brown

most astute observer, the firing pattern would appear random rather than the prewritten target list it had actually been. To the people of Corinair, it was indiscriminate punishment for acts of sedition perpetrated by their fellow citizens—undoubtedly by Followers of the Order. With any luck, that would be enough.

For decades he had served as the planetary commander of the Anti-Insurgency Forces stationed here and on the two other populated worlds in the Darvano system. For decades he had trained his men, recruited Loyalists from the civilian population, and carefully massaged local informants in order to ensure the proper connections needed. Finally, the time that he and his men had trained for had come. As much as he loathed the things he would have to do, he also knew that he had little choice in the matter. If he did not, one of his subordinates surely would, and they might not be as humane about it if given the chance, especially since they all had something to prove. He did not. He had already served the empire and his king with considerable distinction, even if not with the same amount of pride.

His king. The thought rang just as false whether spoken aloud or imagined. Caius was no king. Kings were stately men of courage, honor, wisdom... and above all else, mercy. These were qualities that Caius neither possessed nor understood. The man was nothing more than the heir to the throne of Ta'Akar. His father had been a true king, as had been his father and his father's father before him. Their wisdom had forged a willing alliance throughout the Pentaurus cluster. They had built it from little more than a handful of struggling, hastily thrown together colonies in the wake of a great evil that had nearly destroyed all humanity... or so the legends told. At least they had before Caius, who in all his arrogance had decided to rewrite them in order to feed his own ego.

"Commander Dumar," the young lieutenant said as he stepped up from behind, "we have received an update from our teams at the spaceport."

The commander turned his gaze away from the burning ruins outside to face his subordinate. "What do they report?"

"As suspected, it is the command staff of the Yamaro, as well as her captain."

The commander turned the rest of the way around to face the interior of the room, his attention moving to the large video screen on the far wall. The room was full of dozens of functionaries all going about their tasks, gathering intelligence, creating estimates, contacting informants, and communicating with field units. His command was a picture of efficiency, unlike the empire it served.

A live video feed from the spaceport showed the view from the crowd. He could see a large review platform filled with local dignitaries, many of which he recognized. Behind them and off to one side were the twelve members of the Yamaro's command staff, as well as her captain. "Sir Augustine de Winter," he said as if the name itself left an unpleasant taste in his mouth.

"You know him, sir?"

"I know of him," the commander corrected. "Another pompous Ta'Akar nobleman of questionable skill and valor."

The young lieutenant knew better than to comment on his commander's disdain for the so-called 'nobles' of Ta'Akar society. As with most true men of war, he had little respect for the aristocracy that passed themselves off as honorable and worthy commanders. Such men had little use for honor or patriotism. Their interests were in far more tangible concerns. Men of his ilk were one of the many reasons he had asked for this assignment; so he could finish out his long and distinguished military service without having to deal with such fools.

"They appear to be turning the prisoners over to the Corinairans, sir," the lieutenant concluded.

"Yes, this will not sit well with command; of this I am sure," the commander said. "Have we been able to make contact with the Yamaro?"

"No, sir. Not since she broadcast her surrender a few hours ago."

"Is the ship still in orbit?"

"Yes, sir. Although she appears to be powered down, our scans revealed only minimal life support. The enemy ship—which we have since learned is called the 'Aurora'—still holds station alongside her."

"And the rest of the Yamaro's crew?"

"We believe they are still on board. We stopped receiving telemetry from the Yamaro more than an hour ago. At that time, the ship's sensors showed around two hundred people gathered in two of the primary cargo bays, as well as two dozen more being held in the detention cells."

Commander Dumar watched the video feed as one of the strangers wearing a uniform of unfamiliar design stepped up to the podium, his hand held high by one of the local dignitaries. The action had caused the crowd in attendance to swell into a roar of approval at the arrival of the visitor, and they

5

were chanting something—although the commander could not quite make it out. "What are they saying?" he asked his lieutenant.

"Na-Tan. They are chanting *Na-Tan*. It's the name of the guy in the Legend of Origins," he reminded the commander, "the one that is supposed to..."

"I know of Na-Tan, Lieutenant," the commander interrupted. Just like all of the men under his command, he was well versed in the Legend of Origins, so as to better understand his potential enemies.

"Of course, sir."

The commander stared at the face of the one called Na-Tan displayed on the screen as the camera zoomed in on him. "He appears a bit young to be a legend, don't you think?"

The lieutenant fidgeted uncomfortably, unsure of how to respond. "Uh, yes, sir." The lieutenant waited a few seconds before relaxing at the lack of response from his commander.

"And the other cells? Have they reported in?" the commander wondered.

"All eight cells on our continent have reported they are ready for operations. We are still waiting to hear from the cells on the other continents."

"Very well, Lieutenant. I guess it's about time we earned our pay, then. Send word to the teams at the spaceport. Tell them to begin. Then send flash traffic to all cells. Tell them to commence operations as well."

"Yes, sir," the lieutenant responded as he saluted smartly.

The commander watched the video feed as the young stranger in uniform stepped up to the podium as if to speak. As ugly as things already were on his world, the commander knew they were about to get even uglier.

On the roof of the Anti-Insurgency Command Center, five Kalibri airships sat idling, their ducted fans whirring quietly overhead while the rotor blades were at a neutral pitch. Workers quickly slid extended passenger pods into the cargo bays of two of the five airships while another set of technicians slid a weapons pod into another.

"Are you ready for this, Andre?" the man teased his friend as he checked his gear. They were two of eight heavily armed and well-armored men standing off to the side of the rooftop flight deck. They prepared to board the remaining two airships, both of which were still in their standard configuration with their cargo bays open and empty.

"I've been ready for this for ten long years, my friend," he answered as he slung his assault weapon over his shoulder and secured it to his chest harness.

"Do you think we'll get to rotate back to Takara after this is over?"

"I don't see why not," Andre said. "If this works, we will no longer be of use on this rock."

"And if it doesn't work?"

"Then we'll probably be dead, my friend!" Andre laughed. "Either way, we'll be done with this hellish place."

"What? You won't miss your wife and kids?"

"You mean my nagging wench and our screaming half-breeds?" Andre stated with obvious disdain. "With any luck they're already buried in the rubble."

"Poor Andre. Not everyone ends up with an attractive cover wife," his friend teased as they made their way to their airship.

"The women here do not respect their men. They don't know their place."

"This is not Takara, my friend. And these are not Takaran women," he reminded him as he took his seat in the port side door of the airship, his legs hanging out the side.

"Of this fact I am painfully aware," Andre exclaimed as he took a seat next to his friend in the empty doorway. "You're lucky. You were caught cheating on your cow, so she left you. You got off easy."

"That was not luck, my friend," he said, tapping his head with his index finger.

Andre reached out with his right hand and slapped the canopy three times to signal the pilot that they were ready. "Someday, Bobby, we'll be sitting on the shores of one of Takara's inland seas, drinking cocktails while real women tend to our needs. Then we'll look back on all of this and laugh."

Andre leaned back just enough to cause his harness to lock into place, securely connecting him to the small airship in order to hold them firmly in place while maneuvering during flight. It was a bit uncomfortable and somewhat restrictive, but it was better than falling out of the airship while at altitude. It also left their hands free to scan the area and use their weapons on approach if necessary.

The lead aircraft, the one outfitted with the weapons pod, was the first to lift off, followed immediately by the two airships outfitted with the empty passenger pods.

Andre watched the rooftop of the command center fall away beneath him as his airship leapt upwards, spun ninety degrees to starboard, and then accelerated toward the setting Corinairan sun. Within seconds the command center was just another building amongst many, some damaged and some not. He watched as the devastation caused by one of his mighty empire's warships passed rapidly beneath his dangling feet. He could see the people already fighting amongst themselves. It would be so easy for their operatives to pit these over-emotional Corinairans against one another. The news of the *sign* witnessed by legions of Followers all over the globe had already done much of the work for them. Loyalists had already clashed with Followers even before the bombardment had begun. Now that it had ended, the already enraged tempers of the people below would undoubtedly spin out of control with only the slightest encouragements. Soon, this world's government would collapse and Andre's people could step in and take control once and for all. Finally, they could turn this world into a mirror image of Takara herself. Although in his mind, that would necessitate nothing short of genocide.

He watched as the Corinairans scrambled below him like pigs sniffing for garbage to eat. He wished he could simply start picking them off one by one as they flew overhead, just to get in a little target practice. *Perhaps another time*, he thought.

* * *

The chanting continued to grow as more and more of the crowd joined in the repeated chants of *Na-Tan, Na-Tan, Na-Tan*. Nathan waved to the crowd wearily, unsure of what to do next.

"I believe they are expecting you to speak," Jalea told him, barely audible above the rising din.

Nathan felt a cold chill go down his spine at the thought of addressing the cheering masses. At that moment, the memories of all of his father's political speeches came flooding back to him. He found himself amazed that his father had been able to speak to such crowds as if talking to a neighbor. Surprisingly, Nathan found himself wishing he had paid more attention to those speeches.

Nathan turned to Jessica. "What the hell do I say to them?"

"You... at a loss for words?" she retorted. "That's a first."

"Seriously, Jess. These people think I'm a hero or something. What do I say to thousands of people who think I'm some kind of legend?"

"Say whatever you want. Recite the lyrics to your favorite song. What the hell does it matter? They can't understand you anyway."

"Thanks, you're loads of help, you are."

"Jesus, Nathan. Just wing it. You're good at that. Just remember that what you say here could change the course of this planet's history." Jessica smiled mischievously at him. "So no pressure."

Nathan flashed a mock smile of gratitude at her as he turned back to face the cheering crowd. He was about to open his mouth, still unsure of what to say, when he noticed a disturbance toward the back of the crowd. Two men were swinging blows at another man, pummeling their victim about the face. As the recipient of the blows fell, two others came to his aid, the first one catching the victim as he fell while the second one fought back against the attackers. Moments later, more people joined the fight, and the cheers began to transform into shouts of anger.

The local dignitaries on the platform next to Nathan also noticed the commotion at the back of the crowd, as looks of concern spread across their faces. Several armed security officers charged into the fray from the back of the crowd and tried to separate the combatants, but they too found themselves exchanging blows.

Nathan could hear the comm-units of the security guards on the podium near him blaring reports of the disturbance. "What's happening?" he asked Jalea.

"I am not sure," she admitted. It was apparent by the look on her face that she was just as confused about the cause of the fight as he was.

"I don't like this," Jessica announced as she turned toward Enrique, her former spec-ops partner and now her deputy as the Aurora's chief of security. "Keep a close eye on the prisoners," she ordered. Enrique responded instantly, relaying her sentiments to the two marines guarding the prisoners with no more than a look in their direction and a subtle hand gesture that meant *stay sharp*.

A shot rang out. It was nothing more than a zing and a flash of bright light somewhere in the middle of the scuffle, but it was enough. Jessica recognized the sound of an energy weapon firing. She had heard enough of them over the past week. "GUN!"

At the sound of the gun, the crowd panicked and began to scatter in all directions, their shouts of anger turning into screams of fear. Those that remained had already been drawn into the melee. At least a half-dozen people lay injured on the ground, the result of either the assaults or the panicked crowd as they tried to escape danger.

An instant later, Enrique, the two marines,

and Jessica all had their automatic close-quarters weapons unslung from their shoulders, in their hands, and ready to fire. Everyone on the platform began to scatter, most being ushered off toward the safety of two waiting transport airships that were already spinning up their engines in preparation for a quick departure.

Jessica was in a semi-crouch, tense and ready for combat. She looked around, seeing that Enrique and the two marines had taken similar stances. The prisoners had crouched even lower, some even down on the ground, feeling far more vulnerable while still in restraints. All of them, she noticed, except for Captain de Winter. He appeared to be trying to see what was happening, as if searching for a moment of opportunity.

Enrique noticed him as well, and before Jessica had a chance to say anything, he pushed the nobleman down to the tarmac with his free hand. "Stay down, asshole!"

A Corinairan security officer of upper rank started barking at Nathan and his group in his native tongue. Nathan looked around, unsure of what the officer was trying to tell them. He could see five armed guards as they ran in behind the prisoners to help ensure they remained in custody.

"What's he saying?" Nathan asked no one in particular.

"He wants us to clear the platform and get into one of the transports," Tug explained.

"To go where?" Jessica asked at the top of her lungs over the shouts of the crowd, now fully embroiled in an all-out riot. She looked behind her and saw the armed guards moving in behind the prisoners as if to take them away. "Whoa!" she hollered as she spun her weapon around. "What are they doing with the prisoners?"

Two nearby security guards quickly trained their weapons on Jessica in response to her aggressive motion. Tug reached out and put his hand on the barrel of her rifle and pushed it downward to ensure the guards did not perceive her as a direct threat. "I'm sure they are simply taking them to a secure holding facility," he told her. "They are no longer our concern."

Jessica didn't like that one bit. Nothing made her more nervous than to have something out of her control, and right now she felt as if *everything* was out of her control. All around her there was chaos. There were at least a hundred people rioting not more than ten meters away from them, and the only thing between them and the rioters was a flimsy barricade rail. To make matters worse, at least one person in that conflict was armed and had already fired in anger.

The officer in charge continued barking at them in an unintelligible fashion and pointing toward transport airships a dozen meters away.

"He wants us to board the transport on the left," Tug translated for them. "He says it's for our own safety."

"Where are they taking us?" Nathan asked, still struggling to understand the situation.

"Anywhere is better than here at the moment!" Jessica insisted as she rose slightly and started to lead them quickly toward the transport.

Jessica knew that the sooner they at least got down off the platform, the better. She motioned to everyone else to follow her down. The armed guards had reinforced the barricade by forming a

13

wall of officers between the riotous crowd and the dignitaries and were staying in place long enough for Jessica and the others to get clear as well. A minute later they were at the boarding ramp of the first of two transport airships. Jessica grabbed the officer in charge of the security detail by the shoulder and pulled it back to get him to look at her. "No one is getting on that transport until we know where the hell we're going!" she told him. She didn't care that he did not understand a word she was saying. She was quite sure that her body language communicated her intent.

Jalea stepped in and translated for her, and in a far more respectful tone than Jessica would have chosen. The officer responded back to her without hiding his irritation at Jessica's demeanor. "They wish to take everyone to the local command center," Jalea explained. "Apparently this is not the only location where such hostilities are occurring."

Jessica turned to Nathan. "Maybe we'd better cut this trip short for now and head back to the ship," she strongly suggested. The last thing she wanted to do was to put themselves into the hands of a bunch of people they just met, especially a bunch of armed people.

"We can't leave yet," Nathan insisted. "We just got here!"

"We're not safe here!"

"We haven't been safe since the first jump, Jess! Why should now be any different? Besides, we at least have to get some medical help for Cameron."

Jessica knew he was right, even though she didn't like it. Besides, the XO was her friend as well. "Well, we should at least have Tug take the shuttle back to the ship. It's the only one we've got and we can't afford to lose it down here in all the chaos."

"Agreed," Nathan said.

"I think it would be better if I stayed with you," Tug objected. "I can help you better understand this world and its people."

"Also agreed," Nathan added.

"Well, somebody's gotta fly the shuttle out of here," Jessica insisted.

"Marcus can fly the shuttle," Jalea suggested.

Jessica looked at her with disbelief. "Really? Marcus?" While she had no idea if Marcus really could pilot the shuttle, she suspected that Jalea had only suggested it in order to ensure her continued presence on the surface. Jessica suspected that Jalea, as usual, had her own agenda.

"It's mostly automated," Tug explained. "Even my daughter could fly it."

"Yeah, well, I've got more confidence in your daughter than I do in Marcus," Jessica said. "What about Jalea? She's a pilot, right?" Jessica made the suggestion to test Jalea's reaction. It was obvious by the expression on her face that she did not like the idea.

"She should also stay here," Tug insisted. "She speaks several of the most common languages of this world."

"You speak Corinairan, don't you?" Nathan commented, remembering that Tug had already translated more than once since they arrived on the surface.

"Yes, but not as well as Jalea."

Although uncomfortable with the idea of leaving Marcus at the flight controls of their only way back to the ship, it did make sense to keep Tug on the surface with them. Jessica didn't trust that Jalea would be entirely accurate in her translations, and she didn't want her left alone and unchecked on board the Aurora. She suspected that Jalea had another trick up her sleeve, and if so, she preferred to keep an eye on her.

Tug, on the other hand, was a different story. He had proven himself trustworthy on more than one occasion, most notably during their whirlwind escape from his molo farm on Haven. Marcus had proven himself just as trustworthy, as well as being somewhat resourceful under fire.

Nathan looked at Jessica. "Sound good?" he asked, hoping for her approval.

"Fine," she acquiesced. "Enrique, take the marines back to the shuttle and tell Marcus to fly you back to the ship. You can come back and pick us up later after this all blows over."

"Seriously?" he asked, not convinced that Marcus was the right choice for pilot. He didn't wait for a response, as he already knew the answer. "Let's move out, marines," he ordered as he turned and headed for the shuttle.

The security officer in charge continued to urge them into the transport and appeared relieved when they finally began to move toward the waiting airship. Nathan looked the transport over as they approached. It was about ten meters long and four across at its widest point, and it had large doors that slid open on either side just behind the pilots. It was not terribly attractive to look at, appearing to be a somewhat flattened cylinder that tapered slightly at each end before rounding off. It sat on four squat pairs of heavy-duty wheels as it waited patiently, its four large overhead ducted fans spinning at what must have been an incredible velocity. Nathan assumed that the rotor blades must have been at zero pitch, as he felt no rotor wash as they passed beneath them.

He watched curiously as the massive ducted fans sticking out on each corner of the transport airship wiggled back and forth on their gimbal mounts, the pilot undoubtedly checking their functionality before takeoff. The airships were painted flat black and had little in the way of identifying markings other than simple numbers and letters on their sides. There was, however, some sort of shield or crest painted on the hull just between the cockpit windows and the main door.

The lights on the underside of the airship began to flash as they climbed up the short boarding ramp. The ground crew moved away to avoid the rotor wash that would soon follow. If these pilots were anything like the ones in the fleet back on Earth, they would lift off as soon as possible, especially under the circumstances.

Despite the speed at which the ducted fan rotors were spinning, the airship had seemed unusually quiet to Nathan. As soon as the last passenger boarded and the crew chief stepped back inside, the passive whirring of the rotors intensified into a low roar as they changed their pitch accordingly in order to create the necessary lift.

The transport leapt up off the ground, causing Nathan and the others to be forced down hard against their seats. As a pilot himself, Nathan had experienced rapid ascents on more than one occasion, but the rate at which these airships were gaining altitude made them feel more like rockets than airships.

No more than a few seconds later, the transport

had stopped ascending just as quickly and it turned sharply to port as it swung around on its new course. Nathan looked out the still open doorway as the crew chief activated the hatch controls, causing the small boarding ramp to retract into the underside of the airship and the large side door to slide closed. He could see the crowd below as security fought to subdue what now appeared to be at least a dozen different fights. Just below them a handful of smaller airships darted past and dropped down next to the riot, several more armed guards hopping out of the nimble aircraft as they touched down.

As they continued their departure from the spaceport, Nathan could see numerous pillars of smoke rising from the city. He could only begin to imagine the amount of destruction caused by the Yamaro's bombardment of this world. For at the base of every one of those columns was a smoldering pile of rubble, a raging fire, or a smoking crater... and of course, bodies.

The noise subsided considerably as the door slid closed and locked into place. The crew chief checked the door before he settled back into his seat just behind the pilot, his back facing forward. Through the windows Nathan could see the other transport flying just off their starboard side and slightly behind them. Nathan noticed the others in the cabin donning headsets and followed suit.

"Where are we going?" Nathan asked over his headset.

"Some kind of command center," Jalea answered, after which she began speaking with the crew chief over the headsets in the local Corinairan dialect. "He says we are going to the Disaster Management Command and Control Center," Jalea told them after speaking with the crew chief for several moments.

"Tell him we need to speak to their leaders," Nathan told Jalea.

"Really?" Jessica asked as Jalea translated Nathan's words to the crew chief. "'Take me to your leader.' That's what you're going with?"

"He says the Prime Minister is the most senior government official known to have survived at the moment," Jalea translated back to Nathan.

"Then we should talk to him," Nathan surmised.

"He is in the other transport," Jalea explained. "Apparently, he was the gentleman presenting you to the crowds gathered at the spaceport earlier. He is also en route to the command center."

Nathan rolled his eyes in resignation as he returned his attention to the view outside the windows. He watched as four smaller aircraft streaked past them, taking up positions just ahead of them. They were smaller and only had three ducted fans instead of the four like the larger transports. There appeared to be two fans; one on either side above and slightly forward of the main cargo doors and a third smaller one on the tail. The small ships were heavily armed with a turret-style energy weapon slung under the nose and rocket pods sticking out of each side just behind the cockpit. Other than their armaments, they appeared identical in design to the smaller airships he had seen delivering security personnel to the spaceport on their way out.

"They must be escorts," Jessica observed.

All Nathan could do was wonder why they needed armed escorts in the first place.

* * *

When the Aurora's landing party had first arrived on Corinair, Marcus had chosen to remain with the shuttle after everyone else had disembarked. The last thing he had wanted was to stand in front of a roaring crowd like some kind of celebrity, especially since no more than a few hours ago he had shot down a Corinairan interceptor with a hastily assembled tail gun that had been mounted in the back of this very shuttle. He could easily imagine running into the pilot of that very same interceptor, who would probably still be angry after having to bail out of his disabled ship.

He had watched with dismay as everything around him outside had come unglued. No more than minutes after they had landed, it seemed like the whole planet had spun out of control. Everywhere he looked, people were fighting over one thing or another. He had been in his share of bar fights, but this was getting a bit extreme. As the rioting escalated, he had even considered mounting that little tail gun of his just in case he had to defend the shuttle, but had decided against it for fear that he might attract undue attention. Instead, he had simply chosen to retreat farther back into the ship, ready to close the hatch should trouble come. It was a relief when Enrique and the two marines came bounding up the rear boarding ramp of the shuttle.

"Coming aboard," Enrique yelled as they hit the ramp. The last thing he needed was for Marcus to get trigger-happy and blast a new hole in him.

"What the hell is going on out there?" Marcus demanded.

"The Corinairans are rioting," Enrique told him as he entered the shuttle.

"No kidding. Over what?"

"Don't know; don't care," Enrique answered. "My orders are to get this shuttle back to the Aurora. So fire her up and let's take off."

"Where's the pilot?" Marcus asked.

"I'm looking at him."

Marcus glanced behind him, half expecting to see someone standing there ready to fly the shuttle. "You're serious?"

"The rebel princess said you could fly this thing. Can you?"

"The who? What? Well, yeah, if I have to."

"Well, you have to. So let's get moving. We don't know how long security can keep the crowd under control out there."

Marcus groaned as he turned and headed forward to the cockpit.

"Check the perimeter of the ship to make sure we're all clear to lift off," Enrique instructed the two marines. "But make it quick. I want to get off the ground, pronto."

The two marines ran out the back of the shuttle as ordered, and Enrique turned to join Marcus in the cockpit.

Marcus plopped down in the pilot's seat and activated the auto-launch sequencer. The ship's engines began to spin up, a low vibration translating through her old frame as her reactor plant powered up and her air-breathing turbines ignited. He watched as electronic displays all along the forward console began to light up as all the shuttle's flight controls and monitoring systems began to come online. Marcus mumbled to himself as he looked over the controls, trying to remember what everything in front of him actually did.

Enrique noticed the lack of confidence in his

reluctant pilot's expression. "You *do* know how to fly this thing, right?"

"Yeah, but..."

"But what?"

"But not very well, okay?"

"Well, can you get us back to the Aurora or not?" Enrique asked.

"Sure, I can get you back," Marcus replied confidently. "Gettin' back's the easy part. It's landing that's got me worried." Marcus looked over at Enrique, who was staring at him. "Stop looking at me like that," Marcus insisted. "And tell your boys to get back inside before this thing takes off without them."

Moments later the marines were back on board and the rear boarding ramp was slowly swinging upwards toward its closed position as the shuttle began to rise slowly off the tarmac to begin its journey back to orbit in order to rendezvous with the Aurora.

"Holy crap!" one of the marines exclaimed from the back of the shuttle. As the shuttle rose, the marine hit the stop button, pausing the ramp in its half-open position so he could get a better look outside. As they continued to climb, he could see additional riots breaking out beyond the perimeter of the spaceport. "Sir!" the marine called forward, "are you seeing this?"

Enrique looked out at the riots below as the shuttle passed over the fence line and began its ascent. It took less than a minute for the shuttle to climb too high for him to still make out any detail on the surface, but from what he had seen, there were similar disturbances taking place all over the city. "These people are nuts," he exclaimed, looking at Marcus.

"Yeah, well, them Corinairans tend to get easily overheated, if you know what I mean." A red indicator light flashed on the panel, catching Marcus's attention. He looked at the indicator, read the label, and then frowned.

"What is it?" Enrique asked, noticing the dour expression on Marcus's face.

"You best tell you boys to close that hatch, or the air in here is gonna get thin really quickly."

* * *

Nathan held on tight as the transport skimmed low over the ruins of the city, weaving in between the buildings that were still standing. For such an ungainly looking aircraft, the transport was remarkably maneuverable as it darted back and forth, occasionally bobbing up and down and shifting from side to side, all for no apparent reason. As best he could tell, they weren't exactly taking the most direct route to their destination, and Nathan could not help but notice that they were routinely coming awfully close to not only the buildings they were flying between, but also to the ground below them.

"Is it really necessary for them to fly so low?" Nathan couldn't help but ask as he struggled to maintain his balance in the constantly shifting aircraft.

"The Ta'Akar do the same," Tug explained, "to avoid the portable missiles used by the Karuzari, who are less likely to shoot downward for fear of harming innocent people below."

"And they don't mind putting their people at risk this way?"

"In times of conflict, you do what you must to survive," Tug lamented.

Nathan continued looking out the windows as the scenes of devastation rushed past below him. One moment he would see people helping one another out amidst the rubble. The next moment there would be people fighting each other in the streets for no apparent reason. There were security forces struggling to restore order in the midst of the chaos, but even some of the rescue workers were being attacked while they tried to help those in need.

"What the hell is going on down there?" he wondered aloud as the transport quickly reversed its bank and skirted around a building whose top half appeared to be missing. Nathan held on tight with one hand on the overhead rail to steady himself against the constant wild maneuvering. *Josh would feel right at home here,* he thought.

"Loyalists," the crew chief said over the headsets. His pronunciation of the word was a bit off, but understandable nonetheless, as was the disdain in his voice. "They support Ta'Akar, blame Followers, blame you," he explained in broken Angla.

Nathan was amazed that the wild turns and sudden changes in altitude seemed to have no effect on the crew chief, who remained calm and relaxed despite the constant shifting of the airship.

"Jesus," Jessica exclaimed. "Does everybody around here speak Angla?"

"A few decades ago, yes, everyone still spoke Angla," Tug explained. "Or to be more precise, everyone spoke Angla in addition to their native tongue. There was a time not long ago when all children were taught Angla in school. But as Caius grew more powerful, the restrictions on the language were more rigidly enforced, driving it underground. Now less than half of the population in the cluster still speak it, and even then only in private. Especially on the larger worlds. Other than Takara, the Darvano system *is* the most heavily populated system in the empire. It was originally an ally of the Ta'Akar. They were conquered and forced to accept the rule of Caius just over thirty years ago. I would suspect that most of the older population still remembers the Angla language, even if they haven't spoken it in decades."

As the transport rolled hard to port, Tug looked out the windows down at the fights in the streets. "Notice that most of the aggressors are young males. They were probably born to parents that were either loyal to the Ta'Akar regime or chose to appear that way for safety's sake. These young men were probably never taught the language and believe wholeheartedly in the Doctrine as handed down by Caius."

"You mean they believe Caius is a god?" Nathan asked.

"No one truly believes he is a god," Tug defended as the transport rolled back to port and then dropped back down to just above the rubble, "except maybe for a few zealots here and there."

"Or the criminally insane," Jessica muttered. She too found her knuckles turning white as she gripped the overhead rail.

"I suppose," Tug answered, somewhat amused by her comment as well as her struggle to remain in her seat.

"I still don't understand why they are attacking each other down there," Nathan said.

"The Loyalists blame the Followers of the Order

for the bombardment," Tug told them. "News of the bombardment of Saliya, the planet on which our last base had been hidden, reached this world only days ago. I imagine tensions have been growing between Loyalists and Followers since then."

"So those aren't your people down there fighting the Loyalists?" Jessica surmised.

"No," Tug assured her. "We prefer more covert methods. We would not allow ourselves to be drawn out into open conflict in such a manner. We would lose our anonymity operating in this fashion. And our ability to hide amongst our enemy has always been our biggest strength. The people fighting below are most likely Followers of the Order who are simply defending themselves against attacks by Loyalists."

Jessica noticed that Jalea had remained silent during Tug's explanations. She also noticed that something he had said didn't seem to sit well with her. For a moment, Jessica wondered if the wild ride they were all experiencing might be proving a bit much for Jalea but immediately dismissed the idea.

After listening to their conversation over the headsets, the crew chief felt compelled to add his opinions to the discussion, despite his less than perfect use of the language. "People scared. Loyalists want to be proven to Ta'Akar, so they not be destroyed. Followers believe you," he said, pointing to Nathan. "They believe Na-Tan come to free all, to defeat Caius."

"And what do you believe?" Jessica asked the crew chief.

"I believe Corinair should be free."

"And what about Na-Tan, here?" she added, cocking her head toward Nathan. "Do you believe in him as well?"

The crew chief looked at Nathan, scanning him up and down before poking him once in the shoulder with his gloved finger. "I believe Na-Tan only man. Maybe great man. I not yet know."

Jessica chuckled to herself at the chief's comments. "Yeah, the jury is still out on that one," she joked.

"I don't get it," Nathan said, ignoring Jessica's remark. "If the Ta'Akar are so bad, why don't these people fight back?"

"The punishment for defiance is quite severe," Tug answered. "In the beginning, the people did fight back. That's how the Karuzari were born. But over the decades, most people have accepted their fates. It is easier to live a lie in peace than to die for the truth. As long as life is good, most of them simply do not care."

Nathan looked out the window once more as the transport continued to bank and turn, weaving its way through the burning city. "*Life* doesn't look too good right now."

"True. I believe that the Ta'Akar may have crossed the line this time. The Corinairans are a proud people. Acquiescing to the will of Caius was not an easy thing for them to do. Perhaps now they will find the will to resist."

"Be ready," the crew chief interrupted. "Now fun begins."

"Huh?" Nathan wondered, his eyes looking to Jessica. She only shrugged.

Nathan glanced out the windows again just in time to see that they were leaving the city and crossing out into open country. Below him the industrial areas on the fringe of the city were quickly fading into a countryside dotted with small farmhouses and agricultural fields.

Without warning, Nathan found himself pushed down hard into his seat as the transport leapt upward, gaining altitude at an incredible rate. The sudden acceleration was so severe it nearly knocked the air from his lungs, as he had been unprepared for the airship's alarming rate of ascent. It reminded him of the ride to orbit in the old shuttle that had taken him from the North American Fleet Academy spaceport up to the Aurora when she was still docked at the orbital assembly platform. Only this was worse.

Only moments after they had begun their ascent, alarms went off in the cockpit, followed by the heightened chatter of the flight crew over the headsets.

"What is it?" Nathan asked.

"Missiles," the crew chief answered.

Nathan turned to look forward but could not see past the cockpit console. He turned around in his seat to look out the window behind him at the ground below as it quickly fell away as they gained altitude. Ahead of them and to their left, he could see two small missile contrails arcing upward from the ground. "I've got two contrails to port at ten o'clock low!"

"Two more on this side," Tug announced.

Nathan watched as two of the escorting gunships dove under them toward the incoming missiles on their left. Suddenly, the cabin shook with the sound of at least a half-dozen *clunks* from beyond the aft bulkhead.

"What the hell was that?" Jessica asked, her eyes wide.

"They're probably launching decoys," Tug

explained as he turned around to look aft out his window. "Yes, I see them!"

On either side of the transports, small snub-nosed drones rocketed alongside them, fanning out slowly for several seconds before they started peeling off on different courses. At the same moment, the transport also began to wildly change course in an effort to trick the incoming missiles into locking onto one of the decoys instead of them.

Nathan and the others struggled to cope with the force of their continued upward acceleration. He could feel his heart racing. The airship vibrated violently as it continued to climb. "What is he trying to do, go into orbit?"

"They are probably portable shoulder-launched surface to air missiles. They are very inexpensive weapons and therefore are easily accessible. However, their range and ceiling is limited. The pilot is no doubt trying to get above their maximum effective altitude. We should be out of their range in less than a minute," Tug assured him.

Nathan continued to watch as all four of the escort gunships shrank away from them toward the incoming missiles. Everything felt as if it were going in slow motion. If he had been in a fighter, he would've launched his counter measures and then dispatched intercept missiles to knock down the incoming ordnance. On his world, however, such missiles were a bit on the bulky side. If similar technologies were used on Corinair, he seriously doubted that the weapons would have fit onto those small gunships. He had to wonder exactly how those gunships were planning on dealing with the threats.

In two pairs, the escort gunships dove toward the incoming missiles. Seconds later their nose turrets began firing red streaks of energy that lashed out at the incoming missiles in rapid succession. Three of the incoming missiles were immediately destroyed, but the fourth one found its way through to one of the gunships, striking just behind its cockpit. The explosion tore the port ducted fan assembly completely off and the small gunship toppled over and spun downward, slamming into the ground and exploding a few seconds later.

The remaining three gunships pulled out of their dive only meters above the tree tops, each turning away on different bearings. Two more missiles streaked out from the trees, in pursuit of the pair of gunships turning to the right. The third gunship performed a half loop followed by a half roll, bringing the gunship right-side up again with its nose pointed back at the area from which the last two missiles had been fired.

The pilot of the third gunship switched his weapons selector switch to rockets, causing two small pods to push out from the sides of the small ship just behind the cockpit. He could have used the more precise energy weapons, but time was critical and maximum force had already been authorized by command. He selected the target area on his weapons screen and pressed the small button on his joystick. A millisecond later a hail of miniature rockets leapt from the pods on either side of the gunship and streaked down toward the trees where two of the first four missile launches had originated. As they descended they fanned out evenly. Then, in a blinding flash of red, orange, and white, at least forty square meters of the forest disappeared in smoke and flame as the gunship ceased fire and swung to its left in order to avoid any return fire, but he was not quick enough.

The other two shooters had moved just enough to avoid being targeted before they stopped and fired off two more shots at the gunship that had just fried their cohorts. The third gunship stood little chance as both missiles struck a fraction of a second after they were launched, splitting the small ship into several chunks that fell to the ground in flames, setting yet another part of the forest ablaze.

The crew chief cursed loudly as he slammed his fist against the partial bulkhead that separated the passenger cabin from the cockpit, his sudden display of frustration and anger giving the passengers a start. Jalea tried to say something to the man in his native Corinairan tongue, but the crew chief would have nothing to do with her. He leaned back against his aft facing seat as his eyes welled up. Nathan could see the pain and frustration in the man's gaze.

"His brother was pilot of gunship," a voice announced in heavily accented Angla over the headsets. "He killed two enemy before dying."

Nathan looked forward as the copilot that had just spoken to them turned his head back to check on his crew chief. The copilot said something in Corinairan to his crew chief as he reached his right arm back to grasp the chief's shoulder and offer both comfort and camaraderie. The chief mumbled an appreciative response as he quickly regained his composure.

Down near the surface, the two remaining gunships completed their long, wide turn and came back around in time to note the location of the last two shooters. Within seconds, the remaining shooters were engulfed in a maelstrom of fire and disintegrating trees as more than fifty small rockets exploded across the forest where they had stood only moments before. The remaining two gunships streaked overhead, driving straight through the rising fire and smoke. They pulled away and began to climb upward to rejoin the transports that, by now, had managed to reach a safe altitude, unharmed.

Nathan watched the crew chief as he pulled himself together to carry on with their mission. He wanted to say something to make the poor man feel better, but he didn't know if it would be appropriate. This was a different culture, with different ways and beliefs. A seemingly innocent condolence by Earth standards could be easily misconstrued here. Instead, he just turned away and stared out the window, watching the two surviving gunships as they climbed up to rejoin the transports.

After a few minutes without any conversation, the pilot called to the crew chief. The chief managed to pull himself together, wiping his eyes as he addressed his passengers.

"We will start descent soon. Prepare yourselves. It will be most quickly."

Nathan felt that he had to say something, out of respect if nothing more. He spoke slowly and clearly, hoping he would not be misunderstood. "I am sorry about your brother."

"Thank you," the chief answered. He stared at the

deck for a moment before looking back up. "Many people die today. Good people. Is not right, what Ta'Akar do this day." The chief stared at him for a moment. "You are truly Na-Tan, yes?"

Nathan smiled. "Actually, it's pronounced *Nathan*. What's your name?"

"Montrose," the crew chief responded. "Doran Montrose."

"And your brother, what was his name?"

"Kyle," the chief stated proudly.

The pilot's voice came over the headsets again, and the crew chief braced himself, causing everyone else to follow his example.

The transport began to fall from the sky as if her engines had simply stopped functioning. Nathan felt as if his stomach were about to come out of his mouth as the airship fell back to the planet at an alarming rate. Nearly thirty hair-raising seconds later, their descent ended almost as abruptly as it had begun. The transport flared out, pushing them all down into their seats again with incredible force. Then the transport settled into normal, low-level flight and cruised in over the perimeter wire on approach to the airfield just outside the Disaster Management Command and Control Center.

A minute later, the transport bounced gently as it settled onto the tarmac and began to roll up to its designated unloading position. As they rolled to a stop, Nathan could see the two remaining gunships keeping station in a hover nearby, their noses constantly turning from one side to the other as they kept watch.

A ground crewman opened the door to the transport from the outside. As the door slide open, the small boarding ramp extended outward from the airship and down to the tarmac, turning into three steps. Jalea was the first out, followed by Tug and Jessica. As Nathan followed them out, Chief Montrose grabbed him by his upper arm. "If you fight Ta'Akar, you call us. We fight with you."

Nathan looked into the chief's eyes, seeing a burning intensity. The chief meant what he had said. Nathan looked to the cockpit as well. Both pilots were also looking at him, each with the same serious intent in their eyes. The flight crew said nothing, only nodded in agreement with their crew chief. Nathan returned the nod, his own face adorned with the same intensity as he exited the airship and hopped down onto the tarmac.

His feet on the ground, Nathan felt compelled to turn back to face the crew chief and the flight crew. To his surprise, the crew chief and the pilot both snapped a quick salute. As the airship began to rise up off the tarmac, Nathan returned the salute.

The ground security personnel grabbed his arm to urge him to follow the others to the security of the buildings. Nathan turned and followed Tug, Jalea, Jessica, and the Corinairan security personnel into the main building only ten meters away. Inside, they were greeted by stern-looking men in full body armor brandishing rather ominous looking energy weapons. These men were not the same as the security personnel that they had seen at the spaceport. These men, much like the crew of the transport airship, appeared more seasoned and better equipped. Their uniforms were different as well. While the uniforms of the security personnel at the spaceport were obviously meant to make them easily identifiable as authority figures, the outfits worn by these men were purely functional: flat black with dull gray trim—adorned with nothing more than a name patch, unit patch, and rank insignia.

"Sir," a young man in a black uniform said to Nathan in heavily accented Angla, "I must ask you and your people to relinquish all weapons before entering the command center."

"Hold on just a minute," Jessica began.

Nathan glanced around the room, noticing that the well-armed men had just tensed up a bit. Jessica noticed it as well.

"I really don't think we have much choice in the matter, Jess."

"Your weapons will be returned to you upon departure, sir. But for security reasons, only authorized Corinari personnel are permitted to carry weapons inside this facility."

Jessica slowly unslung her close-quarters automatic weapon, holding it by the barrel stock so as to appear non-threatening to the room full of armed troops. She could tell by their reaction that they all understood the meaning of why she held her weapon in such fashion. "All right then," she said as she handed her rifle and then her handgun to the officer.

Nathan followed suit, as did Tug and Jalea, leaving them all defenseless. Nathan was quite sure that Jessica was not happy about being disarmed, but he was equally sure that she knew it was necessary.

He was about to move forward when the officer cleared his throat and looked at Jessica. She rolled her eyes once and then smiled. "Oops," she exclaimed as she pulled a large combat knife from her belt sheath, as well as a smaller one from her right boot. "Guess I forgot a few."

Nathan looked at her. "Anything else?"

"Just these mini flash-bangs," she admitted, removing four small orange spheres from a pouch on her belt and handing them to the officer.

"You're sure that's everything?" Nathan asked again, a grin forming on his face.

"What, you wanna check my bra?" she remarked, a mischievous smile forming.

Nathan's mind wandered for a moment, as he recalled their encounter in his father's anteroom on the night they first met. It had been a brief but passionate moment shared between two somewhat inebriated strangers. At the time, neither of them had known that they would be serving together, especially out here, a thousand light years from home.

Several of the guards appeared to understand Angla, as they too smiled as the officer-in-charge collected their weapons and placed them in a secure locker.

"Please, follow me," he instructed as he turned and headed for the inner entrance.

The officer led them down a long corridor, passing several doorways and windows looking into various workspaces. Most were filled with personnel busy dealing with the planet-wide crisis.

As they proceeded down the corridor, Jalea moved in close beside Tug as they walked, speaking to him in their own language and in hushed tones in case their escort was conversant in the same tongue.

"I believe it would be best if you let Nathan do the talking," she gently urged.

Tug tried to hide the curious look on his face from the others as they continued down the corridor and around the first corner. "To what end?"

"The Followers on this world now view him as the hero of legend. This can be of great use to our cause."

"I do not care for such tactics. You, more than anyone, should be aware of this fact."

"I'm not suggesting that we take advantage of it, only that you do not purposefully dispel this belief. It may prove too valuable to dismiss, despite your moral objections to such tactics."

"These people are facing the greatest threat to their existence in their entire thousand-year history, Jalea. Don't you think they have the right to know the truth about how this situation was thrust upon them?"

"You mean how the leader of the Karuzari and his former lover planted the notion of a sign from God that Na-Tan, the hero of legend, was about to arrive?"

Tug stared at her as they walked. "I had no foreknowledge of your deceptions. You know that."

"Yes, *I* know that, and of course I would tell them as such. But would they *believe* me?"

Tug was being played and he knew it. It wasn't the first time that Jalea had manipulated events in such a way. She had always had a bad habit of taking matters into her own hands, and in a similarly careless fashion. This time, however, she was risking the lives of billions of innocent people. He could not comprehend how she could justify such actions, yet she seemed to be doing just that.

"They would be more likely to shoot us on the spot," she continued, "or at the very least, arrest us and hand us over to the Ta'Akar as a demonstration of their loyalty."

She took Tug's lack of response as indication of

agreement, and walked ahead of him, a slight look of satisfaction coming across her face.

Tug knew she was right. Depending on who was in control of Corinair at the time their identities were revealed, they would be either embraced as freedom fighters or offered up as traitors to Caius himself. As frustrated as it left him, Tug had little choice but to heed her advice.

After turning another corner, they were led into another windowed room. On one side of the room, there was a large conference table surrounded by at least a dozen chairs. On the other side were several larger more comfortable chairs, as well as a long couch.

"If you'll all please be seated, the Prime Minister will join you shortly."

"Thank you," Nathan responded as the officer left the room, closing the door behind him. After the door closed, a conspicuous *click* was heard. Nathan and Jessica looked at each other, after which Jessica took the few steps back to the door and gently tried to turn the doorknob.

"Yup, it's locked," she announced.

"We're prisoners?" Nathan asked in disbelief. Thirty minutes ago, crowds of Corinairans were cheering, welcoming him as a hero, now they were disarmed and confined.

"I doubt that is their intent," Jalea offered.

"She's right," Tug agreed. "They probably do not want us moving about freely. Security concerns would dictate that you control the movement of personnel during a crisis, especially unfamiliar guests."

"Yeah," Jessica agreed, "especially guests who arrived with guns."

"All right then," Nathan resigned as he turned and followed Jessica away from the door and deeper into the conference room.

"So what do we do now?" Jessica asked as she plopped down on the couch, making herself comfortable.

"What is it about you and couches?" Nathan wondered aloud. Jessica simply shrugged.

"We wait for the Prime Minister to become available," Jalea told him. "I am sure he will explain what is happening in greater detail once he has the opportunity."

Nathan sighed. "I just hope it doesn't take too long. Cameron needs medical help, and I didn't even get a chance to ask them yet."

"What do you suppose is going on out there?" Jessica asked Tug.

"I suspect the Loyalists are blaming the Followers of the Order for what is happening to their world."

Nathan turned back toward Tug, surprised by his words. "You mean for being *bombed* by the Ta'Akar."

"Yes. They see it as punishment for openly defying the Doctrine."

"Well that doesn't make any sense."

"I suspect such attitudes are being fueled by the actions of those who wish such confrontations to occur," Jalea said.

Tug noticed the look of confusion on Nathan's face. "It has been suspected for some time that the Ta'Akar have covert units operating on all of the conquered worlds."

"As well as the worlds that were previously under their control," Jalea added.

"That explains how those assault teams ambushed us so quickly back on Haven," Jessica commented from her seat on the couch.

"Yes, it would," Tug agreed. "If they are operating on this world, at the very least their goal would be to put down any insurrection, and by whatever means available."

"But in that case, the Yamaro just bombed her own troops," Nathan observed. "But why pit the Corinairans against one another?"

"Simple," Jessica interrupted. "It just adds to the chaos. The more chaos, the freer they are to operate without notice or resistance. Hell, I wouldn't be surprised if they're running around disguised as Corinairan military."

"Which means..." Nathan began.

"That we must use caution when choosing who to trust," Jalea finished for him.

"Yeah, kind of ironic, isn't it?" Jessica said, staring at Jalea.

"In fact," Tug said, "it might be better not to trust anyone, at least not completely, for the immediate future."

"Well, at least for now we should be safe in here," Nathan stated.

"If those really were Corinairan transports that picked us up at the spaceport," Jessica pointed out, "and if this really is a Corinairan command facility."

Nathan thought about what she was suggesting, but he also remembered the look on the crew chief's face and the faces of the flight crew as they were getting off the transport. He doubted it had been an act. "You are way too suspicious by nature," he told her.

"Comes with the job," she said with a small laugh, "especially under your command."

CHAPTER TWO

The black, unmarked Kalibri airships maneuvered past the rubble of what was once the largest market plaza in all of Aitkenna. Having taken several strikes from the Yamaro, it was now nothing more than a pile of concrete and steel—and the corpses of those caught in its sudden collapse—with thick columns of black smoke still billowing from the many fires burning under the remains.

The five airships flew in two groups. The first group, with the gunship in the lead and the troop carriers following just behind, turned down the main causeway used by delivery and service vehicles. Most of the citizens of Aitkenna used public transportation systems such as monorails and subways, but there were also service roadways routinely used by various delivery and public service vehicles. That was where they expected to find their target.

"Entering engagement zone," the lead gunship reported over the comms.

"Pivot slightly to port so I can get a visual," Andre ordered the pilot of his airship. The pilot responded immediately, pivoting the small airship slightly to the left as it continued on its flight path, skewed slightly sideways, so that Andre could see the convoy of vehicles on the roadway ahead. "Strike One, target the first and second overpasses directly ahead. As soon as the convoy passes under the first one, take both overpasses out. That'll trap them inside the corridor."

"Strike One copies," the gunship's pilot reported.

"Strike Two, put shooters on either side of the corridor as quickly as possible. As soon as the convoy comes to a stop, keep them pinned down inside their vehicles while we drop in behind them."

"Strike Two copies."

"Strikes Four and Five, hold back until we call you in for extraction."

The remaining two Kalibris configured as passenger ships that were following a half a kilometer behind acknowledged their orders as Andre's airship straightened back out, purposefully falling behind the gunship so as not to get caught in the backwash when he launched his weapons.

"Ten seconds to target," the gunship pilot reported.

"Drop positions," Andre called out. From the cockpit, the pilot switched the passenger restraint system to drop mode.

All four men felt their restraints give slightly, indicating the pilot had initiated drop mode. Just enough cable was released to allow them all to slide off the edge of the decks in order to free hang under the small airship. One end of each high tension cable was connected to a winch built into the deck of the airship. The other end was connected to their harnesses at a balance point in the center of their backs. Just after they slid off the deck, their lines cinched up just enough to hold their backsides up against the bottom of the airship as it swooped in lower in preparation to hover over their drop zone.

As he hung beneath the airship, Andre looked forward as four missiles left the gunship flying ahead of them and struck both overpasses simultaneously. He could feel the heat from the explosion of the overpass behind the convoy as they flew over the fireball and he saw the convoy of four armored troop carriers come to a screeching stop as the overpasses collapsed both in front and in back of them.

Andre could see Strike Two dropping shooters on either side of the corridor. As his own ship descended into position about fifty meters behind the convoy, the shooters moved into position and opened fire on the convoy below as Corinairan security forces tried to exit their vehicles to take up defensive positions. His teams were well trained, however, and they cut down the Corinairan security forces before they had a chance to disperse and put up a proper defense.

Andre's airship came to a hover directly over their drop zone behind the convoy.

"Drop-drop-drop," the pilot announced in well-rehearsed fashion as the ship came to a perfect hover ten meters above the roadway. The pilot activated the winches for all four of the passengers presently hanging under his airship. Andre and the other three members of his squad fell from the airship, the winches braking at the last second to slow them just enough so that their feet barely touched the ground before their drop cables automatically disconnected from the backs of their descent harnesses. The experience was quite like a free-fall, and as usual, Andre's stomach caught up to him just after his feet touched the ground.

Just as rehearsed countless times in the past, all four men dispersed in different directions. Seconds later their descent cables retracted smoothly up into the airship hovering overhead, which quickly climbed away as soon as the cables were secured.

Andre immediately moved up along the left side of the recessed roadway, staying against the corridor wall in a low crouch as he approached the tail end of the convoy with his weapon held ready and tight against his shoulder. The shooters overhead had succeeded in keeping the Corinairan forces pinned down and trapped inside their vehicles, thus he met no resistance on approach.

Pinpoint energy bursts bounced off the armored vehicles, dissipating in little clouds of light as the shooters continued to rain down fire from above. Andre and his partner ran up to the back of the last vehicle. He slid a small flat explosive charge under the vehicle and then rolled off to one side, his partner doing the same in the opposite direction. As soon as his body touched the side wall of the corridor, he covered his head and pressed the remote detonator button on his wrist controller.

The shaped charge exploded, sending a superheated column of plasma up through the bottom of the armored vehicle, engulfing the interior of the vehicle in white-hot flames. The doors, blown open from the blast, fell onto the street, followed by the flailing bodies of the burning soldiers trying in vain to escape the inferno. Andre kept his face covered as he felt the intense heat of the initial blast wash over him. Once the heat subsided, he opened his eyes and watched in fascination as the bodies flailed about for another few seconds. The chemical smell of the plasma fires and the stench of burning human flesh were almost overpowering. He only hoped that the convoy had followed standard Corinairan security procedures for prisoner transport, which dictated that the lead and rear vehicles carried guards and the middle vehicles carried prisoners. If they hadn't, he was sure he would catch hell from Commander Dumar upon their return.

Not wanting to succumb to the same fate, the troops in the lead vehicle of the trapped convoy came piling out in force, screaming at the top of their lungs in typical Corinairan fashion. They fired indiscriminately as they had not had a chance to discern the exact location of their attackers.

Andre let loose a few well-aimed shots of his own, cutting down at least two of the Corinairans. His participation had not been required, as the shooters above had clear lines of fire and could easily handle the floundering security guards. After only a few seconds of intense energy weapons fire, the battle was over.

Andre and the rest of his team rose and charged the middle two vehicles, swinging open the back doors to each.

"It's about bloody time," a distinguished-looking man in his fifties cursed as he stepped out of the vehicle.

"Captain de Winter, I presume?" Andre said.

"Of course, Sergeant, now get these restraints off of me."

"Yes, sir." Andre immediately removed the captain's shackles and tossed them aside.

"We have to get out of here immediately," de Winter ordered.

"The extraction birds will be here in thirty seconds, sir. We'll have you back to command in ten minutes," he assured him as he turned to check on his perimeter.

Captain de Winter grabbed Andre by the shoulder and spun him back around. "I have no intention of going to your command post, Sergeant. We need to get back to the spaceport and commandeer a shuttle."

Andre didn't much care to be manhandled in such fashion, especially by a noble. He, like his commander, had little use for his type. "The only place my birds are going is back to command, sir. My orders were to free you and your staff and to bring you back... and I follow orders. So that leaves you with two choices, sir. Either get in the extraction birds and go back to command, or wait here for Corinairan reinforcements to arrive."

Captain de Winter stared at the arrogant young sergeant. "I outrank you, Sergeant."

"I'm not under your command, sir. So while I do have to show you the proper respect, I do not have to follow *your* orders. If you have a problem with that, you can take it up with *my* CO back at AI command... in ten minutes."

The captain continued to stare at Andre as the extraction birds came down and landed behind them. "Very well, Sergeant. You have your victory... this time," he said as he moved past Andre toward the waiting airships.

Andre didn't turn to watch the captain and his staff board the airships. He had listened to many a story from his commander about the arrogance of Ta'Akar nobility. He had always figured they were the exaggerations of a bitter, aging commander on his last assignment. Now he knew otherwise.

"The vehicles are rigged and ready to blow," his partner reported to Andre.

"Great. Let's withdraw and head back to base," he told him.

The extraction airships were already taking off as his own airship came down to pick them up.

Andre walked back to the idling Kalibri, stepping over the still smoldering bodies of the men from the rear vehicle. He was the last one to arrive at his airship and stopped to turn around and take one last look at the devastation his team had caused. Satisfied that their mission was complete, he sat down on the edge of the airship's deck and slapped the side of the canopy three times. Once again he leaned back slightly and felt the restraint system lock him against the tiny airship as it leapt off the ground and into the evening sky.

They circled around the area to provide cover while the shooters were recovered by Strike Two. Once everyone was clear of the scene, Andre activated his remote detonator and the entire corridor containing the four armored vehicles and the dead guardsmen erupted in a massive white-hot fireball as the plasma charges planted by his team detonated. It would take forensic teams months to figure out who or what had been destroyed by that explosion, and considering all that was going on lately, he doubted that anyone would ever take the time.

Andre had been in the service for over a decade now, and this had been the first real combat action in which he had been involved. He had always heard that until you were under fire, you could not know for sure how you would react. Some men had it, some did not; and no matter how hard you trained, you never knew until the moment came. Today had been Andre's moment, and it had been far more enjoyable than he had anticipated.

* * *

Marcus's eyes nervously darted back and forth

between the auto-flight status and the near-space traffic display. The shuttle had reached orbit a few minutes ago, and as best he could tell, they were rapidly approaching the Aurora. Finally, his guilt got the best of him and forced him to speak. "Uh, we may have a slight problem here," he admitted sheepishly.

Enrique had been aware of Marcus's increasing concerns. "What kind of problem?"

"We're closing on the Aurora, but the auto-flight system isn't locking onto her control signal."

"What are you talking about? What's an auto-flight system? Is that like some kind of autopilot?" Enrique asked.

"Well, it's what pilots the ship, if that's what you mean."

"And it's not working?"

"It's working fine. It's just not receiving a control signal from your damned ship."

"What kind of control signal?" Enrique asked.

"The kind that tells the ship what to do! Without it, the ship doesn't know how to land!"

"Well can't it be flown manually?" Enrique was sure he was stating the obvious. The fact that Marcus was getting so concerned was beginning to worry him as well.

"Yeah, I suppose..."

"You suppose? I thought you said you could fly this thing."

"I can, when everything is working right. I mean, it's all automated and stuff. You just push some buttons, tell it where you want to go, and it takes you there: takeoff, landing... the whole deal from start to finish."

"Did you or did you not tell Jalea you could fly

this thing?"

Marcus grimaced, not wanting to answer. "Well, I may have overstated my abilities just a wee bit." Marcus looked over at Enrique, whose expression was none too favorable. "Oh, come on. Can you blame me? She's a real looker, that one!"

"Oh great!"

"No worries!" Marcus defended. "Just call up your ship and tell them to turn on their auto-flight control system so we can land, simple as that."

"Well why didn't you say that in the first place?" Enrique asked, rolling his eyes as he activated his comm-set. "You had me thinking we were gonna crash and burn on our own flight deck."

"Hey, I'm under a bit of pressure here too, you know."

Enrique just ignored him as he tried to raise the Aurora.

* * *

"That is where she wants it installed," Deliza told him.

"But I do not understand," Vladimir complained. "Why must it be here? Why not in the patch bay? It would be so much easier." Vladimir was wedged into the tiny crawl space at least thirty meters in from the main service tunnel. It had taken him nearly five minutes of crawling and wiggling to get into position, and he still didn't know the purpose of the device he was installing. All he knew was that Nathan had ordered him to install it himself for Doctor Sorenson.

"She did not tell me why, just where," Deliza told him. "Have you found the junction she indicated?"

"Yes, I found the junction she indicated," Vladimir responded, mimicking Deliza's voice.

"Don't get mad at me," she scolded. "I'm just doing as I'm told."

"*Da, konyeshna,*" Vladimir muttered. He pulled out his engineering data pad and plugged in a set of analyzing nodes connected to short cables. Unlike most data pads, the engineering units were slightly larger and had several ports to connect various cables and scanning devices. Vladimir carried it with him in a tool belt everywhere he went while on duty. The tool belt was equipped with a special pouch specifically tailored for the data pad. Without the data pad, he felt incomplete.

He clipped the probes around the insulation of the first set of wires that he had pulled away from the main bundle and activated his data pad. After tapping his headset, he spoke. "Doctor, I am in position. You may begin transmitting the ID signal."

"*Transmitting IDS now,*" Abby answered over the headset.

Vladimir watched his screen but saw no change in the waveform being produced by the probe. "Nyet." He moved the probe to the next wire. "Nyet." He continued moving the probe from wire to wire, checking for a wave form change on his data pad. "Nyet... Nyet... Nyet yeshyo... Nyet..." Suddenly, the waveform spiked. "Ah. Na konyetsna." He rechecked the waveform on his data pad until he was satisfied that he had located the correct wire. "You may discontinue ID signal, Doctor. And please, if you would shut down this circuit, I would very much appreciate it."

Vladimir watched as the waveform returned to the same baseline reading that the other wires had shown. He waited another few seconds until the waveform went completely flat, indicating that the wire was no longer charged and active. The thought had occurred to him that the doctor might use this opportunity to get even with him for all the trouble he had caused her during the initial installation of the jump drive weeks earlier. He could imagine her smile of satisfaction as he received a harmless yet painful electrical shock. However, according to the data pad, revenge was not in the physicist's plans for today—a fact for which Vladimir was grateful.

He carefully cut away a few centimeters of the outer shielding on the small wire and then attached a small compression splicer onto it. Once the tightening screw was turned, the device sunk its teeth into the wire, penetrating the inner insulation to make contact with the wire inside. He then connected the new wire to the compression splicer.

He reached down to his tool belt and felt around for the can of spray-on insulator, but it was nowhere to be found. "Chort," he cursed when he realized it was not where he expected it to be. "Deliza!" he called out in frustration. "Is there a small blue spray can out there?"

Deliza looked around the room by the entrance to the crawlway but did not see the can in question. "I don't see anything." She looked into the tunnel and noticed the small blue can lying on the floor of the tunnel near the intersection into which Vladimir had crawled. "Wait, I see it. It's in the main tunnel, at the intersection behind you. It must have fallen out of your tool belt."

"Can you bring it to me?"

"You want me to crawl up in there?" she said.

"You are small. It will be easy for you," he insisted.

Deliza looked down at her only outfit, the one she had been wearing the morning their farm was attacked and they had been forced to run, leaving everything they owned behind, including all of her clothing. "But I'm not really dressed for this," she pleaded, not wanting to crawl into the dirty tunnel.

"Deliza, please. It will take me forever. You will be fine; I promise."

Deliza rolled her eyes and exhaled in resignation as she climbed up into the tunnel entrance and began crawling through the narrow space. The floor of the long crawlspace was rough, having been textured to provide traction. The walls and ceiling of the tunnel were lined with countless wires, conduits, pipes, and ducting, and there was a fine soot covering everything.

"Why is it so dirty in here?" she complained as she crawled along.

"There was a fire in this part of the ship after our first battle with the Jung," Vladimir explained. "We tried flushing this space out, but it didn't get rid of everything."

"I still don't understand. Who exactly are the Jung?" she asked as she continued crawling down the tunnel.

"We do not know, really. We haven't yet had any contact with them. Our only information comes from communications intercepts and some limited off-world intelligence. All we know is that they have conquered pretty much all of the core worlds of Earth."

"And you think they will attack Earth next?" Deliza stopped and picked up the small blue spray can before continuing.

"We do not know for sure, but it is likely."

"Can you stop them?"

"Probably not. We only have a few ships, and they have many."

"But they don't have a jump drive, do they?"

Vladimir looked at her in amazement as she approached. Not a day went by when her perceptiveness didn't surprise him. Now, it seemed, she was even thinking strategically.

"No, they do not, which is precisely why we need to get home as quickly as possible. If we could install this same drive on at least a few other ships, we might be able to fend off an invasion." Vladimir reached out his hand to take the spray can from her. "Thank you."

"No problem," she said, a hint of sarcasm in her voice as she tried unsuccessfully to wipe the soot from her hands and knees. "Oh God, I'm a mess. I can't go back to the bridge looking like this."

Vladimir smiled. Since Deliza had come on board a few days ago, her father, Tug, had been too busy to spend much time with her despite the fact that her mother had just been killed. Deliza had taken to both Vladimir and Abby right away. Very quickly he had begun to feel like her big brother, which was fine with him. "What is the matter, little one?" he teased. "Might there be someone on the bridge you wish to impress? Perhaps a young pilot or two?"

"Nothing of the sort," Deliza defended. She had already recognized that Vladimir was the type that enjoyed getting reactions out of people, and she was determined never to let him get the upper hand in such games. "A lady should always look presentable," she added.

"Of course," Vladimir conceded. "How silly of me." He took the spray can and squirted the sealant over the compression splice device. Within seconds, the compounds had mixed and had hardened into solid insulation. He tugged at it a few times to ensure that the connection was solid before plugging the other end of the wire into a small, plain metallic box. He activated the device and buried it amongst the wiring.

"Doctor Sorenson, the installation has been completed according to your instructions," he said over his comm-set. "Is there anything else you require of me, or may I return to the repair of my ship?"

"That will be all. Thank you, Ensign."

"Well, at least she is saying thank you now," he muttered as he began to crawl back down the tunnel.

Ten minutes later they were both out of the tunnel and back in the maintenance corridor brushing themselves off. Vladimir couldn't help but chuckle at the sight of Deliza covered with smudges of black soot. "I would not return to the bridge without cleaning up first," he teased. Her only response was an angry glare as she continued to brush herself off as best she could.

"Cheng, Comms," the voice sounded over his comm-set.

"Go ahead."

"Sir, the shuttle is on approach. They're asking that we turn on our auto-flight system?"

"Our what?"

"Auto-flight system, sir. That's what he said."

"Tug asked for that?"

"No, sir. It was Ensign Mendez. Apparently only he and the marines are returning. Marcus is piloting the shuttle."

"*What?*" was clearly heard from Josh in the

background over Vladimir's comm-set.

"We don't have an auto-flight system. We do have an auto-recovery system, but it has not yet been installed. Why would he need such a thing?"

"Sir, this is Josh. Those shuttles are pretty much automated. You can push a few buttons and go just about anywhere. But because of their design, they're a bitch to land if you don't know what you're doing. And trust me, Marcus does not *know what he's doing."*

"Oy." Vladimir looked slightly perplexed. His expertise and experience were limited to the ground warfare training from his time as an infantryman in the European Forces and computer programming and engineering systems that he learned during his four years at the European Fleet Academy.

"The Yamaro probably has one," Deliza offered. She noticed the puzzled look on Vladimir's face. "An auto-landing system, I mean."

"How do you know this?" he asked.

"I didn't get out much, remember?"

Vladimir smiled as he keyed his comm-set again. "Comms, contact Sergeant Weatherly. He's guarding prisoners on the Yamaro. Tell him to see if he can find the auto-flight system and activate it so the shuttle can land there. Then someone can EVA over and fly it back to our hangar deck. If not, the shuttle will have to return to the surface until they can find a real pilot. The last thing we need now is to have the shuttle crashing on our flight deck." Vladimir looked at Deliza again. "That should work, right?"

"Sure," she agreed, shrugging her shoulders. "Can I ask you something?"

"Of course," Vladimir assured her.

"Why do they keep calling you 'Cheng'?"

"It is short for 'Chief Engineer.'"

"Well why don't they just call you 'Chief'?"

"Because I am not a chief, I'm an ensign," he explained as if it should have made perfect sense to her.

"But you just said that you *are* the chief..."

"It's a military thing," he interrupted as he closed the tunnel hatch and started gathering up his equipment.

* * *

"*Shuttle One, Aurora,*" the comm-officer's voice called over Enrique's comm-set.

"Go ahead."

"*We don't have an 'auto-flight' system, at least not yet. We're going to see if the Yamaro has one. Can you hold position while we figure it out?*"

Enrique looked at Marcus. "Can you?"

"Sure," he said as he started looking over the controls. "There's gotta be a hold button around here somewhere."

"Copy that, Aurora. We'll see if we can figure out how to do that. Just hurry it up."

"*Marcus, you stupid ape!*" Josh's voice called over the comm-set. "*Just to the right of the AFCS status display there's a scroll wheel. Roll it until the status display reads, 'Hold position relative to target,' then tap the execute button next to the wheel. That'll hold you where you're at for now.*"

Marcus followed Josh's instructions, carefully and with a bit of apprehension. "Okay, we're holding position," Marcus said with relief. He turned to Enrique. "And tell that boy he'd better hope we *do* crash, because otherwise I'm gonna smack him right in his smart little mouth."

* * *

Everything other than minimal lighting and life support had been powered down on the Yamaro. Sergeant Weatherly and Crewman Raval sat in the captured ship's detention area. Weatherly was reading a book on his data pad and Raval was trying not to fall asleep. Although life support was operating, while the ship was powered down the temperature was a bit colder than normal.

For their protection, the members of the Yamaro's crew that had been involved in the mutiny, either directly or indirectly, had been detained separately from the rest of the crew for fear of retaliations by crewmen that had not agreed with their actions. It was these men that were being detained in the six cells of the Yamaro's brig. The remaining two hundred and fifty crewmen were being held in two of the cargo holds off the port hangar bay until arrangements could be made to transfer them to the surface of Corinair.

"*Aurora to Weatherly,*" the comm-officer's voice called over Sergeant Weatherly's comm-set.

"Weatherly here. Go ahead."

"Are they sending relief?" Crewman Raval begged. He had been sitting there in the cold cell block for what seemed like days, bored out of his mind. Weatherly motioned for him to be silent so he could concentrate on the incoming message.

"A what?" Weatherly said. He looked at Raval. "You have any idea what an 'auto-flight control system' is?"

"Something that automatically controls something

that's flying?" Raval offered, not intending to sound sarcastic.

Weatherly looked at him. "Any idea where it might be located? They want us to turn it on."

"I don't even know where *we* are," Raval admitted.

"There's a separate one for each flight deck," came a voice from one of the cells.

Weatherly turned in his chair to face the cell block. The voice had come from one of the cells nearest him to his left. "Who said that?"

"I did," the voice spoke again.

Weatherly got up and went to the cell door to look inside. A man in his early twenties, in what appeared to be an officer's uniform, slowly stood and made his way to the front of the cell. "I did."

"Who are you?" Weatherly asked.

"Willard, Ensign Michael Willard, son of Robert Willard of Aitkenna."

Weatherly looked the man over with a distrusting eye. "How do you know where the auto-flight control system is?"

"I'm a communications officer. Before being assigned to the bridge, I was assigned to the starboard flight control center. The system you're looking for is located inside the controller's office at the top of each flight deck. I can show you if you like."

"And why should I trust you?" Weatherly asked in a challenging tone.

"I'm the one that surrendered this ship—after I put a good knot on the captain's oversized head, that is."

Ensign Willard's comments brought muffled laughter from many of the cell's occupants. Sergeant Weatherly noticed a look of satisfaction creeping across the ensign's face as he obviously recalled the incident. For a moment, Weatherly wondered what the captain of the Yamaro had done to his crew to warrant such mutinous behavior. "And you're willing to help us out?"

"Aye."

Weatherly thought for a moment, then tapped his comm-set. "Aurora, Weatherly. Give me a few minutes; I think we might have a solution."

The sergeant unlocked the door and pulled the prisoner out of his cell before locking it again. "Just so you know," he told the ensign, "you try anything and I'll put one in the back of your head."

"Understood," the ensign answered as he walked toward the exit.

"The flight control center is just around the next corner," Ensign Willard said, raising his cuffed hands to point further down the corridor.

"You know, where I come from we're more likely to shoot mutineers than give them a trial," Sergeant Weatherly stated as they approached the corner.

"Oh, rest assured; if given the opportunity, I'm quite certain that Captain de Winter will do at least that... if I'm lucky."

"Then why the hell did you do it?" Weatherly asked, still puzzled. "Why would you turn on your captain, your ship?"

Ensign Willard stopped short of the entrance to the flight control center. After looking down for a moment, he turned around to face his inquisitor. "Because I didn't want to turn on my *world*," he stated, looking directly into the sergeant's eyes. "That's *my* world down there. It's where I was born.

It's where I was raised. It's where my family still lives."

Weatherly was slightly taken aback. As far as he knew, this man was a member of the Ta'Akar military. "If you're from Corinair, then what are you doing on a Takaran warship?"

Willard laughed. "None of us are from Takara, at least not most of us. Only the *officers* are Takaran. The rest of us are from worlds the Ta'Akar have conquered." Willard entered the flight control center and made his way across the small room to the main console with Weatherly following behind him. "Many young men on Takaran-controlled worlds are randomly selected to serve in the imperial military, starting on their twentieth birthday."

"That doesn't sound so bad," Weatherly said. "Many of the nations on my world still require service from their citizens. Not ten years, mind you, but you usually end up getting something worthwhile out of it, like a skill or a trade at least."

"Not so for us," Willard told him as he began powering up the flight control console. "If we're lucky, we're put off on a half-decent world when our service has been fulfilled."

"They don't provide you transportation back home?"

"If they happen to be nearby when your time is up, then yes. However, most of us end up on the Takaran home world, or worse."

"Is Takara such a bad place?"

"Not if you are Takaran. Foreign veterans are not exactly welcome. If you are lucky, you will find a job doing some menial task. And in about twenty years you might be able to save up enough credits to book passage home."

Weatherly refrained from commenting further. There was no way for him to know if the ensign was telling him the truth, or leading him on for some other purpose. While he did not have the training that his friend Enrique had, he knew enough to not believe everything he heard, especially not from an enemy prisoner.

"That should do it," Ensign Willard announced. "The AFCS should guide them in automatically now."

Weatherly regarded the young ensign a moment longer. His gut was telling him that the man was being truthful, but it was not his place to make that determination. He would simply pass what he had learned up the chain of command, starting with his friend, Ensign Enrique Mendez of the Aurora's spec-ops unit.

"Thanks," he told the ensign as he reached for his comm-set. "Aurora, Weatherly. The auto-flight system is up and running."

* * *

"*Shuttle One, Aurora.*"

"Finally," Marcus said. "Go ahead."

"*Shuttle One, you are directed to land on the Yamaro, port side flight deck. The auto-flight system should be operating now. Once on board, meet up with Sergeant Weatherly on the flight deck. We'll figure out how to get the shuttle back to the Aurora later.*"

"Ah hell," Marcus complained as he checked the AFCS display for the carrier signal from the Yamaro. "I don't wanna be stuck on the Yamaro for God knows how long."

"It's better than being stuck out here," Enrique

pointed out.

"Don't be too sure. You ever been aboard a Takaran warship? They're kinda creepy inside," Marcus explained as he set the auto-flight system to accept control from the Yamaro. "Then again, I guess that could be just the brig. That was the only part of the ship I ever saw."

The shuttle began moving again, her course changing slightly toward the Yamaro's port side.

"Well, at least they'll probably have better food on board."

Marcus turned, looked at Enrique, and smiled. "Good point. I don't know about you, but I'm already sick of molo."

* * *

"How the hell did a grunt like you figure out how to turn on a Takaran auto-flight doohickey?" Enrique joked as they walked down the shuttle's rear boarding ramp.

"Wasn't me, sir," Sergeant Weatherly admitted. "It was this guy," he added, pointing to Ensign Willard to his left. "This is Ensign Michael Willard, son of Robert of Aitkenna," the sergeant explained, mimicking the fashion in which the ensign had introduced himself earlier.

"Aitkenna," Marcus observed. "You're a Corinairan?"

"Yes, sir. Born and raised. My clan goes all the way back to the original colonies of the Corinairan people," he explained with no small amount of pride.

Enrique looked at the ensign with surprise. "If you don't mind my asking, what the hell are you doing on a Takaran ship, especially one that just tried to glass your planet?"

"I figure that's why he led a mutiny and surrendered the ship," Sergeant Weatherly explained.

"*He* did?" Marcus asked, looking the young ensign over. "He doesn't look like he's got it in him. Hell, he's just a kid."

"Well that *kid* apparently cold-cocked his captain and took the command staff hostage. Seems there's more Corinairans on board as well. Apparently, the enlisted are drafted from various worlds and forced to serve."

"Yup. That's the way it's been for decades. Taxes, resources, and young men to serve in their military. All the worlds conquered by the Ta'Akar have to meet their quotas in order to continue governing themselves." Marcus chuckled once before continuing. "Give us your money, your rocks, and your fresh young lads... That's the running joke."

Enrique stepped closer to Ensign Willard. "So is that why you did it, to save your world?"

"Wouldn't you?" the ensign answered.

Enrique grunted in agreement. "Damn right I would. Thanks."

"For what?" Ensign Willard asked. "Surrendering or turning on the auto-flight system?"

"Well both, I suppose. But I do have one more question. You guys got anything to eat on this bucket? We've been eating nothing but dehydrated crap and molo for days now."

"I believe I can help you there as well."

"Then lead the way," Enrique told him, holding out his hand to point toward the exit.

"Why would you eat molo?" the ensign asked as they headed out of the flight deck. "We won't even feed molo to our dogs."

Enrique cast an accusing glance back at Marcus as he exited the hangar bay.

"Hey, don't look at me. I didn't tell your captain to buy all that disgusting fungus."

The journey from the port side hangar bay was short, as the galley that served the crew of the Yamaro was centrally located. The first thing that Enrique had noticed was that the ship itself was much different on the inside than the Aurora. His ship had numerous pipes, conduits, and ducting running all along the walls and ceilings, leaving very little open wall space. The Yamaro's walls and ceilings were relatively clean, with only the occasional interruption of a strategically placed interface panel or comm-console at shoulder height along the walls.

Another thing that was different was that the bottom edges of the doorways were flush with the floors. On the Aurora, other than a few doors designed to allow equipment to roll through them, the hatchways were always twenty centimeters above the deck. The Yamaro's hatches were automated, disappearing into the bulkheads when activated. Most of the Aurora's hatches were of the hinged type and had to be operated manually—except of course a few of the main hatches that sealed off critical areas or passed through primary bulkheads. All of those were automated.

There was a different aesthetic as well. The Aurora was simple and functional. The Yamaro by comparison was more ornate, with the seal of Caius the Great visible nearly everywhere. While the Aurora's corridors and ceilings were designed with space efficiency as a primary consideration, the Yamaro was designed to impress visitors with its lavish accommodations and gratuitous dimensions integrated in to every facet of its structure. As they approached the galley, Enrique couldn't help but wonder how much it had cost to produce a ship like the Yamaro. While it was impressive, all the extra space and decoration seemed like such a waste.

"How many people did you say it took to crew this ship?" Enrique asked.

"The standard crew compliment is two hundred eighty-six," Ensign Willard told him.

"That's, like, a dozen less than the Aurora. It doesn't seem nearly enough for a ship this size."

"The ship is mostly automated. It takes only a quarter of that number to actually operate her."

"Then why is this ship so big?" Enrique wondered as they entered a mess hall that was obviously designed to seat more than twice the ship's standard crew.

The ensign smiled. "Yes, I can see how that would be misleading." He pointed to a bank of machines built into the far wall of the great room. "The food is dispensed from those machines."

Enrique gestured for him to continue moving toward the food dispensers. As they made their way between the rows of dining tables, the ensign continued his explanation. "You see, it is not uncommon for this ship to carry additional assault forces in addition to her operational crew, hence the need for her size and additional *space*," Willard said, gesturing at the size of the mess hall.

"But you're not carrying any now, right?" Marcus interrupted, looking around as if he expected a squadron of heavily armed men to come charging out from the shadows of the poorly lit room.

"No, not on this patrol. We were on our way to pick up a batch of new recruits to ferry them back to Takara."

"But you're a warship," Enrique said. "Don't they have other ships to perform those tasks, like troop transports or something?"

"Normally, yes. But resources have been depleted in recent years due to the rebellion."

"But still, this is hardly a gunboat. This is a heavily armed cruiser. It seems a poor use of resources if you ask me."

"They don't ask us," the ensign said, another small chuckle peppering his otherwise somber tone. "Besides, rumor has it that Captain de Winter has fallen 'out of favor' with command."

"Ah. I see it flows downhill in your military as well," Enrique commented.

The ensign looked at him quizzically as he tried unsuccessfully to discern his meaning. "It isn't *my* military," he corrected.

Ensign Willard stepped up to the bank of machines. There appeared to be four distinct stations, each appearing identical to the others. "These are the primary food dispensers," he explained. "You simply select what you want to eat, and it will be provided through these compartments on the bottom. The red door is for hot items, the orange for room temperature items, and the blue for cold items."

Enrique looked at the instructions on the screen. "These are all in Takaran."

"Of course," the ensign answered. "We were all required to learn the Takaran language."

"Allow me," Marcus offered as he pushed Enrique

aside and stepped up to the dispenser.

"You read Takaran?" Ensign Willard asked, somewhat surprised.

"Since I was five," he answered, as if it had been a stupid question. "Besides," he added, "after dining with these people for a few days, I think I have a pretty good idea what they like to eat."

"Who says we *like* what we've been eating lately?" Enrique corrected.

Marcus navigated through several menus, after which the display began to show pictures. After scrolling through several pictures of complete meals, he stopped on one. "Whattaya think?" he asked Enrique and the others.

Enrique and Sergeant Weatherly both squeezed in on either side of Marcus to get a better look at the displayed image. It appeared to be some kind of cooked red meat, covered in a light brown sauce. Alongside it was a pale green vegetable that looked something like green beans, but with an abnormal hue.

"What is it?" Weatherly asked.

"It's similar to what I believe you people call *beef*," Marcus told them.

"All right then," Enrique declared. "Order us up some."

Marcus selected the item. The machine made a few faint noises and a half minute later both the hot and cold doors opened at waist level. Marcus pulled a glass of cold water from the cold door, and a meal tray containing the same food that had appeared on the display. "There ya go," he said, handing the food and drink to Enrique. "Food fit for a king."

"No," Ensign Willard corrected, "not in here. But maybe in the officers' mess."

Enrique took the food from Marcus, sniffing the entree. "Smells edible. Order up one for everyone."

"What do I look like, a waiter?"

"More so than a pilot," Enrique quipped. "Are you hungry?" he asked Ensign Willard.

"Actually, yes."

"Remove his restraints," Enrique instructed the sergeant.

Sergeant Weatherly pulled the remote out of his pocket, held it against the metallic cuffs encircling the ensign's hands, and pressed the unlock button. The Takaran restraining devices opened simultaneously. He plucked them from the young ensign's hands and stuck them into the utility pocket on his thigh armor.

"Thank you," the ensign said, rubbing his wrists.

"Least we could do, considering you're feeding us."

The ensign took the food and drink from Enrique, a puzzled look on his face.

"Go ahead, have a seat," Enrique told him as Marcus handed him another plate of food and a glass of water.

Ensign Willard took the food and sat down at the nearest table, with Enrique sitting down across from him. He immediately began shoveling the food into his mouth. He had not eaten since before they had arrived in his home system more than eight hours ago. After a few bites, he noticed that Enrique was watching him intently and had not taken a single bite of his own meal. "You are not hungry?"

"No, I'm hungry all right."

A wave of understanding washed across the ensign's face. "When dining with your enemy, always let him dine first," he said with a smile.

"Something like that," Enrique answered, also smiling.

Ensign Willard continued eating. "I assure you, sir, I have no intentions of poisoning you," he explained between mouthfuls. "On the contrary, you are my only way home."

"I hope you're not offended," Enrique apologized as he took his first bite.

"Of course not. In fact, I'm relieved that those who are to be our *allies* are not fools who would act without forethought."

"Hey, this isn't too bad," Enrique said with surprise as he chewed his first bite of the unusual meat.

"Anything is better than molo," Marcus insisted as he sat down to eat. "Here," he said as he dropped a basket of rolls on the table, "I got us some rolls as well."

"You're right," Sergeant Weatherly commented, "this is pretty good."

"Believe me," Ensign Willard insisted, "the stuff the command staff eats is much better than this."

"How do you know?" Enrique asked. His training in special ops included interrogation, and the act of sharing a meal was an excellent way to get someone to open up to you without their even realizing they were doing so.

"Every junior officer is invited to dine with the captain at least once," he explained as he continued to eat. "Some people think he does this to make you see how the *upper classes* live... as an incentive. But most of us know better."

"Know better about what?"

"Let me put it this way. In the four years that I have served, I have *never* seen an officer of command rank that was *not* Takaran born."

"Why is that?"

"Them Takarans think their shit don't stink," Marcus exclaimed. "Especially them 'well-to-do' bastards."

"Your friend is correct," Ensign Willard told him.

"But aren't you an officer?"

"Technically, yes. But I'm what they refer to as a 'common' officer. My rank is only to allow me access to the areas of the ship that are required to do my job. And even then only because I have unique skills that are of value to them. I am not allowed to roam the upper decks unless I am invited or unless it is in the performance of my duties."

"The upper decks?" Enrique asked.

"The ship is basically divided into four decks. The top two decks are officers' decks, which basically means nobles only. They don't allow non-Takaran born personnel on those decks." Ensign Willard looked at them quizzically. "Haven't you been to the bridge yet?"

"I haven't," Enrique admitted. He looked at Sergeant Weatherly. "Have you?"

"Yes, sir. I was on the original boarding team. Been on board ever since."

"Did you notice the two sets of stairs split by a center walkway?" Ensign Willard asked. "That walkway connects the bridge to the decks where the nobles live and work. The rest of us 'commoners' take the stairs down to the lower decks. Most of the crew never even go up those stairs—just a few of us common officers and the service staff that takes care of the nobles."

Sergeant Weatherly let out a muffled grunt. "That explains why that part of the ship was so much nicer."

Enrique looked at the sergeant.

"Big, wide hallways, luxury suites, recreation center... It was like a cruise ship up there. At first, we thought we had walked onto another ship or something."

Enrique looked back at Ensign Willard. There was something that was bothering him, something that didn't add up. "If there is that much separation of the classes, then how did you get a weapon on the bridge?"

"Who says I had a weapon?" the ensign said, the slightest hint of pride forming on his otherwise somber face.

"You took out a bridge full of nobles without a weapon?" Enrique wasn't buying it.

"There are weapons of use other than knives and guns." The ensign smiled and leaned back in his chair, his meal now finished. "I was a Corinairan long before I was a Takaran communications officer. I will remain a Corinairan long after my tour of duty is over, as will my Corinairan brethren on this ship... one of which worked in environmental control. As soon as the captain ordered the bombardment, I knew I had to act fast to save my world. I sent a covert message to my friend to reduce the atmospheric pressure and oxygen content on the bridge and the upper decks. Takarans are used to a much higher pressure and oxygen content. It took a while—as it had to be done slowly so as not to alarm anyone—but eventually, it made them weak and impaired their mental acuity. When the time came, it was quite easy to overpower both Takaran guards and capture their weapons."

"And the blow to the captain?" Sergeant Weatherly inquired.

"That one was personal." Ensign Willard's grin instantly tripled in size.

* * *

Commander Dumar momentarily glanced at the video feeds from the rooftop security cameras as all five of his Kalibri airships set down safely. His eyes had been fixed on the current action reports scrolling across the large screen built into the planning table in the middle of the command center. He had at least two dozen teams instigating conflicts between Loyalists and Followers in Aitkenna alone. In addition, communiqués from the other posts on his continent reported that they were running similar operations, if not quite as complex as those he was currently running in the planet's capital. This was, after all, the seat of the Corinairan government, and if he was to destabilize them, then this was the place to make it happen.

No more than a few minutes after the airships had returned from the mission to free the command staff of the Yamaro from their captivity, her captain came bursting into the command center. As with any nobleman, he expected everyone around him to gaze in awe upon him, a common trait that the commander found somewhat puzzling as very few of the nobles he had met in his career were visually impressive.

"Commander!" Captain de Winter bellowed as he entered the room and immediately spotted the man in charge standing at the planning table.

The commander continued to watch the various displays built into the table. Live feeds from various sources played in at least a dozen separate windows on the main screen. Most were from handheld digi-cams with live mobile links to the planetary data network. Others were from professional news services still operating within the ruins of the city—the ones that he had allowed to continue broadcasting due to their decidedly Loyalist viewpoints. At catastrophic events, there were always plenty of digi-cams around to record it from every possible angle. It made getting live intelligence considerably easier. As Commander Dumar could control which news agencies were still on the air, he had a greater degree of influence over the population.

"I need to speak with you!" the captain insisted as he approached.

As if to convey his complete lack of interest in or respect for the man, the commander responded without even looking up from his displays. "What can I help you with, Captain?"

"I require ships and armed personnel, the best that you've got."

"You mean like the men who just freed you and your fellow nobles?"

The captain recognized the sarcasm in the commander's voice but chose to ignore it for the moment. Had he been on Takara, he was quite sure that the commander's tone would have been more respectful. "If those are the best that you have, then yes."

"And just what types of *ships* do you require?"

"At least two orbital shuttles escorted by fighters and gunships."

"I'm sorry to disappoint you, Captain, but I'm afraid I can't provide you with all of that at this particular moment."

"Well, when can you?" the captain asked

impatiently.

"If we're lucky, in a few days. But it's more likely to be a few weeks."

"That will not do," the captain objected, his anger at the commander's disrespectful manner growing with each passing moment.

"Well I'm sorry to hear that, Captain." The commander wondered exactly how much longer the exchange could go before the pompous nobleman would lose his temper.

"I don't think you understand the situation, *Commander*." The captain's infliction on the other man's technically subordinate rank was meant to demonstrate his superiority over the commander. "We have to retake the Yamaro and capture that ship..."

"You mean the one that bested you," he interrupted. He knew his remark was pushing the limit, but in his current situation, he didn't much care.

"That arrogant little twit did not best anyone, Commander. My crew mutinied on me at the last second."

Now why doesn't that surprise me? the commander thought.

"Had they not," the captain continued, "I'd be sitting on the Aurora's bridge right now instead of wasting time arguing with you about the priorities of the situation."

The captain's temper had nearly boiled over during his last statement, and the commander felt it was time to put an end to the exchange. "Well at least we agree on that," the commander responded, his head still down and his eyes still on his displays. "It was a waste of time."

"Commander, you do realize that I can give you a *direct* order to…"

That was as much as the commander was going to take. "No, actually you can't, Captain," he interrupted as he raised his head and turned to face the now infuriated captain. "You see, I'm the operational commander for all anti-insurgency operations on this entire planet. And my standing orders are to take whatever actions I deem necessary to prevent acts of sedition or insurrection against the empire. In such situations, I have complete command authority. Only Caius himself could give me a *direct* order at this point, Captain." The commander, although he was correct, fully expected Captain de Winter to escalate their dispute.

"The capture of that ship is far more important than anything happening on this insignificant little world…"

"Is that why you decided to openly bombard it from orbit?" the commander stated without any effort at hiding the accusatory nature of his statement.

"I was well within my authority to do so, Commander. Not that I am required to explain myself to you, but it was necessary in order to force the captain of the Aurora to come out into the open. Besides, you received your warning signal."

"Yes, thank you for that little consideration, Captain."

"Commander…" the captain began in a more subdued voice, "I'm sorry; I didn't get your name."

The commander was surprised at the change in the captain's demeanor. "Dumar, Commander Travon Dumar," he elaborated with conviction, "Operational commander of all Anti-Insurgency Forces in the Darvano system."

"If I might have a word with you in private... please?" Captain de Winter asked.

The captain's use of the word *please* was enough to convince the commander to grant the captain his private discussion. "As you wish," he agreed, turning to exit the command center. "Follow me."

Captain de Winter followed the commander out of the room and into the commander's adjacent office, whose windows opened into the command center itself. Unaccustomed to following anyone, he held his tongue for the moment, intending to play his trump card in private where it would have the greatest effect. His family was quite favored by Caius, and despite the fact that the captain had yet to distinguish himself in his command, his father and his father's father before him had done so on many occasions. He was certain that this fact alone would be enough to force the commander to grant his request.

The commander's office, although not ornately adorned like most offices of command rank, had obviously been occupied by the commander for quite some time. The commander's personal trappings were everywhere, the most obvious of which were the numerous pictures on the wall. Most were of family and friends, as well as a few group shots of comrades he had served with in the past. Of course, there was also the obligatory picture of their leader, Caius the Great. What caught the captain's eye, however, and caused him to pause and reconsider his approach, was the picture to the left of Caius—a photo of an elite squad of royal guards. On the end of the first row was Commander Dumar, somewhat younger to be sure and of lesser rank, but still the highest ranking member of the squad in the picture. *This man has connections of his own*, the captain thought.

"Commander Dumar, my apologies. I allowed my enthusiasm to get the better of me. But I feel it my duty to ensure that you understand the full gravity of my mission."

"*Your* mission, Captain? Or the one that you took upon yourself?"

"Had I waited for command authority in this instance, I'm quite sure it would've been too late."

Too late for you to grab the glory, the commander thought. He had noticed the captain's eyes linger on the pictures on the wall on his way in and recognized their impact on the nobleman. "Perhaps," he said as he took a seat behind his desk. "Continue."

The nobleman chose to remain standing, as a gesture of respect for the man who, while of lower rank, nonetheless had the power to grant him the resources he so desperately needed. "The enemy ship in orbit..."

"The Aurora," the commander interjected, if only to demonstrate to the captain that he was not completely ignorant of the situation.

"Correct." The commander's knowledge of the enemy vessel caused the captain to stumble momentarily in his presentation. "The Aurora... While small and poorly armed, she has a unique piece of technology on board. A device, a propulsion system of some type that gives her the ability to *jump* between two points in space in the blink of an eye."

"Really?" The commander found the idea, although interesting in a tactical sense, difficult to believe. "And how have you determined this device exists?"

"Trust me, Commander. It exists."

"Humor me, Captain. I'm a curious sort."

The captain took a seat across the desk from the commander, seeking to speak on a level of equality, as comrades-in-arms. "During our encounter, the Aurora used this device to repeatedly jump in and out of our shield perimeter, allowing her to deliver an impressive amount of damage to the Yamaro before we could get off a single shot."

"And how far did she jump?"

"We only got a fix on her once or twice during the engagement. Both times she was just over a light minute out. But I believe she can jump much farther than that."

"And on what do you base this assumption?"

"We were transferred to the surface by the same type of shuttle used by the harvesting teams in the Haven system, and I recognized one of the pilots. She was one of the Karuzari cell leaders that escaped our bombardment of the Taroa system. Reinforcements arriving on scene shortly after the Campaglia was destroyed reported a ship of unknown design that seemingly disappeared as they approached weapons range. I believe the Aurora was that ship. As you know, even our fastest ships would take nearly a year to complete the journey between Taroa and Darvano—three times as long if they went to Haven first. Even our comm-drones require a couple of weeks to travel that distance."

"But the Karuzari have no such device, Captain. Such a device would take an entire army of experts decades to create. And they have never had access to such resources."

"The ship is not theirs," the captain smiled.

Suddenly, the news of the *sign* that had swept the planet since late the previous evening was beginning to seem less improbable than he had first believed. "Are you suggesting that the Legend of Origins is true?"

"Of course not," the captain said, his eyebrow raised as a smile came across his face. "That would be in direct violation of the Doctrine," he added in the most politically correct fashion he could muster. "Besides, it's true origins are of little concern, but her technology is of *great* concern, as it should be to you, Commander."

The commander leaned back in his chair for a moment, pondering the captain's conclusions. He had never been one to believe in the Doctrine. He had simply gone along with its administrations like most others, as he suspected was the case with the man sitting across the desk from him at the moment. Unfortunately, if the enemy ship *was* proven to be from Earth, it would be much more difficult to suppress the Followers of the Order. They already believed in the Legend of Origins, as well as in this mythical *Na-Tan* character, who was believed to be the bringer of salvation from the very cradle of humanity long since forgotten. "Indeed," he responded thoughtfully.

"Then you can understand my eagerness. The empire would benefit greatly from the acquisition of such technology, perhaps even beyond measure."

"Perhaps," the commander agreed. "As would your reputation *and* your place in your family history."

"A small consideration by comparison," Captain de Winter assured him. "My only concern is for the glory of the empire."

"Undoubtedly," the commander stated with the slightest touch of sarcasm in his voice. "And if this technology *could* have such an enormous impact on the well-being of the empire, could it not also have an equally *disastrous* effect? Assuming of course that your plans do not go as intended..."

"I assure you, Commander, my actions will prove successful."

"And I'm to base this on what... your recent performance in dealing with this same vessel?"

The captain fought to control his reaction. "The circumstances in which I intend to face this vessel shall be quite different. It is obvious to me now that because of her ability to jump away at a moment's notice, it would be impossible to best her in a traditional battle scenario. Instead, we must find a way to get on board this vessel, covertly if you will."

"And what makes you think that she could be so easily taken by a boarding action?"

The captain smiled, satisfied with the deductive reasoning he was about to bestow upon the commander. "The fact that she is using a dilapidated shuttle not of her own world flown by locals not of her origins is quite telling—as is the youthfulness of her captain. I believe that this ship is insufficiently staffed at the moment, possibly as a result of her initial encounter with the Campaglia."

The commander contemplated the captain's words. If indeed the Aurora was understaffed as the captain suspected, it would greatly increase his chances of a successful boarding action. Not to mention the fact that, if the Yamaro's crew were being held prisoner in her cargo holds as her telemetry had indicated, the Aurora's crew would be further depleted as some of them would be necessary to guard the captives.

"Her captain did seem a bit young," the commander agreed, remembering the news broadcast he had watched earlier.

"Exactly. If we act quickly, we can capture the Aurora's shuttle at the spaceport and use it to get on board."

The commander grimaced. "I'm afraid you're too late, Captain. That shuttle left the spaceport at the same time as you. She actually landed on board the Yamaro minutes before you arrived."

"The Yamaro? Then perhaps she means to ferry her crew to the surface. That might be our opportunity."

"Doubtful. The situation on Corinair is too unstable at the moment. The Corinairan security minister is not dumb enough to bring a couple hundred enemy combatants down to the surface, especially after we so easily liberated the first group to set foot on this world."

"There must be another way," the captain urged, beginning to sound desperate.

"One may still present itself to us," the commander admitted. "But until then, we must take steps to ensure the destruction of that vessel as it poses an unacceptable threat to the empire."

The captain had no intention of letting the Aurora and her technology escape his grasp. He had no choice but to agree with the commander in order to keep his options open for as long as possible. "Of course. But let us not act with undue haste, Commander. It is doubtful that the Aurora is going anywhere for the moment, as her captain is still on the surface."

"Agreed. However, in the meantime, we shall take

steps to seize control of the surface-to-orbit defense missiles currently under the control of the Corinari militia. We may need them."

"They will be of little use against the Aurora, Commander. She will simply jump away before the missiles reach her."

"Perhaps. But at the moment it's all we've got." The commander leaned back in his chair as he recalled a lesson from his days as a cadet. "Better a sword than an empty hand when you set off to slay the dragon."

CHAPTER THREE

Nathan wasn't good at waiting, especially when he was locked in a room with no way out. It had been nearly an hour since their escort had promised them that the Prime Minister of Corinair would be in to speak with them... right before he had closed and locked the door behind him on his way out.

He had been out of contact with his ship since they left two hours earlier, and they had to be concerned. He was sure that Ensign Mendez would have filled Vladimir in on the situation on Corinair once he made it back to the ship. His friend would be worried, but he would be patient. His former roommate was far more patient. In addition, the ship was so banged up from five engagements over nearly twice as many days that there was plenty to keep his chief engineer preoccupied during his absence. In fact, he had complained about the additional burden of being in command while Nathan was on the surface. However, with Cameron still injured and clinging to life in the Aurora's medical facility and Jessica down here with him, Vladimir was technically the only command officer left aboard. They were severely under staffed, and now with the additional burden of guarding the two hundred or so crewmen of the Yamaro, the Aurora had just under thirty personnel on board. The Aurora's normal shift staffing level was one hundred.

Nathan had hoped that the Corinairans, who seemed to have a highly industrialized and technological society, might be able to provide additional staffing. It would undoubtedly be a dangerous proposition for anyone willing to sign onto his crew. However, he hoped that recent events might provide the volunteers he sought.

Of course had Cameron been able to, she surely would have objected to his plan. She had been against any local involvement from the start, feeling strongly that they should make their way back to Earth one ten light-year jump at a time, despite the additional time involved.

Up until now, Nathan had been confident in his decision to defend the Corinairans. After all, it had been his presence that had prompted the attack on their world by the Ta'Akar. He had no way of knowing that such catastrophic events would be the result. He was beginning to wonder, however, if Jalea hadn't suspected such a result would come to pass. It had been her recommendation that brought them to this world after all.

Nathan's thoughts were interrupted by a tap on his shoulder, jarring him back to the situation at hand.

"We've got company," Jessica told him as she rose from the couch.

Nathan looked to the windows along the wall to his left. A procession of armed guards, about a half dozen of them, led an elderly man and several aides. By the looks of the eldest man in the group, he had to be the Prime Minister.

Moments later, the sound of the door lock mechanism releasing its bolt was clearly heard. Tug and Jalea quickly moved over to the same side of the room as Nathan and Jessica as the door swung open.

The first two guards, both with steely looks on their faces, stepped into the room. Their heavy energy weapons were in hand, held firmly across their chests at a forty-five degree angle, barrels up. Nathan could see the green indicator lights on the weapons, which he was pretty sure meant they were charged and ready for use. He glanced at Jessica, who confirmed his suspicion with nothing more than the stern, analytical look on her own face. She too had noticed the state of the guard's weapons, recognizing the potential threat. The two guards stopped momentarily, looked over the four of them and, satisfied that they posed no immediate threat, stepped to opposite sides of the door to allow the others in their party to enter the room.

Four more guards entered next, with pairs going to the right and left. They, too, had fully charged and armed energy rifles held across their chests as they moved to encircle Nathan and his comrades. Nathan and the others moved away from the edges of the room and closer to the conference table in the center, hoping to make room for the armed guards coming around behind them. Nathan was beginning to get an uneasy feeling that the situation might have just taken a turn for the worst. Had they realized that the Yamaro had ruthlessly bombarded their world in order to flush the Aurora out into a fight? Or perhaps they had figured out exactly who he really was and just how damaged and practically defenseless his ship actually was. They might already be sending boarding parties to seize her.

"I don't like this," Jessica said under her breath.

Nathan knew Jessica was looking for a way to

take out the guards and escape what was quickly beginning to look like an arrest. As tough as she was, however, there was no way they could take out all six guards before one or more of them burned their small party down.

"Easy, Jess," Nathan mumbled back. "Let's just see how this plays out."

"No promises."

A slender man, maybe in his thirties and wearing what appeared to be a business suit for this world, entered the room next, followed by the elder man and the other aide.

"Gentlemen, ladies, please forgive the delay, but it could not be helped," the slender man said in perfect although heavily accented, Angla. His speech had a lyrical feel to it, with rolling R's and rough sounding H's, and the vowels he spoke were almost literal in pronunciation and without variation. "May I present the Prime Minister of Corinair."

The elder man stepped forward, presenting himself in standard diplomatic fashion. It was a mannerism that Nathan had often noticed to be common amongst all elected officials and diplomats back on Earth. As a child, he had often wondered if they had all been required to attend special training in order to move and act the same way. The Prime Minister spoke, although in what Nathan assumed was Corinairan. It seemed a more beautiful language now that Nathan could hear it without the distractions and noises of the crowds at the spaceport. Nathan could see where the aide got his accent and pronunciation.

"He is apologizing for keeping us waiting," Jalea translated, "and he wants to know our intent."

"Our intent?" Nathan wondered aloud.

"Forgive our abruptness, sir, but as you might have noticed, we are in the midst of a crisis on our world. Such a situation does not afford the usual diplomatic courtesies one might normally expect. Expediency requires directness, I am afraid. The Prime Minister simply wants to know whose side you are on: the Loyalists or the Followers."

Nathan felt like he was about to step into a trap. He was sure that these people were in fact representatives of the Corinairan government. However, if they *were* impostors, as had been previously considered, the truth could get them all killed, as could hesitation at this point.

"I'm afraid you have me at a disadvantage," Nathan explained. "I do not understand your politics, therefore I have little knowledge as to the position of either group. However, based on what little I do know and if I were forced to guess, I would have to say that we are on the side of those that believe in your Legend of Origins." He hoped that the use of the term might add to their credibility.

The second aide, who appeared to be an officer of some sort, spoke an order in Corinairan. Immediately, all of the guards powered down their weapons and slung them over their shoulders and assumed a slightly less threatening posture. A wave of relief washed over Nathan as he realized that he had given the correct answer.

"Then you are the leader of this group?" the Corinairan translator asked.

"I'm Captain Nathan Scott, of the United Earth Ship Aurora. This is my security chief, Ensign Jessica Nash. And this is Redmond Tugwell and Jalea Torren." Each of them nodded at the Prime Minister in respect. "I assume *this* is your leader," he said, gesturing toward the Prime Minister.

"At the moment, yes. We have yet to confirm the status of all the members of the Corinairan Parliament or the President and her cabinet. Until then, the Prime Minister serves as the head of state for all of Corinair."

The Prime Minister spoke to his aide in their language, pointing at Tug and Jalea.

"Are these two also members of your crew?" the aide inquired in a suspicious tone.

"Not originally, no. They are serving as guides while we are in this region of space. But I have come to trust them as much as any crewman under my command." It was a lie, but a necessary one, at least for the moment. "A question, sir," Nathan continued. "Are we prisoners?"

"No. Restricting you to this room was done only to protect you. Things on the surface are a bit chaotic at the moment. And until more of our troops can be called into service, we must remain locked down... for everyone's protection."

"I understand. Then we are free to go, if we so choose."

"Yes. If you wish to leave, we will return you as safely as possible to the spaceport so that you may return to your ship. But we will retain custody of the prisoners that you handed over to us earlier."

"We didn't exactly *hand them over*," Jessica commented under her breath.

"However," the Prime Minister's aide continued, "I strongly recommend that you remain here for the time being, as it is much safer."

"Yes, of course," Nathan agreed, holding up his hand slightly to urge Jessica to withhold her comments. He had no intention of departing anytime soon, at least not until he tried to get medical care for his executive officer.

"Again, apologies for being direct, but the Prime Minister would like to know the purpose of your visit."

Nathan was a bit confused. As far as these people knew, Nathan and the Aurora arrived out of nowhere and saved their entire planet from destruction. It seemed an odd question to be asking after such an event. Again, he had to wonder how much the Corinairans actually knew about them.

"Captain," Jessica said in hushed tones, ignoring his gestures. "We know little about these people, or their leader for that matter. The less they know about us, the better."

Nathan understood Jessica's point, but his instinct, as usual, was to be open and honest with these people. As a holder of public office, his father was a master at such deceptions. It was a technique that Nathan had always found somewhat distasteful. Given the circumstances of late, he was beginning to understand the necessity of such tactics.

"You should also try to keep your statements in line with the Legend of Origins," Jalea added quietly.

"I'm not telling these people that I'm some kind of hero, if that's what you mean," he objected, trying to keep his voice low enough that the aide would not overhear his protestations.

"She's right, sir," Jessica said. "You might want to turn off your moral compass for the moment, or have you forgotten the stakes?"

Nathan glared at Jessica. He hadn't forgotten what was at stake and she knew it. He had a damaged ship and an injured crew in orbit, and they still had a long way to go in order to get back to Sol and help defend their own world from an invasion by the Jung. "We only wish to help." It was an obvious answer, and not very informative, but it was the best he could muster on short notice.

"Help?" the aide asked. "In what way?"

"By driving the Ta'Akar from your system," Jalea interrupted, "once and for all."

The aide translated Jalea's bold statement for the Prime Minister, who immediately began to ramble on in Corinairan to his aide.

"I may not be armed," Jessica whispered to Jalea from behind, "but I can still just as easily break your neck."

"It may not be as easy as you think," Jalea responded in a similar tone.

"Then it is true," the aide translated for the Prime Minister. "You are the Na-Tan of legend. You are the one who is to lead us to freedom." It was more of a statement than a question, as if the Prime Minister had not really believed it before back at the spaceport, but rather had been playing to the crowd's expectations. Only now he was beginning to believe it was true.

Nathan felt a sinking feeling. There was no turning back from this role. He had to mitigate the situation, downplay it somehow. Then he remembered his brief conversation with the crew chief on the airship. "I am just a man, who happened to be at the right place, at the right time. I only did as any other man would do. I helped someone in need."

"But you are from Earth, are you not?" the aide asked.

"Yes, we are."

"And you are called Na-Tan?"

"Well, Nathan, yes."

"And there was the sign." The aide was obviously getting swept up in the realization to a degree that it appeared there would be no convincing him otherwise.

"The sign?" Nathan asked.

"And your ship is very powerful as well."

"I don't know if I'd go that far..."

"You defeated a Ta'Akar warship; did you not?"

"Well, yes. But it was only a cruiser. And..."

The Prime Minister and the aide again exchanged words in their language before the aide continued.

"The Prime Minister says that when the Ta'Akar warship in orbit fails to report in, more ships will come. Maybe even a capital ship. Can you defeat such a ship?"

Nathan stumbled for a moment, unsure of how to answer.

"We already have." It was Jessica that interrupted this time.

"We did?" Nathan mumbled under his breath.

"Na-Tan defeated the Campaglia at the battle of Taroa," Jalea explained.

The aide excitedly translated her words for the Prime Minister.

"The videos," Jessica reminded him.

Nathan remembered the video footage being broadcast on the wireless nets the night before. The scenes had been horrendous, and the destruction on the planet where the Karuzari base had been hidden was nearly complete. Had they not accidentally jumped into the middle of that engagement—and within the Campaglia's shield perimeter—that entire world would have been destroyed. There had even been gun camera footage that showed the Aurora launching torpedoes at the massive Ta'Akar warship.

At the time, it had been an act of desperation by Captain Roberts, one that had saved their asses as well as the rest of the people still left alive on that world.

"He also defeated three patrol ships in the Korak system, as well as escaping a confrontation with another cruiser in the Haven system only a day ago."

"But this cannot be," the aide protested. "No ship can travel that fast. Even the comm-drones cannot transit such distances in less than a few weeks."

"We can," Nathan said, a smile on his face. "How do you think we got here all the way from Earth?"

The Prime Minister and his aide continued to converse in Corinairan for several minutes, during which Jessica stepped in front of Nathan and turned her back to the Prime Minister in order to speak with Nathan more discreetly.

"He's probably right, you know," Jessica told him quietly. "When the Yamaro doesn't check in, they will send more ships."

"How long until that happens?"

Tug moved in closer to join the conversation. "Even with the high-speed comm-drones, there is always a delay of several weeks with communications between the Ta'Akar command and their ships. By the time they decide something is wrong, contact another ship to investigate, and that ship makes the trip here, it might be a month or more. However, if the Yamaro dispatched a message during the battle, that time might be cut in half. Another warship could arrive in a few weeks, maybe sooner if it was already patrolling nearby."

As Nathan contemplated Tug's words, the Prime Minister's aide broke off his conversation with his superior. "Gentlemen," the aide began, "in light of your rather bold claims, I must ask you what it is you desire of us?"

Nathan could see the apprehension on the man's face. It was obvious that the idea of taking on the Ta'Akar seemed a fool's errand to him. "You need to prepare to defend yourselves, as do we."

"We have no effective means of doing so."

"You have a military, do you not?" Nathan asked, indicating the uniformed and heavily armed men in the room. "You have ships as well. We have seen many leaving your world."

"Those are civilian ships, not military vessels. They are armed, yes, but only for defensive purposes, and certainly not enough to defend themselves against Ta'Akar warships. Our military is primarily ground based. Other than a few squadrons of short range fighters, we have no space borne military assets. The Ta'Akar took them from us decades ago as a condition of our surrender."

"You have missiles," Jessica added, "with nukes. That's a bit more than nothing."

"Not when targeting a heavily shielded warship," the Prime Minister's aide corrected. "We were unable to defend ourselves against just one of their ships. You saw this for yourselves. And now we have the additional burden of the chaotic situation on the surface of Corinair. If the Ta'Akar return, especially in force, we will be destroyed in short order. In our current state of disarray, the population would never support any type of resistance. They will simply march in and take over once and for all. Or worse yet, they will remain in orbit and finish what the Yamaro started."

"If I may, sir," Tug chimed in. "What exactly *is* going on out there?"

"The Loyalists are accusing the Followers of polluting the minds of the Corinairans with lies. They believe that such behavior is the reason for the Yamaro's bombardment."

"It is entirely possible that the actions of the Loyalists are being instigated by Ta'Akar agents operating covertly on your world."

"Yes, we have suspected their presence for some time now. But other than causing general disruption, I fail to understand the purpose of such activities."

"Their goal is to destabilize your government enough to justify seizing control," Tug explained. The Prime Minister's aide looked confused. "The original terms of your surrender allowed you to maintain your self-governance. This was necessary due to the delay in communications over even short interstellar distances. Three decades ago, the problem of communications delay was even greater. Direct administration over conquered worlds was impractical. But the original terms of surrender included a clause that allowed agents of the Ta'Akar to take control of the planetary government should that government become unstable."

"But why now? Was it because of the reports of the sign of Na-Tan's arrival?"

"Possibly, but I believe there are deeper reasons. This event only serves as a convenient excuse," Tug continued. "The anti-aging serum that used to be reserved for the most elite of Ta'Akar society has been increasingly distributed to the lesser classes. Nearly every natural-born Takaran now lives to be several hundred years old. This has caused their population to increase exponentially over the years. Takara itself is dangerously overpopulated. They had originally planned on reforming more worlds within the cluster, but the power requirements for such reformations are massive, requiring great amounts of resources. The rebellion has limited such resources over the last twenty years. Soon, however, they will have their new power generation systems working, and they will be able to reform the worlds they need. But that will take centuries that they do not have. That is why they seek to take control of your world utilizing the loophole in the terms of your surrender. Your population is young, and your world is still mostly undeveloped. Soon, your people will be forced to serve the billions of Takarans that will come to colonize your world, making it their own. Within a few generations, your entire people, your culture, your history will all be erased through attrition."

It was a dire prediction, but the Prime Minister's aide translated Tug's words to his leader. Nathan could tell by the expression on the Prime Minister's face that he did not consider such actions beyond the capabilities of the Ta'Akar Empire.

Nathan watched the Prime Minister. His expression did not change. He showed no signs of horror or denial at the dire forecast-only an increasing look of determination to do what was best for his people. There was a strength in this man. It was the same strength that Nathan had noticed in the flight crew of the airship that had brought them to this facility little more than an hour ago.

"The Prime Minister agrees with your assessment of the situation, sir." The response was aimed at Tug and ended with a nod of respect by the aide. He turned his attention back to Nathan. "He also asks what it is that you suggest we do."

"We will do all that we can to defend your system,

but we have suffered much damage over the last week, and we have many casualties. Unless we can make significant repairs before the Ta'Akar return, we shall not prevail."

"I am sorry, Captain," the aide responded, "but we ourselves are quite overwhelmed at the moment. Until we can get control of the current crisis, there is little we can offer you."

"Can you provide medical assistance?" Nathan asked. "My first officer, she was critically injured during our battle to defend your world. Our ship's physician has done all that she can. But Mister Tugwell here has suggested that your doctors might be able to help—that your facilities might be more extensive, and maybe even more advanced than those on board our ship." Nathan immediately noticed the look of disbelief on the Prime Minister's face as his aide translated Nathan's request.

"Captain, forgive me, but a civilization that can instantaneously travel between the stars must surely have more advanced medical technologies than even the Ta'Akar, let alone our meager world."

Nathan had expected this reaction, as most of the locals they had met thus far had been surprised to find that most of the Aurora's technology was outdated in comparison with their own. "An understandable conclusion, sir, but our jump drive technology is a recent break through, an accidental discovery if you will. In addition, our own medical facilities are overwhelmed with casualties. Believe me when I tell you that any medical assistance you can offer would be most helpful."

Nathan waited anxiously as the aide translated his words. Tug had assured him that the Corinairans had medical capabilities that exceeded those he had seen on board the Aurora. He only prayed that Tug was correct.

"As you might expect, we are also facing a medical crisis due to the bombardment of our world. However, we will dispatch a medical transport to your ship immediately, Captain."

"Thank you, Prime Minister," Nathan said with obvious relief in his voice.

"It is the least we can do, considering all that you have sacrificed on behalf of, not only our world, but others suffering under the oppression of the Ta'Akar."

"Might we be allowed to contact our ship, so that we might alert them of your approach?" Nathan asked. "They are still in a high state of combat readiness and I would not want to see them mistakenly fire on your medical transport."

"Of course. One of the guards will escort you to the communications center."

Nathan turned to Jessica. "You go. Fill Vlad in on what's happening down here."

"Yes, sir."

Nathan returned his attention to the Prime Minister's aide. "My security chief will handle the task, if you don't mind. That way we can continue our discussion about how to defend your world."

"As you wish, Captain."

* * *

"You realize you are wasting your resources," Captain de Winter stated quietly so that no one but the commander would hear.

"Despite your belief to the contrary, Captain, my reasons for capturing some of this world's nuclear weapons have nothing to do with your so-called mission." The commander stood up from the planning table and turned to face the captain. "The fact that I am willing to task some of those missiles for your purposes is a courtesy as much as anything else. I suggest that you remember that."

The captain had been hovering over the commander's shoulder for nearly an hour now, and it was becoming quite a nuisance. The commander understood Captain de Winter's goals, and he certainly understood the strategic importance of either denying the Corinairans use of both the Yamaro and the Aurora or gaining control of them for the Ta'Akar. However, his mission was to take control of this world, and ultimately the entire system, and place it under the direct rule of the Ta'Akar once and for all.

"This is maddening," Captain de Winter exclaimed.

You're telling me, thought the commander.

"This is a highly advanced world, with thousands of space faring vessels. Surely your men are capable of hijacking something that can reach the Aurora."

"Acquiring a ship that can *reach* the Aurora is not the issue, Captain. Being allowed to come close enough to board her is the problem. Considering what she has been through, and what she must surely know is going on down on the planet below her, she will be ready for trouble. I'm afraid the best we can hope for is to get a civilian ship carrying a nuke close enough to detonate and permanently disable if not destroy her."

"There has got to be a way," the captain insisted. "I must have that ship."

"Sir," a subordinate called as he approached the commander, "we just received this message from one of our deep-cover agents." He handed a small data pad over to his superior.

The commander frowned momentarily as he realized the implications of the message. As much as he hated it, the captain was going to get his wish after all. "This must be your lucky day, Captain."

"What is it?"

"It seems the Corinairans are preparing to send a medical shuttle up to the Aurora to ferry down one of her wounded."

"That's our way in!" the captain exclaimed.

"Perhaps," Commander Dumar admitted. "A transport is being dispatched from their command center to the local hospital to pick up medical personnel. *If* we can get a team assembled and get them to the spaceport before the transport arrives, and *if* we can take control of the medical shuttle, then you *might* be able to get on board."

"Excellent! We must depart immediately! How many men can you spare?"

"Weren't you accompanied by twelve of the best officers the Ta'Akar nobility have to offer?"

"Those are staff officers, Commander. I doubt any of them even remember how to hold a gun."

"Then I suggest you refresh their memories, and quickly."

"Commander, surely you can spare a few men?"

"I believe I made my position quite clear on that point, Captain."

"Need I remind you, Commander, of the importance of this mission?"

He didn't. As much as he hated to admit it, the commander knew that the captain was correct. The capture of such technology would make the Ta'Akar nearly invincible. As well, great rewards would be bestowed upon those responsible for her capture. However, he was also aware of the danger such technology presented—not only to his empire, but to anyone who opposed the holders of such capabilities.

"Five men, Captain. That's all I can spare at the moment. But they will be five of my best," he assured him. "In fact, they could probably take the ship without the help of you and your command staff."

"Thank you, Commander."

The commander turned to face de Winter once more, a serious expression on his face. "Be forewarned, Captain. Should you fail to capture the Aurora, I will do everything within my power to destroy her. Even if you're still on board." *Especially if you're still on board*, he thought.

"A reasonable precaution, Commander."

"I will give you one hour, one hour from the time you touch down on her flight decks. If I have not received word of your success, I will do my best to destroy that ship."

"I shall take that ship," the captain promised, "or die trying."

Captain de Winter turned and exited the room to prepare for departure. The commander watched him leave, confident in as well as grateful for the knowledge that, regardless of the outcome, he would not be seeing the pompous nobleman again.

"Corporal," the commander called to a nearby aide, "who's next up?"

"That would be team four, sir," the corporal responded.

"Get them geared up for a boarding action and on the pad in ten minutes. And get Sergeant Tukalov in here immediately. I've got a mission for him."

* * *

Vladimir was frustrated. Ever since Nathan had left the ship to go to the surface of Corinair, nothing had gone right for him. Systems were failing all over the ship—not critical systems, just minor things. However, the constant reports of insignificant system failures were making it impossible for him to get anything done. Every time he would get started on a project, another call would interrupt him. The most he had been able to accomplish in the last hour was to coordinate his repair teams. This frustrated him further as he preferred to roll up his sleeves and get his hands dirty as well. As short staffed as they were, everyone needed to be fixing something.

"*Cheng, Comms,*" the comm-officer called.

Vladimir put down his data pad yet again, rolled his eyes, and tapped his headset to take the call. The bridge had been particularly bothersome, calling him every five minutes to update him on one thing or another. "Yes, this is Cheng. Go ahead."

"*Sir, I've got Ensign Nash on comms.*"

Finally, Vladimir thought, *a real reason to interrupt my work.* "Put her through, Ensign."

"*She's broadcasting over an open frequency, sir. No crypto.*"

"Understood."

"*Vlad, are you there?*" Jessica's voice called over his comm-set.

"Yes. Jessica? Is that you?"

"*Who the hell else would it be?*"

"What is going on? You are overdue for check in. Is everything okay?"

"*I wouldn't say everything is okay, but we're fine.*"

"What do you mean? Why are you broadcasting on this frequency?"

"*We're deep in a command bunker. Things are nuts down here. Riots everywhere,*" she told him.

"Yes, yes. I've been getting reports from Naralena in signals. Something about Loyalists clashing with Followers or something."

"*Yeah, it's complicated. Listen, did the shuttle make it back okay?*"

"Sort of. Please, tell Nathan not to let Marcus fly anything. He does not know what he is doing."

"*Sorry, that was my idea.*"

One of the junior engineers stepped up beside Vladimir, a look of concern on his face. "Excuse me, sir."

"One moment, Jessica." Vladimir turned to his subordinate, irritation on his face. "What is it, Mister Musavi?"

"Sir, we keep having problems with the containment systems on reactor one. It's flirting with the red line, sir. If it crosses the line..."

"Yes, I know, this entire system will be erased from existence," Vladimir finished for him, somewhat overdramatically. "The magnetic field emitters will need to be re-calibrated," Vladimir told him.

"Yes, sir, I know. But it's the only reactor still running. The other three are still offline while repairs are being made to their distribution systems."

"Then we will run on the reserve fusion reactor."

"But we'll be without main propulsion, sir. We wouldn't even be able to break orbit, let alone operate the jump drive."

"But we will not disappear from existence. And it will only be for an hour, two at the most. It must be done, yes? Better to get it done now. Go!"

"Yes, sir."

"I am sorry, Jessica," he said, returning his attention to the comm-set.

"Everything okay up there?"

"No, nothing works, as usual. Every time I get things working, Nathan manages to find someone else to shoot at us. I think I deserve a raise... maybe a promotion as well."

"Vlad, listen, I have a relay from Aurora Actual. Message reads: Vehicle from your college days will arrive within Romeo zero six mikes. Tango X-Ray, X-Ray Oscar, to surface for Romeo X-Ray by friendlies. Do you copy?"

"Wait one," Vladimir told her as he scrambled to figure out the message. After a moment, it all began to make sense to him. "Ah, Da da da." Vladimir keyed his mike to transmit again. "Message from Actual understood, standing by for Tango X-Ray, Romeo zero six mikes." He turned to Deliza, "Finally, some good news for once."

Deliza looked confused, not understanding half of what she had heard.

"We'll try to check back in later," Jessica said over the comms, *"but I can't promise when. Just be ready to pick us up when we call for a ride."*

"Understood," Vladimir said, tapping his comm-set once again to close the channel.

"What was all that about?" Deliza asked.

"It was code," Vladimir said. "Our captain can be very clever at times," he added with a chuckle. "The Corinairans have agreed to send a medevac shuttle to transport Commander Taylor to a hospital on the surface for treatment. They will be here in less than one hour."

"That's the message you got from all that Romeo,

Mike, X-ray stuff?"

"Of course."

Deliza shook her head. "People from Earth are weird."

* * *

Jessica removed the communications headset that the Corinairan comm-tech had given her to use and handed it back to the operator, thanking him. She had never heard Vladimir so frazzled, so stressed out. Of all the people on the crew, he was one of the steadiest she knew. Excitable, yes, but reliable and consistent as well. Perhaps he was starting to feel the pressure of all their struggles over the last week. It was understandable, and he wouldn't be the first crewman to come down with Post Incident Stress Disorder, P.I.S.D., or as they had liked to refer to it, 'pissed.'

Vladimir would be the last person Jessica would expect to be affected. She had seen signs of it with Nathan since day one, but he had managed to control it. He had a few outbursts but then was fine. It was evident in Cameron as well, and she suspected that it was what fueled her desire to turn tail and head home as quickly as possible, leapfrogging it all the way back to Sol.

It happened to everyone, sooner or later. It would probably happen to her as well. They all needed a break, some kind of relief. If they had to go much longer without one, their combat effectiveness, or what little was left of it, was going to disappear rapidly.

Jessica stood from her seat next to the Corinairan comm operator, turning to her escorts. "That should do it, boys," she announced with a smile. "You can take me back to my room now."

As she followed them back down the long corridor, she could see through the windows into the various control rooms. There were always many monitors on the walls, each displaying critical information as well as video feeds from strategic locations throughout the city. She tried as best she could to gather some visual intelligence on the way back, but everything she could see was written in the Corinairan language, which was unreadable to her. From what she did see, she could discern one thing for sure. The planet was in turmoil.

* * *

The staging and gear-up room at the secret Ta'Akar Anti-Insurgency Operations Complex in Aitkenna was bustling with activity. Captain de Winter and the twelve members of his recently freed command staff had donned the uniforms of the local Corinairan military and were being issued weapons by the facility's weapons master.

"These uniforms are rather unimpressive," Captain de Winter commented to his executive officer as he sealed up the torso of his flat black jumpsuit.

"Yes, black and gray," Commander Rishwain said. "Such an imaginative color scheme." He eyed the emblem on the shoulder patch attached to the captain's shoulder. "Even their coat of arms is uninteresting," he added as he picked up the black torso armor from the floor next to him. "And is this what they use for body armor?"

Captain de Winter snickered at the sight of

the simplistic vest. It also was flat black, just like their uniforms, and was composed of multiple hard panels attached to a cloth web designed to hold it all together when worn over the shoulders and torso. It was nothing like the hard, polished body armor the Ta'Akar assault forces commonly used. Even their lowest-level ground forces were more stylishly adorned than the simple military of this world. "Are the officers expected to wear such garments as well?" he asked, noticing his XO's hesitation to put on the cumbersome armor.

"You are if you want to live," a familiar voice called from behind.

Captain de Winter turned around to find Andre, the leader of the team that had freed him and his command staff from captivity an hour earlier. The sight of the brash young sergeant immediately brought a cross look to the captain's face as he realized the implications of the man's presence. He too was fully outfitted in Corinairan military garb and was armed and ready for deployment. He only hoped that the young agent was assigned to one of the teams about to infiltrate the Corinairan surface-to-orbit missile bases and not their team going up to board and capture the Aurora. "Sergeant," the captain began, "I don't think I ever got your family name," he added in a tone meant to intimidate.

"Tukalov, sir," the sergeant answered without hesitation. "And I'd strongly advise you to wear your body armor. Unless, of course, you prefer to be an easy target. In which case, feel free to leave it behind."

"Do they even work?" Commander Rishwain asked with disdain. "They don't appear to be reflective at all."

"They aren't," the sergeant explained as he made his way past them. "They're primarily dissipative—unlike Takaran armor, which reflects incoming energy bolts in countless unanticipated directions. This design doesn't end up inadvertently killing the man next to you via reflected blasts. The Corinari may not be *fashionable*," he added sarcastically, "but they know how to fight." The sergeant continued pushing his way past them without stopping to even look them in the eyes. "You'd be well served to remember that."

Captain de Winter watched with no small degree of irritation as the sergeant exited through the doorway on the far side of the room.

"Friend of yours?" the commander wondered aloud.

"Just another arrogant commoner who has been away from his home world for too long," the captain proclaimed as he donned his body armor. "I fear he has forgotten his place within the very society he defends."

"Then I trust you'll set him straight," his executive officer said.

"In due time, Commander. But for now, we have more pressing matters of which to attend."

Andre stepped out onto the flight deck atop the command center and made his way toward the five men assembled near the first of three Kalibri airships. The men were exchanging jokes as they checked one another's gear, their spirits high as they anticipated the coming mission. It was a chaotic time, with death and destruction all around them, but it was for this that they had spent years in training.

As he approached, Andre was surprised, but not altogether unpleased, to see his friend standing amongst the men. As usual, a broad smile was painted across his face. "You are not a member of this team, Bobby."

"Neither are you," Bobby argued.

"True enough."

"Besides, I didn't want you to get lonely."

"More likely you heard of my mission and wanted to be in on the fun," Andre said as he began to check Bobby's gear.

"I've already had one ground assault today. I need some variety to keep things interesting," he said. Bobby checked Andre's gear in turn. "You know how easily I become bored."

"The sign of a truly unimaginative mind," Andre retorted.

"We can't all be as creative as you, now can we, Sarge?"

"You left out handsome," Andre bragged.

"Is it true?" Bobby asked, after pulling Andre aside from the others. "Are we going to retake the Yamaro?"

"Something like that."

Andre held up his right hand and spun it around in a tight circle, signaling the three small airships to spin up their engines in preparation for departure. He then turned back to his friend. "You stay sharp, Bobby. This one will be much more challenging," he warned as he turned his head and saw Captain de Winter and his command staff coming up the stairs onto the flight deck, "especially with those fools in tow."

Bobby looked over Andre's shoulder at de Winter

and his men, all decked out in standard black Corinairan battle dress, just as they were sporting similar armaments. "You're not serious! But they're a bunch of aristocratic puff 'n fluffs! They'll probably just end up shooting themselves in the foot the first time they draw their weapons."

"As long as they don't shoot *me* in the foot," Andre said. He had no more love or respect for nobles than anyone else in the division, including their esteemed commander.

Bobby rolled his head in dismay. "Is it too late to change my mind?"

"Our team and the good captain will ride the lead ship," Andre ordered, ignoring Bobby's question. "The rest get loaded in the other two. Get them mounted up, Corporal," he ordered as he turned and headed toward captain de Winter and his staff.

"Well, at least it won't be boring," Bobby admitted as he fell in behind Andre.

A feeling of satisfaction washed through Andre, although he did not reveal the fact to anyone. He could see the look of disappointment on the captain's face as he drew near. He was obviously not happy at the idea of having to work with him again, and that made Andre feel like he was doing something right. "Captain de Winter," he began with authority. The sound of the three airships engines required that he now yell in order to be heard. "Your men will ride in the second and third birds, exactly two minutes behind us. We'll take control of the medical shuttle through swift and decisive action. Your men will arrive immediately after we have secured the ship."

"Just a minute, Sergeant..."

The sergeant ignored the captain's attempt to get control of the conversation. Time was short, and he wasn't about to waste it in debate. "If you're about to try and take command of this operation, sir, you're wasting your time." Andre stared him dead in the eyes and did not blink, did not flinch, for what seemed an eternity. He moved a step closer to the captain before continuing. "Those men, Captain, the ones about to board an enemy ship in woefully insufficient numbers, are killers. With guns, knives, or hands, make no mistake; these men know how to kill and have no problem doing so. Can you say the same about your officers?"

Andre stood motionless, continuing to stare as the captain glanced over at his officers. He could see the doubt in the captain's eyes, and he knew his answer.

"And where will I be riding?" the captain asked, deciding not to press the issue.

"With us, in the lead bird, sir," he answered. As much as he didn't like it, technically the captain was in command of this mission, and as such needed to be in the lead airship.

The captain looked to his executive officer, Commander Rishwain. The commander immediately got the hint and ordered his men to follow the sergeant's subordinate to the waiting airships. The captain returned his gaze to the sergeant once more. "Just one question, Sergeant. Why you?"

"Because those are my orders, sir."

"And you always follow orders, like a good little soldier?"

Andre knew the captain was merely trying to lead him into a trap in order to force the issue of command. He knew that he was far more qualified to run the operation than either the captain or any of his officers, but he also fully expected the captain to try and exert some level of control over the mission itself. Andre wasn't about to let himself or his men get killed due to the arrogance of a noble. "No, sir, not always. But this time, I think the mission's purpose is an important one."

Andre continued to stare at the captain, refusing to yield to what he considered an 'inferior officer,' as the expression was commonly used. "Now are you going to board that airship, or am I going to have to leave you behind, sir?"

There was little hesitation on the part of the captain. "Lead the way, Sergeant," the captain said, gesturing with his left hand toward the idling airships.

Andre spun around, turning his back to the captain as he strode off toward the lead airship, the captain following close behind. The sun had completely set by now, and the night had engulfed the city in darkness. Most of her streetlights were out, as much of the city power grid had been disrupted by the bombardment earlier that day. Only those buildings such as their own, ones that were equipped with their own internal power plants, were still lit up. As he skirted the edge of the flight deck, he could see out to the city below. Other than the buildings running on internal power, the only other sources of light came from the many fires still raging out of control. Were he close enough to witness it all first hand, it would surely be a gruesome sight. However, from up here, it appeared exactly as it was to him, a perfect diversion to conceal their activities.

Andre looked over all three airships as he moved toward the lead ship. In accordance with the mission profile, each of them had been given tail numbers that appeared to be of Corinairan military register and displayed the standard crest of the Corinari between the pilot's canopy and the cargo doors. As they planned on flying directly into the Aitkenna spaceport, it would be necessary to appear to be just another Corinari airship ferrying troops around.

As he approached, Andre noticed that the captain's men looked confused; they were mentally unprepared for the idea of sitting in the open sides of the little airships with their feet hanging out. Despite the ground crew checking to make sure each of their harnesses had been properly engaged, many of them still searched for something to hold onto for safety. He wondered how many of them would panic when the tiny airships started maneuvering hard. Despite their relatively simple design, the small ducted fan airships were incredibly agile, and their pilots played to that advantage whenever possible.

"Comm check, Team One," Andre called out. One by one, each of the five members of his team answered, all except the captain. "You would be number six, sir," he explained to Captain de Winter, who was busy searching for a handhold himself.

"Of course, six," he answered.

"Team Two," Andre called out, but there was no response. He looked at the captain.

"Yes. Commander Rishwain, you're the Team Two leader. Count off numerically by rank." Commander Rishwain conducted a comm check for his squad. The senior officer of the nobles in the last airship did the same.

"Control, blue one. Ready for departure," Andre announced as he looked around to ensure that nothing was amiss.

"*Copy blue one,*" the voice came back over the comms. "*Signals Intelligence reports a Corinairan transport is arriving at the hospital now. You should have a ten-minute lead. Good hunting.*"

Andre turned and sat back down on the edge of the lead airship's deck in the same position as before, port side, lead seat. Captain de Winter took a seat next to him, looking a little leery about having his feet hanging out of the small airship. "I suggest you lean back and lock in, Captain," he said with a sneer, as he reached out with his right hand and slapped the side of the pilot's canopy three times.

The captain watched as Andre leaned back, locking his harness into the restraint mechanism. Noticing the sudden increase in noise as the rotors changed their blade pitch, the captain followed the sergeant's advice and immediately did the same, locking himself against the airship as well.

Andre almost burst out laughing at the look on the captain's face as the airship leapt up off the deck, gaining altitude at an alarming rate, and then turned and streaked away into the night.

* * *

"Sergeant Tukalov's team is airborne, sir. Time on target: fifteen minutes."

"Very well," Commander Dumar said. "Bring in the next set of birds and load up the ground assault teams. I want them launched just as soon as that medical shuttle is taken. And send orders to all the other posts to do whatever is necessary to capture the other missile bases. Instruct them to use Karuzari tactics and weapons."

"Yes, sir."

The commander knew that Captain de Winter's attempt to capture the Aurora and in turn retake control of the Yamaro had little chance of success. If the captain was correct in his assumptions about the enemy ship's staffing levels then there was a chance that a swift, decisive action could work. Unfortunately, those assumptions were based on many unknown factors, and everything hinged on their getting on board without conflict. Perhaps the ship was understaffed but carried a full company of ground troops. If that were the case, it would surely spell disaster for the boarding party.

The commander, however, had never been one to play it safe. Instinct had gotten him through many battles in the past, and his instinct now told him that the reward was worth the gamble. For this reason, he had chosen to send one of his best agents to lead the assault. While he had some reservations about Captain de Winter's assumptions as to the state of the Aurora's crew, he was quite sure that the nobleman would be incapable of completing the mission without someone like Sergeant Tukalov calling the shots. There was something else that Captain de Winter was correct about; the capture of the Aurora would be a significant asset for the Empire... especially if she could indeed jump between the stars.

Unfortunately, as great an asset as it might be, it was equally as threatening. It was this that worried the commander the most, and it was the real reason that he had chosen to send some of his men along, especially Andre. The commander had no doubts that the sergeant would do whatever was necessary to complete the mission, even if it meant sacrificing himself.

Despite his confidence in Sergeant Tukalov's skill and dedication, he still had one more concern.

What if they failed? He needed a backup plan, and the only thing he had left was the Corinari land-based surface-to-orbit defense missiles. Due to the communications and response delays inherent in any interstellar civilization, the Corinairans had been granted the use of such weapons in order to defend themselves against attack by other forces outside the Ta'Akar sphere of influence. The weapons had been limited in their range and capabilities, but since they carried nuclear warheads, even a single impact could cripple or even destroy an enemy ship that wasn't protected by the types of shields used by Ta'Akar warships. All the data gathered thus far indicated that the Aurora had no such protection. Then again, she could simply *jump* away once the missiles were detected. Unless...

"Lieutenant Neese," the commander called to his subordinate.

"Yes, sir."

"How long does it take a Corinairan missile to reach a target in orbit around the planet?"

"That depends, sir. The location of the target in relation to the launch point, and the orbital altitude of the target..."

The commander shot a dour look at the young lieutenant. "Assume for the purposes of this discussion that I am referring to the enemy ship currently running alongside the Yamaro, Lieutenant."

The young officer swallowed hard, embarrassed by his failure to anticipate his commander's line of thinking in the matter. "If fired at the most favorable moment, approximately ten minutes, sir."

"And how long do the electromagnetic pulse effects last after detonation?"

"The EMP only lasts a split second, sir. However, depending on the level of protection and the type of technology, the effect can last minutes to months, sir."

"And the radiation?" the commander asked. "How much would that interfere with the enemy's sensors?"

"It's hard to say, as we know nothing about the enemy's level of technology."

"Extrapolate, Lieutenant."

The lieutenant cleared his throat, buying a moment to think. "Well, my first thought would be that if they are advanced enough to jump between the stars, they would be equally advanced in other areas."

"Such as sensors," the commander commented.

"Yes. But they have no shielding, and no energy weapons. At least they showed no use of such technology during their battle with the Yamaro, according to what we learned during the debriefing of her captain and command staff. This might suggest that their advancements, at least for the time being, are limited to only propulsion."

The commander stared at the planning table in front of him, contemplating the lieutenant's comments. It seemed that using the ground-based missiles against the Aurora was still a long shot, but it was a shot.

* * *

The dimly lit flight deck atop the Anti-Insurgency Unit's operations facility was dark, except for the pale blue lighting that spilled out from the bottom edges of the walls out across the deck. The walls were only three meters high—just enough to conceal any activity from the streets below, or from nearby buildings of lesser height. The airships that came and went on this night were unmarked, unlit, and quiet enough that their flights were masked by the noise below. Unless someone were specifically watching the top of the building at the moment one of the airships was in transition, it was doubtful they would be noticed, especially when considering the chaos that still filled the streets of Aitkenna.

There were now four Kalibri airships on the flight deck, all idling with their ducted fan rotors at zero pitch so as to remain quiet and avoid disturbing the air around them while loading. Two of the airships were fitted with extended passenger pods that protruded considerably on either side of the small ships allowing them to carry up to ten passengers each. The other two remained in their standard configuration with an open cargo bay.

Two columns of men dressed in common Corinairan civilian attire and carrying a variety of weapons made their way into the passenger modules of two of the airships. Six others, all heavily armed and dressed in the standard black uniforms of the Corinari, took their seats on the decks of the remaining two airships.

Moments after the last man took his seat, and the passenger airships had closed their doors, the four airships lifted quickly and quietly off the rooftop flight deck and climbed away into the darkness of the night. In less than thirty minutes, they would covertly deposit their passengers near their objective and disappear once again.

* * *

"Maybe in the future you will spend more time in the simulator as a pilot instead of a navigator," Vladimir told Loki as they made their way into the aft topside airlock.

"Right. Just try taking the stick away from Josh and see what happens," Loki protested.

"What are you so worried about?" Vladimir asked as he placed the helmet over Loki's head and locked it in place. The auto-seal engaged with a hiss and the life support pack on his back immediately began pumping breathable air into his helmet. "You have been in space many times."

"In a space *ship*," Loki argued over the comms, "not space itself. There *is* a difference you know."

"Perhaps," Vladimir admitted as he checked Loki's suit and life support systems one last time.

"I still think Josh should go," Loki muttered. "He did volunteer, you know."

"Yes. But Josh must stay here to fly this ship."

"What flying? We're in orbit. All he's doing is flirting with Ensign Yosef."

"You see, he *is* busy," Vladimir said with a smile. "Besides, we need the shuttle back here, not on the Yamaro."

"But Josh loves this kind of stuff."

Vladimir was getting tired of Loki's complaints, and he wanted to get back to his repairs. He had been irritated enough when there was no one available to assist Loki in preparing for his EVA. "Just think of your suit as a tiny space ship."

Loki looked at Vladimir.

"What?" Vladimir asked, shrugging his shoulders.

"That doesn't help."

"Stop whining. It will all be over soon," Vladimir

told him as he stepped out of the airlock, closing the hatch behind him.

"That doesn't help, either!"

"*Depressurizing airlock now,*" Vladimir reported over the comms in Loki's suit.

Loki's breathing rate increased slightly. "This sucks. This sucks. This sucks," he kept repeating to himself.

"*See, like a little girl you are,*" Josh's voice came over the comms from his place at the helm on the bridge.

"Shut up, Josh."

"*Leave her alone,*" Vladimir's voice teased over the comms from the other side of the airlock door.

Loki turned his entire body so that he could see through the small porthole in the airlock door, which was currently filled with Vladimir's smiling face. "Funny."

"*Airlock depressurized,*" Vladimir reported. "*Disabling gravity plating. You are now clear to exit.*"

Loki felt his body become much lighter. The space suit and life support pack together had weighed an extra sixty kilograms, and even walking had been difficult for Loki's wiry frame. Now he was weightless and the weight of the pack meant nothing. He began to drift upward slightly, his feet slowly rising up off the floor.

It wasn't his first time being weightless. After all, he had literally thousands of hours in space, most of which had been out amongst the rings of Haven. However, other than the few times that he had gone into the aft compartment of the harvester during flight, his time in zero G had been primarily spent strapped into his seat in the cockpit. He had hated those times, mostly because Josh's crazy maneuvering usually left him bouncing off the walls of the tiny ship. At least this time that wouldn't be the case.

"*Slow and steady breaths,*" Vladimir said over the comms. Again Loki looked at the engineer's face in the porthole on the airlock door. This time there was no comedic grin, only concerned, sympathetic eyes. He was trying to help Loki calm down.

"Got it," Loki answered, swallowing hard. He concentrated for a moment on his breathing while he slowly floated up toward the hatch overhead. As he approached the ceiling of the airlock, he reached up overhead and grabbed hold of the locking lever on the hatch. "Opening inner hatch."

Loki pulled the hatch lock lever over and the hatch unsealed slightly. He slowly pulled the hatch open to reveal the three-meter long tunnel that lead through the ship's multi-layered hull to the outer hatch, which he could see at the other end of the tunnel above.

The outer hatch was nothing more than a thick, sliding panel, which was operated remotely from either inside the transfer tube, or from the airlock foyer at the console at which Vladimir was currently standing. When he reached the end of the tunnel, he activated the outer hatch and it slowly slid open.

Control my breathing, he thought as the hatch slid open to reveal the blackness of space. Exterior light from the Darvano star spilled into the tunnel at a sharp angle. The light was not directly in his eyes, but it was blinding nonetheless, and Loki had to close his polarized visor in order to reduce the glare.

"Exiting the ship," he announced. *I can't believe I'm doing this,* he thought as he floated up out of the tunnel and into space.

Loki's breathing doubled its pace as soon as his feet cleared the tunnel and he was no longer on board the Aurora. "Oh God. Oh God," he repeated between breaths as he drifted further away. "I'm drifting away!"

"No worries, mate," Josh assured him over the comms. *"If you get too far, I'll just use the old docking thrusters to shimmy right up beside you, nice as you please."*

"Don't you dare!" Loki cried out.

"Hands off, Josh," Vladimir warned. *"Even a bit too much thrust and it would be like hitting a rock with a stick. You would send him flying… if he lived."*

"Really *NOT* helping, guys!"

"Relax, mate. I'm only playing with you. Just use your suit thrusters," Josh reminded him.

"Oh yeah."

"Just a little, first to stop movement away from the ship," Vladimir warned.

Loki flipped up the control pad from his chest piece. A small tug and it extended away from him just enough so that he could see it. He gently placed both of his gloved hands on the control pad and applied a little downward thrust. Tiny jets located on his shoulders squirted their brief burst of propellant, stopping his motion away from the ship. "Okay, I've stopped." Loki took a deep breath and swallowed. His mouth was bone dry. "I'm going to rotate now."

Another small burst of thrust shot out from the back of his left side, causing him to rotate slowly on his vertical axis that ran perpendicular to the ship. He watched as he rotated to his right. As he came around, he could see the landing apron at the aft end of the hangar deck looming in front of him. His eyes were just below the level of the deck, and he could easily see the outer door tucked deep inside the awning that extended out onto the deck to shield the outer doors to the transfer airlock.

The entire hangar deck continued to slide to his left as he rotated to his right. *This isn't so bad,* he thought, his breathing starting to calm down again. Then it happened. The Yamaro slid into his view from the right. She was more than twice the size of the Aurora, and despite the fact that she was badly damaged, all her gun turrets appeared to be pointing right at him. That alone was enough to speed up his breathing once again. "Oh shit!"

"What's wrong?" Vladimir asked over the comms.

"Every single one of her guns is pointed right at us!" Loki cried out as he fired his thrusters again to stop his rotation.

"She's powered down!" Vladimir insisted. *"And her crew is locked up."*

"What about those guns?!" Loki asked. "Why are they pointed at us?"

"That's just the last position her guns were in before the entire ship was powered down."

"Loki? This is Ensign Mendez. I'm on the Yamaro. I promise you, all those guns are cold. I'm waiting for you at the port airlock, just aft of the hangar bay. The one with the flashing lights. You see it?"

"Are you sure? I'm staring right down a whole bunch of gun barrels out here."

"Yeah, I'm sure," Ensign Mendez chuckled. *"Hell, we just ate dinner over here. It wasn't half bad. Get your butt over here and we'll feed you as well."*

Loki started to calm down again. He still didn't like the looks of all those guns, but on closer inspection, the Yamaro did appear to be powered down. He looked her over and finally found the small flashing lights right where Enrique had said they would be... just aft of the port hangar deck. The lights were small and faint from this distance, but they were flashing away. "Okay, okay. I see the flashing lights." Loki swallowed again as he applied forward thrust. "Thrusting forward."

The thrusters on the back of Loki's EVA pack fired, moving him slowly forward. He thrusted again to accelerate a bit more. He watched the hull of the Aurora about ten meters below him as it passed beneath his feet.

"*Slow and easy,*" Josh warned over the comms. "*Don't use too much thrust, or you may not have enough left to slow down when you get there.*"

"I'm a pilot too, Josh. Remember?"

Loki continued to watch the ship as he approached her starboard side. To his left was the landing apron of the flight deck; to his right was the massive drive section, towering far up above him. He was in his own little valley here, tucked safely between two rather large sections of the ship. Although he was floating in a vacuum, at least here he felt relatively safe.

Then the walls of his safe little valley began to subside. First was the landing apron to his left. It had already passed behind him, and to his left he could now see along the entire starboard side of the Aurora, all the way out beyond her bow. He looked to his right; the drive section was about to pass behind him as well.

"*Loki,*" Vladimir stated calmly, "*do not look down.*"

Loki couldn't resist. His neck craned forward slightly so that he could peer down as the Aurora slid under him and away, revealing the planet of

Corinair rotating slowly beneath him.

This time his breathing rate tripled and became very deep. He could feel panic starting to overtake him. "Oh God. Oh shit. Oh God!"

"*I told you to not look down,*" Vladimir scolded.

"*It might have been better had you not said anything at all, mate,*" Josh added. "*You'd better pull it together out there, Loki,*" he warned, "*or you're gonna pass out. Then you'll smack right into the Yamaro and it'll be all over.*"

"*And you think that will help?*" Vladimir asked.

"*I'm just tellin' it to him like it is,*" Josh defended.

Loki could feel his fingers tingling. "There's something... wrong... with my... fingers," he said between breaths. "They're... getting... numb!"

"*You're hyperventilating,*" Vladimir warned. "*You have to take slow, regular breaths. And turn down the oxygen levels in your suit.*"

"What?"

"*Your life support controls. Reduce the oxygen saturation in your suit air. It will slow down your breathing and help you to relax.*"

"*By starving his brain of oxygen?*" Josh wondered aloud.

"*Who's in command here, Josh?*" Vladimir insisted. "*Do it now, Loki. That is an order!*"

Loki had not known Vladimir very long, but it was the first time he had heard the Russian speak with such authority and conviction. It made him instantly respond, and he reached down to his control pad on his left wrist and reduced the amount of oxygen being mixed into the air in his suit. "Okay... I... did... it."

"*Keep trying to slow your breathing down,*" Vladimir urged him, trying to sound as calming as possible.

Loki concentrated on his breathing, but he couldn't stop peeking at the planet below, which wasn't helping much. *I never should have looked down,* he thought.

A few minutes later, his breathing had slowed and the tingling sensation had left his fingers. He was more than three-quarters of the way across, and his view of the Yamaro filled his visor. He could see the airlock hatch, which was wide open and waiting for him.

"How are you doing, Loki?" Vladimir asked.

"Better now," he said as he turned the oxygen level in his suit back up to its normal setting. "I've increased the suit O2 back to normal. I'm almost there."

"Excellent," Vladimir exclaimed.

"Good job, mate," Josh congratulated.

Loki spun himself around using the suit jets in order to point his back toward the Yamaro. He fired the main thrusters on his back again to decrease his closure rate to something that his maneuvering thrusters could manage. Once he was happy with his new rate of approach, he fired his attitude jets one more time to spin around to face the Yamaro again. He was only about twenty meters out now, and would reach her in less than a minute.

As the last few meters disappeared between them, Loki fired his jets once more. From both shoulders and both hips, more propellant squirted out, bringing him to a near stop just before he hit the Yamaro.

"Contact," he announced, as he reached out and grabbed a handhold only a few meters aft of the open airlock. Using the handholds, he pulled himself over to his left until he reached the airlock. He pulled himself inside. Unlike the Aurora's airlock, the artificial gravity in the Yamaro's airlock was always active. As soon as he crossed the threshold, the gravity fields generated by the plating in the floor pulled him downward. Fortunately, he was no more than a few centimeters off the deck, and he barely stumbled as the familiar sensation of gravity swept over him.

"I'm in!" he announced. He could hear both Vladimir and Josh breathe a sigh of relief over the comm-set as the outer airlock door closed behind him.

"*Nicely done, mate,*" Josh told him. "*Nicely done.*"

"Next time, it's your turn," Loki answered.

"*Deal.*"

A few minutes later, the inner airlock door slid open to reveal Ensign Mendez, Sergeant Weatherly, and Ensign Willard of the Yamaro's crew. A cold chill shot up Loki's spine as he eyed the member of the Yamaro's crew standing next to the sergeant. Then he noticed that both Ensign Mendez and Sergeant Weatherly were armed, while the man in the Takaran uniform was not.

"Welcome aboard the Yamaro," the Takaran ensign said with a smile. "You must be our shuttle pilot."

"Yeah, that's me," Loki answered, a look of bewilderment on his face. He looked at Sergeant Weatherly. "What's going on, sir?"

"I'll explain later," Ensign Mendez promised him. "Let's get you out of that suit and get some grub into you."

"Grub?" Loki asked as they helped him out of the airlock.

CHAPTER FOUR

The crew chief, clad in a black flight suit, helmet, and harness, ran out to meet the four person medical team that was making their way across the landing pad atop the hospital.

"Are you my medical team?" the crew chief asked.

"Yes!" the man confirmed. "I'm Doctor Pantor. This is Doctor Galloway, Nurse Brymer, and our med tech, Mister Lenox."

"I'm Chief Montrose," the chief introduced, shaking the hands of each of the men and women in turn. "I'll be your crew chief for the flight out to the spaceport," he informed them as he turned and led them toward the airship that sat idling nearby.

"Who are we going to pick up?" Doctor Pantor asked.

"Rumor says it's one of the officers of that ship that just saved us from the Ta'Akar," the chief told him as he handed the doctor a data pad. "Everything you need to know should be on this pad."

"Really?" The doctor stood reading the data pad as the crew chief helped the two women into the airship, followed by the med tech. "It's a woman," the doctor announced. "Her name is Commander Cameron Taylor. Says here she's the executive officer." The doctor looked surprised. "They've got women in their military?"

"I guess so, Doc," the crew chief said as he pushed

him toward the airship door.

"Why don't we have women serving in our military?" the doctor asked as he climbed on board.

"Probably because they're too smart to volunteer," the chief commented as he hopped in and closed the door.

The crew chief quickly checked that all four of his passengers were belted in and ready to go before he took his own seat directly behind the pilot, facing aft. After plugging the comm wire into his helmet, he informed the flight crew that they were ready for takeoff. "Hold onto your stomachs, boys and girls."

The airship leapt up into the air and quickly sped away from the roof of the hospital. Once clear of the building, it immediately dropped lower and began to weave through the city on its way to the spaceport.

Inside, the passengers held on tight as the airship turned and banked, buffeted and bounced, rose and fell.

"The patient has suffered some serious traumatic injuries," Doctor Pantor read on. "Blunt force mostly from the looks of this. Head, chest, shoulder, abdomen, pelvis... she's a mess, but it looks pretty straight forward."

"They can't handle it on their own?" Doctor Galloway asked as she held on tight.

"We don't know anything about the state of their medical technology, I guess."

"If they can defeat a Takaran warship, I would think they're pretty advanced."

"For all we know, their doctor might be one of the casualties," the med-tech chimed in.

"This report was translated from their doctor. But they could also be overwhelmed with wounded at this point," Doctor Pantor added. "We won't know until we get there."

"Whoever they are, or wherever they are from, they have a few favors coming their way from us," the med tech added.

"They're from Earth," the crew chief told them.

The passengers all looked at him in disbelief.

"Earth? You mean Earth, Earth? The one in the legends?" Doctor Pantor asked. "Are you sure?"

"I met their captain," the chief explained. "He was sitting right where you are now."

The passengers all looked at each other this time.

"You spoke to him?" Doctor Pantor asked.

"A little."

"They speak our language?" Doctor Galloway asked in amazement.

"No. Well, two of them did. But I don't think they were from Earth. I think they were from somewhere in the cluster. But their captain, Nathan, he spoke something very similar to Angla."

"Unbelievable," the med tech exclaimed. "The last thing I thought I'd be doing today would be meeting people from Earth."

"Or any other day, for that matter," Doctor Pantor added.

"What were they like?" the nurse asked.

"Pretty much like us, I suppose. Their captain seemed pretty young. They all seemed pretty shaken as well, like they'd been through a lot recently."

"Well, they did just battle it out with a Takaran warship," the med-tech said. "That would shake me up pretty good."

"I heard on the news," Nurse Brymer said, "people are saying that it's the legend come true. They're saying that their captain *is* Na-tan."

"That's just a myth," Doctor Pantor said,

dismissing her with a wave of his hand. "Nobody believes in that stuff any longer."

"I don't know," she said. "They're rioting in the streets, the Loyalists and the Followers."

"Of the Order?" Doctor Pantor said. "What do you know about the Order?"

Nurse Brymer suddenly became withdrawn. "Nothing, really. I just heard stuff; that's all."

"He is just a man, like any other," Chief Montrose stated. "He just happens to be from Earth."

"And he just *happens* to command a ship that saved us all from certain annihilation," the nurse added.

* * *

A single, black Kalibri airship with Corinari markings and crest swooped in toward the spaceport. Its standard running lights blinking away as it came in over the fence, if anyone took notice, they would assume it was just another military airship ferrying personnel from one place to another. The sky was littered with them on this night.

The airship followed a standard, military-style emergency approach, as had most of their airships that had come and gone from this port over the last few hours. It flew only a few meters above the rows of hangars and open berths, most of which had already emptied during the mass exodus from the planet earlier that day.

Under normal operational conditions, the airship would not have been able to enter the spaceport's traffic pattern without prior authorization. In addition, they would have had to relinquish flight control of their aircraft, allowing the spaceport's automated systems to fly them in and out of the busy complex. Today, however, was different. The events of the last twelve hours had caused so much chaos, and there had been so much death and destruction as a result of the Yamaro's orbital bombardment of the planet, that it was all they could do just to keep the spaceport operational.

At this point, the spaceport had little more than manual air traffic controllers communicating with air and space ships via portable communication equipment. They had literally no tracking facilities in operation, and what little defenses they did have in place were more to keep the crowds of refugees from swarming the complex than to defend against attack from above.

A hastily erected and barricaded gun emplacement, one of dozens that had been quickly deployed to protect the spaceport, tracked the small airship as it came in to land. Although it had identified itself to the traffic controller, it was still considered a higher threat level than the screaming crowds outside the perimeter fence, thus it warranted the attention of the gunners. However, no order to fire had come, as local command believed the pilot's statement that he was delivering security forces to accompany the medevac flight and did not wish to call attention to its mission.

The gunners watched warily as the airship touched gently down on the tarmac not thirty meters from the medevac shuttle that was already idling in preparation for liftoff. Through their electronic gun sights, they could see the six armed men in standard Corinari flat black uniforms scoot off the deck of the small airship after it landed and released its hold on them. As the airship leapt back into the air and sped away, the men left on the tarmac formed up and proceeded in standard military fashion to the wide rear loading ramp of the medevac shuttle. Four of the six men headed up the ramp, leaving two at the foot of the ramp who turned to face away from the shuttle, their weapons held across their chests in a ready state. It seemed quite obvious to the gunners that a Corinari security detail had just taken responsibility for the medevac shuttle's safety. Relieved, the operators returned their guns to their original positions, aimed outward toward the perimeter.

"Sir?" the voice called over his helmet comms.

"What is it, Chief?" the pilot of the medevac shuttle asked as his eyes danced over the cockpit displays in performance of his preflight checks.

"We've got company."

The pilot turned to his left, his eyes meeting his copilot's.

"Are they here already?" the pilot asked, a surprised look on his face.

"Not exactly. We've got Corinari forces coming up the ramp," his crew chief reported.

"That can't be good," his copilot added as she made adjustments to the displays.

The pilot rotated to his left as far as he could while still sitting in his flight seat. He looked down the center aisle that passed from the cockpit to the passenger bay behind them. He could just make out the black-clad men as they made their way through the passenger section.

"As you were," Captain de Winter instructed the medevac shuttle's crew chief, who promptly followed his orders and remained in his jump seat.

"Two here," Sergeant Tukalov told the other two men. "No one comes forward without authorization from me."

The men nodded as they took up positions on either side of the short corridor that led forward to the cockpit.

The crew chief looked up at the man standing next to him, taking special notice of the big weapon he was holding across his chest. "How's it going?" he asked nervously. The guard did not respond, keeping his eyes fixed aft.

"I guess we should have expected this," the copilot said, "considering all that's going on."

Captain de Winter appeared with Sergeant Tukalov at his side, who slid the cockpit door closed behind them. "No need to get up," Captain de Winter told them.

"Who are you? What's going on?" the pilot demanded.

"Nothing to worry about. We're just here to keep you safe. Just do as you're told, complete your mission, and everything will be fine."

The pilot's eyes widened as he recognized Captain de Winter. "You're the one on the news broadcast. You're the captain of that warship, the one that bombed us!" Despite their already enormous size, the pilot's eyes suddenly got even wider. "You're Takaran!"

"You say that as if it's a bad thing," Captain de Winter mused.

Andre reached forward to the center pedestal and switched off the internal comms.

In the aft section, the crew chief's eyes also widened as his pilot's words came across his helmet comms. He turned in his seat in shock to look again at the guards.

The guard next to him looked down at him sternly. "Are we going to have a problem?"

The crew chief swallowed hard. "No, sir."

"Good," the guard said. "Let's keep it that way."

Captain de Winter leaned down, putting his head next to the pilot's. "You might want to show a little more respect for those that rule over you." The captain stood up again before continuing. "Now, in a few minutes, a medical team will arrive. You will do nothing to alert them that anything has changed. Shortly after that, more of my men will join us, at which point you will fly us all into the hangar of the enemy ship in orbit over your pathetic little world."

The pilot's mind was racing. He was the captain of this shuttle, and he was a Corinairan. He, like most Corinairans, hated the Ta'Akar, especially after today. For at least two generations, the Takarans had ruled over them, limited their advancement, limited their growth, and limited their society's potential. Even worse, they had tried to force them to recognize the Takaran leader as a god among men. At that moment, an old adage came back to him: *'You can tell a man what to do, but you cannot tell him what to think or feel.'*

Captain de Winter watched as the pilot placed his hands on his legs and turned to look straight ahead. The captain recognized the position of defiance that the pilot was striking.

The copilot also saw it and followed his example, taking her hands off the controls and placing them on her legs as well.

"I see," Captain de Winter said as he stepped aside. "Sergeant."

Andre stepped forward, pulling out a small data pad from his thigh pocket. He grabbed the pilot's left hand, pulling it forcefully up and away from the pilot's side. He pulled out his data pad and passed it over the back of the pilot's hand, using the pad's scanner to read the small rectangular ident-chip that all subjects of the Ta'Akar Empire were required to have implanted when they reached adulthood. The pad beeped twice in response. Dropping the pilot's hand with obvious contempt, Andre stood upright again, watching the display on his data pad as it retrieved information from the database back at his command center. The sergeant then handed the data pad to Captain de Winter as he turned and resumed his position at the back of the cockpit.

"Hmm, let's see," the captain said as he flipped through the numerous screens of data now pouring into the data pad in his hand. "Ah, there we go," he said as he lowered the data pad and held it in front of the pilot to see.

The pilot looked at the images of his family on the data pad. His wife, Carria, and his sons, Jakob and Wilham. He watched in horror as Captain de Winter continued to leaf through the images with a touch of his finger. "A fine family, indeed. I'm sure your sons would've grown up to be fine young men. A shame really."

The pilot got the point. "What is it you want me to do?"

"It's not like I'm asking you to violate your orders or even to deviate from your flight plan for that matter," Captain de Winter said. "Just complete your mission and deliver us to that ship. That is all."

Captain de Winter stood again, satisfied that he had made his point and secured the cooperation of the pilot. He turned to the copilot. "Now, shall I go through your family album as well?"

She looked at her pilot and saw the resignation in his eyes, the feeling of helplessness. Then she saw the opposite in Captain de Winter's eyes, arrogance and superiority. She too acquiesced.

Captain de Winter turned and looked at Andre, a smug look on his face. "That was easier than I thought."

* * *

"You were right, sir," Loki proclaimed between bites. "This 'grub' is pretty good."

Enrique watched as Loki shoveled the last of his food into his mouth, leaving his plate nearly spotless. "Did you get enough?" he asked somewhat sarcastically.

Loki looked back and forth, his eyes darting between Enrique and Weatherly. "You mean I can have more?"

Enrique laughed. "Ask Ensign Willard here. It's his ship."

Loki looked a bit confused.

"Eat all you want," Ensign Willard told him. "There's enough food on board to feed a few hundred people for several years. And I don't expect we'll need it where we're going."

"Thanks," Loki said, getting up to fetch another plateful from the food dispensers.

"They don't feed you on your ship?" Ensign Willard asked jokingly.

"It's not that they don't feed us," Sergeant Weatherly explained. "It's *what* they feed us."

"Ah, yes, this 'molo' you spoke of. Remind me never to try it."

Enrique leaned back in his chair. "Listen, Ensign..."

"Please, call me Michael."

"Very well, Michael. Do you mind if I ask you a few more questions?"

"Of course not. After what you have done for my world, it is the least I can do."

"Earlier, you said that you weren't scheduled to come to Corinair, that it wasn't on your patrol route. Then why did you come here?"

"As I said before, we were on our way to the Savoy system. We were to pick up a batch of new recruits to bring back to Takara for basic training. Before that, we had been on border duty, so our course for Savoy took us just along the edge of the Darvano system. We happened to pass by just as a comm-drone was departing the system. We intercepted a message about your ship, that it was hiding in the Darvano system."

"But don't those drones travel at something like one hundred times the speed of light?" Enrique wondered. "How could you even see it?"

"We can't, not at that speed. But it can see us, or more accurately it can *detect* us. Comm-drones are programmed to drop back to subluminal velocities when it detects a 'drop-out' signal from a Takaran ship. This allows a ship to add messages to the comm-drone already in transit, instead of having to dispatch one of its own. It also allows the ship's intelligence unit to examine messages contained within the drones and forward anything they suspect to be actionable to the captain."

"He has the authority to take action on his own accord?" Enrique asked, surprised by the information.

"Yes, of course, when appropriate. The distances between systems sometimes necessitate such aggressive measures to ensure timely reactions by the empire."

"I guess that makes sense," Enrique admitted.

"When Captain de Winter realized that the drone we encountered was an unscheduled one, he ordered me to copy all military communiqués from the drone. One of the messages was marked urgent and was encrypted using a top-level cipher. I was ordered to crack the cipher."

"You can do that?" Enrique asked.

"As I explained, those of us with special skills are granted officer's rank, despite our lack of 'noble' blood, so that we may serve on the upper levels."

"So what was in the message," Enrique asked, "the one you cracked?"

"There was a message from the local military intelligence officer on Corinair to Command on Takara-specifically to the commander of fleet intelligence in the royal compound itself. It piqued the captain's interest."

"What was in the message?"

"An informant on Corinair had told the local officer about your ship, that it was hiding in the Darvano system."

"Did the message say where we were hiding?"

"No, just that your ship was hiding somewhere in the system. After that, the captain ordered us to change course and head here. We were little more than half a day away at top speed. And the captain had the reactors running at one hundred and ten percent the entire journey here."

"So he wasn't ordered here," Enrique surmised.

"No, he was not," Ensign Willard confirmed. "I believe he acted of his own accord, in order to secure glory for himself and his family name. You see, the de Winter name has been quite legendary in regards to military service... until the captain had his turn."

"So he hasn't done well for himself."

"His performance has been less than stellar, yes. But in this case, I believe he acted outside of his authority."

"How do you mean?" Enrique asked. "It seems to make perfect sense. If he had waited, we might have been long gone by the time another ship was sent to investigate."

"True, and that was the captain's logic as well. But recent reductions in resources have necessitated certain restrictions on the rules of engagement. Specifically, captains are not permitted to engage enemy ship of equal or superior strength until properly reinforced."

"They don't want to risk losing another ship."

"Correct," Ensign Willard confirmed. "But Captain de Winter deemed your ship an inferior vessel." The ensign smiled. "An obvious misjudgment on his part."

* * *

"And how do you propose we defend ourselves

against an enemy as powerful as the Ta'Akar?" the Prime Minister's aide asked. "We have no fleet," he reiterated.

"Then we'll just have to get one," Nathan said.

"And how do you propose we do that?"

"You have ships, don't you?"

"Yes, but they are not warships," the aide protested. "They are civilian cargo ships and passenger ships. They are only capable of interplanetary travel, due to restrictions in place since our surrender to the Ta'Akar decades ago."

"We can arm them using the rail gun turrets from the Yamaro," Nathan suggested, "maybe even rig some missile launchers to give them greater striking range."

"Captain, you are dreaming if you think we can take on the Ta'Akar using modified cargo ships. We need *real* warships, with *real* weapons and shields, and with the capability of travelling faster than light."

Nathan looked at Tug, remembering the stories he had told him about their failed efforts to capture larger ships in the past. He remembered that they had been unable to get in close enough to board them because of their shields. Such was not the case with the Aurora and her jump drive.

"Then we steal them," Nathan announced, "from your enemy."

"You are proposing that we steal a Ta'Akar warship," the aide said in disbelief. "Are you crazy?"

A small grin began to form on Nathan's face. "I'm proposing we steal several."

"Apologies, Captain, but you are quite mad."

"Who's quite mad?" Jessica asked as she was escorted back into the room, passing the Prime

Minister and his aide on her way back over to Nathan and the others.

"Your captain, here. That's who."

"Oh, without a doubt," she quipped.

"Did you make contact?" Nathan asked.

"Yes, sir. Vlad's all up to date."

"And the shuttle? Did they make it back safely?"

"More or less," she told him.

Nathan looked at her quizzically.

"I'll tell you later," she said under her breath. "After we finish talking about how *mad* you are."

"It is possible," Tug interjected, already seeing where the captain was headed with his idea. "You've already proven that you can jump within the shield perimeter of a warship, as long as that shield is extended far enough. It would just be a matter of more precise targeting, so as to disable the ship without causing more damage than we can repair, as I suspect is the case with the Yamaro."

"Yeah, well, it was our first jump attack. I promise we'll do better next time."

"We would have to act quickly," Tug advised, still deep in thought. "You will only get one or two more opportunities before the Ta'Akar begin running with their shields pulled in tight. It would be best to target single ships running alone, instead of groups so there is no one to witness and report your tactics."

"You guys are forgetting one thing," Jessica warned. "The other guys shoot back, remember? We took a bit of a pounding ourselves. And we don't have shields. Hell, we don't even have torpedoes or missiles for that matter. And we're just about out of ammo for the rail guns."

"Basic slugs for your rail guns should be easy enough to manufacture," Tug theorized, "especially for an industrialized world like Corinair..."

"Excuse me," the Prime Minister's aide interrupted. "Are you seriously proposing to capture one or more Takaran warships?"

"Yes, sir, we are," Tug told him confidently.

The Prime Minister's aide looked to Nathan, a look of utter bewilderment painted across his face.

"But we will need your help," Nathan added.

The aide began translating Nathan's proposal to the Prime Minister, whose face quickly showed a similar expression.

"Captain," Tug whispered, moving closer, "the Yamaro will have many technologies that could be adapted to your vessel. It may take weeks, possibly even months, but if we had an army of technicians..."

"Start with her shields," Jessica insisted, "and then her energy weapons."

"And she might have more fighters on board, or other tactical ships," Nathan said.

The Prime Minister's aide finished his conversation with his superior and returned his attention to Nathan and the others. "Captain, while we appreciate your willingness to fight to protect us, as well as your ingenuity, we still fail to see how you can hope to achieve such a stunning victory over so powerful an enemy. You are but one ship, after all. And even if you are able to capture a few Takaran ships, there are still dozens of them left. They will eventually find you and destroy you; of this you can be sure."

"We have one asset that you are not considering, sir; time." Nathan stepped forward, separating himself from the others for dramatic purposes, moving a step closer to the Prime Minister and his aides. "Our jump drive allows us to navigate anywhere within ten light years in the blink of an eye. That is a tactical advantage of immeasurable proportions. The key is to use this advantage to act quickly and decisively, before the enemy realizes who and what they are fighting. By the time they do, we'll already be invading their home world, long before they have a chance to circle the wagons."

"Circle the wagons?" the aide wondered.

"It's an expression from old Earth history," he explained. "It refers to quickly mounting a defense."

The aide had been translating Nathan's words on the fly, and the Prime Minister was shaking his head in disagreement as he voiced his concerns to his aide.

"What you are proposing would only serve to seal our fate," the aide translated for Nathan. "They will come, and in overwhelming numbers, such that you could not possibly hope to defend yourself. When they do, you will use your *jump drive* to disappear. And where will that leave us?"

"Their numbers are not as many as you might believe, Prime Minister," Tug insisted. "The Karuzari have been whittling away at their forces for decades. Their losses have forced them to abandon their outer worlds in order to maintain control of their primary worlds in the Pentaurus cluster."

"The Karuzari have been destroyed," the aide argued. "We all saw the images of the attack on Taroa. Their destruction was complete."

"No, it was not," Nathan disagreed. "We were there, and we witnessed the escape of several ships. Perhaps dozens of Karuzari escaped."

"Dozens of Karuzari does not make an army, Captain."

"But it is a start. And you could add hundreds if

143

not thousands to their numbers."

"You want the Corinari to join forces with the Karuzari." The aide laughed at the idea. "I was correct the first time, Captain. You are mad. No, we will stand down and take our chances."

"Stand down and take your chances?" Jessica said. "And you're calling him mad?"

"If you stand down, the Ta'Akar will roll over you without blinking and eye," Tug insisted. "They will glass this planet from orbit and then use their reformation technologies to clean up the radiation and make it habitable again in relatively short order. Then they will have this world as their own. In only a few decades, the Corinari will be a long forgotten joke."

"What you people propose is insane! You speak of invasion of the Takaran home world, yet you admittedly cannot even defend this one world should they come in force. What other choice do we have?" the aide pleaded.

"You have the choice to stand up and fight for your freedom!" Nathan yelled back in protest.

"And die in the process!" the aide countered.

Nathan threw up his hands in frustration as he turned around and walked back to where Jessica was standing.

"You will die if you do not," Tug stated, picking up the debate on behalf of Nathan. "Of this I am quite certain. Just as I am certain that giving up and dying is not the true way of the Corinari."

The aide looked at Tug, confusion on his face.

"Yes, I know all about your people," Tug continued, "about your pride and your history. You were once a proud, thriving civilization. Your original settlement was founded from meager stock and supplies, and in less than a millennium you grew from a few hundred to a few *billion*. But when the Ta'Akar threatened you with overwhelming force, you were so afraid that you would lose everything you *had* that you gave up everything you *were*. I understand that; honestly I do. You chose life over death. But make no mistake, sir; that is not the choice you are given on this day. Today your choice is death with honor or death in shame."

There was a silence. There was obvious anger in the aide's eyes. Despite his objections to resistance, he did not care for Tug's characterization of his people.

Jalea took advantage of the silence. "Na-Tan is here now, and he has brought you this wondrous tactical advantage. He and his people are even willing to pledge their lives in the defense of your world. An opportunity such as this shall not come again. A legend comes true but once."

"If the Ta'Akar are allowed to complete their new power source, they will be unstoppable," Tug added.

"You ask too much of us," the aide pleaded in desperation.

"Tell him," Tug insisted. "Tell your leader what we said."

* * *

The black transport airship came in low over the fence line at the Aitkenna spaceport. It flew a careful course just high enough over the parked spacecraft and hangars so as not to disturb anyone on the ground with their rotor wash. Despite the number of ships that had fled the planet before the bombardment, the spaceport was still bustling with activity as people came and went. Some were on their way to Aitkenna to help with the relief efforts. Others were trying to escape the chaos to locations less affected by the orbital attacks.

The airship turned slightly to port to angle itself toward the medevac shuttle that was idling on the tarmac only one hundred meters away. As it grew closer, the airship turned back to starboard while it continued to travel toward the medevac shuttle, sliding sideways to port. As it closed the last twenty meters, it dropped down, flared slightly, and settled gently on the tarmac not ten meters from the medevac shuttle.

The side door to the airship slid open as the airship's rotors changed their pitch to a neutral position, ending the downward wash without shutting down her engines. Chief Montrose hopped down from the airship and then turned around to help the two women, Doctor Galloway and Nurse Brymer, down from the ship. The medical technician came out next, followed by Doctor Pantor.

"Thank you, Chief," the doctor said as he shook the chief's hand.

"You take good care of those people, Doc," the chief said. "I have a feeling they're not done taking care of us yet."

Doctor Pantor nodded his understanding as he backed away from the airship. As he turned and followed his team to the medevac shuttle, he wondered exactly what the chief had meant.

As they reached the bottom of the medevac's loading ramp, the airship that had delivered them began to lift off the ground. It rose quickly, rotating as it climbed. Doctor Pantor stopped at the bottom of the ramp and watched the airship. He could see the chief sliding the door closed as the airship rotated and sped away into the night. He wondered how long that crew had been flying today, and how much longer they would continue to fly before they would succumb to exhaustion. He had heard the stories about the dedication of the Corinari, of the long hours of training they endured in an effort to be ready to defend their world. However, in his lifetime, he had never known them to be called into action. The chaos of this day was the closest they had probably come. He knew that all but the oldest of the Corinari had served in the Ta'Akar military in their youth. Perhaps such a life was all most of them knew by the time they returned. He had been spared such a life. As the son of a prominent public servant and a candidate for medical training, he had avoided Takaran service. At times, he had felt guilty, but his world needed physicians, and medical training took more than a decade. Had he been required to serve prior to attending medical school, his career as a physician would have been drastically shortened. That had always been the argument that had worked with the Ta'Akar, and that was the argument that had eased his guilt as well.

As he headed up the ramp, the view of the back of the medevac shuttle was not what he expected. All the usual equipment was there, along with his three teammates that had gone up the ramp before him. However, the shuttle was packed with Corinari troops, all dressed in combat armor and heavily armed. Including the two guards that followed him up the ramp, there appeared to be more than a dozen men on board. Sixteen he counted as he took his seat next to Doctor Galloway, and it appeared there were two more up in the cockpit with the pilots.

"Are we on the right shuttle?" he asked the crew chief. "The one headed up to the Earth ship?"

"Yes, sir," the chief added nervously.

The doctor was surprised to see the chief so uncomfortable. He had flown missions with him before, and he always seemed like such a relaxed sort. He assumed it was because they were flying with a ship full of armed troops. It was certainly enough to make him nervous.

The loading ramp at the back of the shuttle rose slowly up into the rear of the ship, the outer doors closing over the outside of the ramp once it had fully retracted up into the tail of the shuttle. The whine of the idling engines began to increase as the ship prepared to lift off and begin its journey to rendezvous with the Earth ship in orbit.

"What's with all the troops, chief?" the doctor asked, hoping that a little idle chitchat would ease the chief's obvious tension.

"We're just hitching a ride up, Doc," one of the troops informed him.

The trooper that spoke appeared to be younger and fitter than most of the others. In fact, the doctor noticed that the majority of the troops seemed a bit old to be serving as basic foot soldiers. However, most members of the Corinari served for life, so it stood to reason that there had to be some older men still mixed in with the lower ranks.

The trooper that had spoken noticed the puzzled look on the doctor's face and offered further explanation. "We're going to transfer over to the Yamaro once you've been delivered to the Aurora. There's a few hundred Takarans on that ship that are gonna need to be transferred to the surface. We're just going up to provide security."

"I see," the doctor said, nodding slowly as the shuttle lifted off the tarmac, her engines screaming outside. He turned and looked at Doctor Galloway. "Well I feel safer. How about you?"

* * *

Nathan and the others watched as the aide translated their words to the Prime Minister of Corinair. Nathan wondered what was going through the mind of this man. He had the future of his entire world on his shoulders. Nathan had been a student of history, studying the events of the past, most of which had been buried for a thousand years back on Earth. Until this moment, he had never thought that he would witness history in the making. The decision this man made today would become either the greatest moment in Corinairan history, or the beginning of its doom.

It was an amazing metamorphosis to witness. Over the last hour, this elderly public servant's expression had been one of despair and hopelessness. Over a time span of less than a minute, however, he had changed. Gone was the look of anguish, gone was the despondent expression. It had quickly been replaced with a look of courage, a look of honor. It was a look of hope.

The Prime Minister said something to his aide, something that his aide was surprised to hear. So surprised, in fact, that the aide even questioned the Prime Minister-something that the leader did not appreciate and he made sure that his subordinate understood his incongruity.

Nathan had a feeling that Tug's words had changed the mind of the de facto Corinairan leader, for Tug's demeanor suddenly changed, as did Jalea's. They both spoke the Corinairan language and had already understood what the Prime Minister had told his aide.

The aide turned his attention back to Nathan. "The Prime Minister of Corinair would like to know what we can do to aid you in our defense."

Nathan finally felt like there was a chance, not only for the people of Corinair, but for himself, his ship, and his crew. With the help of the Corinairans, they actually had a chance to defeat the Ta'Akar and obtain the zero-point energy device. With it, they also had a good chance of getting back to Earth in time to help defend her against invasion by the Jung.

"We need people," Nathan began, "technicians, engineers, troops, munitions, ships, supplies... Hell, we need a crew." Nathan took a breath, realizing that he was rambling. "What we need more than anything, right now, is help repairing and rearming our ship. The sooner the better, as we have no idea how long we have until the Ta'Akar will send another ship to investigate the disappearance of the Yamaro."

"The Prime Minister could not commit to such an action," the aide explained. "Only the President can make such a decision, and even then only with the backing of the Council of Representatives."

"I'm sorry, sir, but you are mistaken," Tug argued. "The Prime Minister is currently the most senior government official known to still be alive on all of Corinair. He does have the power to declare a state of war, after which he would have full and unrestricted decision making powers."

"But we are not at war," the aide defended.

"Technically, we have only been punished by our rulers for our open defiance of the Doctrine."

"Funny, it looks like a war to me," Jessica chimed in.

"We have yet to verify that the Prime Minister *is* the most senior member left..."

"Then perhaps *that* is a good place to start," Nathan interrupted, not wanting to waste any time.

The aide quickly translated Tug's words, to which the Prime Minister nodded agreement as he spoke.

"The Prime Minister admits that your knowledge of Corinairan law is quite impressive. It appears you have chosen your guides quite well, Captain. However, it will take time to invoke the official state of war, no matter how quickly we work. And our current crisis requires all of our resources. It will be days, maybe even weeks before we can offer you any significant assistance."

"We may not have that long," Nathan objected.

"It will take the Ta'Akar some time to realize that something is amiss with the Yamaro, and even longer for a ship to arrive to investigate. Your guide said so himself."

"That is true. But we have no idea how long the repairs might take."

"We will do what we can, when we can," the aide insisted.

"But, sir..."

"Captain, please. At least allow us to stop our capital city from burning to the ground. We have riots in the streets and half the people are calling for the heads of our leaders. We have problems right here, right now, and deal with them we must; or come morning there may not be a government left to help you."

Again the aide conferred with his leader, leaving Nathan feeling a bit frustrated at the inaction of the Corinairans.

"Talk about denial," Jessica whispered.

"He just doesn't get it," Nathan mumbled.

"Captain," Jalea began, "these people haven't fought a war in over thirty years. You cannot expect them to suddenly pick up the guns and fall into line behind you."

"She is right," Tug said. "The Corinairans are quite rigid in their governmental procedures. They will follow the letter of their laws right up until the end."

* * *

"Aurora, Aurora. This is Corinairan Medevac Shuttle one four seven, requesting permission to approach for landing."

"*Medevac Shuttle one four seven, this is the Aurora. You are cleared for landing. Approach from astern and well above our longitudinal axis. Begin your descent once you have cleared our stern thrust ports. Upon landing, use transfer bay one for entry.*"

The pilot looked a bit confused by the instructions. "Understood, Aurora. Requesting auto-landing frequency for AFCS approach."

"*Uh, Shuttle one four seven, you are instructed to land manually. Repeat, manual landing. No auto-landing system is available.*"

The pilot of the medevac shuttle looked at his copilot. "Manual landing?"

"Maybe their auto-flight systems were damaged in battle?" the copilot said.

"What's the problem?" Captain de Winter asked.

"They want us to land manually," the pilot explained.

"Then do it," de Winter insisted. "You do know how to land this ship manually, do you not?"

"Of course," the pilot assured him. "I just haven't had to do it in some time, except in practice simulations."

The pilot turned his attention back to the comm system. "Aurora, Shuttle one four seven. Understood. Beginning approach for manual landing. Will enter through transfer bay one."

Captain de Winter left the cockpit and made his way back to the cargo area. He surveyed the passengers. "Well, this is a bit of a wrinkle." He turned to Andre, who had followed him from the cockpit. "They sent two women."

"So?" Andre asked.

"I was planning on having us change clothing with the medical team. That would get us deeper into the ship without raising suspicion."

"Did it ever occur to you that the Corinairans would probably send a security team with their medical staff? I mean, they are sending them into a ship full of strangers, right?"

"Good point," de Winter agreed. He looked at the two men. "You two, remove your clothing."

"What?" Doctor Pantor objected. "We'll do nothing of the sort!"

Captain de Winter turned to Andre. "Can you kill them without mussing up their medical attire?"

"With pleasure," Andre said, taking a step forward.

"All right, all right!" Doctor Pantor agreed.

Minutes later, the two men had removed their medical uniforms and were standing in their underwear.

"Ladies, I assume you have some sort of medical agent that will render these two unconscious for a while?"

"Yes, but..." Doctor Galloway started to say.

"Excellent. About four hours should do it." Captain de Winter noticed Doctor Galloway's hesitation. "Or we could just kill them... Your call."

Doctor Galloway immediately reached for one of the medical bags to do as she was told. A minute later, both men lay unconscious on the deck.

"Stow these two in the forward equipment locker until we're done with them." As two of the anti-insurgency agents began to pick up the first unconscious male member of the medical team, Captain de Winter turned to the women and began to remove his uniform. "Now, ladies, I promise you that if you cooperate in every way, you will all come out of this little adventure unharmed."

Doctor Galloway and Nurse Brymer averted their eyes as both Captain de Winter and his cohort, the sergeant, began to undress.

Captain de Winter picked up the pile of clothing that had been worn by Doctor Pantor. "I believe my mother always wanted me to become a doctor."

"She would be so proud," Andre said in deadpan fashion.

The medevac shuttle fired its topside thrusters briefly, just enough to stop its ascent to a position just above the top of the Aurora's main drive section. Still closing on the Earth ship, the shuttle eventually passed over the top of her main propulsion section.

As the shuttle moved forward of the Aurora's

drive section, it again fired its topside thrusters and began a brisk descent. Its rate of descent, combined with its closure rate on the touchdown marker on the landing apron, put it on a sixty degree attack angle-steep enough that the shuttle had to perform a slight flaring maneuver in order to decrease it closure and descent rate sharply just before touching down on the Aurora's aft flight deck.

Despite his lack of practice at manual landings, the pilot of the medevac shuttle had placed his ship perfectly atop the touchdown marker, at which point the weak artificial gravity generated by the deck plates kicked in to hold her against the deck as she rolled forward. She passed under the hood that extended out over the forward end of the flight deck to shield the transfer bay doors from the outside. The shuttle rolled toward the port side of the deck as it moved forward, aligning itself with the approach path markings on the deck that led to transfer bay one.

The massive door to the transfer bay was already rising to allow them to enter the airlock. The shuttle passed cleanly under the door as it rose, with room to spare, coming to a stop once it was completely inside the transfer bay. As the bay door reversed and began coming back down, they received a message from the Aurora's comm-officer. *"Welcome aboard the Aurora."*

* * *

Vladimir had not slept in days. His ship had been put through so much in the last week. In order to keep her operating, he had been forced to circumvent many repair protocols. One by one, it seemed like each of his previous repairs were beginning to fail, and he secretly feared that his ship might come apart at any moment.

"*Chort,*" he cursed. "We will have to bypass the entire control run until it can be completely replaced."

"Do you even have enough cabling on board to replace it?" Deliza inquired.

"I do not know," Vladimir admitted. "I have not yet had a chance to fully inventory everything on board. There are still so many unopened containers in the cargo holds." Vladimir looked at the schematic displayed on the large monitor built into the top of the console. "We will have to reroute all bridge command and control signals through these lines," he said, pointing at the schematic. "Through here, here, and then finally here." He breathed out a small sigh. "It will cause a small signal delay, but there is no other way. We cannot repair that bundle. It will take too long and there is no guarantee that it will be working at one hundred percent efficiency when we are done."

"How do we do it?" Deliza asked. She recognized the location on the schematic. "We don't have to go back into the dirty tunnel again, do we?"

"No, we just..."

"*Cheng, Comms,*" the voice interrupted over Vladimir's comm-set.

"Go ahead," Vladimir answered, raising his hand to indicate to Deliza to give him a moment.

"*The medevac shuttle from Corinair has just landed and is rolling into the hangar bay now, sir.*"

"Understood. Is there someone there to escort them?"

"*Yes, sir. One of Doctor Sorenson's team is meeting*

them."

"Why not some of our crew?"

"*Our people are all busy with repairs, sir.*"

Vladimir nodded his head as he rolled his eyes. He had ordered everyone to help in repairs where ever possible. Of course, at the time he had not anticipated guests. "Pull the nearest person, preferably two, and have them report to the hangar bay immediately. And make sure they are armed."

"*Yes, sir.*"

"I will join them in medical as soon as possible."

"*Yes, sir.*"

"Unbelievable. You would think they were friends coming over for dinner. Now, where were we?" Vladimir asked, his mind a bit cloudy from fatigue. "Ah, yes. Rerouting the command and control signals. You just have to reprogram routing nodes at each of these points," he explained as he pointed to them on the schematic. "We just tell each of them to pass the bridge C and C signals to the next node on through the new path."

"What about return signals?"

"They will automatically try to return along the same path. But newly initiated signals must know where to go as well, so you must also reprogram all nodes in reverse to detour all signals bound for the bridge across the same new paths."

Deliza looked at him with one eyebrow raised. "Right. Do you always make this much sense?"

"What? It is easy," he said. Deliza looked at him quizzically. "Very well," he declared, "I will do it myself..."

"No, I can do it," she insisted. "It's just basic signal routing, after all. Child's play really."

"Children on your world like to play with signal

routing?"

"I thought it was an Earth expression," Deliza defended. "I heard Abby say it."

"Ah, yes." Vladimir shook his head. "Forgive me, I am very tired."

Deliza looked at Vladimir. He didn't look good. His eyes were red and had bags under them, and his hair was messier than usual. "Maybe you should get some rest."

"Not until all the crew is back and the ship is working," he insisted. "Now, before I go to medical, let me show you how to access and reprogram the nodes. Once you know how, it will only take you minutes."

* * *

"Now, let's just review the rules here, shall we?" Captain de Winter said. He was wearing Doctor Pantor's medical uniform and was putting on his name badge as he stepped closer to Doctor Galloway and Nurse Brymer. "I am Doctor Pantor," he explained, pointing at his name badge. "See? It says so right here." He turned and looked at Andre, who was now wearing the medical technician's uniform. "He is Mister Lenox." He then pointed to the other two anti-insurgency agents, who had removed their assault gear, were dressed only in the plain black uniforms of the Corinari, and no longer carried weapons. "And these four are merely a group of nice young soldiers who are coming along to help carry all of our impressive medical gear."

"You'll never get away with this," Doctor Galloway warned. "This ship has got to be crawling with armed crew. You won't even get out of the hangar."

Captain de Winter squatted down in front of Doctor Galloway and stared at her for a moment. "You might be surprised," he said. "Now, will I have your cooperation, or do I have to kill you both right here and go it alone?"

"What do you need us for?" Nurse Brymer asked. "You already have plenty of people. Aren't we just an unnecessary risk?"

"Perhaps, but the two of you do lend a certain... authenticity to the group. Don't you think?" The captain waited for a moment but got no response. "I'll take your silence as agreement. Just keep in mind that one false move, or one slip of the tongue, and the good sergeant here will break your pretty little necks." The captain turned to the sergeant. "Is everyone ready?"

"Yes, sir."

"Shall we then?" he said, his hand gesturing toward the side door.

The remaining men still clad in body armor and carrying heavy weapons huddled at the back of the cargo bay to avoid being seen by anyone that might be peering in through the side loading door.

The side loading door of the medevac shuttle swung away from the ship and down toward the deck, becoming a gangway as it reached its fully opened position. Sergeant Tukalov, now playing the part of the medical technician, Mister Lenox, peered out into the Aurora's hangar bay. Standing not more than ten meters away was a young woman with a partially healed wound on her forehead, dressed in what appeared to be some sort of medical uniform, although it was unlike the ones that they wore. Hers were just a simple pair of lightweight pants and a pullover top with a shallow V-neck and a single

159

pocket over the left breast. She held some sort of data pad in her left hand and was smiling nervously.

Andre looked both left and right before he made his way down the ramp, a medical satchel in each hand. Captain de Winter came down the ramp behind him.

"Hello," the young lady said. "My name is Doctor Cassandra Evans."

"Ah, then you must be the ship's physician," Captain de Winter said. "I'm Doctor Pantor."

"Oh no, I'm not a medical doctor," she corrected with embarrassment. "My doctorate is in human physiology, not medicine. I'm just here to show you the way to medical."

"I see," the captain said as he waited for Doctor Galloway and Nurse Brymer to reach the bottom of the gangway. "This is Mister Lenox, our medical technician, and this is Doctor Galloway and Nurse Brymer. If you'll just give us a moment to gather our gear, then we'll be ready to go."

"Of course."

Captain de Winter turned and watched as the first two soldiers carried the gurney down the gangway and the next two came down carrying several bags of medical equipment and supplies.

Two members of the Aurora's crew appeared at the starboard entrance to the hangar bay, both carrying close-quarters automatic weapons. They quickly made their way across the hangar deck to the medevac shuttle. Andre and the two soldiers carrying the gurney immediately took notice and began to tense up.

"Easy," Captain de Winter whispered, as he felt his own pulse rate quicken.

The two crewmen continued to approach, but

other than carrying their weapons in a ready position across their chests, they showed no other signs of aggression.

"Excuse me, ma'am," the first crewman said. "We've been ordered to help you escort our guests to medical."

"Okay," she agreed, somewhat confused.

"Sirs, ma'ams," the first crewman began, "Ensign Kamenetskiy has ordered us to safely escort you and your team to and from medical. However, before we can let you come aboard, we will need to inspect your equipment."

"Is there a problem?" Andre asked.

"No, sir. I'm sure the ensign just wanted to ensure your safety. We've got a lot of repairs underway after our last battle, and there are a lot of exposed systems that might react unfavorably with your medical devices."

"I see," Andre said, satisfied for the moment that there was no reason for him to be overly concerned at this point. "Lead the way, gentlemen."

The crewmen that had done the speaking headed out across the hangar bay, not in the direction he had come, but rather down the length of the hangar bay toward the bow of the ship. The Corinairan medical team, both real and impostors, followed behind him with the second crewman from the Aurora and Cassandra bringing up the rear.

Captain de Winter's eyes glanced from side to side as he noticed the condition of the hangar bay. There was the wreckage of two ships, one smaller and more badly damaged, the other identical to the shuttle that had carried him and his men down to the surface of Corinair as prisoners only hours ago. There was also an older model Takaran deep space patrol fighter. He recognized it from pictures he had seen. The design had been abandoned decades ago as the need for FTL capable fighters had been negated by the introduction of larger ships that could carry entire squadrons of short-ranged interceptors, which were easier and less expensive to build and operate. While he had an idea of how the other ships ended up on board the Earth ship, the presence of the old Takaran fighter was somewhat of a mystery, as to his knowledge they had all been decommissioned.

Another surprise was the presence of burn marks on the walls and ceilings of the hangar. There had obviously been a battle involving energy weapons that had taken place in this very bay. However, he had no knowledge of such an action taken on the part of any Ta'Akar ships. Then again, details of the Aurora's activities had been sketchy, and what he did not know had been filled in with many assumptions.

* * *

"So let me see if I've got this straight," Ensign Mendez said. "You intercepted a message headed for command, and your captain took it into his own hands to take action."

"Yes," Ensign Willard answered.

"So command doesn't even know you're here, right?"

"No, they do not."

"But the message about us is still on its way to your command. Did you send them word of your intentions as well?" Mendez asked.

"No, we did not. This action would also be considered a serious breach in protocol."

Enrique thought for a moment. "How long will it take that comm-drone to reach Takaran command?"

"At one hundred times the speed of light? About two weeks. Takara is only four point two light years from Corinair."

"And how long will it take for them to respond?"

"It depends on the location of the responding ship. However, to the best of my knowledge we were the only ship in this sector. It is more likely that the ship will come from Takara herself."

"And how long will that take?"

"It would take ten times as long. Even our fastest ships can only travel at ten times the speed of light, so it would take approximately one hundred and fifty days for a ship to make the journey from Takara to Darvano. But that's assuming they will travel at maximum velocity."

"Then we've got about five, maybe six months before anyone comes looking for us here," Enrique realized.

"Months?" Ensign Willard wondered, unfamiliar with the term.

"It's how we subdivide a standard solar year. Twelve months in a year, thirty days in a month, three hundred and sixty five days in a year..."

Ensign Willard looked puzzled. "Three hundred and sixty-five does not divide evenly by twelve."

"Not all months are thirty days long. It doesn't matter anyway," Mendez insisted. "What type of ship might they send?"

"Procedure would dictate a vessel of equal or greater capability be dispatched. However, the only ship more powerful than a battle carrier like the Yamaro would be a capital ship, and it is doubtful that they would send one of those. There are only three left, two of which are always guarding the Takaran home world. They would only send a capital ship if they were sure of a hostile action."

"What if we could intercept that comm-drone, stop it from delivering the message?"

"That might buy you some time," Ensign Willard said.

"Would they miss it?"

"Doubtful. As I said, it was not a regularly scheduled comm-run. It was dispatched ahead of schedule due to the urgency of the message it carried. As long as the next comm-drone arrived on schedule, they would have no reason to believe anything was amiss in this system. Then you would have until the next yearly patrol came through."

"And when would that be?"

"I do not know," Ensign Willard admitted. "However, I'm sure the Corinairans would have a rough idea, based on past visits. At the very least, they could tell you how long it has been since the last visit."

Ensign Mendez leaned back in his seat. "I'm sure Jess is going to love all of this. She's been dying for some good intel on you guys for a while now."

"I do not consider myself a Takaran," Ensign Willard reminded him. "I am a Corinairan."

"Sorry, I forgot. The uniform and all."

"May I?" Ensign Willard asked, indicating that he wished to remove his uniform jacket.

"Of course."

CHAPTER FIVE

The crewman leading the group of visitors stepped to the right after entering the medical treatment room. Captain de Winter, posing as Doctor Pantor of Corinair, led the rest of them into the room. The room itself was somewhat disheveled, with blood smears on the walls and floors. Every bed was occupied with injured crew, most of who appeared to have been recently injured. Several of the ship's crewmen were busy trying to clean the place up after having finally caught up with the flow of wounded.

"Excuse me," Cassandra said as she squeezed past the sergeant posing as a medical technician. She was trying to make her way to the front of the group in order to make introductions.

The second crewman took up position on the left side of the entrance opposite the first crewman. Andre squatted down and opened up one of the equipment satchels directly in front of the guard on the right side of the door and pretended to look for something in the bag. On the opposite side of the gurney, one of his men playing the part of a Corinairan soldier moved over out of the way, stepping just to the left and in front of the opposite crewman who had taken up position on the left side of the door.

"Doctor Chen," Cassandra called as she made her way to the front of the group.

Doctor Chen turned around to see Cassandra,

who seemed somewhat excited as she approached.

"This is the medical team from Corinair," she stated exuberantly.

"I am Doctor Pantor," Captain de Winter said. He had spoken with a heavy accent, pretending to be not proficient at Angla, just as most Corinairans were supposed to be. It was a difficult task for him, since he had studied several ancient languages, including Angla, during his education. "This is Doctor Galloway and this is Nurse Brymer. And the patient is where?"

"Hello, I'm Doctor Chen. The patient is right over there in bed one," she answered, pointing behind her and to her left.

"Ah, may we look?" Captain de Winter said in his mock accent.

"Of course," Doctor Chen said, turning to lead the way.

The group of visitors moved toward Cameron's bed, including the two crewmen Vladimir had tasked with escorting the Corinairans while on board. At that moment, Andre, who was still squatting on the floor in front of the guard digging in his medical bag, swept his free arm at the moving guard's legs, knocking him off his feet. The crewman fell backwards, landing flat on his back. Andre lunged backwards toward the fallen crewman, landing his elbow into the crewman's throat crushing his larynx.

The other crewman fell just as quickly at the other anti-insurgency agent's hand, which held a small, razor sharp knife that he swept across the man's throat. The crewman, stunned, reached for his gaping wound, gurgling as he fell to the floor only to die a minute later from massive blood loss.

There were screams, not only from other crew

working in the medical treatment room, but also from Doctor Galloway, Nurse Brymer, and Cassandra. The rest of the noblemen quickly dropped their gear and moved into position to help take control of the room.

Doctor Chen also spun around at the sounds of the attack. Her first instinct was to try and run for the alarm button on the wall at the other end of the room. Before she could take a step, she felt a sudden stinging pain in the back of her head as her hair was pulled hard from behind. She found herself falling backward against the man she thought was the Corinairan Doctor Pantor, who had a firm grasp on her hair.

"Going somewhere?" the captain said.

One of the crew working in the far end of the treatment room tried to get to the same alarm button that Doctor Chen had been going for, but as she reached out to slap the red button, a tight energy beam caught her in the shoulder, spinning her around as she fell to the floor, her shoulder still smoldering.

Captain de Winter turned around and saw Andre kneeling next to the crewman who was still coughing and struggling to breathe through his crushed windpipe. Andre was holding a miniature energy pistol that had been concealed in the medical bag he had been rummaging through.

"Nice shot, Sergeant," Captain de Winter told him.

Without looking, Andre moved his small weapon to his left hand and placed it against the temple of the suffocating crewman and pulled the trigger. The beam burned a hole right through his head, boiling blood and brains draining out of the hole on the other side, killing the crewman instantly and putting him out of his misery.

"Oh," the captain winced, "brutal."

"NOBODY MOVES!" one of the noblemen bellowed as he pulled a larger energy handgun from under the gurney mattress. One by one he retrieved weapons and distributed them to the rest of their assault team.

"What, no gun for me?" Captain de Winter asked.

Andre tossed him the miniature energy pistol he had used to kill the crewman.

"Oh gee, thanks. I feel much safer with this."

"It worked on him," Andre said, nodding toward the dead crewman with the hole burnt through his head.

"Good point."

Andre and the other two agents began to move the rest of the Aurora's medical staff into the middle of the room along with the two real members of the Corinairan medical team and Cassandra. Andre immediately began checking adjacent rooms for anyone that might be hiding but found no one.

"All clear," Andre reported when he returned.

"Very well," Captain de Winter said. He looked to Doctor Chen, whose hair he still a firm grasp on with his right hand. "Now, my dear Doctor Chen. If you would be so kind as to direct me to your bridge."

"The what?" she said, struggling to keep her balance as he continued to pull on her hair.

"The room where the captain sits and tells everyone what to do, where they steer the ship."

"Sorry," Doctor Chen said, "I couldn't tell you. As you can see, they keep me pretty busy in here."

"Oh, the brave little Earther, huh?"

"That's Earthling," she correct through clenched

teeth.

The captain spun her around, pulling her directly up against him, looking down into her face with anger. "Don't play with me, young lady," he threatened as he placed his weapon against her temple. "Or I'll ventilate your cranium just like your friend over there."

Doctor Chen glanced over at the dead crewman, his head still smoldering as the blood and cerebral matter oozed from the open hole, but still she said nothing. She only looked the captain directly in the eyes without blinking, determined to show no fear.

Captain de Winter saw a surprising strength in her eyes. "Impressive. You're quite strong for such a tiny thing." A moment later he tossed her aside. Off balance, she fell to the floor.

The captain aimed his weapon at Cameron as she lay unconscious in her bed, being kept alive with machines. "Is this the young lady that we've come to save?" he asked. He moved closer as if to get a better shot. "No, that won't work, will it? She couldn't tell me even if she wanted to." He stopped and turned toward the sergeant. "Sergeant, maybe you can be more persuasive than I."

"Gladly," the sergeant said as he stepped over and grabbed hold of Doctor Chen's hair again and pulled her to her feet. In one smooth motion, he turned her around so her back was against him, his left arm around her neck forcing her head to bend over to her left. He pulled out his weapon, and with one hand set it to its lowest setting: a slow discharge meant to drain the battery pack on the weapon of all energy before storing it. He then held the butt of the weapon's hand grip against her neck so that the bare metal energy transfer nodes were in contact with the doctor's skin. Then, without hesitation, he flipped the discharge switch on the weapon, sending the energy charge into her neck.

Doctor Chen screamed in pain, her body convulsing wildly as the energy of the weapon shot into her body. She felt a burning sensation at the point of contact, and her entire body felt like a million tiny needles were driving deep into her skin.

"Stop it!" Cassandra cried out, unable to bear the sight of the Doctor being tortured.

Andre stopped the torture for a moment.

"You're killing her!" Cassandra cried.

Doctor Chen reached out to her. "No, Cassie..."

Andre again flipped the switch. Her neck glowed red around where the butt of his weapon made contact with her skin as it discharged its energy into her body. She screamed out in pain once more, begging for him to stop as her body shook and twitched.

"Please, stop it!" Cassandra cried out again. "I'll tell you what you want to know!" She began to sob. "Please, just don't hurt her anymore."

Captain de Winter stepped over to Cassandra, who was now holding her hands over her face as she wept. "Answer all my questions, and I promise you no one else in this room will be harmed."

"Straight down the corridor," Cassandra said between sobs, "until you get to the big ramp." She wiped her face. "Then up one deck. It's clearly marked."

"Excellent."

"No," Doctor Chen whimpered. Andre struck her hard in the face with the butt of his gun, breaking her nose and knocking her unconscious. Cassandra screamed again.

Captain de Winter now knew that Cassandra was easy enough to manipulate. "Now, Cassandra, I have another question for you."

"I've told you what you wanted to know," she said, a touch of defiance sneaking into her voice.

"Dear girl, don't make the good sergeant torture another of your friends."

Cassandra looked at him, anger burning in her eyes. "What do you want to know?"

"Tell me why it is that I see so few people aboard this ship."

"There are only about thirty of us left. And everyone is busy with emergency repairs."

"Excellent answer." Captain de Winter smiled broadly, as his assumptions were proving to be correct. "Sergeant, we'll leave one man here to guard these prisoners so they cannot alert anyone in our absence."

"We could just kill them all," Andre suggested. "It would be easier."

"But then who would patch us up if *we* get injured?" the captain pointed out. "This party is just getting started."

"*Team Two, Team One. You are go. Repeat, you are go. Resistance is low, suggest speed over stealth.*"

The anti-insurgency agent standing by on the medevac shuttle touched the comm link around his neck to answer. "Copy Team One, Team Two is moving now. Speed over stealth." He turned to the others. "You heard him. We move fast and take out everyone along the way. Let's move out."

The leader turned to the other agent that was staying behind with the rest of the Yamaro's command staff. "As soon as we leave, wait five minutes, then drop an active jammer out into the bay and wait for our signal."

"If we're jamming comms, how will we get a signal?" the agent asked.

"When those transfer bay doors open, that's your signal."

The last agent nodded his understanding as the leader turned and exited the shuttle.

One other agent, along with three of the Yamaro's command staff, charged down out of the medevac shuttle and ran across the hangar deck. They came to a stop against the side exit where the original escorts had entered the bay. The lead agent peeked around the corner and then disappeared through the hatchway, the other following close behind.

As they charged down the hallway, two crewmen came around the corner carrying loops of signal cable.

"What the..." It was all the first crewman had time to say before an energy bolt struck him in the chest, knocking him backwards. A split second later, the second crewman fell to another blast as the assault team ran past him on their way aft.

"Hold up," the leader called out as he stopped. The other agent dropped to one knee, his weapon aimed ahead down the corridor as he watched for intruders. The members of the Yamaro's command staff, seeing the logical stance the agent had taken, mimicked his position. One of them was even smart enough to aim behind them.

The leader examined the deck layout map on the wall. "We follow this corridor all the way around. At the end there is a ramp that takes us down one deck. Then, at the intersection we turn left and continue aft to engineering. Got it. Let's go."

* * *

"There's one other thing you should remember," Ensign Willard said as he removed his uniform jacket. "We were due to arrive in the Savoy system in approximately four weeks. By the fifth week, the military office in Savoy will report us overdue. That would also trigger action by command."

"But it wouldn't necessarily point to the Darvano system," Enrique argued.

"True, but they would search all systems along the Yamaro's logical route, including Darvano. One scan of the surface of Corinair, which they could accomplish from great range, would alert them to the fact that a Takaran ship had attacked the planet."

"And the jig would be up," Enrique added.

"Jig?"

Enrique waved him off, making a note to himself not to use Earth-based terms and phrases during interrogation of non-Earth humans in the future. "There's still one thing I don't understand. Why bombard Corinair? We weren't even there."

"I believe Captain de Winter did so as a ploy... a way to get your captain to engage the Yamaro in battle. The captain suspected that your ship was equipped with a superluminal propulsion system that made even our high-speed comm-drones appear pale in comparison. After your captain refused de Winter's offer to join forces, it was the only way he could keep you from simply vanishing."

Enrique was surprised, as he hadn't realized that the captain of the Yamaro had contacted Captain Scott directly prior to their battle.

"This act of aggression against the people of Corinair, although possibly warranted according to their original terms of surrender, was also a serious violation of protocol."

"How so?"

"An attack against an entire world, especially one that has not taken an aggressive posture, must be approved by Caius himself."

"He went against his own king? What the hell was he thinking?" Enrique said.

"He was sure that he would capture the Aurora and her technology. That would have not only gotten his inappropriate actions excused, it would have undoubtedly regained the honor of his entire family and possibly even earned him a spot in the Admiralty."

"All or nothing, huh?"

"Yes. His previous failures had made him desperate. He would have stopped at nothing in order to achieve his goals. As with most nobles, his concept of right and wrong is measured by what is best for himself, above all else."

"Well, at least he's past history now," Enrique commented.

"What do you mean?"

"He's on his way to a Corinairan prison, if not an execution."

Ensign Willard's eyes widened. "He is not in your custody?"

"No, we handed him and his command staff over to the Corinairans just a couple of hours ago."

"Then it is not over," Ensign Willard insisted, becoming quite agitated.

Loki stopped eating, startled by Ensign Willard's sudden change in demeanor, as was Sergeant

Weatherly.

"What are you talking about?" Enrique asked.

"You do not understand. There are operatives of the Ta'Akar everywhere, especially on Corinair."

"Relax," Enrique told him. "I saw about twenty armed guards take them away. Trust me; he's done for."

"No! You will see! They will free him and he will come for you! He will come for us all! He must be stopped!"

"Calm down!" Enrique insisted. He looked at Sergeant Weatherly, who immediately rose from his seat by Loki at the next table and moved closer to them.

"Oh God," Willard exclaimed, "I should have killed him when I had the chance."

"Listen, I'll call the ship. I'll have them call down to Corinair. We'll have them double the guards, triple them even."

"He must be killed! Don't you get it?"

"Relax! I'm calling right now," he promised as he tapped his head set. "Aurora, this is Mendez." He waited a few seconds for an answer. "Aurora, Mendez. Do you copy?" Again he got no response, only static. "Aurora, come in." He looked at Willard, whose expression grew even more despondent. "We're probably just too deep in the ship for these to work properly," he told him. "Marcus, you and Loki head back to the shuttle and try to raise the Aurora."

"Where are you going?" Marcus asked.

"We'll take him back to the brig for now. It's also on the port side and right up against the hull, so we might be able to make contact from there. Call me if you make contact first."

* * *

"Two men is not exactly my idea of an effective strike team," Andre whispered as they made their way up the ramp to the command deck, crouching low with their weapons held high and ready as they advanced.

"I count five," Captain de Winter said.

Sergeant Tukalov looked behind himself and his partner at the captain and the two noblemen following him. The captain looked calm and relaxed. He was either ignorant or truly thought that he was too important to be injured. The two noblemen behind him, however, appeared to be on the verge of an anxiety attack.

Andre smiled. "I only count two."

"Funny," de Winter remarked, feigning a smile. "Besides, you heard her. There are only thirty of them left, and most of them are busy trying to fix their poor little ship. There can't be more than a handful of them left on the bridge."

"I just keep thinking of the words of my CO," the sergeant said as his head came to deck level. He halted momentarily as he checked to make sure there was no one that would notice them as they crested the top.

"And what words of wisdom did your esteemed commander offer?" de Winter asked.

Andre smiled. "Never trust a noble." Andre and the second agent continued up the ramp onto the command deck.

De Winter turned and looked at the two nervous noblemen crouched behind him. For a moment, he thought he saw their weapons shaking. He turned back around and continued to follow the sergeant. "There might be some truth to that," de Winter mumbled to himself.

They quickly made their way to end of the main corridor, which split to either side at the end.

"Left or right, sir?" Andre asked.

"Left."

Andre looked at the captain, surprised that he sounded so sure of himself.

"A hunch," Captain de Winter admitted.

Andre went around the corner on the left and continued down the hall, the second agent and de Winter following him. They immediately came to a right turn, at which Andre stopped to peek around with a quick, smooth motion. Andre looked back to the second agent, communicating the presence of one armed guard with hand gestures. The second agent nodded his understanding. Andre followed with another set of gestures indicating his plan, which drew another nod of confirmation. He held up three fingers, then two, then... suddenly there was a noise. Andre held up a flat hand indicating a hold.

"Excuse me, Corporal," a women's voice said from the open hatchway. "Could you help us move this console?"

"Yes, ma'am," the guard at the hatchway answered.

Andre peeked around the corner again, just in time to see the guard at the entrance to the bridge turn his back to them to step through the hatchway. He quickly gestured for his teammate to go.

The second agent came charging around the corner with surprisingly little noise, walking at a near jog along the left side of the corridor with his weapon up high and pointed dead ahead at the man entering the hatchway with his back to them. Andre came around at the same time, staying along the right side of the corridor as they advanced. If they were lucky, they would get close enough to take down the unsuspecting guard from behind without even firing a shot, which would have alerted others on the bridge, and Andre had no idea how many of them there were or if they were armed as well. Unfortunately, Captain de Winter decided to join them, and in not as quiet a fashion.

The guard turned his head to look back as he noticed the sound of footfalls. In a split second he saw two armed men advancing toward him. His eyes widened as he tried to bring his gun around, but he was too late. A flurry of energy blasts struck him in the face and chest, knocking him backwards into the bridge.

Andre heard a woman's scream followed by the sound of at least two male voices shouting as he ran down the hallway toward the bridge. Not three seconds later he was stepping gingerly over the dead guard's smoking body. Andre sensed a man moving to his left and went into a roll as he landed. He came up firing, striking the moving man in the shoulder.

The second agent came in right behind him, but stopped and crouched, using the dead guard for cover as he sized up the situation. There was a terrified blonde woman on the far side whose hands were already up in the air. There was another equally terrified woman in a uniform to his left. Her hands were also up, as were the hands of the young man standing next to her.

"Nobody moves!" the second agent ordered as he slowly rose from his crouched stance. He glanced to his right. "I've got another room to my right."

Captain de Winter came in next, holding his miniature energy pistol. "Check it out," he ordered.

The second agent backed away toward the entrance to the captain's ready room at the back of the bridge, making room for the two nervous noblemen to join the party from the corridor.

"Is that a gun?" Josh asked, trying not to laugh at the captain's tiny pistol.

Captain de Winter did not take kindly to the crack and immediately fired his weapon, narrowly missing Josh's leg and striking the back of the navigator's chair.

"Whoa!" Josh yelled.

De Winter looked at his weapon then back at Josh. "Yes, I suppose it is a gun."

"It was a joke!" Josh defended. "I was kidding!"

"Please refrain from shooting people, Captain," Andre advised as he rose from the floor. "One of them might be the pilot."

"Yeah!" Josh agreed. "Don't shoot the pilot!" he declared, pointing at himself. "That's me, the pilot."

De Winter looked disappointed. "You got to shoot someone."

"Pilot's don't usually guard the entrance," Andre said as he reached down and grabbed the close-quarters automatic weapon from the dead guard, "with a gun."

De Winter ignored the sergeant as he strolled into the middle of the room, looking around the bridge. "Not much to look at," he commented, "very... functional." He looked at his two officers, still standing just inside the entrance, waiting for something to do. He gestured for them to take up positions, a look of complete dissatisfaction on his face. "Get him over there with the others," the captain ordered the fumbling noblemen, gesturing toward the wounded comm-officer lying on the floor, holding his injured shoulder.

"You," Andre said, pointing to Josh, "which console is your tactical station?"

Josh pointed hesitantly toward the tactical station not more than a meter in front of the sergeant.

"Josh," Kaylah scolded under her breath.

Andre stepped up onto the center command platform and sat down at the tactical station directly behind the captain's chair. He spent several seconds examining the console.

"Is there a problem, Sergeant?" de Winter asked.

"It's in Angla, I think."

"You don't speak Angla?"

"I am Takaran," he growled. "We don't need to speak Angla."

De Winter moved over behind him and looked at the console. After a few moments spent looking over the controls, he spoke. "This one operates the hangar bay doors."

* * *

Vladimir reached the end of the central corridor and started up the main ramp that led up one deck and emptied into the main circular corridor that encircled the Aurora's hangar bay. Although there were still weeks, maybe months, worth of work to be done before the ship would be in decent shape again, he welcomed this little break. After he ensured that Cameron was safely in the hands of the Corinairan doctors, he would visit his quarters, take a quick shower, and change into clean clothes. On the way back, he thought he might even get something to eat. Although most of their meals still involved hefty servings of molo, when combined with some of the emergency meal kits that had been scavenged from the forward escape pods, it made for a pretty decent meal.

He was a little worried about Nathan and the others still stuck on the surface below, especially with the reports he had received from Naralena about riots in the streets of Aitkenna. The multilingual Volonese woman—who had been stranded on board as a result of their hasty departure from the Haven system—was working in their newly formed signals intelligence office and had turned into quite an asset.

Unfortunately, there was nothing he could do to help his friends at the moment. He had sent Loki to retrieve their shuttle, and after that, all he could do was wait for Nathan to call in to be picked up. Besides, Jessica was with him on the surface, and if anyone could protect him, it was her.

Vladimir stopped halfway up the starboard ramp leading up to the main deck as he heard strange sounds. Some sort of energy discharge, and several of them. It was faint, but very reminiscent of the weapons used by the troops that had attack them on Tug's farm back on Haven. Next, he heard two faint thuds. He instinctively crouched down low, his mind racing. He had no weapon, and the armory was on the other side of the noises. That's when he heard a voice. It was in a language he didn't understand. However, he was sure of two things: they weren't friendlies, and they were headed his way.

* * *

"The doors," the agent guarding the medevac cockpit announced. "They're opening. Prepare to take off," he ordered the pilot. He turned and yelled down the short corridor that led from the cockpit to the cargo area. "They made it! They took the bridge!" Cheers erupted from the back of the shuttle.

After he had dropped the jamming pod into the hangar bay, the agent ordered the pilot to depart the Aurora and head for the Yamaro. With its engines already spun up, the shuttle was able to immediately begin its roll out into the transfer airlock. Wasting no time, the pilot eased the shuttle forward, sliding just under the inner doors as they rose. As he rolled to a stop, the doors began to close behind him. In a few more minutes, the transfer bay would be depressurized and the outer doors would open. Then he would begin the second phase of the worst mission of his career.

* * *

Allet and Deliza were busy reconfiguring the routing nodes to redirect all signals between the bridge and engineering to their new transmission path.

Vladimir came running into the middle of engineering, causing Deliza to jump, a small squeal erupting from her mouth. "Everyone! We've been boarded!" he announced. "Go now! Get out! Get out! They will be here any moment!"

Two crewmen that were working on repairing one of the damaged consoles immediately dropped their tools. "Where do we go?"

"Anywhere!" Vladimir instructed. "Go down one deck, try to circle back and reach the armory."

"I don't even know where the armory is!" one of them said.

"We're civilian technicians, remember?" said the other.

Vladimir rolled his eyes. "Then just hide! Go!"

Allet looked confused, until Deliza excitedly translated. He grabbed her and pushed her toward the other exit, yelling orders at her in his language.

Deliza ran to the other exit across the room, stopping at the doorway and turning around. "What are you doing?" she called to Vladimir.

"Where is my gun belt?" he cried. "I left it in here!" Jessica had ordered all fleet personnel to carry a side arm ever since they were first boarded back in the Taroa system, but Vladimir had taken his off while climbing around in the service tunnels. Now he cursed himself for not putting it back on.

Deliza looked quickly around the room but saw nothing except loose tools and equipment. She looked toward Vladimir and Allet who were both frantically searching for a weapon of any kind.

"Look in there!" Vladimir shouted at Deliza, pointing to the room behind her.

Deliza spun around and frantically searched the room. Finally, she spotted the gun belt draped over the edge of a seat at one of the systems monitoring consoles. "I found it," she yelled as she ran toward it.

Allet had already taken up a position to the left of the hatchway holding a large piece of damaged metal pipe. It wasn't a weapon, but it was better than nothing. Unable to find anything suitable, Vladimir took a position on the other side of the hatchway. He looked at Allet holding the pipe across the hatchway from him. "Go low," he whispered, motioning with his hands. "I'll go high."

A moment later, the first member of the boarding party entered the room. He came in at a slow walk, crouched low. He immediately turned toward Allet to his right, not because he saw him but rather because that was the direction he was supposed to check. Allet was already crouched low, expecting to swing his pipe at the attacker's knees, but the attacker's already crouched stance required a different tactic. Allet swung the pipe upwards, striking the enemy hard under his chin, driving his head up and back and sending his weapon flying out of his hands. Allet immediately dove toward the loose gun that had landed deeper in the room.

The second boarder came in right behind the first one but went left instead of right. Vladimir lunged into, letting out a groan as he and the enemy agent went tumbling over. They wrestled for a few seconds, but Vladimir was quickly able to get behind the man. His old infantry training kicked in, and in a quick motion, he yanked the enemy agent's chin around, snapping his neck.

The third boarder was right behind the first two and immediately opened fire through the hatchway, spraying the room with red bolts of energy that instantly burnt holes through any organic matter and ricocheted off the bulkheads, decks, and overheads.

Allet dove for cover behind the nearest console as the energy blasts danced around the room, the enemy weapon still in his hands. Vladimir managed to roll, pulling the body of the man whose neck he had just snapped over on top of him. The dead man's body armor absorbed the energy blasts, preventing them from reaching Vladimir.

Gunshots rang out in rapid succession. At least a dozen or more sounded, ricocheting off of everything. Everything except the enemy that had been standing in the hatchway spraying the room with energy blasts. His armor was designed to dissipate energy, not stop solid projectiles, and the three rounds that struck him blew right through his torso, killing him instantly and dropping him where he stood.

The sound of weapons fire, both energy and projectile, having stopped, Vladimir pushed the dead man's body off to one side and peeked in the direction that the gunfire had come from. There stood Deliza, smoking pistol in hand and shaking with fear, her eyes wide.

The respite was short lived, and the room was immediately lit up with energy weapons fire once more as a fourth man opened fire from behind the corpse lying in the hatchway. This time, the red bolts were flying in both directions.

Deliza screamed, dropping the gun and running back into the other room.

"Vlad!" Allet cried as he returned fire from his position behind the console.

Vladimir looked and saw that Allet was trying to cover his retreat. He quickly scrambled on hands and knees across the floor toward Allet's position, staying low enough to avoid being hit by Allet's return fire.

Vladimir made it behind the console with Allet just as several energy bolts struck the wall directly behind him. For the moment, he was safe.

"Thank you, my friend," he panted, staring at Allet in disbelief. This quiet man who had spent his every waking moment working to repair and sometimes even upgrade this ship, was now risking his very life to defend them, and without a moment's hesitation.

Allet continued returning fire, pressing the trigger as quickly as he could. He muttered something to Vladimir in his own language. He repeated himself several times, finally gesturing with his head toward the same doorway that Deliza had been standing in moments ago. Vladimir got the hint.

He jumped up and ran toward the other door as Allet continued returning weapons fire in rapid fashion, diving through the doorway and onto the floor in the next room.

Deliza screamed as he tumbled into the room. Vladimir quickly got to his feet.

"Where is the gun?" he asked frantically.

"I dropped it!"

"Where?"

Deliza pointed back toward the other room where the firefight still raged.

"What?"

"I'm sorry! It was loud!" she cried.

Vladimir grabbed her and held her, trying to comfort her.

"Did I kill him?" she sobbed.

"Yes, yes. You did. I am very proud," he told her, looking around the room.

"What?"

"Go," he told her, pointing, "into the service tunnel."

"What? Why?"

"Go now!" He pushed her hard toward the tunnel entrance, nearly knocking her over. "GO!"

Deliza stumbled over to the tunnel and quickly climbed up inside, scrambling to get deeper.

Vladimir quickly moved back over to the doorway, keeping himself out of the line of sight of the attacker at the main entrance to engineering. He could see Allet holding his ground from behind the main console, firing red energy bolts as fast as he could.

"Allet!" Vladimir called.

Allet looked to his right and spotted Vladimir standing in the next room, but the Russian's hands were empty. Allet saw the gun that Deliza had dropped to the left of the door, the slide still back and the chamber empty.

Another enemy soldier appeared at the hatchway and joined his cohort in spraying the room with energy bolts. Allet had little choice but to run. He made a mad dash for the doorway toward Vladimir, firing his weapon the entire time. He only made it three steps before one of the red beams struck him in the left leg, knocking both his legs out from under him. He went down hard, bouncing once off the floor.

Vladimir watched in horror. It seemed like everything was moving in slow motion as he watched the Karuzari's body bounce a few centimeters up from the floor. His body fell back down just as another energy beam struck him in the top of his head, causing the right half to explode outward, sending pieces of bone, blood, and brains spraying up and outward into the air.

"ALLET!" Vladimir yelled, but there was no movement.

The weapons fire continued for what seemed like an eternity to Vladimir as he stood there staring. In actuality it was only seconds. As soon as the enemy realized they had killed the only threat, they began to slowly move forward.

Vladimir caught a glimpse of one of the enemy's gun muzzles and reacted instantly. He ran across the room and climbed into the tunnel entrance, scurrying after Deliza. "Quickly," he called ahead to her in a hushed shout. "We must get to the next junction quickly."

Deliza crawled through the tunnel as quickly as she could. Her knees were bleeding from the textured non-slip surface. The rough surface had already torn through the thin tights she had been wearing under her skirt. Her hands were holding up much better, partly due to the amount of work she had done around her father's molo farm back on Haven.

"Quickly. Quickly. Quickly," Vladimir called from behind.

"I'm moving as fast as I can," she defended as she scurried along.

The tunnel was rapidly becoming darker as she moved farther along. Finally, Deliza reached the first tunnel junction. It led off the main tunnel to the left, going downward at a sharp angle. Afraid to go down the steep drop headfirst, she managed to turn around in the cramped tunnel and go in feet first.

Deliza slid down the four-meter long tunnel before she reached the level portion at the bottom. It was darker here, with only the slightest bit of light spilling down from the main tunnel now. It was even dustier here than it had been in the main tunnel. She coughed as the dust she had disturbed during her landing swirled about her.

"Look out!" Vladimir warned as he came sliding down the tunnel headfirst. He slammed into her right shoulder, pushing her further into the level portion of the dark tunnel below and kicking up even more dust. She moved to her left, as this tunnel was both wider and taller than the first one.

"Forgive me," Vladimir apologized as he rolled onto his back and struggled to right himself. "Oh, my head. I think it hit your shoulder."

"Yeah, I'm sure of it," she said as she rubbed her painful shoulder. "Why didn't you turn around and come down feet first?"

"I am not as small as you."

A voice called from the distance. Vladimir became silent. "Ssh."

Another voice responded to the first, this one slightly louder. Vladimir could not understand their language, but he did recognize it. They were speaking Takaran; he was sure of it.

Vladimir looked at Deliza. He could barely make out her face in the darkness, but from what little he could see, he could tell she was petrified. "What did he say?" he asked in a barely audible whisper.

Before she could translate for him, the more distant voice spoke again. It was a little louder now, as if the speaker had joined his comrade in the second room where the service tunnel entrance was located.

The closer of the two men spoke again, only this time he was quite loud, as if he were in the main tunnel itself. Vladimir's hope began to vanish. He had no idea where this tunnel led, and without lighting, they would never be able to navigate the tunnel system, not in the dark. If they came into the tunnels after them, they were doomed.

The louder voice continued speaking. The more distant voice immediately answered.

"Oh no," Deliza whispered as they heard the

sound of the hatch sliding closed. In the total darkness, they also heard the sound of the tunnel hatch locking mechanism being engaged. "Now what do we do?"

"Let me think," Vladimir said as he sat panting in the pitch-black service tunnel.

* * *

The medevac shuttle rolled briskly out of the transfer airlock and onto the exposed flight deck. It came to a stop in the middle of the deck and then fired its thrusters to push it gently upwards and away from the Aurora. As it rose slowly, the shuttle rotated quickly to port until it was perpendicular to the Aurora's flight path. Another blast of its rear-facing maneuvering thrusters and it began to move away from the Aurora on its way to the Yamaro.

* * *

"Aurora, Aurora. This is Ensign Mendez aboard the Yamaro. Do you copy?" Enrique sighed in frustration. "It's no use. I get nothing but static."

"Maybe the batteries are dying?" Sergeant Weatherly wondered.

"No way," Enrique said. "These things will last a week without a recharge, and this one came off the rack only a couple days ago."

"May I listen?" Ensign Willard asked.

"To what?"

"Please?"

Enrique shrugged and handed him the comm-set. "Suit yourself."

Ensign Willard placed the comm-set onto his ear

and listened intently.

Enrique and Sergeant Willard both spun around with their weapons high when someone appeared at the hatchway.

"Jesus," Enrique exclaimed. "You guys scared the shit outta me!" he added, lowering his weapon. "I thought I told you to call in."

"We tried," Marcus defended. "Nobody answered."

"Did you manage to make contact with the ship?"

"No," Loki said. "No one's answering. Not on the Aurora's channels or anything else. We got nothing but static."

"Yeah, us too," Enrique said.

"Oh no," Willard interrupted. Everyone turned to look at him. "It's not static; it's white noise."

"What?" Enrique asked.

"Like the kind generated by a Takaran jamming pod."

"A what?" This time it was Marcus that asked.

"Very simple devices. Multi-band high-power transmitters. They transmit white noise on all frequencies. It interferes with all transmission within a ten-kilometer range. It is standard practice to deploy one during any Takaran assault action." Ensign Willard's voice showed genuine concern. "That means they are here."

"We didn't see anyone," Marcus insisted.

"Yeah, the hangar bay was clear," Loki added.

"There's two hangar bays on this ship, right?" Enrique asked Willard.

"Yes, port and starboard."

"They could be on the Aurora," Sergeant Weatherly pointed out.

"Maybe, but if they are there's nothing we can do about it," Enrique said. "Hell, we can't even warn them as long as that jamming pod is active. We have to assume they're coming here. That's all we can do." Enrique turned to Crewman Rival. "You, Marcus, and Loki go back down and check both hangar decks."

"Me, sir?" Crewman Rival wondered, "but I'm just a systems tech."

"You do know how to use that weapon, don't you? I mean, you were trained how to shoot, right?"

"Uh, yes sir," Crewman Rival admitted reluctantly.

"Then go check out the starboard hangar bay. After that, go to the cargo bays and pick up the two goobers that were assigned to guard them and bring them back here."

"What about all those prisoners?" Crewman Rival asked.

"They're locked up, right? They'll be fine for now," Enrique insisted.

"Why are you sending us down there?" Marcus asked, also not terribly crazy about the idea.

"Well I can't send him alone," Enrique stated as he handed his automatic weapon to Marcus. "Besides, I need you two to guard our ride."

"How the hell are we supposed to do that?" Marcus grumbled.

"You still have that big-ass gun in the back of the shuttle, don't you?"

"Yeah."

"Then re-park the shuttle with its rear door pointed toward the hangar bay airlock doors. If they open the doors, blast the shit out of them."

"And if that don't stop them?"

"Then blast a whole in the hull and depressurize the whole damned bay," Enrique spelled out for him.

"Case you hadn't noticed, we ain't got no spacesuits neither," Marcus protested.

"I do," Loki said. "Or I did. Do you think there's time for me to put it back on?"

"Shut up, kid."

"If it comes to that, just close your back hatch as soon as you take your last shot."

"The ramp don't come up that fast..."

"Then hold your fucking breath," Enrique said, getting frustrated.

"Come on," Loki told Marcus, pushing him toward the exit. "Let's get this over with."

"Your plan sucks," Marcus protested on his way out.

Loki glanced at Enrique as the three of them headed out. "It's better than most of the plans Josh comes up with," he admitted as he accepted the automatic hand gun being offered to him by Sergeant Weatherly.

"If they make it aboard, they will head straight for the bridge," Willard told him.

"The bridge? Wouldn't they try to free their crew first?"

"Doubtful, as most of them are not Takarans. In fact, many are from Corinair."

"But still, why the bridge? This ship is too busted up to go anywhere."

"But her weapons systems are still mostly intact. If powered up, she could do considerable damage to your ship before they had a chance to escape. She could even resume bombarding the planet below."

"The Aurora's main reactors are offline for repairs. She's not going anywhere right now."

* * *

The medevac shuttle slowly rolled into the Yamaro's brightly lit port side hangar bay, coming to a stop just before it reached the mining shuttle the Aurora had been using since they escaped the Haven system a few days ago. Its clam-shell rear doors already opened, the cargo ramp came down as the shuttle rolled to a stop, the ramp touching the deck a split second after the shuttle had stopped rolling.

The sound of the metal ramp striking the deck reverberated throughout the empty hangar bay as six heavily armed men came charging out, down the ramp, and into the hangar bay. Just as soon as the last man's foot came off the ramp, it began to retract back up into the medevac shuttle.

The two groups of intruders split out in opposite directions as they left the ramp, three to each side. The group on the right immediately took up fire support positions to cover the team on the left as they made their way to the ragged-looking mining shuttle. One man positioned himself on one knee and stood guard at the bottom of the mining shuttle's ramp as the other two charged up the ramp and inside the shuttle.

Less than a minute later, the two men came running back down the ramp, moving quickly away from the mining shuttle with the last man rising from his kneeling position beside the ramp to follow. A moment later, there was a loud *bang* accompanied by a flash of red-orange light from inside the mining shuttle and black smoke started pouring out the back of the shuttle, wafting its way out into the massive hangar bay.

The first team made its way across the bay and joined up with the second team, after which they continued across the hangar bay, disappearing through one of the many exits that led deeper into the Yamaro.

CHAPTER SIX

Bright flood lights illuminated the tall grass that surrounded the compound as it swayed in the late night breeze. For at least thirty meters in all directions, the night appeared as day. Normally, the perimeter would not be so brightly lit, as doing so always drew complaints from the surrounding towns. However, roving spotlights were insufficient when the missile base was in a high state of alert, and on this night, *all* Corinairan military installations were in such a state.

The guards monitoring the perimeter detection systems behaved no differently tonight than from any other night. Their eyes jumped from one display to another, keeping an eye on the various video feeds, motion detection systems, and automated gun turrets located strategically around the base. Everything appeared as it usually did, just more brightly lit.

In the tree line just beyond the grassy perimeter, four teams of men, all dressed in predominantly dark-colored civilian clothing, hid amongst the rocks, fallen trees, and heavy brush. The missile base had been built in the middle of a dense forest full of extremely old Jespin trees. Most of them never lived beyond a century, toppling when their bases weakened due to various molds found on the forest floor. Once fallen, their dead trunks remained for decades before significantly decaying. This collection of fallen timber made the approach through the forest an arduous task at the least. Trying to make the passage through the thick forest bed at night was nearly impossible, unless you were properly equipped.

Each three-man team had made their way through the thick forest in relatively short order using standard issue visual-enhancement systems. The maneuver had been well rehearsed over the years in similarly wooded areas. In fact, some of the areas they had chosen to train in had been more densely packed, making tonight's passage seem easy by comparison.

The teams had all taken up well hidden positions along the edge of the tree line, one team on each of the four sides of the small base. Each team had a sniper, a tech operator, and a leader who also acted as the spotter.

"All teams are in position around the Aitkenna missile base, sir."

Commander Dumar showed no emotional reaction, as usual. "Start your hack, Lieutenant."

"Yes, sir." The lieutenant signaled the technician sitting at a terminal nearby with a simple nod. The technician immediately started typing furiously at his keyboard as streams of computer code flowed across his screen. The little green status light on the implant at the base of his neck flickered madly as streams of data moved back and forth between the computer system and the operator's implant. His eyes didn't seem to move, only stared straight ahead at the screen full of scrolling code, as if in a transcendent state.

Back in the security station at the Aitkenna missile base, one by one each of the video displays on the wall before them went dark. No sounds, no warnings. They just shut off.

"What the..."

Technicians began to scramble to determine the cause of the problem as their controls also began to rapidly shut down. The shift commander immediately picked up the comm-set to report an emergency when all the lights went out, leaving them in total darkness.

"Hello? Hello?" the shift commander called through the dead comm-set as the emergency battery-powered lighting flickered to life, bathing the room in a dull, red glow.

Outside the base, the bright flood lights suddenly shut down, allowing the darkness of the night to return. There were no sirens, no alarms, only the distant shouts of guards calling out to each other over dead comm-systems. No one knew what was happening, but they all knew what to do; they each stood their ground and prepared for attack.

One by one, each of the guards that had been walking the perimeter began to fall to enemy sniper fire. Invisible pinpoint beams of focused energy bored instant holes through their foreheads, dropping them into the tall grass. There were no cries of pain, no shouts for help, only instant death.

The automated turrets, however, each had their own internal power sources. Independently controlled by artificial intelligence algorithms, they frantically tracked back and forth along their designated fire zones, searching for targets of opportunity.

The tech operators in each team tossed small devices up into the air. The devices, each similar in proportion to a human finger, flew up and made their way in high arcs to the automated defense turrets. Each one attached itself to a turret's control boxes. Seconds later, the operators activated the small devices. A flash of bluish-white light came from each device as it released its destructive energy into the turret's control boxes, rendering them useless. The turrets stopped their frantic search for targets, no longer having any algorithms to follow. They would still be able to fire, but unless a target just happened to wander across their targeting point, they would be ineffective.

The teams all exited the tree line and dashed across the grassy perimeter, dropping at the edge of the outer fence. The first team's tech operator pulled out a small canister with a twin nozzle applicator. He quickly sprayed a circle on the fence about a meter in diameter. The two chemical agents mixed and immediately dissolved the metal fencing, creating a neat series of cuts. The other team member pulled the loose piece of fencing back and laid it aside, creating an opening through which the tech operator passed, after which each of them followed. The process was repeated two more times in order to quickly pass through all three layers of the perimeter fence that was supposed to keep the missile base secure from intruders.

Within minutes, the intruders had swept through the small missile base and had executed the three dozen men inside. The entire operation had taken less than five minutes and had been virtually silent.

"Strike teams report Aitkenna missile base is secured, sir," the lieutenant reported.

"Excellent," Commander Dumar said. "Restore their operational controls and tell them to begin preparing their strike packages."

"Yes, sir." Again the lieutenant signaled the operator whose implant light began to flash as he started restoring functionality to the Aitkenna missile base that was now under the control of the Takaran Anti-Insurgency Command.

* * *

Another aide burst into the room, announcing his urgent news in Corinairan as he entered. Before he could finish passing his message to the Prime Minister, the elder leader turned and exited the room, also in a hurry.

"Gentlemen, ladies," the aide who had been acting as translator said in brisk fashion, "forgive us, but a matter of some urgency requires our attention." He signaled the guards to withdraw before continuing. "We will return as soon as the situation allows." With that, the aide also left the room, followed by the last two guards who closed the door behind them.

"Anybody feel the need to check the lock?" Jessica asked sarcastically.

"What the hell was that all about?" Nathan asked Tug.

"I did not hear everything," Tug told him, "only the first few words before his superiors chastised the carrier of the message for speaking too openly."

"They said something about the Aitkenna missile site," Jalea added. "I believe it is under siege."

"Yes, that's what I heard as well," Tug agreed.

Nathan could see the deep concern on both their faces. "What missiles?"

"The nuclear ones?" Jessica surmised, hoping she was incorrect.

"The ones they shot at the Yamaro?" Nathan said as he made the connection.

"Yes. If the Corinari have lost control of those missiles..." Tug began.

"I'm not liking the sound of this," Jessica interrupted.

"Who has got control of them then?" Nathan asked.

"I did not hear them say," Tug admitted. "Perhaps because they did not know themselves."

"Any guesses?" Jessica asked.

"If the Followers of the Order have taken control, they could use them to destroy the Yamaro in an act of vengeance," Jalea said.

"Possibly," Tug said, although it was obvious by his tone that he did not feel that was the case.

"But that doesn't make any sense," Jessica argued.

"Vengeance seldom does," Tug told her.

"But that ship is an asset," she added. "Even without propulsion, it's still an effective orbital weapons platform."

"To you and I, yes. But to a group of angry Followers who just had their friends, family, homes... their very lives destroyed, that ship is a symbol of oppression. Destroying it would serve as a symbol of rebellion, a rallying cry if you will."

"That doesn't make it any less stupid," Jessica

said.

"But would the nukes even do the job?" Nathan asked.

"In its current state, without any shields to protect it, yes," Tug assured him.

"We could call up to the ship, tell them to power up their shields," Jessica suggested.

"That might be interpreted in an unfavorable light," Jalea warned.

"Quite possibly," Tug agreed.

"You said *if* it's the Followers..." Nathan said.

"Yes. I do not believe the Followers of the Order are so militant in their nature. It's more likely the Loyalists," Tug said. "Which would mean their goal might be to destroy the Aurora."

"After we saved their asses?" Nathan found the idea to be preposterous.

"They see you as the enemy of the Ta'Akar. Destroying you after a Ta'Akar ship failed to do so would be looked upon as an extreme demonstration of loyalty on the part of the Corinairans."

"So the Ta'Akar wouldn't come and finish the job the Yamaro started."

"Yes."

"There's one other possibility," Jalea offered with some hesitation.

Everyone looked at her, waiting for her to explain.

"The Loyalists could also use the missiles to strike other nations on Corinair."

"What?" Nathan looked confused.

"She's right," Tug said, realizing the implications. "Captain, you have to understand the complexity of the Corinairan politics."

"Give us the short version," Nathan insisted. "I don't think we have time for the long one."

"There are five nation-states on Corinair," Tug began. "Some are fiercely loyal to the Empire; others only pretend to be so. The division is roughly equal."

"I thought this guy was the Prime Minister of the entire planet," Jessica said.

"He is. Again, the politics are complex. There exists a structure of unity and cooperation between the nations, but it is somewhat delicate."

"Sound familiar?" Jessica commented to Nathan.

"Unfortunately, each nation has its own missile bases. They are supposed to be for defense of each nation against aggression from space."

"Aren't the Ta'Akar supposed to do that?"

"Yes, but the Ta'Akar are not always close at hand, and interstellar communication, even within the cluster, takes weeks. And since the Karuzari have weakened the Ta'Akar over time, they were forced to provide the missile systems in order to appease the Corinairans as well as to live up to the terms of their original surrender."

"The empire has to protect them," Nathan surmised.

"Correct."

"But why nuke themselves?" Nathan asked.

"I agree; it does not make sense," Tug said, "unless the people that have taken control of the missile site are only pretending to be Loyalists."

"The Ta'Akar?" Jessica wondered aloud.

"More specifically, their anti-insurgency teams. This nation, Hakai, is generally perceived as loyal to the empire."

"You could've fooled me," Jessica commented.

"As I said, no one is openly disloyal to the empire. If the Ta'Akar agents use the missiles of Hakai to strike a nation perceived as disloyal, say,

Melentor…"

"You're talking about a nuclear war," Nathan said ominously.

"There is no planetary government more unstable than one that is engaged in a nuclear war amongst its own nations," Tug explained.

"The Ta'Akar agents would seize control after the last missiles had struck and take direct control of the planet," Jalea concluded.

Tug looked at Nathan. "Captain, I believe that is the most likely scenario."

"But you really don't know for sure, do you?" Nathan said.

"No, I do not."

Nathan sighed. "So, we've got three possible scenarios then. Loyalists looking to shoot us down, followers looking to shoot the Yamaro down, or Takaran agents looking to start a nuclear war in order to seize control of the planet. This story just keeps getting better and better, doesn't it?"

"Captain, we need to contact the ship again, and pronto," Jessica warned him.

"Yes, we should have them move the prisoners off the Yamaro and onto the Aurora, just in case."

"No, you don't understand. When I spoke with Vlad, he was complaining about how many systems were damaged."

"Like what?" Nathan asked, his concern showing.

"He didn't say, but he sounded really stressed. I know that we were only running on one reactor when we left. If they're still running on only one reactor…"

"They couldn't jump if they wanted to," Nathan added.

"They'd be a sitting duck for those missiles,"

Jessica said.

Nathan immediately went to the windows and started banging on them to get the attention of the guards. Within moments, the door opened.

"We need to speak with the Prime Minister right now," he demanded. The guard looked at him with a puzzled expression until Jalea translated. The guard seemed reluctant to deliver the message, but Jalea argued the point until he finally gave in, closing the door again.

"He has agreed to deliver your request," Jalea said, "but he cannot guarantee that the Prime Minister will come."

Nathan watched through the windows as the guard went down the hallway, supposedly to deliver the message to the Prime Minister. "We need a plan," he said as he watched the guard walk away, "a way to deal with the threat, in case the Corinairans can't."

"Or won't," Jessica added, drawing a look of concern from Nathan.

* * *

Five hundred kilometers west of Aitkenna at the Wellerton missile complex, the floodlights began to switch off one by one. This was followed by small flashes of blue-white light from the backs of each of the automated turrets that normally protected the base from intruders.

This particular base was located at the top of a rocky hill whose steep terrain made it impossible to take by ground. Instead, strike teams used a frontal assault on the main gate, bursting through it with a remotely controlled vehicle full of explosives. It was a trick that had been made infamous by the

Karuzari and to this day remained an effective one.

The remote missile complex, being guarded primarily by automated systems, was not heavily manned. The base commander had recalled all off-duty personnel to return to the post during the crisis, but many had been unable to find a way to report. Most of the main roads were ruined, and much of the public transit system was either damaged or otherwise overloaded. Most of the men had simply reported to the nearest military post they could reach, awaiting transportation to their normal duty stations.

The remote vehicle burst through the front gates, exploding a few meters past the fence line. The explosion collapsed the guard post and decimated all three layers of security fence for fifty meters in either direction. The heat from the blast had been so intense that most of the fencing, as well as the fence posts, had melted into heaps of red-hot metal that lay on the ground, still bubbling after the initial blast cleared.

Moments after the blast, at least thirty armed men dressed in civilian attire came charging in, weapons firing indiscriminately in all directions. Chaos ensued as the dozen guards that had come rushing out of the main building to reinforce the missing gate guards were mowed down by enemy fire before they had a chance to defend themselves. Oddly enough, the incoming fire from the civilians had been so poorly aimed that it had not been anywhere near the scrambling guards. The shots that had killed them had been precise, from a different angle and from some distance away.

The eyes of the base commander and his subordinates behind their consoles widened as the angry hoard rushed into the command center. They pulled their side arms to return fire, ducking behind consoles, chairs, and any other cover they could find. While they did manage to kill at least a half dozen of their attackers, they were quickly overwhelmed and eventually cut down in a stream of red and green energy bolts.

The squad leader of the attacking forces made his way through the cheering men to the main console, checking that everything was still intact. Their siege had depended on the reflective nature of the Corinairan console designs, and by using lower energy settings on their weapons, they had managed to kill the defenders without damaging the delicate equipment. By using the built-in override functions required by the Ta'Akar in all Corinari military assets, he now had full control of all the missiles left in the launchers.

The squad leader picked up his comm-unit and keyed it to transmit. "Command, Four. Objective achieved. This position is go." He turned to the cheering men. "Tobias!" he called out. "Get over here!"

Tobias made his way through the cheering men to join his squad leader, sitting down at the console beside him.

"Re-target these birds," he ordered. "I want them ready to launch in twenty minutes."

"No problem, sir."

The squad leader turned back to the cheering men. "All right! Everyone outside! I need perimeter guards until we get the turrets back online. Move it!"

* * *

Vladimir had never spent much time this deep inside the service tunnels of the Aurora. Now that the invaders had sealed the entrance shut, there was absolutely no illumination to be found. The inky blackness was all consuming to the point that he could no longer see his own hands.

Despite the fact that the tunnels had their own air circulation systems, it felt stuffy to him. He wasn't sure if it was warmer in this part of the tunnels or if he was just hot from all the excitement. It also smelled of hydraulics, rubber, silicone, and of course, of the black soot that was to be found everywhere inside these tunnels as a result of the shipboard fire that had occurred during one of several battles they had been in over the last week. Vladimir was no longer sure which battle it had been. In fact, it seemed as if they had all run together in his mind, like they were all one long battle. All the fighting, the killing, the struggling to keep the ship together—just trying to stay alive—was really starting to get to him. All he really wanted to do right now was lay quietly in the darkness and wait for it all to pass. Unfortunately, he knew he didn't have that luxury. Even if he did, it simply wasn't in his nature. Deliza's sobs served to remind him of that fact.

"Try not to cry," he said as sympathetically as he could. "We will be safe here."

"I know," Deliza sobbed.

"Then why are you crying?"

"I don't think I'm cut out for all of this," she admitted between sobs.

"For what? Being trapped in a dark, dirty, smelly, service tunnel? Who is?"

"No, not that. All of this." She continued to sob.

"It is not so bad," he tried to joke.

"I just killed a man," she half whispered, not wanting to admit it to herself.

"Nyet, nyet, nyet," he insisted. "It was in self-defense."

"He wasn't trying to kill me."

"But he was trying to kill your friends and take your ship..."

"Oh God," she exclaimed, as she suddenly remembered. "My little sister."

Even in the total darkness, Vladimir could tell that she was quickly becoming more distraught. "She was helping in the kitchen, yes? She will be fine. Why would they hurt her?"

"Who were they?" Deliza asked as she tried to calm herself down.

"I do not know," Vladimir admitted. "I have never seen those uniforms before."

"They said the other team had taken the bridge," she told Vladimir as she realized that although he would have heard them speaking, he would not have understood their words.

"You understood them?" Vladimir asked.

"Yes, they were speaking Takaran," she told him. "We had to learn it in school. Everyone does." Deliza then realized what was going on. "If they have taken the bridge and engineering, then..."

"They have taken control of the ship," Vladimir finished for her.

"Then we are going to die in here?"

"No," he said resolutely.

"How can you be so sure?"

"Because I am too good looking to die in this grimy tunnel," he joked, "as are you." He could tell his joke had not helped. "And because I am a very lucky man. I always have been."

"That's it? Because you're cute and lucky?"

"You do not think I am cute?" he asked, trying to distract her from the apparent hopelessness of their situation.

"I don't know. I can't see you," she responded, a bit of her usual sarcasm sneaking back into her voice.

"Wait, I have an idea," Vladimir said. He struggled for a moment to reposition himself in the dark, cramped tunnel. He reached into the utility pocket on his thigh and pulled out his trusty little data pad. The engineering version was designed to be more rugged than those carried by the command and medical staff. If it hadn't, his would've surely been damaged beyond use by now. He felt his hands along the side of the unit until he found the small slider switch and turned the unit on. The little screen was only about ten centimeters wide and twenty high, but the light from the display was enough to provide illumination out for nearly a meter. It was faint, but it was enough for them to see their surroundings as well as one another. "There, that's better," he said as he held it up like a flashlight. He pointed the screen toward Deliza to see her face. What he saw made him chuckle. Her face was covered with black soot. Her tears had run down her face and created lines that she had then wiped away, causing big smudges across her cheeks. It reminded him of the way they used to paint their faces when he was in the European Infantry to blend in with their surroundings.

"What?" she asked.

"I'm sorry, but your face is very dirty."

She instinctively put her hands to her cheeks,

not realizing that they were even dirtier and only compounding the problem, causing him to giggle even more. She reached out and grabbed the data pad, turning it toward him to light his face. Now it was her turn to laugh. His face was nearly all black. Only his eyes and his neck were still relatively clean. "You should see your face," she giggled.

Vladimir stopped laughing, noticing something on the data pad's display screen. He hadn't cleared the view from his last use. The screen displayed the schematic showing the rerouting patterns that he had given to Deliza and Allet to perform. "Deliza, did you finish rerouting the command and control signals like I asked?"

"Yes," she told him, recognizing the change in his tone. "It was easy. Why do you ask?"

"Because I think I know way we can stop them," he told her as he scrambled to turn around and head back out the way they had come. "But we have to hurry, as we have a long way yet to travel."

"But we can't see, at least not with that thing."

"There are emergency chemical flashlights in the main tunnel," he told her as he repositioned himself flat against one wall. "Now squeeze past me and I will boost you back up to the main tunnel."

* * *

"*We have secured engineering,*" the leader of the second team reported over the hardwired comm-system. "*But we lost three men in the attack.*"

"How many of them were there?"

"*Two that we saw, and a young girl.*"

"Two engineers and a young girl managed to kill three heavily armed Takaran soldiers?" Captain de

210

Winter said, anger in his voice.

"More like three nobles playing soldier," Andre mumbled, just barely loud enough for the captain to overhear. He recognized the voice of the man reporting as one of his own and was quite confident that the other agent had survived as well.

Captain de Winter did not respond to the sergeant's remark, choosing only to cast a sidelong glare in his direction as he continued his conversation over the comms. "I trust you eliminated the offending combatants?"

"One of them, yes. The other one and the girl escaped into a service tunnel, which we secured. There are no other exits from that tunnel in this area, so as far as we can tell, they are trapped in there for now."

Captain de Winter rolled his eyes and turned toward Andre. "Any suggestions?"

Andre stepped up to the comm station to speak. "I will send someone to you. Two of you will sweep forward while the third one stays behind to hold engineering."

"Understood."

Andre switched off the comm and turned to Bobby, who was standing near the exit keeping an eye on the corridor outside. "Go to the hangar bay and deactivate the jamming pod, then meet up with them in engineering and conduct the sweep yourself."

"And if we encounter anyone?" Bobby asked, already knowing the answer but needing to hear it from his sergeant first.

"Kill them," Andre ordered without hesitation. "We don't have the manpower to deal with prisoners."

"Understood."

Andre grabbed Bobby's arm as he turned to leave, adding, "I don't care who they are: man, woman, or child. Kill them where they stand."

"No problem," Bobby answered, seeing the serious look in the eyes of his friend.

Andre turned back to de Winter. "Any objections?" he asked, more as an offer of cooperation than an actual concern.

The captain smiled. "You're beginning to grow on me, Sergeant."

Next, de Winter turned back toward the center of the bridge. "Now, which one of you was the pilot again?" He looked at Josh. "Ah, yes, the young lad with the quick tongue. You might want to take your station and prepare to get underway."

Josh didn't move, instead crossing his arms in defiance. Captain de Winter could see the hesitation in his eyes. "Are you sure you want to do this, young man?"

"I'm not flying you anywhere," Josh said, his voice slightly cracking.

De Winter thumbed the safety on his small handgun into the off position as he began to raise it toward Josh.

Josh's eyes grew wide, his voice trembling as he spoke. "I'm the only pilot left on board this ship," he said, swallowing hard. "If you kill me, who's going to fly it?"

"You might be surprised to know," the captain began as he moved closer to Josh, "that I'm a pretty fair pilot myself. I'm sure I can figure it all out, given time." The captain stopped his advance, his gun now pointed directly at Josh's trembling face. "Fortunately for you, I don't have that kind of time."

De Winter spun around and fired his weapon at

the wounded comm-officer sitting to his left, next to Kaylah. The tight beam struck him in the chest, burning a thumb-sized hole in the front and out the back, spraying blood and tissue from the exit wound and striking the comm station behind him. Sparks flew from the damaged displays as the comm officer fell to the floor in a heap. Kaylah screamed and jumped but froze instantly when the captain's gun moved to point toward her next.

"Will you perform your duties as pilot, or do I have to execute her as well?" de Winter asked Josh coldly.

Josh said nothing, looking at Kaylah's terrified expression. He dropped his hands, turned, and took his seat at the helm, ready to pilot the ship.

De Winter turned back toward Andre. "You know, I'm starting to like this little gun after all. It's really quite effective."

"Maybe you could dial it down a little, Captain," Andre advised, trying to control his anger. "I believe you also killed the communications console."

"Sorry," the captain said. "I guess I got carried away."

* * *

Marcus looked at Loki as they followed Crewman Rival down the wide, angular corridors of the Yamaro on their way back to the midsection of the ship where the port and starboard hangar bays were located. "You do know how to use that thing, right?"

"Works the same as ours, doesn't it?" Loki said.

"Sort of. It's just got a bit more of a kick," Marcus told him. "And it's louder."

"Just squeeze this, right?" Loki asked, pointing

the weapon upward.

"Just keep the damn thing pointed away from me," Marcus insisted.

"If this is the safety, then what's this other one for?"

"It ejects the thing in the handle. I think they called it a 'magazine.'"

"What's a magazine?"

"It's the thing that holds the bullets."

"What are bullets?"

"The little pieces of metal that shoot outta the end of your gun, dumbass."

"Really?" Loki looked at his gun. "I've never heard of such a thing. It doesn't seem like it would be anywhere near as effective. How many bullets does it hold?"

Marcus looked at him. "You know, I never thought to ask."

"Seems like it would be a good thing to know." He looked at his gun again. "What do you think? Fifty? A hundred?"

"Probably more like two hundred," Marcus guessed. "What good would it be with only a hundred bullets?"

"Yeah, you're probably right." Loki flipped off the safety. Marcus immediately became nervous.

"You might want to leave the safety on, kiddo."

Loki held the gun out in front of him, sighting down the barrel. "Relax. I'm just getting a feel for it," he said as the came around the corner.

"You're both wrong," Crewman Rival said, "each magazine only holds..." Crewman Rival stopped dead in his tracks.

Loki found himself looking down his barrel at six heavily armed men in flat black assault gear, all crouched down as they walked forward briskly, their weapons up and ready.

"Oh shit," Loki exclaimed. He instinctively pulled the trigger on his gun. It fired, flame spitting out the end of the barrel as the gun kicked up and back. The bullet landed squarely in the neck of one of the nobles, sending a large chunk of flesh and blood flying. The wounded man's first reflex was to reach for the searing pain in his neck as his body spun around from the force of the bullet's impact, causing him to lose his balance and fall against the men behind him.

"RUN!" Crewman Rival ordered as he raised his weapon and opened fire. Before he got more than a few poorly aimed shots off, he was cut down by energy weapons fire from the intruders. He fell over backwards, bullets from his still firing weapon spraying the bulkhead as he twisted and went down.

Marcus raised his own weapon, a close-quarters automatic weapon given to him by Enrique. He pulled the trigger and held it for a moment, sending at least a dozen rounds toward the enemy. Another noble was hit in the leg, also sending him down but not killing him. "Take cover, kid!" he yelled as he fired again.

Loki quickly fell to his left, tucking in behind an upright support against the wall. It wasn't much cover, but it was all that was available. He stared at Crewman Rival's smoldering body in the corridor, a look of terror and pain frozen on the dead man's face.

Marcus, on the other hand, was safely tucked behind the corner of the corridor on the opposite side from Loki. "Stop staring and shoot some more, kid!" Marcus yelled.

Loki held his gun out without looking and repeatedly pulled the trigger. Another twenty rounds flew down the hallway, ricocheting off the bulkheads and not striking any of the intended targets. Once Loki's magazine was empty, the slide on the gun locked open. "What the hell?!" he cried out as energy blasts struck the upright support he was hiding behind. "It's broken!"

"It ain't broke, you idiot! It's outta bullets!"

"That wasn't two hundred bullets! Hell, that wasn't even a hundred!"

"Yeah, your gun sucks!" Marcus bellowed as he brought his gun around the corner and opened up. "Run for it, kid!"

As Marcus sprayed bullets down the corridor from side to side, Loki ran from behind his cover and headed back the way they had come as fast as his feet would carry him.

"DIE, YOU FUCKERS!" Marcus yelled as he gleefully continued firing. Then his gun stopped firing. He looked down at his weapon and saw that the breach was locked in the open position, and nothing happened when he pressed his trigger. "Uh oh."

Loki continued running around the next corner. As he rounded the corner, he looked back over his shoulder. The sound of Marcus's gun had stopped. It was quickly replaced by the sound of energy weapons fire and Marcus screaming at the top of his lungs as he came running around the corner behind him.

"THESE GUNS SUCK!" Marcus yelled as he came around the corner, energy blasts slamming the bulkheads behind him.

They continued to run as fast as they could,

rounding the next corner into an even longer corridor. As they continued to run, Marcus realized that they would never make it to the end of the corridor. The enemy troops chasing them were about to come around the corner behind them and would have a clear shot. "Wait!" he called out to Loki as he stopped running. "Down the ladder!"

"What?" Loki asked in confusion as he too came to a sudden stop.

"We'll never make it down this corridor! Just do it, kid!" he ordered as he grabbed him by the shirt and yanked him toward the ladder. "GO!"

Loki quickly climbed down the ladder. Marcus followed, but before his body had passed the floor level, the enemy troops came running around the corner and saw him, opening fire. Marcus fell the rest of the way down, landing unceremoniously on the deck below. "Keep going!" he yelled as he got back to his feet. "They're right on our ass!"

They continued running for a full minute before Marcus realized something was wrong. He slowed down, eventually coming to a stop. He turned around and looked behind him, intently staring down the corridor and listening.

Loki noticed that Marcus had stopped and ceased running himself. "What are you doing?"

Marcus waved his hand at Loki, motioning for him to keep his voice down. After a few moments, he turned back to Loki, a surprised look on his face. "They're not behind us anymore."

"Are you sure?" Loki was equally surprised.

Marcus shrugged. "Maybe they ain't after us."

"Where do you think they're headed?" Loki wondered.

"If they're after the ship, they'll head for the

bridge for sure. If they're after the crew, they'll be going to the cargo bays and the brig. But if they head for engineering…" Marcus paused in mid-sentence.

"What?" Loki asked. "What does it mean if they head for engineering?"

"My guess would be that they'll overload the reactors and blow up the ship."

"But they were headed forward, toward the bridge, right?"

"The ones we met, sure." Marcus took in a deep breath. "Either way, we need to get back to the brig and warn the others." He took off on a jog again. "Come on."

* * *

Ensign Mendez and Sergeant Weatherly quickly turned toward the hatch as they heard someone approaching at a dead run. If it was an enemy, they weren't trying to be stealthy. A moment later, Marcus and Loki stumbled through the hatchway into the brig's main foyer where Mendez and Weatherly were waiting with Ensign Willard from the Yamaro's crew. Enrique stared at them, expecting an answer as to why they had returned so quickly.

Marcus looked up at him, trying to catch his breath. "Problem," was all he could get out.

"They're here," Loki announced, not being as winded as the older and heavier Marcus.

"Who's here? Where's Rival?" Enrique asked.

"He's dead," Loki answered.

"Who were they? Takarans?" Enrique inquired.

"I don't know," Loki said. "I didn't ask."

"They weren't…dressed like…Takarans," Marcus added. "Dressed in black…from head to toe…wearing soft armor...no markings."

"That sounds like the Corinari," Ensign Willard told Enrique.

"Who the hell are the Corinari?" Enrique asked.

"Specially trained divisions, highly skilled combatants. When Corinair surrendered to the Ta'Akar decades ago, they had to give up most of their advanced weaponry. To make up for this, they created a special branch of the military called the Corinari. They are highly trained and very dedicated. The skills make them more effective while having to use less advanced weapons and technology."

"Why would the Corinari attack us?" Enrique wondered. "We just saved their butts, didn't we?"

"Maybe they, too, have lost contact with us. If they believed this ship had somehow fallen into the wrong hands, they might try to retake it."

"So we might be exchanging fire with friendlies?"

"It is possible," Ensign Willard admitted, "but I do not believe it is the case. The Corinari would've identified themselves when they saw two civilians. They would not have fired indiscriminately either. They shoot with pinpoint accuracy. If these two had indeed exchanged gunfire with the Corinari, they would not be alive to speak of it." Willard turned to Marcus and Loki. "No offense intended."

"Okay, so we're back to Takarans." Enrique turned to Marcus and Loki. "How many of them were there, and which way were they headed?"

"At least a dozen," Loki exclaimed.

Marcus turned and looked at Loki funny. "There were six," he corrected. "And we killed two of them."

"Oh God, I'm pretty sure I killed one," Loki admitted.

"Don't brag, kid," Marcus interrupted. "You fired

at least twenty times and only hit one of them."

"Yeah, well..." Loki turned to Enrique, his expression turning sour. "Hey, what's up with these guns having so few bullets?"

"Sorry about that," Enrique apologized, "I guess I should've warned you about that." He looked at Marcus, noticing that he was unarmed. "Where's the gun I gave you? It had a lot more than twenty rounds in it."

"Uh, I must've dropped it," Marcus admitted sheepishly. "It was outta bullets anyway."

Enrique pulled a pair of full magazines out of his combat vest pocket and held them up for Marcus to see, a sneer on his face.

"Oh, sorry," Marcus apologized.

"My fault," Enrique admitted. "I should have given you the extra magazines." He turned to Sergeant Weatherly, handing the magazines over for the sergeant to use in his own weapon. "Any idea where they were heading?"

"Forward, for sure," Marcus told him. "I figure they're headed for the bridge, seeing as how they didn't follow us when we went down a level."

"Are you sure they just didn't see you go down a level?" Enrique challenged.

"I'm sure. One of them looked right at me when I was about halfway down the ladder. Made eye contact with him I did, right before he opened up on me."

"Is that where you got this?" Enrique asked, reaching out and sticking his finger in a hole burnt through the shoulder of Marcus's jacket.

Marcus looked at the hole. "Damn, this is my favorite coat, too."

"We should assume there are two teams," Enrique

began theorizing aloud. "One headed to the bridge, the other to engineering. Those are the two spots you need to capture if you want to seize control of a ship."

"Not necessarily," Willard disagreed, "at least not in the case of the Yamaro. She is of a newer design—extremely automated. She can be easily controlled from the bridge with only a few men."

"But what about life support, power generation, propulsion..."

"There are no dedicated interfaces for any of those systems anywhere other than on the bridge. The only time anyone goes to engineering is to make repairs or perform routine maintenance. And then they use portable consoles that they simply plug into any number of interface ports."

"If we had one of those portable consoles, could we take control from another location?" Enrique asked.

"No, you could not. Bridge consoles always take priority over portables."

Enrique thought for a moment. "Okay, so there are at least four of them headed for the bridge. We have to assume that there is more than one team, maybe even several. And there's gotta be at least a few guys guarding whatever ship they used to come on board. So they're probably down in the hangar bay right now as well. If we got a look at the size of their transport ship, that might give us an indication of how many combatants we're dealing with."

"There isn't time for all that," Willard insisted. "They will reach the bridge in minutes. They may be there already."

"We locked up the bridge once we powered everything down," Sergeant Weatherly reminded

Enrique.

"That will only slow them down five or ten minutes at best," Ensign Willard insisted. "Given time, they will gain entry. And once they do, there will be no stopping them. They can simply vent the rest of the ship into space and be done with us."

"Jeez, this is not good," Enrique said. "There are only the two of us, and all we've got is a few hundred rounds between your weapon and my handgun."

"We've still got two more guys down guarding the prisoners in the cargo bay," Weatherly pointed out.

"It'll take too long to retrieve them. I'm afraid it's just the two of us, Sarge."

"Make that the three of us," Ensign Willard interjected.

Enrique looked at him for a moment. "You sure?"

"You will need my expertise with the systems on this ship," Willard told him.

"Add us and that makes five," Loki added.

"No. I need you two to go meet up with the two guards, then go and secure our shuttle. If we fail to stop them, we're going to need a way off this bucket and fast," Enrique explained. "Besides, three on four isn't too bad."

"How about four?" a voice came from one of the cells.

They all turned and looked in the direction of the cells.

"Five," another voice sounded. Then another called out, "Six." Then, "Seven." Then, "Eight."

Enrique walked over to the row of cells looking at the five men that had stepped forward. As he moved closer all the men in the cells stood and came forward, as if indicating that they too would volunteer to fight. "Why would you guys want to fight?"

"None of us are Takaran," Number Five stated, "and none of us wish to suffocate in here when the Takarans take the bridge and rob us of air."

Enrique looked long and hard at the men. They were all young and strong, and he had no doubt that at some point the Takarans would have given them at least some basic combat training. Still, Enrique was unsure. He turned and looked at Ensign Willard, who he had grown to trust over the last hour.

"They were all forced to serve, just as I was," Willard stated. "A few of them are of Corinair as well, just like I am."

"We're still gonna need guns," Weatherly pointed out.

"I am an armory technician," Number Six offered. "I can get us into the armory down the corridor. We will have all the weapons we need."

Enrique looked back at Willard, the doubt on his face subsiding. "Looks like we've got ourselves a few fire teams, Sergeant." Enrique smiled at Ensign Willard. "Let 'em out."

CHAPTER SEVEN

The main operations room at the Aitkenna Disaster Management Command Center was buzzing with activity as various technicians, specialists, and command personnel dealt with a myriad of problems afflicting the capital city that night, as well as the entire nation of Hakai.

Nathan and the others had been retrieved from the conference room where they had been waiting for what had seemed like an eternity after the Prime Minister had been suddenly whisked away by his aides. In order to reach this room, they had traveled through a maze of corridors as well as descended several levels. As best they could tell, by now they had to be several levels below the surface at the least.

They were led through a doorway that opened onto the mezzanine level overlooking the main operations center. Below, there were three large display screens, each reaching from waist high to the ceiling, more than two floors, and were at least twice as wide as they were high. While the center display showed whatever video feed was the most critical at the moment, the massive displays on either side showed maps: one of the nation of Hakai, the other of its capital, the city of Aitkenna. Each map was littered with color coded dots. Most of them were a combination of dots: brown, orange, and red. The red dots sat mostly at the center of the larger orange ones, which in turn sat somewhat near the center of the still larger brown ones. The dots overlaid on the map of Aitkenna were much larger than the ones overlaid on the map of Hakai.

As they walked over to one side of the mezzanine, Nathan could see the rows of consoles and the workers manning them on the ground level below. In addition, there were numerous additional workers, possibly higher ranking personnel than the operators, moving furiously back and forth as they checked on the subordinates they were responsible for overseeing.

The mezzanine level was similar in layout but with only a single row of four consoles and their operators, along with one control officer. The Prime Minister stood behind the technicians at their consoles instead of being seated in the row of overstuffed chairs arranged on a small raised platform behind them. The platform reminded Nathan of the command platform back on the bridge of the Aurora, where both his command chair and the tactical station were situated.

"Those must be where the bombs hit," Jessica said, nodding toward the map of Aitkenna.

"What, the red dots?" Nathan asked. "What are the orange and brown ones, fallout?"

"My guess, red for impact, orange for blast radius, and brown... fallout maybe? Or shock wave damage?"

The Prime Minister was obviously very upset at something that one of his aides was telling him. There was a lot of shouting going on, and Nathan got the impression that something wasn't going as expected. He noticed that Tug and Jalea were both listening intently to the exchange between the Prime Minister and his aides.

"What's going on?" Nathan asked. "What's he so pissed about?"

"It seems that several of their missile bases are no longer under their control," Tug explained. "The Prime Minister is demanding to know how missile bases could be so easily compromised."

"A good question," Jessica said, a mixture of sarcasm and accusation in her tone.

Another demand from the Prime Minister resulted in video footage being displayed on the main center display screen. The image was the view from a security camera at one of the missile installations.

"What is that?" Nathan asked Tug.

"I believe it is from one of the missile bases."

The image showed the brightly lit main gate of the facility. There was a sudden flash of blue-white light near one of the gun turrets, after which the image went dark. A few moments later the camera view switched to night vision, showing surrealistic green-hued images. A vehicle suddenly burst through the main gate, exploded a few seconds later, and caused the view from the camera to switch off.

"Whoa," Jessica muttered. "Nothing subtle about that."

"Why did everything just turn off?" Nathan asked. "The lights I mean..."

"I do not know," Tug said, contemplating the cause.

The view was replaced by a feed from another camera. The image also showed the main gate, or where the main gate had once been. Now it was only a black shallow crater covered with puddles of melted fencing and debris, much of which was still burning. At least a dozen men came charging into view in a loose unorganized fashion. They were obviously civilians, evidenced by their clothing and mixed assortment of weapons, as well as the chaotic method in which they fought. Their numbers and their fire power, however, were obviously enough to overwhelm the guards who had been depending on the automated turrets to protect them against such an attack. The bolts of energy danced back and forth between the two sides, with the majority of the fire coming from the civilian attackers. The firefight was over in less than a minute, and the civilians disappeared into the buildings of the missile complex.

"I believe this was recorded only minutes ago," Tug theorized.

"It was like someone just turned everything off right before they attacked," Jessica said.

"Captain," Tug began. He was deliberately speaking in hushed tones to avoid being overheard, despite the fact that most of the people around them did not speak Angla. "All of the missile bases were provided by the Ta'Akar as part of the defense structure that they put in place when the original Corinairan military complex was dismantled. As I said earlier, the bases were meant to defend Corinair against unknown aggressors until such time as the Ta'Akar arrived to defend them. If these bases are being taken offline at the moment they are attacked, it is likely being done by Ta'Akar agents operating on the planet."

"You're saying they have back doors built into the Corinairan systems," Jessica said.

"Back doors?"

"A secret way to remotely access and take control

of a system," Nathan explained, "one that is usually unknown to the owners of the system."

"Precisely. All Corinairan military assets are required to have such override capabilities available for use by the Ta'Akar. These are known and tolerated by the Corinairans. But we have always suspected that all Ta'Akar systems have such hidden access channels. This is one of the reasons we always overhauled any systems we liberated from the Ta'Akar," Tug explained, "to remove the 'back doors' as you call them."

"Something else is happening," Jessica said, pointing toward the main display screen once again.

A different video feed was coming in. At first it was from a single source—a shaky, fairly dark image, lit only by the flicker of burning debris and the frequent blasts from energy weapons. The blasts appeared to be coming from men atop armored vehicles. Soon, the single image was joined by three others. They appeared to be coming from handheld cameras carried by either reporters or civilians. The images were being sent live across the planetary network for all to see.

"Is this live?" Nathan asked.

"Yes, I believe so," Tug agreed.

"How can that be?" Jessica asked. "Most of this city is in ruins. How can their network still be functioning?"

"The networks of Corinair," Jalea explained, "just as on most worlds, are quite robust. They are a combination of underground hardlines, ground-based wireless, and satellite-based networks. It is highly unlikely that all three networks would be completely taken down by any attack. At most, there might be additional latencies wherever the hardlines were down and either wireless or satellite based networks had to take over."

"Captain," Jessica wondered, "are those armored personnel carriers?"

"Those are Corinairan troops," Nathan realized. "They're fighting with their own citizens?"

One of the feeds was being provided by a news reporter on the scene, who was narrating over the video footage being transmitted.

"The reporter is saying the crowds are composed of Karuzari." Jalea listened intently before continuing her translation. "They are intent on seizing control of military assets in order to reinvigorate their movement." Jalea turned to look at Nathan. "Captain, Hakai is predominantly composed of Loyalists. Of this I am quite certain. The Karuzari would not be present in this area."

"Yes, they would probably be hiding in Melentor," Tug agreed.

"This doesn't make any sense," Nathan declared.

Nathan watched in horror as the angry mob managed to reach up and grab soldiers, pulling them down off the vehicle into the crowd where they were savagely beaten.

The Prime Minister was furious, barking orders at his aides and the military leaders nearest him.

An image flashed across the screen. A symbol of some kind. It was on a banner being waived by several men.

"What was that?" Nathan asked.

"It is the symbol of the Karuzari," Jalea admitted.

"Captain," Tug began, pulling Nathan back away from the guards in order to hide their conversation, "this is not as it seems. It is a ruse; I am sure of it."

"How can you be sure?" Nathan asked. "I mean,

look at it," he said, pointing toward the screen.

"Captain, too many factors do not add up."

"Such as?"

"First, as Jalea said, the Karuzari would not *hide* amongst Loyalists; it is unsafe. Second, the Corinari are extremely competent warriors. The members of their military serve for life. What they lack in equipment and weapons, they make up for in training and expertise. You saw the way those soldiers in the video were firing—blindly, and mostly over the heads of the crowd. Even local security forces are more effective."

"Maybe they were just trying to scare them?" Nathan surmised.

"The Corinari do not use their weapons to scare, Captain. They use them to kill. They do not pull them unless that is their intent. Those impostors were pulled from their vehicles like frightened school children."

"Yeah, considering how much firepower they had to be carrying, it doesn't seem like it should be that easy, does it?"

"And finally, the strategy does not follow the edicts of the Karuzari. We do not attack missile bases, especially those not operated by the Ta'Akar. And we go to great lengths to avoid civilian casualties. These people are killing indiscriminately. That is not our way; believe me."

A Corinari guard standing just within earshot overheard Tug's comments and quickly drew his weapon and aimed it at Tug. "DO NOT MOVE!" he ordered in perfect Angla.

Jessica was standing a step back from Nathan and somewhat in between Tug and the armed guard. Her left arm instinctively shot out and up, knocking the guard's gun upward. An instant later, her right hand swung across, striking the guard hard in the abdomen and causing him to double over slightly, but not as much as she had hoped. The guard's arms swung upward as a result of Jessica's blow, his left hand coming free from the weapon still held by his right hand. His torso straightened and his head turned to the right just in time to evade Jessica's upward thrust with her right hand. He spun around to his right, pivoting on his right foot as his body coiled down into a crouching position. As he came around, his left foot shot out and swept at Jessica's legs, taking them out from under her.

Jessica landed squarely on her back and found herself looking up into the barrel of the guard's energy weapon as he held it in both hands, his arms extended forward and down at her as he stood in a half squat over her. "Damn," she commented, surprised by the guard's speed and expertise.

At the same time, every other guard in the command center around them also drew their weapons. Several of them moved in front of the Prime Minister in order to shield him from attack. The rest of the guards moved quickly in a highly trained fashion into combat positions.

Nathan's hands immediately went up when he realized every weapon in the room was trained on them. His mouth hung open as well, as he had never seen anyone get the drop on Jessica in such a manner. "Whoa, whoa, whoa!" he cried out. "Don't shoot!"

The senior officer in the room began barking orders in Corinairan. The guard that had first pulled his weapon was being asked his reasons for taking such actions. That much Nathan was sure of even though he couldn't understand what they were saying. However, when the guard's answer included the word *Karuzari*, a sinking feeling hit him in the gut.

"What's going on?" Nathan asked calmly of Tug.

"I'm afraid the guard speaks Angla," Tug admitted. "He is telling his commander that we are members of the Karuzari."

"Great," Nathan muttered. More words were being exchanged between the officer in charge, the Prime Minister, and his aide.

"Is this true, Captain?" the Prime Minister's aide asked. "Are you Karuzari?"

"No, we are not," Nathan answered without hesitation.

The aide looked at Tug and Jalea. "And your *guides*, are *they* Karuzari?"

This time Nathan hesitated, looking to Tug for any indication of how to answer the question.

"Yes, we are," Tug admitted.

With a flick of the wrist from the Corinairan officer in charge, the guards moved in and grabbed Tug, Jalea, and Nathan. Two more moved over and picked Jessica up off the floor.

"This one," said the guard that had taken down Jessica. He moved closer to Tug. "He spoke of the Karuzari as if he were one of them."

"And you were aware of their affiliations, Captain?" the aide questioned.

"Not at first, no," Nathan tried to explain.

"But you knew they were Karuzari when you brought them here, to Corinair, did you not?"

Nathan knew that there would be little use in lying to them at this point. "Yes, I did. But the Karuzari are no threat to you."

The aide translated back to the Prime Minister, whose response was neither a short nor happy one.

"Perhaps you are not the hero of legend the Followers of the Order believe you to be, Captain," the aide translated back for the Prime Minister. "Perhaps you are, instead, the cause of our ultimate demise."

Nathan looked confused. "Excuse me?"

"These people are undoubtedly the reason the Ta'Akar have attacked us," the aide continued. "They mean to punish us for harboring them."

"How would they even know the Karuzari were here?" Nathan asked. "The Ta'Akar came for us. They contacted me and asked us to join forces with them…"

"Captain…" Jessica interrupted from her position on the floor.

"When I refused, they attacked your world," he said, ignoring Jessica's protestations, "hoping that, instead of jumping away, I would stay and defend Corinair."

"It's exactly as the legend says…" Jalea tried to slip in.

"No, it's not," Nathan disagreed. "We're not here because of some legend, and I'm not some kind of hero. Hell, I'm not even supposed to be the captain."

His last statement left the aide somewhat confused, but he continued to translate Nathan's words for his leader. After he finished, there was silence. The Prime Minister simply looked at Nathan as if he expected some type of explanation.

"We're not even supposed to be here," Nathan said, deciding it was time to come clean with the Corinairans. If they were ever going to trust one another enough to go into battle together, they had to know the truth first. "And by here I don't mean here, here. I mean this whole region of space. We were just supposed to perform a test of the new jump drive. A single hop, barely even a light year, to just outside our own system. But we were ambushed, there was an antimatter explosion at the same time we jumped, and we ended up standing toe to toe with a Takaran capital ship. Since then it has been a constant struggle to survive. We're a thousand light years from home, and *our* world, Earth, she needs *our* jump drive in order to defend herself against our own enemies. It's the only one in existence, and if we can get our hands on the Takaran zero-point energy device, we might be able to get back home in time to help defend our world against our own enemies." Nathan lowered his gaze for a moment, breathing a sigh of relief. It felt good to let it all out, to level with the Corinairans. "I didn't mean for any of this to happen," he said, raising his gaze again and locking eyes with the Prime Minister as he spoke. "This is entirely my fault."

* * *

The Takaran anti-insurgency agent that had led the group of civilian Loyalists against this missile base stood on the rooftop landing pad of the control center. From this vantage point, he could see down all sides of the mountaintop base. The steep, rocky faces had made the main road leading to the front gate the only way into the compound, and had required a brute force attack in order to breech base security. To all the ignorant civilians that had followed him and his small team of covert agents in the attack, it had appeared to be a simple, brute force attack. The overall strategy was to embolden the civilian Loyalists of Corinair to continue their attacks against the Followers of the Order, as well as the Corinairan government. Thanks to the influence of the Anti-Insurgency Unit, the Loyalists foolishly believed that an overt demonstration of their loyalty to the empire would earn their world a reprieve.

It wasn't entirely true, and everyone in the unit knew it. The Corinairan government had not done anything to justify any action be taken against them, but the Takarans also knew that deep down the Corinairans hated the Ta'Akar for what they had done to their once proud world. It was this wounded pride that had made it so easy to acquire the loyalty of the weak-minded of their population. Such people needed something to belong to, something they could take pride in. When given the choice of claiming allegiance to a fallen, beaten world, or to a strong new empire, the choice for many had been easy enough.

Those same men now stood guard at the ruined gates of the complex against an enemy that would never come. It gave them something to do, something to make them feel empowered. They were defending what they had taken from the ones they believed responsible for the destruction that had rained down upon them from above. They would raise their weapons in defense, but unfortunately for them, in the end, their weapons would be pointed in the wrong direction.

The squad leader made his way down the stairs from the rooftop landing pad. "How's it going, Tobias?" the squad leader asked as he entered the control room.

"Re-targeting is complete, sir. Missiles will be

ready to fire in a few minutes."

"Good job. Our ride will be here momentarily. We'll be on the roof waiting for them. As soon as the bird touches down, you launch the missiles and then make a beeline for the roof, or we'll leave you behind. Understood?"

"Yes, sir," Tobias answered. "What about the civilians outside?"

"Casualties of war, my friend," the squad leader said with a smile as he turned to exit the room.

"Oh, that's cold, sir," Tobias commented, a grin of his own appearing.

At first, the civilians guarding the gates were surprised to see a small Kalibri airship land on the roof of the command center. They were sure that it was the Corinairan military coming in to retake their base, and they scrambled to move into a position from which to attack.

Alarms sounded and the doors in the missile silos began to open. The civilian Loyalists that had assisted in the capture of the base scattered in all directions as they realized that, at any moment, they could be incinerated by the thrust wash of departing missiles.

"What the hell are they doing?!" one of the civilians called out as he ran, but no one heard his query. With a deafening roar, all six silos began to spew smoke and fire out of their opening, the blasts rising high into the night sky. The entire compound was instantly bathed in a red-orange glow, turning the entire area into a scene from hell itself.

Almost simultaneously, the tips of six missiles began to rise up from out of their silos. They were nearly masked by the smoke and fire, but within seconds, the missiles were completely out of their silos and rapidly climbing into the night. At first, their contrails of fire struck the ground below, spreading out laterally in all directions, but as they continued to rise, the tails eventually no longer touched the ground.

Hiding behind the relative safety of the control buildings, some of the Corinairans that had helped seize the missile silo watched in astonishment as the missiles climbed away. They watched, wondering if they were being sent to destroy the enemy ship sitting in orbit that had defeated the Yamaro earlier that day. As they covered their ears against the din and watched the bright orange fireballs rise up into the darkness, not one of them noticed the small Kalibri airship taking off from the roof of the control center behind them with six pairs of legs hanging off the sides.

* * *

An alarm sounded from one of the consoles in front of the Prime Minister. At the same time, the massive center display screen on the far wall of the main floor of the command center changed to show a global map of Corinair. The loudspeaker was repeating a phrase, one which seemed to draw considerable attention from the Corinairans, including the Prime Minister, whose attention was now focused on the new problem.

"What is it?" Nathan asked Tug.

"There's been a missile launch," Tug explained.

Nathan could see that Tug was considerably disturbed. "By who?"

"By Hakai," Tug said.

"Who are they shooting at?" Jessica asked more urgently. Jessica looked at the guard hovering over her with his gun aimed at her face. "Can I get up now?"

"I don't know yet," Tug admitted.

"Prime Minister," Nathan shouted above the noise, "what is going on? What are you targeting?"

"They did not fire them," Jalea said as she struggled to overhear more details of the numerous exchanges that were going on among the controllers and the command staff present.

"Wait, isn't this Hakai?" Nathan asked.

"Yes," Jalea said. "The missile launch was from a Hakai installation, but the Hakai did not initiate it. The launch was from one of the captured sites."

"Prime Minister," Nathan repeated more fervently, "I demand to know who you are targeting!"

Another alarm sounded. Nathan looked to the main display downstairs. A new set of lines representing another missile track appeared. This time, it was from another continent on the map.

"What the hell is going on?" Jessica asked as she got back on her feet.

"The nation of Melentor has also launched," Tug told them grimly. "The Hakai missiles must be targeting the Melentorans. They are responding in similar fashion."

"Are you saying a nuclear war has just started?" Nathan could feel his body becoming cold, as if the hand of death itself had just touched him.

"They are low-yield tactical warheads," Tug assured them. "We are safe in here."

"Oh, I feel so much better. Thanks," Nathan said.

A map of the local area appeared on the screen

to the left. Two small triangles appeared from what seemed to be the Aitkenna spaceport.

"They have dispatched strike aircraft," Tug said, "to destroy that missile base."

"They're trying to keep it from escalating," Jessica observed.

"Precisely," Tug said. "However, it may be too late."

They watched as the missile tracks on the main display grew longer and stretched out across the map toward one another.

"How long?" Nathan asked.

"Perhaps thirty minutes," Tug answered, "maybe less."

* * *

The two Corinairan interceptors streaked along no more than a few hundred meters above the ground as they closed on the Wellerton missile base. Even though it was over five hundred kilometers away, it had only taken them a few minutes to get within firing range.

Two missiles leapt from the wings of both interceptors, accelerating away at incredible speed as the aircraft that had launched them banked away to port. The missiles flew for less than a minute before they began to arc upward. They continued to climb for another twenty seconds before they finally reached the apex of their trajectories and began their terminal dive onto their target.

One missile would have been enough to destroy the entire base on its own, but the Hakai were not taking any chances. All four of the missiles struck the base at evenly spaced locations. There was a blinding flash of blue-white light, followed by a thunderous boom that could be felt for at least a hundred kilometers, and could probably be heard even farther out. There was no ball of fire, not even much smoke, but the rugged, rocky terrain on which the missile base had once stood was now a smooth, slightly rounded mound of rubble. The remaining unused missiles residing deep underground would remain buried for some time to come, as would the radioactive materials contained within their warheads.

* * *

"They are trying to make it look as if the Loyalists are leading the revolt," Jalea said, realizing it herself for the first time.

"Who," Nathan wondered aloud, "the Takarans?"

"Yes. Don't you see? It is the only thing that makes sense."

"She may be right," Tug agreed. "The Loyalists simply aren't organized enough to make such things happen. This is all too well coordinated to be a collection of random acts by those with similar imperial loyalties. Even with this world's robust communications network, it would be a monumental task, one that would require *military* precision."

"The Anti-Insurgency Units," Jessica realized.

"Yes. They must have multiple units operating all over the planet, and all according to a carefully laid out plan," Tug explained.

"You'd think they would already know this," Jessica added.

"Yes," Tug agreed. "In fact, they probably do, or at least suspect it. At the very least they would be aware of a Takaran presence on their world, one far greater than the standard Takaran military and political offices that are present on all worlds within the empire."

"Sir, you do realize your people are being deceived?" Tug said.

"Yes, we're quite aware of that fact," the aide said. "Thank you."

"Then what do you intend to do about it?" Nathan asked.

"We're doing what we can, Captain," the aide assured them. "But with all the rioting going on in the streets, our limited military resources are rapidly becoming overburdened and ineffective. Right now, our own people are our worst enemy."

"You have to talk to them, let them know the truth," Tug suggested.

"We don't even know who to speak with," the aide argued. "They have no organization, no leadership, no delegates..."

"Of course not. They're simply people responding to unprovoked attacks."

"That is my point," the aide said in frustration. "Without a delegate or a representative with which to communicate..."

"Then simply speak to all of them at once," Tug insisted. "Both sides, all sides, everyone. Broadcast it across all media, video, news services, the entire planetary network. You can even tie in all the comm-sets every Corinairan carries around in their pockets."

"They will not listen to us," the aide translated from the Prime Minister. "They no longer trust us to protect them, to do what is in their best interests."

"Then let Na-Tan speak to them," Jalea suggested.

Nathan and Tug both turned to look at Jalea in shock. "What?" Nathan wondered aloud.

There was a moment of silence in the room. The aide translated Jalea's suggestion to the Prime Minister, who appeared intrigued by the idea.

"Your world is mostly made up of Followers of the Order," she continued. "Everyone knows this; they just don't speak of it openly. Your people keep this fact very well hidden. Why do you think there are secret places where Followers of the Order congregate in nearly every district?"

"What do you propose?" the aide asked, obviously prompted to do so by his superior.

"You saw the way they behaved at the spaceport. They see Na-Tan as their hero..."

"Which he clearly is not," the aide countered. "He said as much himself."

"That may be true," Jalea admitted. "Then again, it may not. Who knows if the legend is true? Who cares? Na-Tan doesn't know, but then again, he didn't even know that people from Earth had made it out this far into space. Was his coming here an accident, or was it destiny? Again, we do not know. But he has brought you two very powerful weapons on this day: his ability to jump between the stars, and the power, the inspiration that the Legend of Origins provides for the people of Corinair. These are far more powerful than any weapon the Ta'Akar possess. But they only work to your advantage."

"She's right," Jessica admitted. "A bit melodramatic, but right."

"Let him speak," Jalea continued to plead. "Let them hear his words. Let him call them to arms in defense of their world."

The aide finished translating their words for the

Prime Minister, who stared at them, particularly at Nathan himself.

Nathan could feel his scrutiny. He could feel that he was being sized up. It was like he could read the old politician's mind. He was trying very hard to make a leap of faith, one that he knew his world needed, but it could all go terribly wrong, and that was what was holding him back. Nathan returned his gaze as confidently as he could. "I can do this."

* * *

Altogether, there had been twenty-four members of the Yamaro's crew in the cells, of which more than half were Corinairans. Rather than risk them all roaming the corridors unarmed, Enrique had chosen to leave six behind at the brig with Marcus and Loki. Once they had secured the nearest armory, they would send two of their eighteen back to the brig loaded down with as many weapons as they could carry. At that time, they could return to the hangar bay with sufficient forces to secure both the bay and their shuttle.

In groups of six—each led by either Enrique, Sergeant Weatherly, or Ensign Willard—they made their way forward through the corridors of the Yamaro. It had taken them only minutes to reach the nearest armory, and as promised, the Yamaro crewman Enrique now called Number Six had opened the armory doors with ease by simply placing his hand on the wall scanner.

The doors to the armory slid open slowly and evenly, disappearing into the bulkheads. Enrique stepped into the dark room, which tripped the sensors and activated the lighting. He looked around as the lights came on, marveling at racks of weapons: pistols, snub-nosed rifles, long-range rifles, and even some very mean-looking weapons with large bore barrels that Enrique was afraid to ask about.

"Damn," Enrique exclaimed as he walked into the room, gazing at the racks of weapons.

"Now we're talkin'," Weatherly added.

Directly on their heels, Ensign Willard and the rest of the volunteers quickly started grabbing weapons.

"Everyone, listen up," Willard announced. "Each of you take a rifle, a pistol, and a few stun grenades. And a few of you take a boomer as well."

Enrique and Weatherly watched as the volunteers from the Yamaro's crew raided the shelves to arm up. It was a little unnerving to watch eighteen men who had, up until a few minutes ago, been members of a captured enemy crew start taking on weapons, and for a horrifying moment, Enrique wondered if he might have made a terrible mistake.

He watched as the volunteers took their weapons, checking them to be sure they were operational with obviously practiced hands. These men knew how to use these weapons, that much he was sure of. "What are *boomers*?" Enrique asked, leaning in toward Willard.

Ensign Willard picked up one of the short, large bore weapons and held it up for Enrique and Weatherly to see. It was a little more than half a meter long and the barrel was as big around as a man's wrist. The back of it had a rather unattractive squared box, with handles at the front and back. "This is a boomer. It'll blow through just about anything. As the saying goes, 'There's no hiding from a boomer.'"

"Why is it called a boomer?" Enrique asked.

"Because everything it hits goes *boom*," he explained.

"I'll take one of those," Sergeant Weatherly announced, taking the mean-looking weapon from Ensign Willard's hands with a smile on his face.

"Be warned," Willard cautioned him, "You only get four shots, and then it is useless."

"Better take more than one, then," the sergeant said.

"And be careful what you shoot at with them," Willard added. "For example, don't shoot at an exterior wall, or you may find yourself floating in space."

Enrique looked at the sergeant. "Ask before you shoot, okay?"

"Yes, sir," Weatherly promised.

The two men tasked with taking weapons back to the brig to arm the others stepped up to depart, loaded down with at least a dozen rifles and pistols, as well as a few boomers.

Enrique noticed the boomers. "Don't give any boomers to Marcus or Loki. Understood?"

"Yes, sir," the volunteers promised before they departed.

The now fully armed volunteers had lined up along the armory shelves to indicate their readiness. Enrique looked them over. Each of them carried an energy rifle, an energy pistol, and several stun grenades. In addition to Sergeant Weatherly, four more of them carried a boomer as well. They were an impressive bunch. If the enemy boarding party were only one team of four, they were sure to come out on top.

"I think we've got them outgunned, Ensign," Enrique announced.

"You should be aware, sir, that the entrances to the bridge are designed to be quite defensible should they come under attack by a boarding party. They will have superior positions, both in terms of cover and fields of fire."

"Great, good to know. But they are still only four guys."

"We hope," Willard reminded him.

"A good friend of mine once told me that sometimes it's better not to think about something too much and to just do it," Enrique told Ensign Willard. "I'm pretty sure she was talking about a time like this." Enrique held out his hand, indicating that Ensign Willard should lead the way.

"Let's move out," Willard announced on his way out of the armory.

* * *

Getting back up into the main service tunnel had been difficult enough. The side tunnel they had escaped into was smaller and had dropped off at a forty-five degree angle from the main tunnel, dropping nearly three meters. Vladimir had been able to push Deliza back up the incline from underneath easily enough, despite her protestations against being pushed into a space in complete darkness, even though she had already been in there today. However, it had been far more difficult for Vladimir, who had to try and jump up several times to grab the ledge and pull himself up the incline. It too was covered with soot, like every other surface inside the tunnels, and he had been unable to keep hold. Had it not been for Deliza's help, he never would have made it back up into the main tunnel.

Once back in the main tunnel, it was a short distance to the nearest emergency box where they found the first flash light. They continued on for some distance, changing tunnels at least three times. They picked up a few more flashlights along the way, just in case the first ones they had located died out, as they had no idea how long they would be trapped inside the service spaces of the Aurora.

Vladimir stopped again to check on their location. He pretty much knew where they were, but they had limited time and he did not want to make a mistake and waste valuable time back tracking. Besides, it gave Deliza an occasional break from crawling.

"My knees hurt so much," she complained.

"We are almost to the routing node," Vladimir assured her. "From there I can connect the data pad and send commands to any system on the ship as if I were on the bridge or at the main engineering console."

"What are you going to do then?"

"I do not know yet, but I will think of something." He studied the tunnel map on the data pad one more time. "Okay, another fifty meters, and then we come to the last junction on the right. Then another fifty meters and we are there."

"Another hundred meters? Can't I just wait here?"

"No, I cannot leave you behind," he told her as he put the data pad back into his pocket. "Besides, I may need your help." Vladimir put the small tubular flashlight back in his mouth so his hands would be free to crawl and started making his way down the tunnel again on his hands and knees. Deliza, on the other hand, refused to put the flashlight in her mouth, choosing instead to hold it in her right hand, despite the fact that it made it even more difficult to crawl.

"Whatever you have in mind had better work," she told him. "Or guys with guns will be the last thing you have to worry about."

"*Oiy, ya biyoos*," he teased.

* * *

"Now then, on to more important issues," de Winter began, "like how it is that you are able to travel so quickly between systems." The captain began to move about the bridge, looking over each console as he passed. He started with the main flight console at the front of the Aurora's bridge. He bent over slightly and looked at all the controls and display surfaces. "This must be your helm," he said, looking at Josh's console on the right, "which would make that one navigation, I suppose." He looked closer at the displays and noticed that many of them were written in Angla, while others were written in a similar looking alphabet. "Odd, some of this is in Angla."

"I've been translating it a little at a time," Josh admitted, "to make it easier for me to use."

"I wouldn't do too much of that if I were you," de Winter said, "or we might not need you much longer." He continued looking over the helm and navigation stations. "This all looks pretty standard." De Winter stood straight again. "Perhaps it's a separate system, something apart from the standard propulsion and maneuvering systems one might expect to use on a ship such as this." He looked around, trying to determine which station might be the one he was looking for. For the first time, he noticed the amount of damage that the bridge had suffered in recent days. "You know, you really ought to fix this place up a bit."

De Winter moved to the sensor station to the left of the navigation console next, moving past Kaylah without a word to her. "No, not this one either," he said after a brief inspection. He looked at the aft station next, to the left of Kaylah's, stepping over the dead comm-officer's body. "This is obviously just communications."

He turned back toward the center of the bridge. "That's tactical, and those two over there are obviously not working, so that leaves just that one," he surmised, pointing to Abby's console near the starboard exit. "Is that your station?" he asked Abby, who was standing next to the helm. She said nothing, but he could tell by the look in her eyes that he was on the right track. He moved closer to her, making his way across the bridge. "It is, isn't it?" He smiled, quite happy with himself for figuring it out. "Oh my dear, you must tell me all about it. What it's called, how it works... I want to know *everything*."

"I'm sorry; I'm just an operator. I don't know how it works," Abby lied.

"Come now," de Winter said. "I'm sure you know far more than you realize. You see, we humans pick up so much information without even thinking about it. For example, the young woman over there, she's obviously a member of this crew, as was that poor chap over there. I know what you're thinking; that was an easy one, what with the uniforms and all. Now this smart-mouthed young man here, he's not a member of the crew. I can tell by his accent. He's either from Haven or has spent considerable time there. You, on the other hand, you're also not a member of this crew, but then again, you aren't from this part of space either. You're from Earth, just like the rest of them. Even though you only spoke a few words, I can tell that your accent is not of this region of space. And you're far too delicate to be a member of the crew. You don't have the look of someone who has endured vigorous training. You have the look of a clinician, a scientist perhaps."

"You flatter me, sir. But I'm afraid I am merely a technical specialist, a glorified systems operator."

"Then I guess you'll just have to show me how to operate the *system* that allows this ship to jump about from place to place as it does. That was quite a neat little trick, after all. The way you repeatedly jumped inside my shields in order to fire on us. Quite clever it was. I'll give your captain credit for coming up with that one." Captain de Winter stepped closer to her, staring down at her. He was a good deal taller than Abby, who was rather petite to begin with, and dressed in his flat black assault gear, he was quite intimidating.

"I think it's time that you returned to your station, young lady," he said in a rather sinister tone. "We have much to discuss."

Abby stood her ground for a moment then looked up into his eyes, a look of defiance on her face. Her disobedience, as subtle as it might have been, was instantly met with by the back of Captain de Winter's hand, almost knocking her over. A short, startled scream escaped her lips as a result of the blow. Josh instinctively moved as if to defend her, but the captain raised his pistol at him again without anything more than a look.

"You do not want to test me, madam," the captain

told her as he turned back to look in her eyes. "Trust me; you do not."

After a moment, Abby looked away and moved toward her station.

A satisfied smile came across de Winter's face. "As soon as the jamming pod is deactivated, contact the boarding team on the Yamaro and check their progress, Sergeant."

* * *

Loki nervously kept his handgun pointed at the hatchway leading from the brig to the corridor. Before they had left, Enrique had shown him how to reload it and had given him a few extra magazines, but now it was the only defense they had should another team find them.

His eyes widened as he heard footsteps coming toward them. "Someone's coming," he told Marcus.

"Easy, kid," Marcus warned. "Don't shoot until you know who you're shooting at."

Loki swallowed hard, his gun held up high, his hands gripped tightly around the handle. He thumbed the safety off as the footsteps grew louder. Two men suddenly appeared from around the distant corner, each of them loaded down with multiple weapons. Loki immediately recognized them as two of the prisoners that had volunteered to help defend the ship, returning with weapons exactly as Enrique had promised.

Loki breathed a sigh of relief. "They're back," he announced to the others waiting in the brig, "with guns."

The two crewmen carrying the weapons entered the brig and deposited the weapons on the table at the guard station.

"What the hell are these?" Marcus asked as he reached for one of the boomers.

"They are very destructive," the crewman told him, taking the boomer out of his reach. "And very dangerous if you do not know how to use them correctly."

"I think I can figure it out," Marcus said confidently.

"I'm sorry, but we were instructed not to give them to either of you."

"Instructed by who?" Marcus asked.

"By your commander."

Marcus grunted as he reached for one of the other energy rifles. "He ain't my commander."

"We must get moving immediately," the crewmen said. "There are ten of us, so we will split into two teams of five. I will lead one group. Corporal Lewis will lead the other."

"Who the hell put you in charge?" Marcus challenged.

"Do you have any military training, sir?"

"Well, no, but..."

"All of us do. Besides the two of you are our pilots, are you not? You should not be put at risk. You will follow us. We will protect you."

"Well, when you put it that way..." Marcus agreed. "What do we call you?"

"I am Corporal Eckert." The corporal turned to the men. "Everyone ready?" They all nodded their readiness. "Let's move out."

The men started filing out through the hatchway, their weapons all held ready. Marcus and Loki were the last two out of the brig.

"Pilot my ass," Loki sneered. "If you were any

kind of a pilot, we wouldn't be here."

"Shut up, kid."

* * *

"Please tell me we're there," Deliza said, coughing, when Vladimir stopped in front of her.

Vladimir shined his light on the terminal box on the wall, checking the numbers on the box against the schematic on his data pad. "Yes, I believe this is the place." He repositioned himself on his knees facing the metal box on the wall and began removing the four thumb screws that held on the cover plate.

Deliza collapsed on the floor of the tunnel, rolling over on her back. She had been crawling for what seemed like forever, despite the fact that it had probably only been about twenty minutes. She didn't even care that she was lying in soot. After all, she had been breathing it the entire time, due to the fact the she had been following Vladimir as he kicked up the soot in front of her.

Vladimir had noticed her coughing when it had started nearly ten minutes ago. He knew that she had probably inhaled a lot of soot. They both had, but there was nothing he could do about that now. Perhaps, once they regained control of the ship, Doctor Chen could give her something to fix her up.

Vladimir laughed at himself on the inside. He had no doubt that they would regain control of the ship. The thought of failure had never entered his mind. He had always been that way, confident and self-assured. His mother had recognized this trait in him at an early age. When he was only a child, about five years of age, he had expected to go to the park on a Sunday morning, just as he and his

father had always done. However, his father had
been called into work unexpectedly and could not
take him to the park. Undaunted, young Vladimir
had announced that he was going to the park
anyway, on his own. His mother, who was busy with
his younger twin sisters had paid no mind to his
proclamation and had continued going about her
daily chores. Hours later, his father had been forced
to leave work in order to search for his missing son.
To his surprise, he had found him exactly where he
said he would be: at the park, some five kilometers
from their home on the other side of town.

His entire life, he had always set forth on each task
with the absolute certainty that he would complete
it successfully, and this time was no different, even
if he didn't have a plan of action just yet.

"So, have you figured out what you are going to
do?" Deliza asked in between coughs.

"No, not yet. I will connect the data pad to the
routing node and use it as an interface terminal. I
will have to use the on-screen keyboard, so it will be
a slow process. But I should be able to at least slow
them down by rerouting command signals coming
from the bridge. That might at least buy us some
time."

"Time for what?"

"Time for me to figure out what to do," Vladimir
defended. "Or time for help to arrive."

"What help?"

"From the surface. Jessica will be trying to
check in soon. If we do not answer, she will become
suspicious and send help."

"Are you sure? Maybe she'll just think the comms
are broken. Everything else is."

Vladimir looked over at her lying on the floor,

coughing. "You are not helping," he told her, removing the cover plate. "She will become suspicious. It is in her nature; you will see." With the cover plate removed, Vladimir was able to see the routing node with all its little green flashing lights. He pulled out the connector cable from the data pad and plugged it into the interface port on the routing node. Data began flashing across the pad's screen as it began communicating with the routing node. Finally, after a few moments, the data pad was properly linked to the system. "There, it is connected." He began shuffling through various screens of data, trying to see what commands were passing through the routing node.

"What do you see? Is there something we can do?"

"Ssh, I'm busy."

Deliza's curiosity overcame her discomfort, and she rolled over and moved closer to Vladimir, getting on her knees despite the pain. She wanted to see what he was looking at. "What is that?"

"They are command packets," he told her. "Each one contains an instruction to be relayed to another place on the network."

"How do you know what's in them?"

"You have to open them and look."

"That'll take forever," she objected. "There are millions of them."

"Yes, but don't look at individual packets. Look at strings. They have ID tags on them that indicate their point of origin, destination, type, and priority. So we can set filters to only show us packets heading from bridge to engineering for example."

"But that'll only narrow them down to the tens of thousands."

"True, but then we can apply more filters, like only show us priority flight commands. Then we can issue reroute instructions, sending them off to where ever we choose, even in an endless loop."

"Nice," she said. "It's like hacking."

Vladimir looked at her. "You have hacking on your world?"

"If you have computers, you have hackers. Why, don't you?"

"Of course. How do you think I passed history?" he admitted with a smile.

CHAPTER EIGHT

"How many people are we talking about here?" Nathan asked as they hurried along the corridor.

"Several million, at least," Tug told him as he followed behind.

"Several million?" Nathan said, stopping and turning to look at Tug.

"At least."

"Well, at least I won't be up their alone," Nathan said as he continued down the corridor. "You're coming with me."

"Why me?" Tug asked.

"There are Karuzari hiding on this world, right? It might help if they see you as well."

"There are far fewer Karuzari on this world than you might think, Captain."

"That may be so," Nathan conceded as they turned and entered the media room, "but if this is going to work, we need to show them all a unified leadership. You, me, and the Prime Minister. We all have to stand together on this, or it doesn't stand a snowball's chance in hell."

"A what?" Tug asked, unfamiliar with the phrase.

Nathan and the others followed the Prime Minister and his entourage across the room and over to the podium. Behind it was a plain background with the same coat of arms that Nathan had seen on the side of the airship that had brought them to the command center.

Bright flood lights snapped on, nearly blinding Nathan for a moment until his eyes adjusted. A few meters away from him, several men stood behind large cameras mounted on stands that moved so smoothly across the floor that they almost appeared to float.

A man stepped up and aligned each of them. Nathan stood to the left of the Prime Minister, who himself stood directly behind the podium. To the Prime Minister's right stood Tug. The Prime Minister's translator stood to Nathan's left.

"Any idea what you're going to say?" Jessica asked him as she began to back away.

"Not a clue," Nathan admitted nervously.

"Wing it," she said with a wink. "That's what you're good at, Skipper."

Nathan feigned a smile at her as one of the men standing behind the cameras began to countdown in Corinairan.

A red light atop one of the three cameras lit up, and a moment later the Prime Minister began speaking in Corinairan. He continued for several minutes, during which time the translator whispered the Angla translation to Nathan. Nathan didn't hear half of what the translator said, as he was too busy trying to figure out what he would say when it was his turn to speak.

Before he knew it, his turn had come. Nathan stepped over to the podium as the Prime Minister nodded to him and stepped back out of the way. He looked into the camera as he cleared his throat. "People of Corinair, I am Nathan Scott, and I'm the captain of the United Earth Ship Aurora."

Nathan paused a moment as he thought about

his words. For years, his father had chastised him for not thinking before speaking. He could recall at least a dozen times when failing to do just that had gotten him into trouble. However, as often as it had gotten him into trouble, it had also gotten him out of it. It was a dichotomy of sorts that he never fully understood, at least not until this very moment. For now, Nathan realized that what had always worked so well for him in the past had been nothing less than the truth. Good or bad, in the end, the truth had always gotten him that which he sought. He wondered how that had come to be. He had grown up in a family of politicians: his father, his grandfather, and his great grandfather. All of them had been politicians. He had grown up watching his father massage the truth in order to achieve the results that each listener wished to hear, and somewhere along the way, Nathan had developed a dislike for the practice. In the end, that had probably been why he had such an intense dislike for politics. Perhaps that was also why he seemed to be a natural leader. It wasn't just that he had a trustworthy face; it was because he was trustworthy. In fact, he could hear his mother's voice saying, *'Oh Nathan, I can always trust you to do the right thing.'* That's when he knew what he had to say. "I am not Na-Tan."

The Prime Minister's aide, who was translating aloud for the benefit of the audience, most of which did not speak Angla, suddenly stopped his translation, looking to the Prime Minister for guidance. Nathan turned and glared at him. The Prime Minister bowed his head at the aide, indicating that he should continue to translate, which he did.

Nathan could see the look of concern in the eyes of everyone in the room: the cameramen, the technicians, the various aides, even the soldiers. All of them had the same look, except for Jessica, who had made her way quietly through the room until she was as close as she could get to the main camera without getting in the way. Somehow, she had known that Nathan would need a familiar face to get him through this, the face of someone he could trust.

"I am not a legend. In fact, until we accidentally ended up in this region of space, we knew nothing about your legends. We didn't even know you were out here. But you are. Somehow, during the worst disaster in human history, your forefathers managed to start anew well out of reach of the plague that nearly destroyed us all. You all originally came from Earth; we all did, even the Ta'Akar. Even Caius, unfortunately."

Nathan looked at Jessica again. She was smiling. "Your legends state that your people fled the core worlds of Earth in order to escape a great evil. That, in a sense, is true as well. But that particular evil has long since disappeared. However, there is always a new evil waiting to take its place. My world, Earth... well, we have our own evil. They're called the Jung. Your evil goes by a different name—Caius the Great, ruler of the Ta'Akar Empire. As I speak to you today, his agents are stirring up trouble on Corinair. They're pitting brother against brother, Loyalists against Followers, and the truth is they care about neither of you. They only care about what is best for them. They only want control of your world."

Nathan's posture changed, as if he had become more relaxed. "'Then why don't they just take it?' you're probably wondering. 'After all, they are the most powerful force in the entire sector, are they not?'" Nathan paused again, this time for dramatic effect, just as he had seen his father do on many occasions. "Well, they're not, actually. You see, they've been fighting the Karuzari for decades. And they're down to a handful of ships. That's why they've been abandoning their outermost colonies. That's why they require *your* young men to serve in *their* military. That's why they require so many of your resources. And perhaps that's why only one ship came looking for us today."

Again, the faces of the Corinairans in the room became concerned. "That's right; the Ta'Akar came here looking for us. In fact, the captain of the Yamaro called me and tried to convince me to join forces with the Ta'Akar because he knew that our jump drive was the key that would allow the Ta'Akar to conquer this entire region of space. If combined with their new energy source, they would undoubtedly be able to conquer the entire galaxy. But I refused his invitation. In exchange, he attacked your world. He knew that if he attacked only us, we would simply jump away. But if he attacked you, then I would feel obligated to defend your world. Well, he was right; I did. But that hardly makes me a legend."

Again, Nathan paused, but only to collect his thoughts. "Maybe that makes me a great man; I don't know. That judgment is not mine to make. It's yours. The things that I chose to do today were chosen not because they were the right thing to do, but because they were the only thing to do. If this makes me a legend then so be it; I am Na-Tan. But I alone cannot save you. You have to save yourselves. You have to stop fighting each other, Loyalists and Followers, and you have to start working together. The Ta'Akar will return, sooner or later. We have to be ready to fight! We have to be ready to win! And we have to start now! Lay down your arms. Return to what's left of your homes, and care for your loved ones. The time to fight will come. We will call for you soon enough."

Nathan stared at the camera for several seconds. *Did they understand him? Did they realize what was at stake?* These people had turned the other cheek for over thirty years, despite the fact that they came from a long line of strong and determined people. Would they even consider taking control of their destiny once again?

Nathan finally turned and looked to Tug standing next to him. He could see the emotion in Tug's eyes, and he knew that Tug could see the pain in his own. Nathan stepped back to stand by the Prime Minister, allowing Tug to take the podium.

The Karuzari had long ago chosen to speak an ancient dialect of the rarely visited world of Palee. Although a difficult language to master, it had the distinct advantage of not being understood by those around them that were not of their clan. He chose to begin his address in Palee, but only long enough to establish his identity to any Karuzari that were listening. He knew that there were no more than a few dozen Karuzari at best hiding on Corinair, but those that were would undoubtedly be listening to all broadcasts.

The Prime Minister's translator looked a bit panicked, as he did not understand the Palee language. For all they knew, Tug was passing top secret information to his subordinates. Just as the Prime Minister was about to order the guards to seize Tug, he began speaking Angla instead. He could easily have spoken well enough in Corinairan to be understood, but his Angla was better and he hoped to present a unified front by speaking the same language as Nathan.

"My name is Redmond Tugwell, and I am the leader of the Karuzari."

* * *

Commander Dumar stared at the video display. There was something about this man, this leader of the Karuzari. His name was not familiar to him, yet there was something about him: his mannerisms, his voice, the way he carried himself. Had he met him in battle? Had he seen him on a street corner? For all he knew, he could have been one of his children's school teachers.

"I order all Karuzari," the man on the video screen continued, *"wherever you may be hiding, to stand down. Do not engage in combat with anyone, even if you suspect they are agents of the Ta'Akar. Remain in your homes and await further instructions from myself or from Captain Scott. We will call for you in the days to come. For now, take cover and be safe."*

The man on the screen was not of Corinair; of that much the commander was sure. His appearance was not manicured like most Corinairans. He was a man of labor, a man of the soil... a farmer, perhaps. The commander immediately dismissed the notion, as he was too well spoken to be a farmer. Yet he did have the appearance of a man who spent much of his time outdoors.

He remembered that Captain de Winter had said that he believed the Aurora had been in the Haven system recently. The shuttle they had come down in was of the type used in that remote, backwater system. However, the commander had never been to the Haven system. If he had met this man before, it could only be one of three places: on the battlefield, here on Corinair, or on his home world of Takara.

"Lieutenant, run an ID search on the second speaker in that video, the older one. Every ID database from every world in the Empire. I want to know his identity."

"Yes, sir."

* * *

The Takaran anti-insurgency agent peered around the corner from the opening of the corridor into the Yamaro's main command deck foyer. The section was open in the middle around a central court yard punctuated by a circular security desk. The foyer was two decks high, with an upper level balcony that wrapped around the foyer's upper deck. There was a pair of staircases at each end of the room that led to the second level. At the forward end, the stair cases formed a direct route to the landing balcony outside the command and control center's port and starboard entrances.

One of the Yamaro's command staff also peeked around the corner. "That's it," he said in a whisper. "The C&C is right up those stairs." He looked around for a moment. "It looks clear," he announced as he started to move.

The agent grabbed the nobleman, pulling him back behind him. "Not so fast," he instructed, rolling his eyes in dismay. "You ever wonder why it's clear?" He looked at the nobleman, who still didn't seem to have a clue. The agent realized that the old axiom that *nobility is bestowed on any fool born into it* was more true than he ever imagined. "It's the command and control center. Why wouldn't it be guarded?"

"The ship is powered down," the nobleman pointed out. "Perhaps they were not expecting us."

"I would be," the agent muttered to himself.

"Regardless, we won't discover why if we stay here."

The agent looked at the nobleman. "After you, sir."

The nobleman hesitated for a moment, wondering if the anti-insurgency agent was perhaps right. Unfortunately, he had little choice in the matter and was forced to take off running in a low crouch across the foyer and directly up the stairs.

The agent watched for a moment, scanning the foyer for any signs of an ambush. Part of him wanted it to happen, just to teach all these arrogant nobles a lesson, but the Yamaro's officer made it across the foyer and was headed up the stairs, all without incident.

"Let's move," he decided, rising and heading out into the foyer. The other two noblemen crouching behind him followed, the second one keeping an eye out behind them as they progressed up the stairs.

The first nobleman reached the port entrance to the bridge and immediately crouched to the right of the doorway in front of the access control panel. He placed his hand on the panel's scanning bed, expecting his palm print to be read in order to gain access to the command center. Nothing happened. He removed his hand and tried again, yet there was still no reaction.

The agent had already come up and taken up a position behind the first nobleman as he struggled with the uncooperative access control panel.

"Problem?"

"It's not accepting my palm print as ID."

"Maybe it doesn't like you," the agent responded. "Psst," he called to one of the nearby nobles crouching behind the armored wall that ran along the entire landing and across to the starboard side of the C&C. "Get over here." The nobleman moved closer. The agent grabbed his hand and thrust it toward the first nobleman. "Try his hand."

The second nobleman got the hint and moved in closer to try and gain access using his hand, but he also had no luck. "It doesn't work."

"No kidding," the agent said. "Back on the wall." The second nobleman moved back over to the wall, allowing the first one to move back over to the access panel.

"I guess we know why they weren't guarding it," the agent decided.

"They must have reprogrammed it, removed our access files," the first nobleman told him.

"How would *they* know how to do that?"

"They wouldn't," the nobleman agreed, "but that little worm Willard would."

"The officer that mutinied?"

"Yes, but he wasn't really an officer. He was only a common officer; his duties were limited, as was his access to the command decks."

"Apparently not limited enough," the agent commented. "Can you bypass it?"

"It might take a while to crack the command codes," he warned.

"How long is a while?"

"Ten, fifteen minutes, maybe longer. We could get in immediately if we had the captain's command codes."

The agent turned on his comm-set but found that it was still being jammed by the electronic countermeasures device they had left running in the Aurora's hangar bay. "No good," he said as he turned his comm-set back off again. "The jammer is still running. You'll have to crack it."

* * *

Ensign Willard quickly led Enrique and the other seven volunteers from the Yamaro's crew through the corridors on their way forward, stopping at each corner to check that the next section was clear before progressing. It took longer, but Enrique had been worried that there might be more than one team on board. He was also concerned that the boarding party may have laid traps along their way in order to delay any pursuers. So far, there had been signs of neither. Enrique only hoped that Sergeant Weatherly's team, which was approaching from the starboard side, was experiencing similar luck.

"How good of a defensive position will they have?" Enrique asked as he followed in a fast walking crouch behind Ensign Willard.

"Very good, I'm afraid. Both entrances to the bridge are at the top of the stairs that lead up from the foyer. There is a balcony across the aft end of the C&C that connects the port and starboard entrances. The entire balcony wall is a meter-high armor plate. If they are still trying to bypass the security lockout, they will be able to rain down fire on us from behind this wall. There are even firing ports built into the wall, so that they do not have to expose themselves in order to fire."

"And if they have already bypassed the lockout?"

"Then we will have less than five minutes to reach the shuttle in the hangar bay before they vent the ship's atmosphere into space."

"Great," Enrique said as they continued forward. "No pressure, then."

* * *

Corporal Eckert moved very slowly in order to avoid being noticed as he peeked around the corner into the hangar bay. The bay was empty, except for a medevac shuttle and a very old cargo shuttle that appeared to have smoke wafting out the back of it.

"You said you came in an old cargo shuttle?" the corporal asked.

"Yeah. Why?" Marcus answered.

"I do not think you will be leaving in it," the corporal told him.

"What?"

"It appears to have been disabled. There is smoke coming from the rear loading hatch."

"Son of a bitch," Marcus swore.

"You mean I came all the way over here for nothing?" Loki said.

"Can you fly that?" Corporal Eckert asked.

Loki moved closer to Eckert and peered around him, seeing the medevac shuttle. "I suppose so," he said as he leaned back. "How hard can it be?"

"That's what I thought," Marcus sneered.

Eckert looked again. "I see at least three people in the cockpit. Possibly the flight crew."

"Then they can fly it," Loki said.

"If they're willing to cooperate," Eckert pointed out.

"Oh they'll cooperate," Marcus said.

Eckert thought for a moment. "There could be more of them inside the back. That shuttle is big enough to hold at least a dozen men."

"Why would they leave that many behind?" Marcus asked. "Seems to me they'd want to take as many men as possible, seeing as how they were intent on capturing the bridge."

"True, but they would leave at least a few to guard their only means of escape." Corporal Eckert turned to his second. "Lewis, take your team and circle around the far side of the bay, aft of that shuttle so that you have a clear line of fire into the rear hatch. We will try to flush them out. I will watch for your signal."

Corporal Lewis and his group of men rose and headed back in the direction they had come.

"How do you plan on flushing them out?" Marcus asked.

"We will open fire on them from the front," Corporal Eckert explained.

"That don't sound like such a hot idea to me," Marcus argued.

"That ship has no weapons. If there are troops inside, they will have to come out the back and take up positions on either side to defend the shuttle. They will then be exposed to Corporal Lewis's fire team."

"So we're just supposed to go charging out there, guns a blazing?" Marcus asked.

"Yes, that is the plan."

"Still don't sound like such a hot idea."

* * *

Enrique stood with his back tight against the wall of the corridor that led to the port side of the command deck foyer. To his right were Ensign Willard and the seven volunteers on his squad, all lined up against the wall in similar fashion.

Enrique watched across the open foyer to his left, his eyes on the starboard corridor directly opposite his position, waiting for Sergeant Weatherly's fire team, who had approached from starboard, to get into position. Although they had only arrived a minute ago, as the seconds passed, he became nervous, wondering if they had encountered another boarding party on their way.

The single quick peek he had allowed himself had revealed exactly what Ensign Willard had described, a pair of stairs leading up to the command center on the second level, with meter-high armored walls complete with firing ports. Taking that position away from even a group as small as four men was going to be difficult.

Luckily, a moment later Sergeant Weatherly's team moved into position on the other side of the foyer, taking up a similar posture. Enrique ensured that he had eye contact with the marine before beginning a series of hand gestures meant to communicate the enemy strength and position, as well as what Enrique's plan of action entailed. Once he finished his gestures, the well-trained sergeant repeated the exact same set of gestures to prove that he understood his instructions.

Enrique turned to his team and began whispering. "I need one man with a boomer. When we lay down cover fire, you and one just like you from the far side are going to take position behind that central station out there in the middle of the courtyard.

270

Whenever we open up, you'll pop up and blast at them with that thing. Got it?"

The first man with a boomer nodded as he stepped forward, readying himself to run. Enrique held up his hand for the sergeant to see from the other side. Once he had his attention, he held up three fingers, then two fingers, then one... "GO!"

Enrique swung out to his left, bringing his energy rifle to bear on the command balcony above and to his left and opened fire. At the same time, Sergeant Weatherly did the same, showering the command balcony from his side as well. A split second later, a volunteer from each side of the foyer went charging across, their energy rifles blazing and a boomer swinging on their backs.

The sudden onslaught caught the two Takaran noblemen standing watch by surprise. Being inexperienced with actual combat, they followed their first instincts, which was to duck and cover, despite the fact that they were behind considerable amounts of reflective armored plating.

The Takaran anti-insurgency agent spun around and saw the two noblemen cowering behind the armored wall. "What are you doing?" he shouted. "Return fire!"

The nearest noblemen looked at the agent like he was crazy.

"Through the firing ports, you idiots!"

The nobleman realized his error, lifted his weapon to the nearest port in the armored wall, and took aim, firing rather indiscriminately but at least in the general direction of the incoming fire.

For a brief second, Enrique thought the enemy was not going to return fire. That moment had passed rather quickly, and now red bolts of energy were raining down from the firing ports in the wall above. The energy rounds struck near neither him nor any of his men, but they were frequent enough and within close enough proximity to keep them all pinned down for the moment.

Enrique swung out again and opened fire but was forced back by return fire almost immediately. The two men with boomers hiding behind the center station out in the middle of the courtyard rose up anyway and fired their big guns. The sound was horrendous, creating a thunderous slap-back effect as it echoed off the metal bulkheads in the courtyard. The energy blasts raining down from the command balcony did not stop and one of the men firing the boomers was hit directly in the face before he could get a second shot off.

Enrique had hoped that the boomers would damage the armored wall. If so, a few more shots might reduce the amount of usable cover the boarding party had up there. However, the blasts appeared to reflect off the armored balcony walls, most of their energy bouncing up into the ceiling above and causing considerable damage to those unarmored sections instead. While it did send metal and panels falling from above, it fell nowhere near the command balcony where the Takaran boarding party was still free to fire upon them at will.

They repeated the process two more times, but with similar negative results. The fourth attempt only got the second boomer shooter killed as well.

"I need two more boomers out there!" Enrique ordered. He swung out yet again, Ensign Willard stepping behind him to join in the covering fire. Another boomer-carrying volunteer went scurrying out but was cut down before he reached the cover of the center station. The Takarans firing through the ports in the armored wall had become more accustomed to the incoming fire, and their cover fire no longer seemed to have the desired effect of making the enemy pause to take cover.

"This is not working!" Enrique announced angrily.

* * *

"They are in position," Corporal Eckert announced from his position just outside the Yamaro's port hangar bay.

"How do you know?" Marcus asked.

"Because I can see them." The corporal rose. "It is time."

"I still think this is a dumb idea," Marcus insisted.

Corporal Eckert strode out into the hangar bay toward the front of the medevac shuttle at a rather leisurely pace, his weapon held across his chest. Reluctantly, Marcus, Loki, and the rest of the team followed.

"This is dumb," Marcus continued to mumble.

"All right, we all heard you the first five times you said it," Loki objected.

"Just making sure everyone is fully aware of my feelings on the matter."

They continued to walk toward the medevac shuttle for another few meters until Corporal Eckert stopped.

"They ain't doin' nothin'," Marcus said. "Do they even see us?"

"Who are they?" the pilot asked no one in particular.

The guard jumped up from his seat at the back of the medevac cockpit, where he had been sitting, nervously waiting for word from the boarding party. He looked at the five armed men standing in a line not more than ten meters from the front of the ship.

"What are they doing?" the copilot wondered.

Nearly at once, the five unknown men raised their weapons and opened fire. Not a single shot struck the shuttle. Instead, the bolts of energy slid close to the sides and above the ship. It was enough to startle the guard inside who reflexively raised his hands in defense.

The copilot saw her opportunity and jammed her right elbow hard into the guard's abdomen, causing him to double over. With both hands clenched together, she swung them upwards into the guard's nose, knocking him backwards.

The pilot, his eyes wide from shock at his normally demur copilot's spontaneous attack, quickly climbed out of his flight seat and dove aft on top of the stunned guard. His copilot quickly followed, slapping the button to deploy the rear loading ramp as she rose from her seat.

"Cease fire!" Corporal Eckert ordered. He could see through the medevac's cockpit windows that something was going on inside. The people had disappeared from view, although he could see an occasional head or fist—even a foot he thought—appear from time to time. Then he noticed that the rear ramp was coming down. "The rear ramp is opening!" he shouted. "Lewis, move in!" he ordered as he took off running toward the rear of the ship.

All five of them charged along the port side of the

medevac shuttle as the ramp came down at the aft end of the ship. Corporal Lewis and his men charged in from the other side of the hangar bay, approaching directly toward the aft end of the shuttle with their weapons up and pointed straight ahead, ready to fire. They leapt up on to the lowering ramp even before it touched the deck, charging up into the ship without delay.

They continued charging forward, their attention drawn to the sounds of a scuffle coming from the cockpit. They paid no attention to the wide-eyed crew chief, bound and gagged as he was to his aft-facing jump seat in the cargo area.

"Do not move!" Corporal Lewis shouted repeatedly as they charged up the narrow corridor that led from the cargo area into the cockpit. "I said do not move!" Corporal Lewis stepped to his left to make room for the man behind him. "Hands where I can see them!" he shouted at what looked like a pile of three people on the deck of the cockpit. "Take them aft!" he ordered his men.

One by one, the copilot, the pilot, and finally the Takaran nobleman that had been guarding them, were half dragged down the narrow corridor to the cargo area in the back half of the ship. Corporal Eckert came up the boarding ramp, followed by Marcus, Loki, and the other two members of their team. "What's your status?" Corporal Eckert inquired as he entered.

"We found this one tied up in his seat," Corporal Lewis started, "and these three wrestling in the cockpit."

"Any of them armed?"

"Just the guy in black," Lewis said. "I'm pretty sure the rest of them are the flight crew for this ship."

The medevac pilot looked up from the deck at all the armed men now in the back of his shuttle. They were all wearing Takaran military uniforms, yet they had stormed the ship and were taking the Takaran officer captive as well.

"Who are you?" he asked, somewhat confused.

"We are Corinairans serving on this ship," Corporal Eckert explained. "But we have mutinied."

"Really?" the pilot asked, a bit surprised. "Well, there are six more of them out there," the copilot informed them.

"Four," Marcus said with no small amount of pride.

"We are aware of the others in your party," Corporal Eckert told her.

"It's not *our* party," she corrected. "We were hijacked before we even took off from Aitkenna."

"It was your captain," the pilot added.

Corporal Eckert's expression soured. Corporal Lewis reached down and rolled the guard over to see his face.

"Commander Tomlinson," Corporal Lewis said, recognizing the man who had been one of his superiors only hours ago.

"Release me and I'll see to it that all of you are spared," the nobleman sputtered.

"I don't think so," Corporal Eckert stated coldly. He pulled out his handgun and dialed it down to its lowest deadly setting and took aim. "Takaran justice for a Takaran nobleman." The corporal fired his weapon, sending a beam of reddish orange into the commander's face, burning a massive gap where his nose had previously been located.

The cargo area was silent. Only the sound of the

commander's still sizzling face could be heard. "Get rid of him," the corporal ordered.

"Are you crazy?" the pilot said. "You can't just execute a man in cold blood like that..."

"I just did..."

"It's not right..."

"Not right?! That man killed three of us during the mutiny. He would've spaced over a hundred others in the blink of an eye. He hijacked your ship, threatened your lives."

"He should have been brought back to face charges," the pilot insisted.

"That's what they did the first time, and look where it got us... fighting for our lives, yet again! No! This is the only thing they understand, strength and force!"

"I'm with you," Marcus chimed in.

"That man was a noble," Corporal Lewis reminded him. "There will be consequences."

"We are already way beyond mere consequences," Corporal Eckert told him.

Two of the volunteers dragged the dead nobleman's body out the back of the shuttle, dumping his corpse unceremoniously on the deck outside.

"I think you should know," the pilot began, "they had us deliver twelve other troops, including your captain and one of our doctors and a nurse, to the other ship, the one from Earth."

"*One* of your doctors?" Corporal Lewis asked. "Where are the others?"

"In there," the pilot told him, pointing to the port cargo storage lockers.

Corporal Lewis opened the locker and saw two men in their underwear. They weren't moving. "Are they dead?" he asked.

"No, just drugged."

"Why are they in their underwear?" Lewis asked as he removed the medevac crew chief's gag.

"They switched places with them, took their clothes," the medevac crew chief explained.

"That's how they got on board the Aurora," Loki realized.

"Why would a Corinairan medevac shuttle be going to your ship?"

"Our XO was badly injured," Loki explained. "That's why our captain took the prisoners down to Corinair. He hoped that by presenting them to the Corinairans as prisoners, it would buy him a favor, medical care for Commander Taylor."

"He's trying to capture the Aurora's jump drive," Marcus surmised. Loki looked at Marcus in shock. "What? I can put a few brain cells together now and again."

"We've gotta tell Ensign Mendez," Loki said as he turned and headed quickly down the boarding ramp.

"Wait, kid!" Marcus called out after him. He turned and looked at Corporal Eckert as he started backing down the ramp to follow Loki. "Can you spare a couple guys, least ways so we don't get lost?"

"You two," Eckert said, pointing to two volunteers, "get them back to command."

* * *

"It's no use!" Willard shouted. "The energy from the boomers is just reflecting off the armor. If we could just hit it head on, we wouldn't lose so much energy to reflection!"

Enrique scanned the foyer. The only way they

could get a straight on shot would be from the second level at the far end. "What about from the back balcony?"

"The only way up there is the far stairs!" Ensign Willard told him. "They would cut you down before you got half way up!"

Enrique continued looking as he fired at the balcony. "What about the floors?"

"The what?"

"The floors! What if we used the boomers to shoot upward from underneath?"

"It's too dangerous!" Willard protested. "You'd never make it there alive! Even if you did, the balcony might collapse on top of you when you opened fire!"

"We need this ship!" Enrique insisted.

"It won't even fly. The engines are shot!"

"The tech on this ship alone is worth saving. It could give the Aurora a chance! It could give Earth a chance!" Enrique knew what he had to do. "Cover me!" he shouted as he made a mad dash for the center station. Willard jumped out and opened up on the balcony again, firing as rapidly as his weapon would allow.

Enrique ran for the center station in the middle of the courtyard, bending over and grabbing the boomer that the previous man had dropped when he had been gunned down moments ago. As he neared the center station, an energy round caught his left shoulder, spinning him around as he fell, his momentum carrying him the last meter to safety behind the big circular metal security station in the middle of the courtyard.

Enrique winced at the pain in his shoulder. He looked at the wound, pulling at his uniform. He was lucky; it had just grazed him. It hurt, and he doubted that he could lift that arm above his head, but he could still use it. He was still in the fight.

He looked around. There were at least six bodies lying around him. Each of them volunteers, members of the Yamaro's crew that had mutinied. They had fought to prevent the death of the rest of their crew still locked in the cargo bays. Those men had not participated in the mutiny; they hadn't even known about it.

Enrique realized someone was yelling at him. Someone on his left. He looked and saw Sergeant Weatherly. He was yelling something, but he couldn't quite make it out above the noise of the energy weapons and the rounds of energy destroying some things and ricocheting off of others. "GRENADES!" Enrique yelled as he reached for another boomer from one of the dead men's hands. "GRENADES!" he yelled to Willard this time. He looked back at Sergeant Weatherly. He was pulling grenades from his pockets. Enrique looked back to Willard. He was doing the same.

Enrique grabbed two grenades of his own, pulled the pins, and tossed them blindly over his head toward the balcony occupied by the enemy. He looked over at Weatherly and saw him tossing a few more. Enrique rolled to his right, using his still good shoulder to struggle to his knees. He closed his eyes as the pain in his shoulder intensified with movement. As luck would have it, the grenades he had just thrown went off, creating a blinding flash and sending a deafening thunder, as well as a sonic shock wave, across the room.

Enrique's hearing had disappeared. Still rising, he opened his eyes just enough to see Willard's arm come down after throwing his own grenades.

He closed his eyes tight and grabbed the counter to steady himself, knowing there were a few more grenades yet to go off.

There were two more flashes, followed by the thunder claps and shock waves, and then two more after that. His head rang and his body felt numb, the shock wave nearly knocked him over. If he hadn't been holding onto the counter, he would've gone down for sure.

In the face of flying debris, Enrique ran around the left side of the counter and charged forward toward the port staircase. Willard and Weatherly, from opposite sides of the room, were firing madly. The few remaining volunteers left alive stepped out into the line of fire to join them. Three more of them were cut down almost immediately. Enrique fired both boomers at the same time. The sound was nearly as horrendous as the stun grenades, but by now his hearing was so muffled that he hardly noticed. He continued running forward with all his strength as energy bolts struck the floor to his left and the center counter to his right. He could feel the heat of every bolt that flew past him, though they made no sound and moved so quickly that he could not see them as they streamed by.

An energy bolt caught his right foot, blowing it clean off the end of his leg. He stumbled forward, screaming, even though he still heard nothing more than a low constant rumble. He hit the deck face first, bloodying his nose if not breaking it.

Everything seemed to be moving in slow motion. His vision was blurred now, probably from the blow to his nose, and he could feel something wet and hot in his mouth and throat, probably blood. He was pretty sure he was sliding along the floor now.

The slide seemed to last forever, but eventually it stopped. He rolled over, his senses reeling, his vision still blurry, and his hearing all but gone. It was darker here, and there was something over him, above him. It was the balcony.

Enrique lifted both arms, looking at his hands. They were both still holding the boomers. He looked upward at the dark shadowy object above him. There were flashes of light coming from the outer edge. He was sure now. It was the balcony from where the enemy was cutting down his men, his friends. He took aim as best he could and fired. Not once, not twice, three times. There were huge flashes of light, and he could feel millions of tiny, burning hot things hitting his body, his arms, his face. Then the light was replaced by something dark coming toward him rapidly.

"NO!" Sergeant Weatherly called out as the balcony collapsed.

Ensign Willard watched in horror from the other side as the balcony fell, landing directly on top of Enrique. The firing stopped. There was nothing left but the sound of bits and pieces of the balcony still falling.

Sergeant Weatherly immediately came rushing out from cover, trying to get to Enrique, but it was no use. That entire section of the balcony had broken apart and come down in several large sections, undoubtedly crushing the brave Ensign. The rest of the balcony had come loose and fallen, hanging now at a forty-five degree angle. The sudden blast had knocked the only remaining member of the Takaran boarding party off the balcony to where he now lay, moaning in pain.

Weatherly stood there for nearly a minute,

staring at the pile of rubble that had just crushed his friend. When he finally realized that the last enemy was still alive and lying next to the heroic ensign, he pulled his handgun out and shot the injured Takaran officer several times in the head, all without even looking at him.

Marcus, Loki, and two more volunteers came running out from the corridor. They were nearly out of breath after running all the way from the hangar deck.

"Holy shit," Loki said as he came to a halt. Marcus and the other two were speechless. Loki looked around. Eighteen men had originally gone to fight this battle. Now there were only four of them left alive. "Where's Ensign Mendez?" Loki asked.

"He's dead," Willard answered.

"What?" Loki couldn't believe what he was hearing.

Willard looked at Loki and the others. "Why are you here?"

"We captured a medevac shuttle on the hangar deck. They brought those guys here. They said they left twelve guys on the Aurora, dressed as doctors or something."

Weatherly immediately turned his head toward Loki, whose words pulled him from his grief and snapped him back to reality. "What did you say?"

"The Aurora has been boarded," Loki told him. "We've got to do something."

"Damn right we do," Sergeant Weatherly announced as he headed back toward the corridor. "Let's move!"

* * *

283

"Did you get it to work?" Deliza asked. She had been holding the flashlight for what seemed like forever, providing light for Vladimir to see what he was doing in the dark tunnel.

"Nyet. I cannot get the routing node to reroute priority data streams to my pad. I cannot convince it that the data pad is a console."

"That's because it's not."

"Really?"

"Sorry," Deliza apologized. "Why don't you just ask it to send you copies of the data stream?"

"I cannot control anything with only copies of the data streams," he told her.

"But at least you'd be able to see what is going on."

Vladimir looked at her for a moment. "Good point." He returned to his data pad and began tapping the on-screen keyboard furiously.

"Thank you."

"Ah, it worked," he said gleefully. "I can see everything: life support, propulsion, main power..." Vladimir suddenly stopped.

"What?"

"Oh bozhe," Vladimir exclaimed.

"What is it? What's wrong?"

"Mister Musavi finished recalibrating the magnetic containment field emitters on the number one antimatter reactor."

"But that's a good thing, right?"

Vladimir looked at her. "He already initiated the automatic restart."

"But that's good. We'll have light in here again..."

"Nyet, Deliza. You do not understand. When the reactor comes back online, they will have full power. They'll be able to get underway. They could even

284

jump the ship... all the way back to Takara."

* * *

"Andre, I'm at the hangar bay now," Bobby said over his comm-set. "I've disabled the jamming pod."

"*Copy. Did you run into any of the crew along the way?*" Andre asked over the comms.

"Just two guys carrying some equipment. I took them both out and stowed them in a nearby cabin."

"*Good. Avoid contact if you can, at least until you hook up with Team Two in engineering. Remember, our numbers are few, so don't take any unnecessary chances now that we have the upper hand.*"

"Understood. Proceeding to engineering. Minimal contact."

Bobby looked around the hangar bay. For a warship, it seemed odd to him that the hangar bay only had a single, outdated, Takaran deep space interceptor, an old cargo shuttle that had seen much better days, and a wrecked spacecraft that was so busted up he couldn't quite tell what kind of ship it had once been. In addition to the odd collection of spacecraft in various stages of disrepair, the forward end of the hangar was filled with crates of varied size and shape. The place looked more like a cargo bay than a flight deck.

* * *

"Lieutenant Brayerton," Captain de Winter's voice called over the nobleman's comm-set.

"Yes, sir."

"We have control of the bridge and engineering. What's your status?"

"All quiet here, sir."

"Good. We'll be conducting a sweep of the ship shortly. When the others join you, eliminate all the prisoners in medical."

The nobleman's eyes widened slightly. He turned away from the prisoners, fearing that they would notice the change in his expression, thus discerning that something was wrong. "All of them, sir?" he said under his breath. "Even the medical staff?"

"All of them, Lieutenant. We haven't the manpower to babysit prisoners whilst flying this ship back to Takara. Is that clear?"

"Yes, sir." The lieutenant tapped his comm-set to end the call. He hadn't expected to have to kill everyone. In fact, he had expected that they would be released and allowed to return to the surface of Corinair in the same medevac shuttle that had brought them here. He saw no reason to murder the medical staff and the wounded. Surely they were no threat to them.

It wasn't right, not even by Takaran practices, which at times could be quite ruthless. Much had changed under the rule of Caius. Those that were willing to do what must be done were rewarded. Those that did not were punished. His career thus far, while unblemished, had also been less than noteworthy. If they managed to get this ship, the magic *jump* ship, the one that destroyed the mighty Campaglia back to the home world, all of that would change. If he had to kill a dozen or so unarmed persons in order to achieve his own acclaims, then so be it. He only hoped that the others would reach him so that he wouldn't have to do it alone.

The lieutenant's thoughts were interrupted by a beeping sound coming from the bio-monitors on the bed in the far back corner of the treatment room. The ship's doctor, a petite woman with short black hair and oriental features, started to rise from her seat against the back wall of the room as if to tend to the cause of the alarm. "What are you doing?" he asked her. "Sit back down!"

The doctor froze, saying something that he could not quite understand. Some of the words seemed familiar yet incorrectly pronounced and in a strange order. She was pointing toward the sound as well.

"I said sit down!" he reiterated, pointing his weapon at her to emphasize his point. The doctor's hands went up in submission, and she again pleaded in her strange language. "I don't understand what you're saying!" he told her.

"She says she needs to tend to the patient," the female Corinairan doctor explained, her hands also up to show that she wasn't trying to present a threat.

"You speak their language?"

"They speak something very similar to Angla."

"You speak Angla?"

"Yes, I learned it in my advanced studies."

"It is a forbidden language," he reminded her. "I could execute you based on your own admission of guilt." He didn't really have any desire to do so, but the excuse might ease his mind about having to execute her later. In fact, if they all spoke a forbidden language, it would give him an excuse under Takaran law.

"Then how would you understand what they're saying?"

"One moment," he instructed her as he activated his comm-set. "Captain, Brayerton."

"Yes, what is it, Lieutenant?"

"The medical staff is requesting permission to

tend to a patient. I believe it is the same patient that the Corinairans were intending on treating."

There was a pause before Captain de Winter responded. *"Allow them to treat whomever they need. If you do not, they may become fearful for their lives and attempt escape. And you are but one man."*

The lieutenant turned away again before speaking. "I am armed, sir, and I'm quite certain I can handle a bunch of doctors."

"Just see that you do, Lieutenant," the captain said before ending the communication.

The Takaran lieutenant turned back to the doctors. "You may treat the patient. But I shall be watching."

"Thank you," the Corinairan doctor said.

* * *

"The static is gone," Willard exclaimed as they jogged through the corridors of the Yamaro on their way from the command center to the port hangar bay. "The comms are working," he added as he tapped his comm-set to open a call. "Corporal Eckert, can you hear me?"

"Yes, I hear you," Eckert answered over the comms. *"What's your status?"*

"We stopped them before they got into command. We are safe for now. And you?"

"We have secured a medevac shuttle..."

"Yes, we heard. We are headed your way now. How many men do you have?"

"There are six of us here."

"We have eight, including the four you sent." There was a pause. Ensign Willard knew that Corporal Eckert was probably shocked that so few had survived the battle.

"*Sir, that means we are down to fourteen total.*"

"There are two more of our guys guarding the prisoners in the cargo bays," Sergeant Weatherly reminded Ensign Willard as they continued their jog back to the port hangar bay.

"They will need to remain at their posts," Willard said. "There will be many among the remaining prisoners who will not be so willing to fight to save the lives of those they were recently trying to kill."

"Wait a minute," Weatherly demanded, grabbing Ensign Willard from behind. The entire group suddenly stopped their jog. "What the hell are you talking about?"

"We need more men if we hope to regain control of your ship," Willard insisted. "Those are the only men at our disposal."

"The pilot said there were twelve of them," Loki added.

"That we know of," Willard corrected. "They may already have been reinforced. Even if they haven't, they are undoubtedly well armed, and perhaps even well trained. And we will not have the element of surprise on our side. They will see us coming."

"I suppose you've got more Corinairans mixed in with the rest of them down there." Sergeant Weatherly challenged him.

"Perhaps. I do not personally know every Corinairan on board."

"Then how can you trust them to fight with us?" Weatherly asked.

It was a reasonable question, one to which Ensign Willard had a reasonable answer.

"If the Ta'Akar take control of the Aurora, they will surely blast this ship and everyone on her to hell. If they fight, at least they have a chance. We have been under the foot of the Ta'Akar for too many decades. Perhaps this is the moment when everything changes."

Sergeant Weatherly looked Ensign Willard in the eyes for several long seconds. He had come to trust this man, as had Enrique, as he suspected Captain Scott would as well. "You'd better be right about this."

"I watched a man I met only an hour ago give his life to save everything and everyone on this ship, on the world below, and on your home world. Now it's our turn." Ensign Willard keyed his comm-set again. "Corporal Eckert. Go to the cargo bays and call for all men who wish to fight for their freedom."

"*Yes, sir.*"

* * *

Deliza thought she heard something. A strange sound of some sort. It was fairly quiet in the tunnels, quiet enough that she could hear the two of them breathe as Vladimir tapped away at his data pad, but the sound kept coming. "Uh, Vladimir?" Deliza said. "Do you hear that?"

"Hear what?"

"That sound."

Vladimir stopped tapping for a moment. His head came up from his data pad, his eyes darting side to side and his head cocking as he tried to locate the sound. He looked down at the floor of the tunnel next to him, at his comm-set that he had taken off and laid there. He picked it up. "It's coming from my comm-set." He put it on and heard voices. "It's working again. I can hear someone talking."

"Who is it?"

"I am not sure. I don't recognize..." Vladimir recognized the next speaker and became excited. "Hello, hello? Can you hear me? Loki, is that you?"

"Yeah, this is Loki. Is that you, Vlad?"

"Da, da, da! It is me. We have been boarded, they have taken engineering and the bridge."

"Cheng, Weatherly. Can you go secure?"

"Yes, of course. One moment." Vladimir took off his comm-set and turned on the encryption before putting it back on. "Weatherly, Cheng. I have gone secure. How do you copy?"

"I hold you same." His voice was tinnier and there were little chirps at the beginning and end of each transmission as a result of the software that automatically encrypted and decrypted the communications at each end. *"Do you have an ID or a force count on the enemy?"*

"Nyet... I mean, negative on both. We only saw five when they tried to take engineering. We took out three of them before escaping into the service tunnels."

"Copy that."

"Where are you? Are you on board?" Vladimir asked, his desperate need for hope evident in his voice.

"Negative, but we're working on it."

"You must act quickly," Vladimir instructed. "We are still running on the backup fusion generator, so the ship cannot break orbit or use any weapons. But the primary antimatter reactor has already begun its auto start sequence. They will have full power in twenty minutes at the most. I believe they will try to escape and take the ship to Takara."

"Yeah, that's what we figured as well."

"Sergeant, we cannot let that happen. Do you understand? Even if it means destroying the ship."

"Understood, sir. Where are you now? Are you secure?"

"Yes, Deliza and I are trapped in the service tunnels. I have managed to access the ship's command and control network using my data pad. I am trying to find way to at least slow them down."

"Copy that. Keep at it. We're putting together a strike team now. We expect to make a boarding attempt in ten or less."

"Can you power up the Yamaro's rail guns? Maybe you can disable us enough to prevent their escape."

"No, sir. We no longer have access to the Yamaro's C&C."

"Why not?"

"We were also boarded, sir. A couple dozen of the Yamaro's crew helped us fight off the enemy, but we had heavy losses and there was a lot of damage." Weatherly paused a moment before continuing. *"We lost Ensign Mendez, sir."*

"Nye mozhet bit!" Vladimir exclaimed. After he composed himself, he muttered the only words that came to mind, "Understood." Vladimir sighed. "Hurry, Sergeant."

"Yes, sir."

Vladimir looked at Deliza. "They will come soon." He tried to look confident, even though for the first time in as long as he could remember, he had his doubts. "Everything will be okay."

Deliza nodded. She could see the doubt in Vladimir's eyes but knew that he would never let anyone know that those doubts existed within him. Her father was the same way.

CHAPTER NINE

There were only a half dozen cells in the Yamaro's brig, so when the Aurora's boarding party had first taken control of the ship immediately after her surrender, her crew had been confined to the two massive cargo bays located aft and below the hangar decks on either side of the ship. The bays were more than large enough to house the nearly three hundred crewmen, and even had toilet facilities as well as plenty of food and water stored in large cargo modules. It was boring, and it was not very comfortable, but they were safe and had one another for company.

The prisoners had broken off into various groups, the most common of which was by planet of origin. While most of the Corinairans had been separated and held in the brig, many of them had never been asked about their place of origin. Most had simply been corralled to the nearest cargo bay for holding until transportation to the surface of Corinair could be arranged.

They had spent much of their time in the cargo bays contemplating their disposition. Most of them had never known who they had been fighting and who it was that had taken them prisoner. Eventually, a few who knew the answers got mixed in with those that did not. Not long after which knew they were being held by people from Earth.

There had even been a rumor that the captain of the Earth ship was the legendary Na-Tan from the Legend of Origins. This spawned from a crewman from communications that had overheard news broadcasts from Corinair about the *sign of Na-Tan* that had been witnessed by tens of thousands the night before. Although most of the crew had dismissed such beliefs as myth before they reached puberty, it had still become the most common topic of conversation during their imprisonment.

There were only a handful of Corinairans in the port cargo bay, eight of them in all. They had soon clustered together, spending much of their time reminiscing about their youth on their shared home world prior to their forced enlistment in the Takaran military. Less than ten percent of those inducted got to serve aboard spaceships. Most inductees were forced to serve as foot soldiers stationed on the surface of some of the worst worlds in the empire. Those stuck on such worlds rarely made it back to their own worlds after their service was fulfilled, instead being left to scratch out a meager existence on whatever world they happened to occupy when they were discharged. That was about the only reason any inductees ever re-enlisted for a second tour.

By comparison, however, those serving on ships had a much better chance of returning home. In fact, if they had served well and were favored by a nobleman of command rank, they might even be able to serve a few extra months in exchange for passage to at least get close to their planet of origin.

Dexter lay on the large crate, his legs dangling over the edge as he stared at the ceiling high above him. "I don't care if he was trying to protect the home world," he announced, interrupting the two men arguing from atop the crate next to him. "He had no right to put us all in this predicament. I was three days from getting out, I was. And Lieutenant Brayerton favored me, he did. I was sure to get an early boot so as to return home."

"And what would you have returned home to, Dex?" one of the other men argued. "We were bombing the hell out of our own world, our mothers and fathers, our lads and ladies. If not for that Na-Tan fella, we'd have no home to go to."

"I'm not convinced of that, Sal. The captain had a few tricks left up his sleeve, he did."

"You heard the others, Dex. That Earth ship just kept appearing out of nowhere, slipping inside our shields and hammering away at us, then disappearing again just as magically as she had appeared to begin with. How the hell was the captain gonna defend against that?"

"He'd a found a way. I'd bet my life on it."

"Well, it's certainly nice to know that you've got so much faith in the Lord de Winter," his friend jeered.

Dexter sat up with a start. "I've got no faith in the bastard, Sal. You know that as well as anyone. But I *do* know what a sneaky little weasel he can be when he puts his mind to it."

Their conversation was interrupted when the cargo doors began to open. Splitting down the middle, they slid slowly to either side just enough to allow a man to pass between the doors before they stopped moving. No sooner had they stopped than five members of the Yamaro's crew stepped through the opening.

"Well I'll be damned," Dexter said, recognizing

that his fellow Corinairans were heavily armed. "They've taken back the ship!" he announced, jumping down from his crate to follow the others as they crowded the area in front of the exit.

"Remain where you are!" Corporal Eckert ordered.

"What's the good word?" Dexter asked.

"We need volunteers," the corporal announced, "Corinairan volunteers."

"Volunteers for what?" someone shouted.

"Captain de Winter and his staff managed to escape from Corinair and we believe he has taken control of the Earth ship. We intend to take it back."

"Are you joking?" Dexter asked. The crowd agreed, and the level of noise increased drastically as the crowd began to shout out questions and talk amongst themselves.

"Quiet down!" Corporal Eckert ordered. "They already tried to take back this ship, but we stopped them."

"We?" Dexter wondered. "Have you gone over to the other side now?"

"They fight for *us*," the corporal told them, "for *all* of us. They fight and they die, not only for Corinair, but for everyone."

"Against the Ta'Akar?" Dexter shouted in disbelief. "That'll be a short battle!"

Corporal Eckert looked at Dexter. "Those people died protecting you, Dex."

"Weren't no one shooting at us, Eckie, least ways not that I noticed."

"If they take control of the Aurora, they will destroy this ship to keep it out of the hands of the Corinari."

The prisoners exploded at the news. If the Yamaro was going to become a target they wanted off as soon as possible. Corporal Eckert realized that he had no right to keep them locked up on a ship that could be under fire at any moment. Especially since they had no way to defend themselves.

"Any Corinairans who are willing to fight, follow me now," Corporal Eckert told them.

"What about those of us who aren't?" Dexter asked. "You gonna give us a ride down to the surface?"

"We don't have any shuttles available," Corporal Eckert said.

"What about the Corinairans? Surely they can send up a few transports?"

"Corinair is in turmoil. Between the bombardment and the riots..."

"Riots?" Dexter interrupted. "What riots?"

"Between Loyalists and Followers, at least that's what we heard."

"The escape pods!" someone shouted.

"Yes, of course," Corporal Eckert agreed. "Anyone wishing to get off the ship is free to use an escape pod. That should get you safely to the surface. Now, those who wish to fight for their freedom, for the freedom of Corinair, step forward now."

Corporal Eckert watched as one by one, eight men stepped forward. Dexter hadn't moved.

Sal turned around and looked at Dexter. "Get your ass over here, Dex, or I'll rat you out to your mum when I get back to the surface." Dexter shook his head and reluctantly stepped forward.

The tenth man to join was someone that Corporal Eckert did not recognize. "Where are you from?" he asked the man as he put his hand out to stop him from advancing.

"Omotosso," the man answered.

"This is not your fight. You are not of this world."

"The way I see it, sooner or later, this is gonna be everyone's fight." The corporal stared at him for a moment, unsure if he should allow the Omotossan to join them. "Besides, you ever been to Omotosso?" he said with a dour smile. "Consider me an immigrant."

"As you wish," the corporal agreed, nodding his head in respect as he turned and lead the group of volunteers out the door.

"Good of you to join us, Dex," Sal teased.

"Escape pods are death traps anyway," Dex grumbled as they followed the corporal out of the cargo bay.

"I guess you'd know, wouldn't you."

"What are you trying to say?" Dexter asked defensively.

"Nothing just making an observation. I mean, you are the escape pod maintenance technician, aren't you?"

"Careful," Dexter warned.

* * *

"Sir," Andre said, "we still have not been able to raise Team Three."

"What about the medevac shuttle?" de Winter asked.

"They are also not responding."

"Are they still on the Yamaro?"

"Yes, sir. They have not moved since they landed."

"Damn," de Winter cursed. "I was hoping to get at least a few loyal crewmen over to help man this ship for the voyage back to Takara." The captain's demeanor quickly changed, lightening up. "Oh well. I guess there's nothing else keeping us here, is there?" Captain de Winter walked around and sat down in the command chair in the middle of the command podium. "As soon as full power is restored, I want you to target all weapons on the Yamaro, Sergeant. I don't want to leave anything behind for the Corinairans to salvage."

"Yes, sir."

Captain de Winter sat confidently in the command chair as he contemplated his triumphant return to Takara. While no captain had ever returned to the home world after losing their ship to an enemy in battle, neither had any captain ever returned with a prize that would change the entire future of the empire. Caius would have no choice but to bestow the rank of admiral upon him, making him the first in his long family line to have achieved such rank. Money, lands, and power would soon follow, and his less than stellar early career would be a distant memory. No longer would he spend his days rotting in a warship out in the cold of space. The rest of his days would be spent under the golden sun of Takara, reveling in the trappings of his position and status in Takaran society.

"Captain," Andre added. "I should also point out that we have been unable to make contact with Commander Dumar, and there are only ten minutes left in which to do so, or he will launch a strike against both ships."

"Why have you not been able to contact them?"

"You shot the comm-station, sir," Andre reminded him, gesturing toward the damaged station with the body of the dead comm-officer still lying against it.

"Yes, of course."

"If we could reach the medevac shuttle, we could have them send word..."

"Not to worry, Sergeant," de Winter assured him. "It will take at least ten minutes for the missiles to reach us, by which time full power will have been restored and we will simply disappear."

"Don't you think that's cutting it a little close?"

"Do you have any suggestions, Sergeant?"

"Send the sweep team back to the hangar deck. There were a couple of old ships in there: a cargo shuttle and an old Takaran interceptor. Maybe they can get one of their long-range comm units working."

"Very well," de Winter agreed. "See to it, Sergeant."

* * *

"Gentlemen," Bobby greeted his fellow agents as he entered the Aurora's engineering section. "Situation?"

"All secure here, sir."

"And what about the two that escaped?" Bobby asked.

"They went into the service tunnel in the next room. We locked the hatch behind them. We checked the layout, and as best we could tell, they could move around quite a bit in there. It's like a maze. But it also looks like all the exits are closed."

"*Bobby, come in,*" Andre called over the comms.

"Go ahead, Andre."

"*Where are you?*"

"I'm in engineering. I'm about to start my sweep forward."

"*That can wait,*" Andre told him. "*I want you to go back to the hangar deck, see if you can get the long-range comms working in one of those old ships, and get a status report back to Commander Dumar so he doesn't try to shoot us out of orbit anytime soon.*"

"Understood. We're on our way." Bobby turned to the two agents. "Which one of you is best at comm repairs?"

"I am," the second agent said. "Why?"

"We've got an urgent call to make."

* * *

Two columns of fifteen men jogged into the Yamaro's port hangar bay. They were all carrying energy rifles and handguns. In addition, they each wore the torso section of Takaran assault armor as well as the helmets complete with their built in comm gear. They also had stun grenades on the gun belts worn around their waists.

Ensign Willard looked surprised as the columns of heavily armed troops made their way across the massive bay. Corporal Eckert noticed the stunned look on the Ensign's face as he drew closer.

"We took the time to raid the nearest armory on our way over," the corporal told Ensign Willard. "We didn't have time to don all the armor, so we just chose the pieces most likely to keep us alive."

"Good thinking, Corporal."

"Do you wish to address the men, sir?"

"No time for that now, Corporal. I'll brief them en route. Get them on board."

"It's going to be packed tight in there," Marcus pointed out.

"Luckily, it's a short trip," Willard reminded him.

"Come on, kid," Marcus said, grabbing Loki by the shoulder. "Let's get on board first. The last ones in are the first ones out and the first to die."

Sergeant Weatherly watched as the two columns of heavily armed Corinairans, who had moments ago still been members of an enemy crew, made their way past and up the boarding ramp into the medevac shuttle. "You are going to tell them not to shoot at us, right?"

Ensign Willard smiled. "Do not worry, Sergeant. We are not going to take the Aurora from you," he said with a pat on the sergeant's shoulder. "We intend to take it *from* the Takarans and *return* it to you."

"Just checking," he said as he turned to follow the men into the shuttle.

* * *

Commander Dumar watched the tactical map displayed on the planning table in front of him. "How long to max range?"

"The Corinari interceptors will reach maximum missile range in five minutes, sir," the lieutenant reported.

"Any word yet from Captain de Winter or Sergeant Tukalov?"

"No, sir, and we've been hailing them repeatedly for some time now. They still have fifteen minutes to their deadline, sir."

The commander frowned and rubbed his chin. "Unfortunately, we're going to lose our only orbital strike asset in less than five minutes."

"Yes, sir."

"Tell the Aitkenna team to re-target their missiles: two on the Aurora and two on the Yamaro. Tell them to launch immediately and then abandon the site before it's too late."

"Yes, sir."

"And continue trying to hail Sergeant Tukalov,"

the commander added.

* * *

The two black interceptors streaked through the night, skimming the treetops at four times the speed of sound as they closed on the Aitkenna missile base. Although the Aitkenna site had been closer to their base than the Wellerton site, the Aitkenna installation had only four of her original twenty missiles left. The Wellerton site had been fully loaded, hence her twenty missiles were of far more danger in the hands of others than the Aitkenna site had been and therefore had been dealt with first.

If the interceptor wing based at the Aitkenna spaceport had been at full strength, both targets could have easily been dealt with simultaneously. However, all but two of their wing had gone up to fight the Yamaro during her bombardment of Corinair. These two interceptors were the only ones left in the immediate area.

"Command, Black Dog One. Locked on target. Max range in thirty seconds. Requesting weapons free."

Black Dog One, Command, the controller's voice responded. *You are cleared to engage, max force.*

"Black Dog One copies. Twenty seconds to launch."

The pilot looked down at his targeting display on the forward console, located just above the center console they jokingly referred to as the *nut buster.* His long-range missiles showed that they were locked on the Aitkenna missile site. He reached over to the left side of his console and flipped a switch to arm the selected weapon. "Two scooters armed," he announced. With his right thumb, he flipped a small switch on the side of the flight control stick being held by his right hand. "Pickle is hot. Ten seconds."

He watched as the range display rapidly ticked away the distance to the maximum effective range of the long-range, hypersonic cruise missiles that they referred to as scooters. The scrolling number still displayed in red as it rapidly approached zero. A few seconds later, it turned green, flashed the phrase *Max Range* three times and then continued counting down, this time the distance to the target.

The pilot depressed the firing button on the side of his flight control stick with his thumb two times. "Scooter two. Scooter two," he declared, announcing the launch of two scooter missiles.

Outside the interceptor, two panels along the underside of the fuselage quickly slid open. A split second later, two weapons, each just under three meters in length and about a meter across dropped out of the aircraft and fell away. They looked like flattened cigars, with stubby wings at the nose and slightly larger ones at the tail. A moment later the first weapon's engine fired and the missile streaked ahead of the interceptor. The second missile did the same, and within seconds the two weapons had accelerated to more than ten times the speed of sound. A moment later, the same process played out under the second interceptor as well.

The pilot watched his weapons display as the missiles rocketed ahead of him. "Tracking four scooters, four locks. Time to impact: three minutes."

"Copy Black Dog flight. Command is tracking four good scooters."

The scooters were fire-and-forget weapons under normal circumstances, but this entire day had been anything but normal, and the pilot chose to continue on toward his target, just in case. He and his wingman each carried two more scooters, as well as several short-range missiles that were nearly as deadly against a ground target. If the first scooters missed, he might have time for another round.

* * *

"We've got incoming ordnance!" the sensor operator announced. "Four scooters, two minutes out."

The squad leader spun his head to his left to look at the missile operator.

"Re-targeting complete," the missile operator announced, and not a moment too soon.

"Launch all missiles!" the squad leader ordered.

The missile operator looked at the squad leader as he moved over and put his hand on the second missile launch key at the other end of the console, just over four meters away.

"Launch in three......two......one......launch."

Both men turned their missile launch keys to the firing position. Everyone watched the main tracking screen on the wall in front of them. A row of twenty screens across the top of the main screen showed all the missile silos, of which only four were left. The other sixteen missiles had been launched at the Yamaro earlier in the day. They watched as the four missiles rose from their silos, clearing the ground level doors and leaping into the dawn's breaking light outside.

"Four good launches," the missile operator announced. "Turning over control of all weapons to command."

"Tell that Kalibri to meet us on the roof now!" the squad leader ordered. "We've got a minute and a half until this based is turned into slag!" he added as everyone rose from their seats and started out the door.

* * *

The medevac shuttle flew out of the Yamaro's port hangar deck and into space, heading toward the aft end of the ship. As soon as it cleared the launch tunnel, it turned to starboard heading away from the Yamaro and toward the Aurora. It was flying a bit faster than normal, despite the fact that the Aurora was quite nearby, as they had little time to spare.

* * *

"*Cheng, Weatherly. Inbound, ETA three mikes,*" Sergeant Weatherly reported over the comm-set. "*Any idea how we're gonna get the hangar doors open?*"

"Yes, but it is rather drastic," Vladimir admitted.

"*Talk to me, Cheng.*"

"The doors are designed to open automatically for any ship trying to enter while the ship's power is down. This is to facilitate rescue of the crew if the ship is dead in space."

"*Are you telling me you're gonna turn the ship off?*"

"I said it was drastic," Vladimir defended.

"*That's not drastic, Sir; that's crazy.*"

"Drastic, crazy, same thing," he said as he tapped buttons on the data pad.

"*Any other ideas,*" Weatherly asked, "*like, maybe just opening the doors?*"

"Nyet. All data streams from the bridge have command priority. If I tried to open the doors, they would simply override them, and then they would know that you were coming as well."

"*Don't they already know?*" Weatherly asked. "*I mean, can't they see us coming.*"

"That is why I am shutting everything down...... right......now!" Vladimir tapped the key on his data pad to send the command string he had just written.

"What did you just do?" Deliza asked. Even though she had heard every word he had said to the sergeant, she still couldn't believe it.

"I turned the ship off," Vladimir said calmly.

"You what? How can you do that? All that stuff about command data streams having priority and..."

"The command string I sent does not take effect until after each and every element has already reached its destination." Vladimir looked at the time indicator on the data pad. "It should happen in a few seconds."

She looked at him, a smile forming on her face. "You made a cyber-bomb."

"Da," Vladimir answered confidently.

"But what about gravity and life support and..."

"It is not a problem," Vladimir interrupted. "Artificial gravity systems in main areas are self-powered. They have backup generators that will run for hours."

"What about the environmental systems?" Deliza wondered.

"Do not worry, there is plenty of air to breath, even without the recyclers. We would freeze long before we would suffocate," he assured her. Deliza just looked at him. Vladimir ignored her expression as he checked the ship's digital time display on his data pad again. "Ship will power down, right...now."

All throughout the Aurora, everything began to quickly shutdown. Lights began shutting off everywhere, plunging the entire ship into complete darkness. A moment later, all the circulation fans that constantly cycled air throughout the ship also shut down. The ship was now as dark and as silent as it could possibly be. A few moments later, emergency battery powered lighting started to kick on in key areas of the ship such as the bridge, medical, engineering, and the hangar bay. In addition, small battery-powered lights evenly spaced along the bottom edge of the ship's many corridors also lit up. The lights would all run for several hours, after which handheld units would be the only source of light available. It would take the oxygen many more hours to diminish down to levels that would no longer support life, especially considering how few people were left on board.

* * *

The pilot of the medevac shuttle looked out the forward windows of his ship just as the Aurora's running lights all turned off.

"What the..."

The copilot also looked out the window. "What happened?"

"Uh, somebody!" the pilot called out.

Loki came forward through the narrow passageway to see what was wrong in the cockpit. As soon as he got there, he saw what they were talking about. "She's dark!" Loki turned around. "Hey, Sarge! All the Aurora's lights just went out!"

The sergeant pushed his way forward between the men. They were packed into the cargo area of the small medevac shuttle, shoulder to shoulder. "Holy shit!" he exclaimed as he arrived in the cockpit. "The crazy bastard did it." He turned and shouted toward the cargo bay. "It looks like we're in business!"

* * *

"Sir, the medevac shuttle..."

Andre never finished his sentence as the lights on the bridge all went dark. A moment later, emergency lighting kicked in, washing the room in an amber-white glow.

"What's happening?" de Winter demanded, suddenly standing and waving his little gun around to make sure none of the Aurora's crew tried anything.

Both nobles guarding the room stepped forward, their weapons held high and ready.

Andre looked at his console. There were no lights, no displays. It was completely dead. He looked around the bridge. All the other consoles were also dead. He also noticed that the circulation fans had stopped, resulting in an unsettling lack of background noise.

"We've lost all power," Andre said, not quite believing it was possible even though he was witnessing it happen.

"That's not possible," Captain de Winter.

"Apparently it is," Andre disagreed.

"Maybe we damaged this ship more than we

thought in the first place."

"I don't think so, sir," Andre said. "Just before the power went out, I saw the medevac shuttle leaving the Yamaro."

"Maybe their comms are down and they're simply returning to report in person."

"More likely they've failed and those are more of the Aurora's crew returning," Andre offered. "Either way, we'd better get someone down there."

Andre didn't wait for approval from Captain de Winter. "Bobby, Lian, double-time it for the hangar deck. We may have hostiles inbound. We'll meet you there."

"*Copy. We're on our way*," Bobby reported.

"*On my way*," Lian reported from engineering.

Andre pointed at one of the nobles, "You, come with," he ordered as he headed out.

"Wait!" de Winter shouted. "We need to hold this bridge!"

"There's only three of them, two of which are women. The two of you are armed. Besides, if they are attacking we need to stop them while they're still bottled up in the shuttle."

* * *

The lights in the medical treatment room all went out at once, plunging the room into complete darkness. Lieutenant Brayerton had been standing at the foot of Commander Taylor's bed in order to keep an eye on what the doctors were up to as they treated the patient while still keeping an eye on everyone else in the room.

"NOBODY MOVE!" the lieutenant ordered, his voice slightly panicked. There was an electronic whine that started low in pitch. It was coming from his left, where the doctors had been working on their patient. The whine quickly rose in tone and within two seconds it was inaudible to the human ear.

The emergency lighting kicked in, flooding the room with dim, amber-hued light coming from battery-powered lighting in the upper corners of the room. When the lieutenant's eyes managed to refocus in the subdued lighting, he realized someone was holding two oval metal objects up to his face and coming at him. The objects were attached to the wall next to the gurney with long, coiled, insulated wires.

"CLEAR!" Doctor Chen shouted. There was a blue flash of light as energy leapt from the defibrillator paddles in the doctor's hands to the lieutenant's face. A loud *pop* was heard and the Takaran nobleman fell in a heap to the floor.

A nearby patient moved into action, nearly falling out of his bed as he did so. His monitoring leads pulled loose from his body and started setting off alarms on the bio-monitor on the wall above his bed. His IV line ripped free from the puncture site on the inside of his elbow, sending blood trickling down his arm as he stumbled over and nearly fell on top of the unconscious enemy lieutenant. The man used his good arm to pull the rifle away from the Takaran and remove his handgun from his holster, tossing it to Cassandra who stood nearby watching in shock.

"Nice move, Doc," the crewman congratulated her. "But why'd you warn him?"

"What?" Doctor Chen asked. She was standing there, still holding the defibrillator paddles in her hands, stunned by the fact that she had just sent three hundred joules of electrical energy into a man's head.

"Clear?" the crewman reminded her.

"Oh, that. Just habit I guess." She looked at the paddles, realized that she no longer needed them, and set them back into their hooks on the wall of Commander Taylor's treatment cubicle.

"Are you okay, Doctor?" Cassandra asked, noticing the look on Doctor Chen's face.

"Yes, I'm fine," she promised, her composure returning. "Give me that," she ordered, taking the handgun from Cassandra. "We should check the corridor for others."

* * *

"They've fired," the lieutenant announced. "We're tracking four scooters headed for the Aitkenna site."

Commander Dumar didn't even raise his head. "Has the Aitkenna site launched?"

"Wait one," the lieutenant said, raising his hand with one finger as he listened to reports coming in over his comm-set.

Commander Dumar grew impatient. "Lieutenant?"

"Confirmed, sir. Aitkenna base reports four good launches. We have control of all four, and the team is bugging out now. They've got one minute to get clear before the incoming missiles take out the base."

"Very well," the commander sighed. If the Aurora was still in good shape, there was a pretty good chance she would either jump away before the missiles struck or power out of orbit under normal propulsion. Either way she would avoid destruction. There was nothing he could do about it now. Either it would work or it would not. At least the Yamaro would be destroyed, as she had neither the shields nor the propulsion to avoid her fate. Either way, this would all be over in ten minutes.

* * *

Ensign Willard stood at the forward end of the tightly packed cargo compartment of the medevac shuttle. "Gentlemen, listen up! A man on the inside has managed to shut the Aurora completely down, so we're going into a dark ship with minimal emergency lighting. We have no idea what to expect. We know that there are at least twelve enemy targets on board, but there could be more, a lot more. We do not expect any of the Aurora's surviving crew to be armed, so if you see someone with a weapon, kill them on the spot. And no boomers. We don't know enough about this ship to know where it's safe to use them and where it's not. So leave them behind just to be safe."

Willard looked at the men, who were all standing at packed into the small cabin shoulder to shoulder. "We have to assume they know we're coming, so expect heavy resistance when the doors open. Your best chance of survival is to get out of the ship quickly and spread out. Find cover as quickly as you can." Willard looked around again then looked forward toward Sergeant Weatherly in the cockpit. The sergeant held up one finger. Willard turned back toward the men. "One minute!"

He looked over the volunteers. They were all Corinairans, with the exception of one man from Earth, two men from Haven, and one rather large Omotossan. They were all young, mostly between the ages of twenty to twenty five. They had all gone through basic combat training at the beginning of their forced service to the Ta'Akar, but none of them had the type of training required for what they were about to attempt. He wished at that moment that he had a shuttle full of Corinari warriors, who were highly trained and ready to give their lives in defense of their world. Nevertheless, these men, despite their inadequate training, were about to make the same sacrifice. They deserved the same respect, and the same pride.

From the front of the compartment, Ensign Willard straightened up and shouted, "CORINARI!"

In unison, the volunteers responded, "HUP! HUP! HUP!"

Dexter and Sal stood at the back of the shuttle. Each of them looked at the other.

"I don't think we're in the most favored position back here, Sal," Dexter said.

"Yeah, you could be right about that."

"Relax, guys," the Omotossan told them. "At least you'll die fighting for your own world instead of someone else's."

Dexter turned and looked over his shoulder at the Omotossan. "Thanks. That helps a lot, really."

* * *

"How did we do?" Nathan asked Jessica as they made their way back through the corridors to the command center.

"Tug did fine," she said. "You, on the other hand, said way too much, as usual," Jessica smiled at him, "exactly as I figured you would."

"I guess it's a good thing that I didn't go into politics," Nathan admitted. "I don't think that speech is going to move any mountains."

"Do not worry, Captain," Tug said. "I believe your straight-to-the-point style will have the desired effect."

"I hope you're right," Nathan said as they entered the command center again.

Without warning, cheering erupted from the main floor below them. Nathan and the others looked to the main display screen. All the missile tracks had vanished.

"What happened?" Nathan asked.

"The Hakai missiles were destroyed," Tug realized by listening to the chatter as they entered the room. He was obviously surprised himself. "The Melentorans must have re-targeted to intercept the incoming missiles only, instead of retaliating against Hakai."

"Perhaps your speech had the desired effect after all," the Prime Minister's aide offered.

"Well at least one country on this rock doesn't have their head up their ass," Jessica said, quite loudly.

The Prime Minister's aide turned to her as he spoke. "I'm not sure how the word *ass* translates into Corinairan. I expect it would be best not to try."

The cheers were short-lived as another launch alarm sounded. Nathan already knew what that sound meant, his head turning to the left to look at the main display screens in the room below. Four stubby lines appeared coming from the Aitkenna missile site.

"Now what?" Nathan asked.

"The Aitkenna missile site has launched," the aide stated.

"Who are they targeting?"

"We do not yet know. They are still climbing."

"What does that mean?" Nathan asked, fearing he already knew the answer.

"Either their target is on the other side of the planet or it's..."

"...orbital," Nathan finished for him. "We need to contact my ship."

"Yes, of course, Captain," the aide promised, signaling to one of the technicians in the room. "Immediately."

"I thought you were going to take out that base," Jessica wondered aloud.

"We are trying," the aide defended. "As you can see, the interceptors have already launched their missiles."

"Too late," Jessica scolded.

One of the communications technicians spoke to the aide in Corinairan.

"What did he say?" Nathan asked.

"The Aurora is not answering their hails," Tug translated.

"We will continue trying, Captain," the aide assured him.

Nathan felt a cold chill go down his spine.

* * *

"TEN SECONDS!" Willard shouted from the front of the medevac's cargo bay.

As the boarding ramp began to lower, Dexter closed his eyes, not wanting to see the deadly shot that he was sure was about to hit him, but nothing happened, except that he was pushed forward by the Omotossan behind him. He opened his eyes and charged down the ramp, raising his weapon to firing position as he descended. Sal was to his

316

right as they descended the boarding ramp together, followed by the rest of the Corinari volunteers. Each column peeled off in opposite directions, fanning out on either side of the shuttle.

The medevac shuttle had rolled straight into the middle of the dimly lit hangar bay. Vladimir had been correct in his assumptions. The entire transfer process through the airlock had been completely automated, the system being powered by its own emergency power generation systems that activated when the system sensed a ship trying to enter the hangar. Luckily, it had assumed they were a rescue ship. The flight crew of the medevac shuttle watched through the front windows as the men disembarked out the rear. So far, they saw no signs of the enemy, but that would change in a moment.

Bobby was not an amateur. He had taken one of the agents with him to the starboard side of the hangar bay and sent the other agent to port, hoping to trap whoever was trying to come on board in a crossfire. Had the boarding party come up the center of the bay, his plan would have worked beautifully. However, the volunteers from the Yamaro's crew had come out of the back of the shuttle and immediately spread to either side of the bay looking for cover.

Bobby stepped into the hatchway of the dimly lit hangar deck and immediately opened fire on the column of men coming around the starboard side of the medevac shuttle. He had already taken out three men when the other agent stepped in next to him and joined in the attack. Within seconds, half the starboard column was either dead or injured, and the rest were scrambling for cover that simply wasn't there. The best they could do was hug the bulkheads of the hangar bay, trying to tuck in behind the vertical beams protruding slightly from the walls. Unable to step out to take aim, the volunteers simply held out their weapons and fired blindly. Since most of them were technicians who hadn't fired a weapon since basic training years ago, their fire was ineffective at best.

Red and amber bolts of energy danced back and forth between the two forces for several minutes. On either side of the massive bay, the volunteers were pinned up against the walls with no decent cover from which to effectively return fire. The only good cover was toward the front of the hangar bay, and the enemy firing positions were between the volunteers and the forward end of the bay. It was only a matter of time until they were picked off one by one.

"We've got them pinned down in the aft end of the hangar deck!" Bobby reported over his comm-set.

"We're approaching medical!" Andre responded as they jogged down the corridor headed aft. "We'll be there in two minutes!"

"Come in from the forward end of the bay!" Bobby told him. *"You've got good cover and you'll be able to pick them off easily!"*

"Copy that!"

Doctor Chen leaned out the doorway into the corridor. She could hear the sounds of energy weapons fire coming from the hangar bay. "I hear something." She turned to see Crewman Davies limping over with the rifle in his good hand.

"What is it?" he asked.

"It sounds like weapons fire."

Davies listened for himself. "It's coming from the hangar bay." Then he heard something else. "Someone's coming," he said as he quickly closed the hatch. He listened as the footfalls passed them by then cracked the hatch just enough to see two of the enemy soldiers running towards the hangar bay. "Two bad guys just ran past. I think they're headed for the hangar bay."

"Do you think our guys are fighting back?" Doctor Chen asked.

"Probably," he said as he stepped through the hatch.

"Where do you think you're going?" she demanded.

"Those two guys running toward the fight can't be good news for our side," he said. "Maybe I can sneak up behind them and take them out."

"You can barely walk! You should be in bed!"

"I can go back to bed later, Doc," he insisted as he started limping down the corridor.

Doctor Chen turned to Cassandra. "Keep everyone inside and lock the hatch after I leave."

Cassandra, her eyes wide, nodded agreement.

Andre and the Takaran nobleman entered the hangar deck and took up positions behind some cargo crates. After sizing up the layout, Andre immediately opened fire, picking off the Corinari volunteers with ease. The nobleman tried as well but was not as successful. Within seconds, another four men had fallen to Andre's marksmanship.

"We've got new shooters at twelve o'clock!" Weatherly hollered over the comm-set. He was stuck behind one of the forward-most upright beams along the port bulkhead of the hangar bay and was having a hard time getting any shots off without revealing himself so much that he might get hit himself. Normally, he would've charged forth into the jaws of death. However, other than Marcus and Loki—both of which were still in the medevac shuttle—he was the only member of the group that even knew where the bridge was located. "Their angle is too good. We're getting torn up out here."

"They're getting slaughtered," the copilot exclaimed. "We've got to do something."

"Hold on," the pilot announced. The pilot quickly fired up the shuttles engines again. "Ensign Willard!" the pilot called over his comm-set. "Tell everyone to get down!"

"*What?*"

"I've got an idea!"

"What are you going to do?"

"You'll know it when it happens!"

The pilot began inching the ship slowly forward, moving deeper into the hangar bay. As he progressed, he angled the ship to the right. He continued rolling forward until he was just about even with the port and starboard hatches from which the enemy troops were firing. Moments later, he turned sharply to port, coming to an abrupt stop when his nose was facing the port hatchway.

"Disengage the automatic thrust pod controls and go manual," he ordered his copilot.

She quickly began punching buttons on her side console. A moment later she responded. "Thrust pods set to manual."

"Swing the forward pods straight ahead and the aft pods to the rear!"

"Yes, sir," she answered as she realized what he was up to.

The pilot looked out the forward window directly into the eyes of the enemy shooter in the port hatchway. He watched as the shooter's eyes widened when he saw the thrust pods swinging up toward him. The shooter started firing madly at the cockpit windows, shattering them.

"Get down!" the pilot ordered as he ducked to his left onto the center console.

The copilot was not fast enough and took an energy blast straight to her face, killing her instantly.

"Everyone get under the middle of the ship!" the pilot ordered over the comm-set. "NOW! NOW! NOW!"

Outside the shuttle in the Aurora's hangar bay, the surviving volunteers all began firing wildly as they made a mad dash toward the middle of the shuttle, which now sat astride the hangar deck with her nose pointed to port and her tail pointed to starboard. Her forward engine pods had rotated up and forward and her aft pods had rotated up and back. As the men scrambled to her midsection, she fired all four of her thrust pods at once. They weren't even at one tenth of their maximum power, but the roar inside the hangar bay was deafening.

Andre and the nobleman saw what was happening. The thrust from the medevac shuttle was preventing any of those men from even sticking their guns through the hatch to fire.

Andre rose up and started pouring fire under the sideways shuttle in an attempt to kill the men now scrambling underneath to get into position to open fire on the port and starboard hatches. As he also stood to fire, a blast from behind sent the nobleman next to Andre flying forward, falling over his cover to land in a smoldering heap on the other side. Andre quickly spun around and fired madly, charging back through the hatch into the corridor in pursuit of the assailants.

The shuttles engine's died down again and the volunteers charged forward toward both the port and starboard hatches, firing madly as they advanced. Several more of them fell to enemy fire as they charged through the hatchways, but within seconds the Takaran agents were cut down by overwhelming numbers.

More volunteers charged forward toward the hatchway at the far end of the hangar bay where only moments ago a third set of shooters had been firing.

"Regroup! Regroup!" Willard shouted. Now that the bay was clear he knew he needed to get his men back together in order to complete their mission.

"We've gotta push forward and get to the bridge!" Sergeant Weatherly told him. "The other shooter went back into the forward corridors. Give me a few guys so I can chase him down."

"Give me a minute to regroup," Willard said. His men were scattered about, and the entire bay was in chaos, with small fires having broken out due to the thrust from the medevac shuttle's engines.

"We don't have a minute," Weatherly argued. He looked about and spied Marcus and Loki coming down the ramp of the medevac shuttle. Their assignment had been to guard the ship and prevent any un-friendlies from entering. "You two," he yelled, pointing at Marcus and Loki, "Come with me!"

Willard watched as Marcus and Loki went jogging past on their way forward in pursuit of Sergeant Weatherly who was nearly to the hatchway at the forward end of the bay by now. He looked about and spotted Dexter, Sal, and the Omotossan returning through the starboard hatchway. "You three, follow them!"

Andre came charging down the corridor in pursuit of the people that had shot the nobleman next to him from behind. As he turned the corner, he saw two people duck into a side room.

Doctor Chen suddenly found herself tumbling forward into the darkness, her momentum carrying her forward as she floated about a meter and a half above the floor, rotating head over heels at a forty-five degree angle to the deck. It had never occurred to her that while the ship was powered down, not every compartment would have gravity.

There was just enough light coming in from the open hatch behind her to see the rows of plush, high-backed chairs just before she slammed into them shoulder first. She managed to grab hold of the back of the first chair and prevent herself from careening over the top of them and continuing across the room. She looked around quickly and saw Crewman Davies scrambling to push himself down off the ceiling.

The darkness was pierced by a sudden flash of light and the sound of an energy weapon being discharged. She screamed briefly as she saw Crewman Davies go tumbling across the room, smoke and blood wafting from his smoldering chest wound. She turned toward the hatch and saw the same Takaran soldier that had tortured her earlier. Her gun still in hand she raised her weapon and fired several times, but she found it nearly impossible to get a good aim while floating in zero gravity.

Despite her poor aim, Andre felt it best to duck back from the hatchway in case she got lucky. He peeked carefully around the edge of the hatch, speaking calmly to her. "Relinquish your weapon and I will let you live."

"Fuck you!" Doctor Chen declared in anger as she raised her arm and fired again.

Her shots were even more off target this time, as her body movements were causing her to rotate away from the hatch slightly. Andre peeked around the edge of the hatchway again and saw that she would no longer have a good angle to fire until she finished rotating back around.

He stepped into the hatchway and took aim, responding to her declaration. "I think not," he stated as he moved his finger to the trigger button to fire.

It was too late. An energy blast struck him in the back of the head, blowing the back side of it clean off, sending bits and pieces flying in all directions. With the force coming from behind him, most of the blood and tissue sprayed into the weightless room, drifting toward the doctor.

Doctor Chen whimpered in disgust, her eyes closed as the dead Takaran's blood and tissue began striking her about her face and upper body. When she opened her eyes again, she found that the dead man's body was floating toward her. In a gruesome fashion, the dead Takaran's body continued floating forward, passing by her and traveling across the room until it reached the far side where it collided with the floating body of Crewman Davies. "Oh God," she mumbled in disgust.

Sergeant Weatherly appeared in the hatchway a moment later, his weapon raised. "Are you okay, Doc?" the sergeant asked as he checked the room for any other threats.

"No," she replied weakly. "I'm not."

"Are you injured?"

"Not physically," she told him.

"Push off and come to me, Doc," the sergeant instructed as Marcus and Loki came up behind him in the corridor.

"Damn," Marcus exclaimed, seeing the blood and bodies floating around the dimly lit room. Loki said nothing.

Doctor Chen managed to push off the chairs and float back toward the hatch, where Sergeant Weatherly reached in and grabbed her, pulling her back into the corridor and into normal gravity once again.

"You two get her back to medical, then meet me at the entrance to the bridge."

"Sure, Sarge," Marcus answered.

Sergeant Weatherly released the Doctor, gently handing her over to Marcus and Loki as Dexter, Sal, and the Omotossan caught up to them. "You three follow me," he told them as he started jogging down the corridor again, headed forward.

* * *

"We have still not been able to contact your ship," the Prime Minister's aide told Nathan. "However, we will continue to try."

"Is there anything you can do? Can you shoot down those missiles somehow?" Nathan pleaded.

"We do not have any anti-missile assets available in this area. They have either been used, captured, or destroyed."

"Jesus," Nathan exclaimed, feeling utterly helpless. "There has got to be some way to contact them..."

"Wait," Jalea interrupted. "The comm-unit. I had one on me when we came."

"What comm-unit? What are you talking about?" Nathan asked.

"When we first came to Corinair, I purchased comm-units so that we could communicate. I purchased one for Tug, one for myself, and one for Marcus. If he still has it on him, we might be able to contact him that way."

"Where is it?"

"They took it from me when the removed our weapons, at the security checkpoint on the way in."

Nathan turned back to the Prime Minister's aide. Before he could ask, the aide was already in motion.

"I will send for the device immediately," he assured them before turning to assign the task to one of his subordinates.

Tug stared at the main display on the far wall down below. "Excuse me, sir," he said to the Prime Minister's aide, "but those interceptors—

the ones that just destroyed the Aitkenna missile installation—are they for atmospheric flight only?"

"No, they are multi-role interceptors. They are capable of operating in space as well, but their range was limited by our treaty with the Ta'Akar. They can only reach high planetary orbit and cannot depart the orbit of Corinair without first refueling."

"But they can achieve escape velocity," Tug stated for clarification.

"Yes, quite easily."

"Can they catch a missile?"

The Prime Minister's aide looked at Tug for a moment as his mind pondered the idea. "Yes," he finally said somewhat tentatively, "I believe they can." The aide turned to the Prime Ministers and began translating the idea. The Prime Minister quickly agreed, gesturing for his aide to stop wasting time talking to him and get on the task. The aide relayed the orders to the military leaders in the room, who in turn began relaying instructions to their communications technicians.

* * *

The pilot of the lead interceptor had just watched his missiles destroy the Aitkenna missile installation. Unfortunately, it had been about a minute too late, and he was already watching the contrails of four nuclear missiles climbing into the light of the dawn. The surreal sight was interrupted by his comms.

"*Black Dog One, Command. Standby to copy action orders.*"

"Command, Black Dog One. Go with action orders," the pilot responded.

"*Black Dog One, Command. Pursue all missiles*

launched from Aitkenna missile base and destroy if possible. Repeat. Pursue and destroy all missiles launched from Aitkenna missile base. You are weapons free and cleared for maximum force."

"Black Dog One copies action orders. Pursuing Aitkenna missiles, weapons free for max force. Don't worry, Command, we'll get 'em." The pilot quickly toggled his comms to speak to his wingman in the second interceptor flying to his starboard and slight behind him. "Two, Leader. Did you copy?"

"*You bet, boss,*" his wingman answered over the comms. "*Let's put it to the stops and head for the black.*"

The pilot advanced his throttle to its maximum setting and then armed his orbital ascent drive. "Arming OAD. Pitching up." He pulled back on his stick and started climbing.

Outside the interceptors, a pair of thrust ports located on the back of the externally mounted ascent drives opened up in preparation for firing.

"Passing six thousand KPH," the pilot announced as he continued to slowly pitch his nose up toward a vertical. He could see that his course was already leading the targets by a good amount. "Wings back," he ordered, pressing a button on his console. "OAD burn in three......two......one......ignition."

The pilot pressed the ignition button on the throttle for his orbital ascent drive. The drive ignited in a burst of flame shooting out of the thrust ports, which immediately tightened into a focused stream of thrust, causing the interceptor to leap forward. The pilot grunted as the sudden acceleration pressed him hard back into his seat and his body instantly took on five times the normal gravity on Corinair.

"OAD burning," the pilot grunted over the comms.

"Going vertical," he added as he finished pitching upwards. His aircraft was now flying upward at an angle of only twenty degrees short of absolute vertical in relation to the surface below him. "Passing eight thousand KPH. Time to max firing range is five minutes."

* * *

"Sergeant Tukalov, respond!" the Captain de Winter shouted into his comm-set. He looked about the bridge in frustration. The last transmission he had received from any of his men had been in the midst of a gun battle in the hangar bay. The fact that he could no longer make contact with any of them was not a good sign. Even Lieutenant Brayerton who had been left guarding the prisoners in medical was not answering. It all could only mean one thing; he and the other nobleman on the bridge were all that were left of the boarding party. That undoubtedly meant that an armed force was headed his way. There would be more than just two of them. That left the captain with only one viable option: escape.

"Where are the nearest escape pods?" the captain asked.

Josh turned around from the helm to face the captain. "The escape pods! What, are you kidding me?" The look on his face was one of disgust and disbelief. "After all that big talk, now you want to run away and hide?"

Captain de Winter was in no mood to be ridiculed, especially not while he was still holding a gun, which he immediately raised and pointed angrily at Josh. "I will not ask again!"

Josh stood reflexively, his hands shooting up and

away from his side. "In the corridor, just outside!" he answered quickly to avoid being fried by the captain's small but deadly hand gun. "There are four of them on either side. Take your pick."

De Winter signaled to the other nobleman standing nearest the exit. "Go!" he ordered as he stepped back toward Abby. He reached down and grabbed her arm. "You're coming with me," he ordered, fully expecting her to comply.

Abby slapped his hand away. "I will not! Get your hands off..."

Her words were cut off as the back of de Winter's left hand smashed across her face, bloodying her lip and her nose.

Josh started toward de Winter, instinctively wanting to protect Abby. The captain saw his advance out of the corner of his eye and pressed his trigger. A small reddish-amber beam shot out and struck Josh in the abdomen, knocking him backwards over the helm and onto the cowling on the other side. Kaylah screamed and went charging toward Josh, scrambling over the navigation console to get to him.

De Winter grabbed Abby again, this time by her hair, and pulled her to her feet. "Come with me, or you die!"

Sergeant Weatherly and Dexter were crouched down outside the bridge, hidden just around the corner at the next intersection. From his position, he could see the nobleman guarding the entrance, but the man seemed distracted by whatever was happening on the bridge. Directly across the intersection from him, Sal and the Omotossan crouched in a similar fashion.

As he was sizing up the situation, an energy blast was heard coming from the bridge. There was a flash of reddish-amber light, a scream, and the sound of someone falling hard. At that moment, Sergeant Weatherly knew there was no time to come up with a plan, they just had to charge in, guns blazing, and hope for the best. People were dying in there. He only hoped that the medevac pilot's report of only twelve men being delivered to the Aurora was an accurate one, or else he was about to make a very big mistake.

The Omotossan wasn't doing that much thinking. As soon as he heard the gun blast and the scream, he was up and running toward the entrance to the bridge, his rifle firing away. The sergeant immediately followed, with Dexter and Sal reluctantly bringing up the rear.

The first few shots from the Omotossan missed, giving the nobleman time to turn and bring his own weapon to bear. As the Takaran returned fire, the Omotossan's next shot landed squarely in the nobleman's chest, knocking him backward.

The Omotossan went down, stumbling forward onto his knees, finally bending over into a crumpled heap on the floor right in front of Sergeant Weatherly. The sergeant continued moving forward, stepping onto the dead Omotossan and leaping forward to tackle the nobleman. The Omotossan's fire had been absorbed by the nobleman's armored vest, and even now the Takaran nobleman was scrambling to get back to his feet, still able to fight.

Dexter and Sal came charging down the corridor right behind the sergeant, screaming at the top of their lungs to psych themselves up as they charged.

Captain de Winter pivoted toward the commotion

at the entrance, dragging the struggling Abby in front of him as a shield. He raised his weapon and fired toward the sergeant and the nobleman, the latter of which was struggling to keep the sergeant's combat knife away from his throat.

Sergeant Weatherly saw the captain firing, and pivoted himself, pulling the struggling nobleman off balance, which allowed the sergeant to move the nobleman into Captain de Winter's line of fire. The blast from the captain's small hand gun struck the nobleman's back, his armor again absorbing the energy. The force of the blast pushed the nobleman forward into the sergeant's knife, which was positioned directly in front of the Takaran's throat. There was a gasp of escaped air followed by a gurgling sound, and the nobleman froze, a horrified look on his face.

Abby raised her left hand, inadvertently striking de Winter in the face. Unaccustomed to being struck in any fashion, the captain released his hold on the physicist and reached for his face, allowing her to fall away to the side.

Dexter and Sal charged clumsily into the bridge behind the now dead Omotossan and Sergeant Weatherly, their weapons firing wildly. Several of their shots inadvertently struck Captain de Winter. The first two were absorbed by his body armor, resulting in nothing more than being knocked off balance. The third shot, however, struck his left shoulder, spinning him around as he went down. As his knees hit the floor, a fourth shot struck the side of his face, blowing half of his head away, sending it spraying across the console behind him.

Behind Sal and Dexter, back by the hatchway, the nobleman's body went limp and the sergeant let him drop to the side. He stepped forward, his bloody knife still in his hand, looking around the bridge. Other than himself, Dexter, and Sal, the only other people moving on the bridge were Abby and Kaylah. Josh was wounded but appeared to still be alive for now. A feeling of elation washed over the sergeant at that moment as he realized they had done it; they had retaken their ship.

"Did you see that?" Dexter proclaimed excitedly. "I blew the captain's face clean off, I did!"

"You did? I did?" Sal argued.

"What are you saying? Your shots weren't anywhere near him."

"My shots were the only ones that were near him. Yours were on the ceiling for the most part."

"Oh, it figures!" Dexter complained. "It's just like you to try and steal my moment of glory!"

Marcus and Loki ran up the ramp to the command deck on their way to join in the assault on the Aurora's bridge. They had been running ever since they left Doctor Chen back at medical. Marcus was beginning to get tired of all the physical exertion. He was not a young man, and his body had been reminding him of that fact all day long.

As they continued down the main corridor toward the bridge, an electronic alert sounded from his pocket. At first Marcus couldn't ascertain from where the sound was emanating.

"I think your pocket is beeping," Loki told him as they reached the bridge.

Marcus stopped just outside the hatchway to the bridge, letting Loki go in ahead of him as he pulled the forgotten comm-unit out of his pants pocket.

"Hello?"

"*Marcus, is that you?*"

"Who the hell were you expecting?" he said between breaths.

"*Is everyone all right?*" Jalea asked over the comm-unit.

"Jalea?" Marcus said as he stepped into the bridge and looked around. "Shit."

"*What?*"

"No, not you."

"*What is going on there? Is the ship all right?*" There was some noise over the comm-unit, like it was being roughly handled. Then Nathan's voice came over the device. "*Marcus, listen up! You've got missiles inbound...*"

Marcus quickly handed the comm-unit to Sergeant Weatherly. "I think you'd better take this," he said, switching the unit to speaker mode.

Sergeant Weatherly took the device from Marcus, staring at it momentarily. It reminded him of the portable phones everyone carried back on Earth. "This is Sergeant Weatherly."

"*Sergeant, what's going on there?*" Nathan asked over the comm-set.

"We just took back the ship, sir."

"*The ship? What ship? What do you mean*, took back? *Who had taken it?*"

"Sir," the sergeant interrupted, "the captain of the Yamaro and some of his men, the ones that you took down to the surface. Somehow they managed to sneak back on dressed as medical staff. They came aboard the medevac shuttle the Corinairans sent up."

"*Sergeant, I thought you were on the Yamaro.*"

"Yes, sir, I was. They attacked us there as well.

After we put them down there, we came over here..."

"*Where's Vladimir?*" Nathan demanded.

"The Cheng is in one of the service tunnels, sir. They trapped him and Deliza in..."

"*Sergeant, listen,*" Nathan interrupted, "*you've got four nukes inbound. They'll be there in just over five minutes. You have got to get the ship out of there! Do you understand?*"

"Yes, sir. One moment; I'll contact Cheng over comms." The sergeant tapped his comm-set to place the call. "Cheng, Weatherly."

"*Yes, Sergeant. What is your status?*"

"We've retaken the ship, sir. I'm on the bridge now. We believe all hostiles have been eliminated."

"*Excellent news, Sergeant. Good work!*"

"Sir, I've got the captain on some kind of portable comm thing. He's still on the surface. He says there are four nukes headed our way, and that we have to get out of here now."

"*Oh bozhe moi,*" Vladimir exclaimed. Weatherly didn't understand what the Russian was saying, but he was pretty sure it wasn't good. "*Sergeant, we do not have any power. How long until the missiles reach us?*"

"Captain said five minutes, sir." There was a pause. "Sir?"

"*Sergeant,*" Vladimir began somberly, "*we will not have power back in time.*"

Sergeant Weatherly looked at the others.

"What?" Dexter exclaimed. "You mean to tell me that after surviving all of that, we're gonna be blown outta orbit by our own missiles?"

* * *

"*Sir,*" Sergeant Weatherly said over the comm-unit. "*I'm afraid there's nothing we can do. We're sitting ducks up here. Cheng had to kill all power so the transfer airlocks would go into rescue mode and let us in. He can't get the power back up in time for us to take evasive action. Is there anything you can do from your end, sir?*"

Nathan could hear the desperation in the sergeant's voice. He was a good man, strong and loyal to the end. Hearing the worry in the man's voice didn't make Nathan feel any better about the situation. "We're working on it, Sarge."

"*Yes, sir.*" Nathan was quiet for a moment. He looked to Tug. "How long until the interceptors are able to fire?"

Tug looked at the main display on the far wall below. It had switched from a wide area map of the Hakai nation to the tactical plot of the interceptors on their way to engage the missiles bound for the Aurora and the Yamaro in orbit over Corinair. "Two minutes."

"We've got a plan working here, Sergeant. We'll know in three minutes."

"*Yes, sir.*"

* * *

"Command, Black Dog flight. Clearing atmosphere. Cannons in thirty seconds," the pilot reported as the light of dawn faded into the blackness of space. The planet Corinair rotated below them now as they continued to accelerate.

"*Copy Black Dog. In the black, cannons thirty.*"

The pilot switched back to his ship-to-ship frequency as the buffeting stopped and they left the atmosphere behind. They were no longer on a vertical trajectory, having come over onto a course more parallel to the surface as they chased the missiles into orbit.

"This is gonna be a bitch of a shot, Jonas. We're coming in nearly vertical under those missiles, so their thrust is gonna disperse most of the cannon's energy. We're going to have to tag them just outside the engine bells but still hit the bottom bulkheads in order to rupture their fuel tanks and light 'em up."

"*Can't we just shoot them in their sides and be done with it?*" his wingman asked.

"Their fuselages are reflective. At this angle they'll just bounce off. They were designed that way to make them more difficult to shoot down when they're coming right at you."

"*Great. We just had to build them good, didn't we?!*"

"Ten seconds. Cannons hot." The pilot watched as the distance to the targets slowly counted down. He was traveling considerably more than escape velocity now. Under normal circumstances, they would've burned just long enough to reach a velocity slightly faster than the missiles they pursued, allowing them to coast up on their targets. But the timing of the launch required that the missiles burn their engines all the way to their targets in order to reach them. They had to shoot at hot targets, which made it all the more difficult as they could only make minor adjustments in their course to try and hit their targets.

"Here we go!" the pilot announced. "Firing cannons!" The pilot depressed the cannon trigger on his flight control stick. Brilliant blue-white beams of energy shot out of either side of his nose in staccato bursts. "Damn it!" he swore. The brilliant burn of the missiles was becoming blinding as they grew closer. All he saw were four white-orange balls that grew larger and larger with each passing second. He continued firing, trying to swing his nose slightly from side to side in the hopes of striking that exposed portion of the bottom of the missile between the outer edge of the engine bell and the edge of the missile's body.

At last, one of the missiles burst open and the fuel ignited in a massive fireball. The interceptors had no choice but to fly right through the fireball of propellant, unable to maneuver around it at such speeds.

"Nice shot, Jonas," the pilot congratulated his wingman.

* * *

"*Command, Black Dog Two! Splash one! Still firing!*" the call came over the comms. Several members of the military staff made triumphant noises, but no one was getting too excited just yet. There were still three missiles left, and time was running out.

"Two minutes to impact," Tug said softly as they watched the display screens.

Nathan stood their staring. He had never felt so helpless in all his life. Everything that had come to be important to him was embodied in that ship, that crew. Those were his people up there, his friends. He should be there with them right now, ready to die with them—not standing here on the surface of some alien world, watching it all being played out on video screens in the hands of others. He had never felt guiltier in his life.

Jessica could see the despair in Nathan's eyes as she stepped closer and took his hand. Neither of them looked at each other. They just kept staring, holding hands.

* * *

"Come on," the pilot mumbled. "Hold still." Another missile exploded without warning. "Oh yeah! Command, Black Dog One! Splash Two! Still firing!" he announced as they flew through the fireball of the second missile.

A piece of debris not quite vaporized by the explosion struck the interceptor hard. The pilot could feel the tail of the ship jump sideways a few degrees. Alarms started going off in the cockpit. First one, then two, then ten. "Command, Black Dog One. I'm declaring an emergency. I've got multiple alarms..."

Something hot touched the pilot's backside. Before he knew what was happening, a bright white-orange ball of flame leapt out around him from behind. His breath suddenly left his lungs as his faceplate began to melt away. Then everything went black.

"Shit!" Jonas exclaimed from the cockpit of his interceptor as he watched his leader's ship explode. "Command, Black Dog Two! One is down! Repeat, One is down! He must've taken a debris hit in a fuel tank or something!"

"Black Dog Two, command copies. One is down.

Are you still operational?"

Jonas looked around at his instruments. "Yeah, Black Dog Two is good," he reported. He took a deep breath and repositioned himself, mentally regrouping. "Black Dog Two, re-engaging."

Jonas squeezed his trigger again, firing away with his energy cannons once more. He swept the nose of his interceptor back and forth, but he just couldn't seem to get the beams to find the sweet spot.

"Command, Black Dog Two. This isn't working. I've got an idea. How much time do I have?"

"Black Dog Two, Command. Two minutes to impact."

"Copy, two minutes. Black Dog Two is accelerating."

Jonas kicked in his secondary boosters in the same manner he would as if he were attempting to climb to a higher orbit. His rate of closure increased dramatically, and within thirty seconds the two missiles were starting to fall below him as he climbed to a higher altitude than they were traveling. A few more seconds passed and the nearest missile was now below him and slightly ahead. He cut his engines and pitched his nose down, bringing his guns to bear on the missile below. At such a sharp angle, his beams cut the missile in half, rupturing its fuel tank and igniting the fuel inside. The missile exploded.

"Splash three!" he reported gleefully. His triumph was short lived as he realized that he was too close to the exploding missile. Now his interceptor was spinning wildly and he was rapidly losing speed in relation to the missile. His interceptor fell behind the missile rapidly, passing through the its contrail and scorching the outside of his ship. About then, everything in his interceptor shut down.

"Oh shit," he exclaimed over a dead radio. He flipped switches and pressed buttons, but everything was dead. For several seconds he continued fidgeting, but nothing was working. Then he saw little puffs of smoke beginning to fill the cockpit. "Command, Black Dog Two, ejecting!" he announced as he reached down between his legs and pulled his ejection handles.

* * *

"The third missile has been destroyed," Tug reported. He looked grimly at Nathan.

"What is it?" Nathan asked.

"The second interceptor has also been lost," Tug told him with saddened eyes.

"How long?"

"Less than a minute," Tug answered. "I am sorry, Nathan."

Nathan stared at the orbital tracking display, his eyes fixed on the symbol that represented the Aurora. In a few seconds, the symbol that represented the last missile would converge on the Aurora or the Yamaro. It did not matter which ship was struck, as the explosion from one ship would undoubtedly destroy the other. This was the end of everything. Without the Aurora, he and Jessica were stranded on a world that could not defend itself against an enemy that would eventually destroy their entire civilization, replacing it with their own. Worse still was the fact that the Earth would not get its jump drive back and would probably fall victim to a Jung invasion.

He had failed, in every sense of the word.

* * *

Commander Dumar looked down at the images displayed on his table top, his attention on the flashing icons on the orbital track display. The Corinari interceptors had taken out three of the missiles, but it had cost them both of their ships and there was still one missile left. At that moment, his attention was drawn away by a flashing light on a side screen. The light indicated that the ID search he had started earlier had found a match for the second, older man that had identified himself as the leader of the Karuzari. He read the ID description, his eyes widening. He looked at the matching picture, one taken more than thirty years ago, and his mouth fell open.

"No," he muttered to himself in disbelief, "it cannot be." He called out to his subordinate. "Lieutenant!"

The lieutenant responded instantly. "Yes, sir."

"Time to impact?"

"Sixty seconds, sir," the lieutenant answered.

"Clear this room, NOW!"

The commander's startled assistant quickly ordered more than a dozen confused personnel out of the command center. As soon as he was sure the room was cleared, he turned to exit himself.

"Wait!" the commander called, halting the young lieutenant in his tracks. "Not you; I need you," he told him. The commander pointed to the next console over from him. "There."

The confused lieutenant made his way over to the indicated console, unsure of what his next task might be.

"Log into that console, and confirm my abort order," the commander instructed.

"Sir?"

"You heard me!"

"Yes, sir," the lieutenant assured him as he typed. "But why would you want to abort the missile..."

"No time to explain. Just enter your code and confirm. Then be ready to turn your key to abort on my count."

"But sir, those ships are a direct threat to..."

"Lieutenant," the commander said, this time in a more pleading tone, "I don't have time to explain everything. You just have to trust that what I am doing is for the benefit of Takara." The commander stared into the eyes of the nervous lieutenant for several seconds before continuing. "Three...... two......one......abort," he said, turning his key to the abort setting. At the same time, the lieutenant swallowed hard and turned his key as well. The green light next to the missile key on each console flashed red three times then went off.

The commander looked at the display screen just in time to see the last missile track disappear. He breathed out a sigh of relief as he realized the last missile had been successfully aborted.

"Sir, perhaps now you can tell me why we just allowed the enemy ship to survive," the lieutenant asked as he moved closer to his commander. He looked down and saw the ID match on the table top display. His mouth also dropped open in disbelief. "This cannot be correct."

"It is," the commander told him.

"But, sir, that would mean..." The lieutenant never finished his sentence. It was cut short by the sudden, excruciating pain of a knife being thrust into his abdomen.

"Yes," the commander whispered. He grabbed hold of the lieutenant's collar and lowered him back against the table. The expression on the young man's face was one of shock and disbelief, as his face grew pale and the life quickly drained out of him.

"I'm sorry you had to see that," the commander said as he lowered the lieutenant down onto the floor, "but there is far more at stake here than you realize, and I cannot take the chance that the wrong people might learn what you and I now know."

The commander withdrew his knife, wiping the blade on the dead lieutenant's clothing before replacing it into its sheath under his tunic. He quickly returned his attention to the console and began furiously typing commands to initiate a complete emergency wipe of all of the command center's files, including the video of the Earth ship's captain and the leader of the Karuzari. Realizing that the data wipe alone might not be enough, he also keyed in a command string that only he knew.

Commander Dumar pressed the execute button, beginning the wipe, and slowly backed away from the madly flickering computer screens. He watched as the wipe took place. Moments later, the center screen flashed the message '*Self Destruct Sequence Initiated.*'

Commander Dumar looked around the room, knowing full well that this would be the last time he would see it. He had another task to perform, and he could not send others to do it. He had to do it himself. He had to be sure it was done properly.

CHAPTER TEN

It had been three days since the events that had nearly plunged the Corinairans into a planetary civil war. They had seen death and destruction on a scale not experienced since the great Pentaurus wars more than thirty years ago. Friends, neighbors, and family members had been unwittingly pitted against one another. Nations had come to the brink of nuclear exchange, and visitors from the birthplace of humanity had come to their rescue in their hour of need. It did not matter if one believed in the Legend of Na-Tan or not. They had all witnessed the actions of the Aurora's captain and her crew.

So they lined the streets of Aitkenna on this cold and rainy dawn. They stood along the main roadway that led from the spaceport, through the center of the city, and to the Walk of Heroes located in the central park of the city. The walk was nearly six kilometers long, wrapping its way around the middle of the massive park. On either side of the broad walkway were the graves of men and women that had sacrificed themselves to protect their world. Their graves were close together as there had been so many over the years, each marked with only a simple headstone showing their portrait and name laser-etched into the stone. Built into the walkway at the foot of each grave was a display screen built into the stone that, when tapped with one's foot, projected a life-sized holographic image of the person buried there. In this way, these heroes would live on for as long as their world survived.

Once a year, on Memorial Day, citizens would come to pay their respects to the fallen heroes. They would make their way down the walkway, tapping each display so that their heroes would come to life again, at least for a moment. It was usually an awe-inspiring sight to see hundreds if not thousands of holograms on display. However, it had been over three decades since any heroes had been buried here, and every year the interest in the Memorial Day tradition had waned a little bit more. This day was different. On this day, the Walk of Heroes was not only lined with holograms of the deceased, but it was also lined with the living. They stood shoulder to shoulder here, in the thousands, to watch as the ones that had fought and died for them in the recent struggle were brought forth for burial. There were hundreds of them, all carried by their brothers and sisters in arms.

The procession had started at daybreak and was led by an honor guard in traditional Corinari dress uniforms. They were the typical nondescript black that they usually wore, only the dress version was fully trimmed in gold, and each one of them wore their service medals with pride. The honor guard was followed by a drum and bagpipe corps, playing the battle hymn of the Corinari over and over again.

For some strange reason, Nathan never tired of hearing the same lilting melody, verse after verse, as the procession made its way down the walkway. Nathan stared straight ahead as he guided the casket containing the body of Captain William Roberts, the Aurora's original captain and the only man that Nathan had ever served under, if only briefly. He walked along the left side of the captain's casket, his right hand grasping the anti-gravity control handle to gently float the casket down the ceremonial walkway.

Immediately behind him, Sergeant Weatherly guided the casket of Commander Montero, the Aurora's original executive officer. Next was Vladimir escorting the casket of his mentor, the original chief engineer, Lieutenant Commander Patel. Finally, there was Jessica, who stoically guided the casket carrying the remains of her trusted friend, Ensign Enrique Mendez of Special Operations.

In fact, nearly all of the Aurora's surviving crew had come down, in the best uniforms they could manage, to accept the gracious offer from the Corinairans to bury their fallen warriors amongst the Corinairan heroes of the past. Only a handful had remained behind to man the ship, which was not going anywhere due to the amount of damage it had sustained in recent days. The Corinari, who were well aware that there were Takaran agents still operating on Corinair, had insisted on assigning a full company of men to guard the Aurora and keep her safe.

When the number of surviving members of the Aurora's crew had proved insufficient to escort her dead, members of the Corinari eagerly volunteered to do the honors. They had mixed in nicely with the Aurora's crew, and it sent a message of cooperation and respect to both their peoples.

The decision to bury their dead here on this alien world so far away from their birth place had been difficult for Nathan. In the end, the decision had been a political one, as the Corinairans had been rather insistent on bestowing such honors upon the Aurora's fallen crew.

Nathan suspected that the event would be a cathartic one for his people. They needed to get over the trauma of the last two weeks. They needed to move on. If they had been back on Earth, they all would have been required to report for stress debriefing. Out here, the luxury of that type of psychotherapy was not available. They still had much work to do in the days ahead. They had a ship to repair and they had a war to fight. Nathan only hoped the Corinairans would be able to provide the assistance they needed in order to accomplish their goals and somehow, eventually, get home again.

The procession reached the first empty grave sites along the walk. As they did so, the bagpipes ended their repetitive melody, leaving only the drums pounding their incessant beat as the two columns of casket bearers continued on until the last casket reached the first empty grave site. With a heavy strike of the drums the beat ended and the procession stopped. The bearers rotated their caskets ninety degrees inward toward the center of the broad walkway and then stepped backward until the caskets were positioned over the open grave sites.

A new beat started and the bagpipes began a burial hymn. In unison, the caskets began to descent toward the gravesites below them. The caskets themselves were equipped with levitation devices that Nathan guessed worked on principles similar to the artificial gravity plating they used on board the Aurora. It was something that had been discussed on Earth but had yet to be tested in practical applications. The devices were being controlled remotely, and the presence of pallbearers had been more for show and tradition than for anything else.

As the caskets began their descent, Nathan and the others stepped back, all in unison with the hundreds of pallbearers performing their duties that day. Then he felt the urge, as usual, to 'wing it,' as Jessica would say.

"Crew of the Aurora," he bellowed, "AH-TEN-SHUN!" Every member of the Aurora's crew in attendance snapped to attention at their grave sites. "COMPANY, SA-LUTE!" Again, in perfect unison, the members of the Aurora's crew raised their hands to the side of their heads in perfect military salute, holding it until the caskets reached the bottom, and Nathan dropped his hand back to his side. Following Nathan's example, the Corinari had repeated the same gesture for their own fallen comrades. Finally, all the dead heroes were laid to rest. Normally, their holographic projectors would have already been active and would be displaying their images. Recent events, however, had made it impossible to get such measures in place in time. The Corinairans promised that, eventually, every member of the Aurora's crew would have a holographic image on display as well. That thought alone had made Nathan feel much better than he had expected.

As previously instructed, the pallbearers assembled in the center of the broad path and marched up to the front of the podium that had been erected in the middle of the Walk of Heroes. Several hundred of them lined up several rows deep along either side of the walkway, with the twenty members of the crew of the Aurora that had attended in the front row. They stood there proudly as the Prime Minister of Corinair, who was eventually confirmed as the most senior surviving member of the government, made a moving speech in Corinairan. Jalea and Tug, who had come along, were standing behind Nathan and the others, allowing Jalea to translate for the crew of the Aurora. The Prime Minister spoke of the hardships they had all endured over the last few days, and he spoke of the difficult times that lie ahead of them. He recalled the decisions his predecessors had made to surrender to the Ta'Akar thirty-five years ago in order to prevent their complete destruction. He told the people of Corinair that a new parliament would have to be formed in order to begin discussions on how to handle the current crisis as well as the looming threat that the Ta'Akar now presented. He spoke of the possibility of maintaining the peace through reasonable negotiations and how he believed that the inappropriate actions of one Takaran nobleman did not have to unravel decades of peace and prosperity.

The crowd was not buying the Prime Minister's opinions as he might have hoped. Even Nathan, who did not speak a word of Corinairan, could tell that the crowd was growing more discontented with each word the Prime Minister spoke.

"What the hell is this guy talking about?" Nathan whispered as he stood at parade rest, his hands held squarely behind his back like everyone else in the formation. "Peace with the Ta'Akar? Does he really believe that's possible after all that's happened here?"

"He is looking for a way out for his world," Tug said. "He doesn't believe the people will support going to war. He doesn't think the people believe they can win."

"You mean *he* doesn't believe they can win,"

Jessica corrected.

"If these people aren't willing to fight, then what the hell are we doing here?" Nathan wondered.

"They are willing to fight," Tug promised him. "They just need someone to lead them."

Nathan looked at the crowd. They were continuing to grow impatient, some of them beginning to talk amongst themselves in louder and more disgruntled tones. Nathan recognized one of the Corinari, the man from the airship that had taken them on that wild ride from the Aitkenna spaceport to the command center. It was Chief Montrose. He had carried his brother to be buried here today, just as Nathan and his people had carried their shipmates. Their eyes met and the chief nodded respectfully. Without warning, the chief yelled, "Na-Tan!" at the top of his lungs.

The Prime Minister stumbled momentarily in his speech but did not stop. A strange look of surprise made its way into his expression for a moment before the politician in him overcame the momentary distraction and he returned to his confident and serious demeanor.

Someone else in the ranks did the same, hollering, "Na-Tan!" Nathan looked around but couldn't see who had yelled the second time. Then there was a third, this time someone in the general crowd. Then a fourth, and a fifth, and a sixth.

Chief Montrose stepped forward and began yelling, "Na-Tan!" over and over until the entire crowd eventually joined in.

Nathan was astonished by the chanting. It was just as it had happened before, when he had first arrived at the Aitkenna spaceport after the initial bombardment and subsequent battle with the

Yamaro. But that had been a few thousand people at the most. This was tens of thousands of people, and they were all chanting his name, or at least the legendary version of it.

"I think they want you to speak," Jessica yelled.

Nathan looked at Tug. The man had become somewhat of a father figure to Nathan over the past week.

"They just need someone to lead them, Nathan," Tug repeated, "and that someone is you."

"How can I lead these people? I know nothing about them. I don't even speak their language."

"More of them speak Angla than you might think," Tug assured him, "and I will translate for the rest. I do have some experience in speaking to large crowds, even Corinairan ones."

Nathan looked at him again, his eyes pleading. "None of this was supposed to happen this way."

"You can't outrun your fate, Nathan," Tug reminded him. "Sooner or later, it catches up to you."

Nathan turned around to look at Vladimir.

As usual, Vladimir flashed a smile his way. "Go, Nathan. You can do this."

Nathan looked back out to the crowd chanting his name. He took a deep breath, pulled his uniform shirt down to present as good an image as the worn uniform allowed, and he took his first step forward on his way to the podium.

The crowd roared in approval. Half of them were screaming, the other half were still chanting, "Na-Tan!" as he made his way to the podium, with Tug following closely behind.

The Prime Minister had already given up trying to finish his speech and stepped back out of the way, gesturing with both hands enthusiastically toward Nathan. It was obvious to him now what the people of Corinair wanted, and what they needed, and it wasn't him.

Nathan stepped up to the podium as the crowds continued to cheer. He waved to them, just as he had seen his father do countless times in the past at any one of the numerous political speeches he had been forced to attend. Now he was thankful that he had done so. He continued to wave for what seemed like an eternity. Eventually, his waves became gestures pleading for the noise to die down so that he could speak. The cheering eventually subsided, leaving only the repetitive chants of "Na-Tan". Finally, those too fell in volume to an almost whispered chant before they died out completely.

At that moment, as he was about to open his mouth, every speech ever recorded in Earth history, from both before and after the great bio-digital plague, came flooding back into Nathan's mind. He was a student of history; it had been his subject of study during his higher education back on Earth. He had read speeches from men and women, both great and small, from all the pivotal moments through the course of humanity on that small blue planet from whence they had all come. Many of them were simply variations of the same theme, the very same theme that was at the root of this pivotal moment in, not only the Corinairan history, but in the history of the entire Pentaurus cluster. At that moment, Nathan knew exactly what he had to say.

"History is replete with struggles between good and evil, between right and wrong, between freedom and oppression. These battles are not new to the human animal. The spirit that is humanity must be fed. It must be nurtured. It must be loved. But above all else, it must be respected. Any person who tries to put themselves above humanity and impose their will, their beliefs, upon the body of humanity shall be defeated. It may take years. It may take decades. It may take centuries. In the case of the great plague that forced your migration to the Pentaurus cluster, it took a millennium. But it was defeated."

Nathan looked out across the great park, scanning the sea of faces. He recognized only a few of them, but he noticed a familiarity in them all. They were just as he was. They were distraught. They were traumatized, and they needed something to believe in.

"The Ta'Akar came after us for one reason, and it was not because we represent a truth that their leader had been denying for over a century. They came after us because they knew that our ability to jump between the stars represented the most powerful weapon imaginable. They knew that if they could capture that technology and incorporate it into their own ships, they could conquer not only the Pentaurus cluster, but quite possibly the entire galaxy. But more importantly, they knew that the very same technology could also be the key to their ultimate defeat. For the jump drive is more than just a way to travel amongst the heavens. The jump drive is hope—hope for an Earth reborn and for worlds oppressed. It is hope for our future. And *hope* is the most powerful weapon imaginable."

The crowds again cheered a mixture of affirmations and the recurring chant of "Na-Tan." After a minute, Nathan again motioned for quiet, a gesture that was eventually obeyed by the masses in attendance.

"Many great men over history have reminded us that the price of freedom is the blood of those that seek it. Today, the people of Corinair, the crew of the Aurora, and volunteers from the crew of the Yamaro have all made the first payments. It is now time for us all to pay the balance due. You have been held down under the boot of Caius for far too long. The time to fight is NOW!"

The previous cheers and chants were nothing compared to the final approval now offered by the tens of thousands gathered on the Walk of Heroes. Their ovation roared as a mighty thunder that shook the morning dew from the trees. The people of Corinair were united once again, and they were ready to follow their new leader, the one they called Na-Tan.

* * *

Nathan sat in a comfortable chair next to Cameron's hospital bed where she still lay in an unconscious state. The doctors of Corinair had spent hours in surgical repairs of her broken body. They had even coaxed millions of microscopic nanites to repair the damaged portions of her brain, but even with all their medical wonders, in the end, it all came down to a waiting game. Commander Taylor would either come out of her coma with all her mental faculties intact, or she would spend the rest of her days in a comatose state. She had shown signs of waking for more than a day now, and the doctors felt comfortable enough to predict that she might wake up at any time.

Nathan had nearly refused to attend the funeral ceremonies, preferring instead to be at Cameron's side should she suddenly wake. In the end, Vladimir had convinced him that his duty was first to his crew, and second to the people of Corinair. Although his friend assured Nathan that Cameron would understand, it was not until Abby had agreed to come down and stay by Cameron's side in his absence that he finally agreed to fulfill his obligations at the funeral.

Once that task had been completed, he had returned post haste to her side. It was neither love nor friendship that brought him back to her side. It was respect. Cameron was family, just as much as any of his sisters, and even his brother, back on Earth. Besides, it also gave him a chance for some peace and quiet.

The Corinairans had a much different approach to medicine than the people of his world. Their hospitals were more like resorts or spas. Cameron's room was ornately decorated and was filled with fresh flowers and various candles. Almost hourly, an attendant would enter the room and snuff out one scented candle to light another. The attendant explained that the variation of smells helped to stimulate healing of the body. Some of the smells were quite relaxing, while others were not so much.

Nathan had dozed off in his comfortable chair. Jessica, as usual, had immediately found the couch and, small though it was, had managed to curl up and fall asleep in it. Before he had also dozed off, Nathan had wondered if Jessica had ever actually slept in a proper bed. He had made a mental note as he drifted off to visit her quarters on board the Aurora someday, just to see if she even had a bed.

The attendant entered the room quietly so as not to disturb Nathan and Jessica. Again she snuffed out the burning candle and lit the next one in the series that had been designed by the aromatherapy specialists. As she was about to leave, she noticed the patient moving her head. The attendant stopped, watching the patient in amazement as her eyes began to flutter slightly.

The attendant quickly moved over to Nathan and touched his arm. "Sir, sir," she prompted. Nathan opened his eyes, briskly looking around to identify his surroundings. "I believe she's waking up, sir."

Nathan quickly adjusted himself, sitting upright in his chair and leaning forward to look at Cameron as the attendant backed away and quietly slipped out the door.

Cameron opened her eyes, slowly at first. She looked around at the unfamiliar but pleasant room. Then she saw Nathan and frowned. "What are you doing here?" she questioned.

"Where else would I be?"

She looked around some more, realizing she wasn't on board the Aurora, and neither was the Aurora's captain. "Who's watching the ship?"

Typical Cameron, Nathan thought with a smile. *All business.* "Relax. Vlad's in command for now."

"Oh, great." She reached up and felt the bandages on her head. She also noticed the IV line in her arm. Then it all started coming back to her. "How long have I been out?"

"Three or four days, I think."

"Three or four days?" Her head fell back against her pillow. "Did I miss anything?"

"Oh, not much," Nathan said as he turned and looked at Jessica who was now waking up as well. "We fought off the Yamaro, survived a planet-wide riot, recaptured our ship from the bad guys... the usual stuff."

"Oh," Jessica interrupted as she rose from the couch and came to the other side of Cameron's bed, "and Nathan became a legend."

"A what?"

"Never mind," Nathan told her as the doctors rushed into the room to check on Cameron now that she was awake. "We'll tell you all about it later, when you're stronger."

Nathan rose from his chair and backed away from Cameron's hospital bed to make room for the doctor's and specialists seeking to check on their patient's condition. He smiled and waved at Cameron as he and Jessica exited the room.

Tug and Jalea rose from their seats in the intensive care unit's lobby when they saw Nathan and Jessica coming. Tug felt a huge sense of relief as he saw the smiles on their faces when they approached. "She is well?"

"Yeah, she just woke up," Nathan told him. "The doctors are with her now. I think she's going to be fine."

"That is wonderful news, Nathan. Wonderful indeed."

"I think the doctors are going to be with her for a while. So maybe we should get some work done. There's a lot to do..."

"And little time to do it in," Tug finished for him.

"We're going to need a lot of help, Tug. The ship is pretty busted up and I have almost no crew left."

"I think there is something outside that you should see," he told Nathan, intentionally being secretive in his manner.

Nathan looked concerned, glancing at Jessica.

"Go ahead, Skipper," Jessica told him. "I'll stay with Cam until you get back."

Nathan followed Tug out of the lobby and down the corridor, at the end of which they stepped into an elevator to take them down to the ground floor.

"What's this all about?" Nathan inquired. "What do I need to see?"

"Don't worry," Tug told him. "It's something good; I promise."

The elevator stopped and they stepped out into the main ground floor lobby. Nathan followed Tug across the expansive lobby and out the front doors of the hospital. Gathered just outside were thousands of men and women, most of them in Corinari uniforms. They were lined up in four single-file lines. At the head of each was a table with several people also in uniform that were signing them in.

"You asked for volunteers," Tug said proudly, holding his hand out at his side to gesture toward the lines of thousands.

At that moment, a man in uniform working one of the sign-in tables stood and shouted. "CORINARI!" Nathan recognized him immediately. It was Chief Montrose.

The crowd responded in unison. "HUP! HUP! HUP!"

* * *

The lines did not shorten as the day wore on. The men and women worked the sign-in tables tirelessly throughout the day.

"Can you believe these lines?" the man said to the fellow standing in front of him.

"Yes, they are impressive," the man in front of him agreed.

"I've been out here since sunrise," the first man exclaimed.

"As have we all."

"I lost my parents in the bombardment," the first man said solemnly. "That's why I'm here. I'm ready to kick some Takaran ass!"

The man in front of him turned to look back over his shoulder in response to the other man's declaration. "The time will come; I am sure."

"Did you lose anybody?"

"No, I was fortunate," the second man told him. "My wife and children survived unharmed."

"Then why are you here? Shouldn't you be home taking care of them?"

"They are quite capable of taking care of themselves. Besides, I believe I can do more to protect them here."

"Yeah, I guess so."

"Next!" the man at the sign-in table called out. The second man, now being at the head of his line, stepped up to the sign-in table.

"Here to join up?" the man at the table asked.

"Yes, I would like to volunteer."

"What skills can you offer?" the man at the table asked.

"I have extensive experience in assault tactics, covert operations, and intelligence."

The man behind the table smiled, obviously impressed. "Anything else?"

"I am also a qualified and experienced pilot."

The man behind the table looked him over. He was a bit older than most of the volunteers, maybe even a bit too old. However, no one knew how long this war was going to last, and it was quite possible that in the end it would take the efforts of every man, woman, and child in order to win their freedom from the Ta'Akar.

"Why not?" the man behind the table finally agreed as he scribbled on his paper. "What's your name, sir?"

"Dumar," the man said. "Travon Dumar."

14577642R00213

Printed in Great Britain
by Amazon.co.uk, Ltd.,
Marston Gate.